For You _Debbie_

By the way, Rob
calls me Maricius
(my childhood name)

e

For Debbie
We hope you enjoy this novel.

Rob Ritchey

Book design by Nancy Viall Shoemaker, West Barnstable Press
www.westbarnstablepress.com

For my wife, Maricris

Along life's journey there walks a queen
she feels one's sorrow, she knows one's dream
her crown is sunlight
her robe the earth
to know her is to know rebirth
the thorns of life lay at her feet
each thorn she feels springs forth a seed
the seeds hold wisdom,
knowledge, gold
each holds one's story to unfold
to know their story
one must decide
to hear the whispered voice
inside

Maricris

Acknowledgements

A little over four years has elapsed since I began this novel. It probably would not be in print today if it had not been for the people who encouraged and supported me. First and foremost, I want to thank my wife, Maricris, who partnered with me on this project. The story would never have reached this point without her commitment and diligence, both with the lion's share of editing and her intuitive guidance of the novel's personalities, particularly the two strong female characters, Marriette and Jen, who she came to know and understand as well as I have.

I'm grateful to Mary Ellen McTague who read the book in its most crude form early on. Her encouragement and unflagging enthusiasm for the story is greatly appreciated. Longtime friend, Marlene Denessen, PhD, scoured the later version of the novel, word by word and provided needed criticism and further guidance. I would also like to thank Betty Nietz, William Blaisdell, Joseph Calvert, Dave Feightner, Matt Feightner, Wade Ritchey, Steve Ritchey, Peggy Holtman, Paulette English, Jayne Stearns, Mary Hart, Nancy Viall Shoemaker and Ann Hart for their direct and important input into this project.

Foreword

I never conceived of, nor planned on writing a novel. However, the experience of doing so was beyond rewarding. Writing this was clearly the most interesting thing I've ever done in my life. It was joyful hard work and often emotionally taxing. Unlike painting, which to me is a kind of soothing anesthesia and detachment from thought, writing occupied my attention constantly. Often, my experience seemed that of a detached observer consciously watching my brain operate independently. I discovered that doing the research, reading, and interviewing, saturated me to the point where I would stop and wait about 48 hours and then watch the "pen" reliably release a new batch of material onto the page as if I had nothing to do with it.

Also important is to acknowledge what drove the writing of this novel. As both an active duty physician in the United States Army and as a civilian, I had the honor of listening to the accounts of World War II, Korea, and Vietnam combat veterans who revealed not so much their stories of war, but the stories of their troubled lives after returning home.

The experience of fear and violence leaves a lifetime of powerful images and feelings which injure the brain and wreak emotional and physical havoc unless effectively treated. In this regard, I will mention, unnamed, a patient of mine who has recently passed. Always wearing his 8th Air Force ball cap while present at appointments, he was just a 20-year-old airman on B-17 bombers when he flew 35 missions over Germany in '44 and '45. At the end of his time there, despite the horrors and devastation he witnessed around him, he remarkably went home without a physical scratch. He then suffered in silence the bizarre images of war he carried which tortured him day after day, night after night, killing him a little bit more, every day, for 75 more years.

Rob Ritchey
July 2020

Prologue:

Walking towards Civilization

A young West African man, known as Havra, stands at elevation gazing out upon a vast grassy plain glowing orange in the setting sun, a long view stretching to the horizon. Below him lies a strand of deciduous trees more numerous at this site with the presence of water. Beyond this grove their numbers diminish, scattered and smaller, transitioning into an African prairie.

Havra is weary from his day of travel by foot, another day further from his ancestral home. He is tall, broad-shouldered, and sinewy, a handsome man with keen, attentive eyes. When he walks, he walks slowly, but this is uncommon. On the trail he covers ground quickly, not in a run, but with an efficient lope.

On the left side of Havra's neck is a distinctive tribal tattoo of a raptor head with its exaggerated crest feathers and hooked beak. He wears khaki cargo shorts cinched at the waist with a traditional goatskin belt and carries a backpack of collected accoutrements of Civilization he deems useful for his journey. As the terrain becomes rocky, light hiking boots and socks feel good. Havra carries matches, a pocketknife, and a semi-automatic Russian sidearm, heavy along with its ammunition. It is the weapon removed from the body of the Malevolent Other who murdered his only son. He regrets both its weight and its presence, yet feels safer with it. He has made himself familiar with its equalizing power.

Havra fears the evil that killed his young son. This is a new and unnatural source of fear, present as a tightness in his chest and Dreams Unwelcome. Knowledge of the current threat has forced him to walk away from his familiar past into an uncertain future.

Distant Ancestors also paused at this vista to take in their surroundings. They were the Original humans as referred to in his native language. They looked like him and, in more ancient times, shared this land and climbed these hills with hominin variants who would not make the evolutionary cut.

In a scale measured in hundreds of thousands of years, waves of human precursors migrated north from their African environment of origin, mixing with or displacing those who came before them. Generation after generation, early Originals left the human cradle moving with expansion of their numbers along the saltwater coast, its shores and estuaries replete with sustenance. The ancient hominin trails, their early tools, and encampments of the True Exodus, were now long since dissolved in a deeper ocean.

The Originals were supremely social animals, able to flourish in the varied environments they encountered as they dispersed throughout all habitable regions of the earth. The modern Originals, who left the African continent 50,000 years prior, settled in the Middle East where all the necessary conditions were present for the birth of a great social change: Civilization. They brought to the Middle East improved language skills, conscious thought, shared intentions, and a plethora of adaptive characteristics not yet sufficiently present in their predecessors.

For the Original populations not leaving Africa, such as Havra's grandfather's tribe, the arrival of those from distant continents, beginning some five hundred years ago, brought disruption to the stability of the comparatively unchanged Original culture. These foreigners, who were no longer perceptibly Original, were returning, if you will, to Africa with their advanced technologies to conquer and supplant. They were referred to as the Others.

Havra had experienced little of the Others, as he lived in a region devoid of attractions to them. There were no large beasts to hunt, and no resources the Others believed worth taking from the earth to be used elsewhere. The only Others Havra had known were university anthropologists who were solely interested in his people's culture instead of their resources or their labor. In his native language, he referred to them as the Friendly Others. Since his birth in 1940, Havra was constantly in the presence of the Friendly Others, who acquainted him with their languages and provided glimpses of Civilization. As the result of this unique opportunity, he acquired a rather complete education.

The Originals and the Friendly Others coexisted in harmony, until change was forced upon Havra's tribe, by the threat of Disruptive & Malevolent Others encroaching on their territory and culture. After a recent and tragic event, his small tribal band of 50 Originals decided to disperse among other local subtribes with whom they were familiar.

Now, distant from familiar territory, Havra discards his traditional clothing in favor of items left for him by the students, a visible indication of his commitment to seek a new life in Civilization.

As Havra looks out over the same landscape viewed by his Ancestors, he sees a precious continuum that instills a feeling of Original Sacredness and spiritual oneness with Nature. He senses this in an innate and intuitive way, assembled prior to experience. In his Originality, he was never set apart from Nature with the construct of a Great Other.

Yet, there is a dichotomy that has grown within him since he was a child. The Good and Friendly Others – the anthropologists – were present throughout each year of his life. Season after season they sought information about his people's Originality, but now that his people were no longer perfectly Original, the Friendly Others would not be back to study them.

However, the presence of the Friendly Others' culture, so different from his, crept into his being and provided him with the gift of Civilization's knowledge. Each year, with every new visiting student, new skills were available for him to learn, so Havra became accustomed to pass into and out from a duality of worlds.

On this day in September of the year 1972, Havra stands upon this precipice watching the last rays of the setting sun reach out across the savanna. He feels imperfect and unprepared. Leaning on a walking stick, he gazes on the darkening horizon. The future no longer exists for him in the disappearing environment of the Original world, so he is committed to encounter Civilization and take his chances.

Sitting down on a rocky outcropping, he grasps the shaft of his walking stick, supporting his chin against it. Only the Ancestors and Ancestral Presence of his son are with him. This new loneliness feels foreign and unnatural.

His mind frequently wanders back to thoughts of the last student to stay with his tribe. His relationship with her grew intimate during the two years she was present. Havra misses her. Her absence, this loss, is another source of enduring sadness. He imagines her climbing the embankment to join him as the evening light fades. Closing his eyes, he recalls his last moments with her before she leaves to begin the long journey home to her Canada, her image disappearing forever into the dust of the departing vehicle.

Tonight, he will make his bed under the trees in the sand and dry leaves to fall asleep while gazing into the milky depths of a starry sky. Tomorrow, he will walk another day closer to his encounter with Civilization.

Marriette LaFleur Roy

Part 1

– Chapter 1 –

The Long Trip Back Home
Friday, June 30, 1972   Montreal, Quebec

A young woman, a graduate student from McGill University, arrived at the city airport of Paris from Gibraltar with only a few hours remaining before her connecting flight to Canada. She was exhausted and disheveled after her long journey from an anthropology site in West Africa. Between flights, the best she could manage was airport food and an abbreviated sponge bath in a bathroom at the Villeneuve-Orly.

After two years in West Africa, she was making her way back to Montreal and then on to her family home in northern Vermont. At this point, she had been traveling four long days. The journey had started with a truck picking her up at the study site, driving her to a rail head where she met several other anthropology graduate students leaving from another location. Both students and instructors were part of a scheduled exit from the continent. Others were expected to meet at the capital where a charter flight would return them and their equipment to Gibraltar for a connecting flight to Paris.

Throughout the journey, her thoughts drift to her departure from the tribal camp. She relives the images of looking out of the truck window back at the tribal family she had just spent the last two years with. Her daydream focuses on the tall young African man with whom she became so close.

Her belongings secured at the back of the vehicle, she sits in the front seat next to the driver. The tribal family gathers around the vehicle to touch her once again before she is gone. They have greatly enriched her life. For them change is coming quickly. Their future is uncertain.

As the driver shifts the truck into gear preparing to move forward, the tall young man leans into the cab window and kisses her lips. She grasps his hand one last time. As the vehicle moves away, she leans out the window and focuses on his face until he becomes part of a receding portrait of the group, an image vanishing into the accumulating cloud of dust. He is gone forever. She never anticipated such sadness and never expected an intimate relationship. She replays the scene over and over again.

Marriette Catherine LaFleur is the daughter of a French-Canadien family who moved to the United States when she was an infant. She will be 30 years of age in the fall. Because of her isolation on the African continent, there had been little communication with her family for nearly two years. She hoped her parents had received the telegram she sent from Gibraltar and would be waiting in Montreal upon her arrival.

Françoise and Gil LaFleur had two children. Their daughter, living in a remote region of West Africa, was a constant source of stress from the day they saw her off to Europe. The mail delivery to the study site was unreliable. They had been contacted by a graduate student returning from the location a year prior, informing them that their daughter was doing well. This reassurance and the uncommon arrival of her letters provided only ephemeral relief.

The return to civilization proved disconcerting for Marriette. At the French airport there were crowds and long noisy lines of people moving shoulder to shoulder. The hot, gritty smell of summer in the city permeated the concourse. Marriette had long been accustomed to the quiet of the African wilderness. The days and nights were filled with natural sounds only. The nighttime sky shone bright with stars. It was now a world left behind.

Throughout Villeneuve-Orly airport she noticed young women dressed in fanciful clothes. In the women's bathroom mirror, Marriette looked at the reflection of her soiled khaki shorts and shirt. Her hair was matted, still loosely held in a braid. Next to her stood a young woman, a contemporary wearing meticulous make up, dressed in a miniskirt and flowing blouse. Despite their contrasting physical presence, Marriette's disheveled appearance could not disguise her striking features with smoky blue eyes against her dark chestnut hair. She caught the woman's furtive and dismissive glance in the mirror. The girl hurried to replace her lipstick in its small case, impatient to leave the bathroom and be distant from the beautiful, but curiously unkempt, tall woman beside her.

Blaring loudspeakers and the deafening roar of jet engines provoked a headache. Marriette froze in the air conditioning at the airport after having baked in the heat of the poorly acclimatized aircraft. Her feet burned from walking on concrete in shoes she had worn little in the past year. She soon boarded the Air Canada 707 to Montreal, occupying a middle seat between two large men. The man sitting to her left spent the flight snoring, occasionally falling against her shoulder which necessitated her pushing him back into his seat. The traveler on her right nervously chain-smoked and went back-and-forth to the bathroom more times than seemed necessary. She is unable to fall asleep until only an hour remained in the flight and then was awakened with the announcements of arrival preparation.

Now on the ground in Montreal, the Air France aircraft taxied to its gate. Moments later, the rear door opened as a stairway was rolled to the fuselage. The sleeping man pried himself out of his seat and removed his bag from the storage bin above. He glanced at Marriette asking if she had a nice flight. She could only manage an icy stare and shrug of her shoulders.

Marriette descended the mobile staircase and made her way across the tarmac, stopping momentarily along the way to fix the unraveling braid in her long hair. She entered the terminal door behind the other passengers. Not carrying much more than her passport, she cleared customs quickly. The arrival area was crowded with people waiting for friends and relatives returning from Europe. She then noticed her father waving in the crowd.

Weaving her way through a sea of people, Marriette flew into his arms. They held onto each other without a word. Moments later, she spoke to him in their native French, her face still resting on his shoulder.

"Daddy, I'm so glad to be home. I will never go away like that again."

Swallowing hard, he responded softly, "You don't know how much of a relief it is to see you, my darling."

Looking at her father for the first time in two years, she realized he wasn't smiling. Although it was clear he was relieved to see his daughter, the presumed joy of this event was missing.

"Where is Mom, Daddy?"

"She's at home."

"Is Mom alright?"

Struggling to hold his emotions in check, her father uttered the words, "Pierre a été tué au combat. Il y a trois mois."

Staring into her father's eyes, Marriette exhaled, "Excusez-moi?"

"Pierre was killed in action three months ago," her father whispered back.

Marriette collapsed onto a nearby bench bursting into tears, hiding her face in her hands.

As her father held her, she cried out her brother's name as if speaking to him. Through her sobs it was difficult to understand the meaning of her words.

"Tu m'as promis, Pierre. Tu m'as sauve' la vie et maintenant tu es parti!" (You promised me, Pierre. You saved my life and now you're gone!)

Marriette and her father remained there for a long while. The room had emptied. Her father explained that Pierre was reported as MIA for almost two months before a Special Forces envoy in dress uniform arrived at the bakery one afternoon. Her brother's body was brought home and buried a month ago at Green Mountain National Cemetery only blocks away from the family home.

Pierre's secret military life had been of great concern. Pierre joined the Army after graduating from high school in 1962. He soon found his way into the Special Forces. After serving on active duty for seven years, he was honorably discharged in 1969. His parents had urged him to attempt civilian life and he acquiesced. He tried to work at the family bakery and ease into the family tradition, but that lasted but a month. One afternoon he surprised his parents, announcing that he was leaving for Minnesota to meet up with some Army friends. He said he missed his brothers and needed to be with them. Pierre was gone again. However, he kept in touch with Marriette who, at the time, was a pharmacology major at McGill.

Pierre chose to live in the deep woods of Minnesota as a lumberjack until he might feel differently and change direction. When Marriette informed Pierre she would be studying in remote West Africa for two years, he insisted she visit him prior to leaving so he might provide her with necessary survival training. She spent a week with him in the wilderness. Pierre accompanied her back to Vermont where he continued to prepare her. It all seemed excessive to Marriette, yet she felt it important to spend time with her brother, sensing the precarious nature of his existence. Now, the first news returning home was of his death.

After the initial shock of her father's revelation, they attempted to collect her two steamer trunks. Only one was found traveling the carousel behind them. Marriette was in no mood to chase down the other. The explanation given to them was that the missing trunk would probably ship on the next day's flight and be sent directly to McGill University. They loaded the single trunk onto a cart and left for the parking lot.

During the two-and-a-half hour drive home to Montpelier, Gil LaFleur occasionally glanced over at his beautiful and exhausted daughter. Marriette lay curled up asleep on the front seat with her head resting against her father's leg. Her long hair was tangled, and tears had cleaned lighter patches on her cheeks. Her clothes were tattered and soiled. She smelled like an ashtray at best. During the long trip, Gil occasionally rested his hand on his daughter's arm as she slept, as if to reassure himself that she was still there. He was grateful beyond words to have his daughter, alive and well, beside him.

The LaFleurs owned the building that housed the family business. LaFleur's Bakery was located on the ground floor while the family occupied the two floors above. Marriette and her brother grew up there having always taken part in their family's business. The LaFleur family had established the bakery in Montreal in 1922. Gil and Françoise took the family expertise and moved to Montpelier in 1944.

After Marriette graduated from high school, she worked at the bakery full time. It was hers to inherit. But in a few years, she became dissatisfied with her direction in life and wanted to move on. By then it was clear to her parents that she had no interest in carrying on the family tradition - a tradition that had begun in France generations ago. It was something Gil and Françoise had envisioned and hoped for, as parents do, but they understood and supported her decision. With an abundance of enthusiasm, Marriette entered McGill in the fall of 1966, five years behind her peers.

****

As Gil parked the station wagon in the back parking lot, he called softly to his sleeping daughter. Marriette awoke somewhat disoriented. Her eyes still closed, she inhaled the aroma of French bread baking. It smelled like home! Opening her eyes, she saw her mother running down the open back stairs. Gil stopped Franchise's descent to brief her on their daughter's condition.

"It's been a very long trip back home for Marriette," whispered Gil. "I told her about Pierre. She seems to be in one piece, but completely exhausted. She's been asleep since we left the airport."

Still lying on the front seat, Marriette looked up through the windshield seeing her mother talking with her father on the stairway. She was relieved to be home and felt safe again.

Marriette got out of the car and embraced her mother as her father joined them. Not much was needed to be said at that moment. They climbed the stairs to the second floor and entered the kitchen. The comforting smell of bread baking below circulated throughout the house, same as it ever was.

Marriette walked through the kitchen and down the corridor into the front parlor. Nothing had changed. Her home looked the same. Alone on a small table near the front-facing windows was a formal picture of her brother in dress uniform. Staring at the portrait, Marriette gazed into her brother's steely cerulean eyes. A black silken cloth was draped around the picture. Her brother's Green Beret hung over a corner of the brass frame. Marriette picked up the beret.

"Did this come back with Pierre?" she asked.

"Yes," her father replied. "Not much else."

Marriette held it to her nose and cheek for a moment before placing it on her head, carefully draping the smooth fold in the felt to the side of her right eyebrow, aligning the red and yellow striped 5th SFG flash over her left eye as she had seen her brother do.

She noticed his dog tags on the table. The long chain with one tag was discolored, from a fire perhaps. The other, on the smaller chain now attached to the longer, was relatively clean and shiny. She gathered up the tags and chains and coiled them into her palm, closing her fist around them. Marriette held them to her chest, shutting her eyes tightly. She then returned the beret to the corner of the portrait but placed Pierre's tags around her neck.

"I feel as though I need to wear these for a while," she said aloud. "I owe it to him."

The words puzzled Marriette's mother who was standing at her daughter's side with her head resting against hers. Françoise had little understanding of why Pierre put himself in such dangerous situations and then paid with his life.

Although grieving his loss, Marriette knew Pierre had lived in his element. It wasn't so much about the war in Vietnam or other places he was sent to in the world. It was about experiencing the intensity of his specialized job. He was the archetype of the universal warrior, the soldier of fortune with allegiance to his brothers in arms. Away from this environment of risk and danger, Pierre felt an emptiness, and depression set in. Separation led some to drink and smoke dope, while others added more formidable drugs, lawlessness or hard labor. Pierre reenlisted.

Later in the afternoon, Marriette began feeling the effects of the time zone difference, mixed with the accumulated fatigue of travel. She promised her parents that they would talk more in the morning. She excused herself and went off to take a long shower.

As the hot water poured over her head, Marriette felt Africa washing away. She watched as the stain of soapy orange silt accumulated in a pool, swirling on the tile floor before disappearing down the drain. She revisited images of her African family. She thought of her deep affection for the tall young man whose hand she held onto until the last possible moment only days ago.

Marriette studied the dog tags now resting between her breasts, rubbing the tarnished tag to see if it might easily shine again. It would not. She had lost track of time. The cloud of steam around her had disappeared. The hot water was beginning to cool quickly. Her hair was finally clean; she felt much better. In her bedroom Marriette found a pair of blue jeans and a familiar tank top, but putting them on seemed like clothing from a distant past.

Gil and Franchise's lanky daughter walked into the parlor still combing her long chestnut hair, surprising them with her transformation.

"There's my beautiful girl," Gil called, from his red Naugahyde easy chair.

"I'm really tired," Marriette admitted, "but I want to walk downtown to buy a few new things. I don't want to wait until tomorrow. I'll be right back."

"Do you want me to come with you, honey?" her dad asked as he stood up.

Marriette walked up to her father and hugged him.

"No, Daddy, but tomorrow we will. It feels so strange being back. It's so good to be home, but it feels like I'm in two places at the same time."

Clutching the pocketbook which still held her checkbook and driver's license in it, she gave each of her parents a kiss.

Smiling, she said with amusement, "Well, I guess my checking account still has money in it. I haven't spent any of it lately."

Marriette went out the back door and trotted down the stairs. She walked along the sidewalk, crossing the bridge over the river into town. Well aware of her disorientation, the trip to town seemed a gentle way to reacquaint herself with civilization.

Within an hour she had purchased some jeans, tops, underwear, socks and a comfortable pair of shoes. Marriette also replaced her pocketbook with a small leather backpack, emptying the contents of the old into the new. She put the old pocketbook, jeans and top into a Goodwill container that she passed on her way home. She dug out two dimes from her new jeans pocket, inserting them into the old red Coca-Cola machine still standing out in front of the hardware store, the iconic green glass bottles aligned vertically behind the white access door. Marriette lingered on a park bench drinking the Coke while watching townspeople pass by. She purposely tapped her feet on the cement sidewalk reminding herself that she was solidly on the ground in Vermont – and really home.

On the walk back to the bakery, she looked down State Street in the direction of the cemetery. As she did, she pressed her palm to her chest feeling the dog tags beneath her tank top.

When she arrived home, Marriette explained to her parents that she already felt more acclimated just doing a few ordinary activities of civilization. She apologized for her need to retire early and went right to bed. As she crawled in between the fresh cotton sheets, the idea of being back in her own bed felt strange, yet so comfortable.

The next morning, before opening her eyes, Marriette became aware of the traffic noise outside her windows and the gentle rhythmic hum of machinery at work in the bakery. At 11 a.m., the room was bright with the late morning sun. Her head still deep in her pillow, she squinted one eye open as she considered what she might want to accomplish on this new day. The flutter of a pigeon brushing against the screen, as it came to rest on the ledge outside the window, startled her. She propped herself up on one elbow to watch the pigeon march back-and-forth along the outside sill.

Suddenly, an awareness emerged that her brother was not off on a mission somewhere. She sat up in bed, occupied by a wave of sadness. Marriette walked across the room and knelt at the window, resting her elbows on the sill. She looked out from the third floor through a break in the tree line toward the cemetery across the river where her brother's body lay. His loss felt unbearable and Marriette knew she must focus elsewhere. She stood up, stretched, and made ready to join her parents who were both at work in the bakery below.

The three walked to a favorite restaurant for lunch. After eating, Marriette's desire was to go to the state park for a swim. Her mother was happy to join her. The late spring days in Vermont had not yet warmed the lake but, after a quick swim in the cold clear water, they lay on big rocks warmed by the sun at the water's edge. This provided an opportunity to discuss the loss of Pierre.

Françoise felt that Pierre's death was inevitable. Although she had never given up all hope, she had hardened her heart against the notification she predicted would eventually come.

She searched for what she might have done or not done to cause him to become who he was. It confounded her that he chose to do what he did and be so proud of it. Marriette's attempt to explain what motivated Pierre seemed inadequate and not fully comprehended by her mother, at least for the time.

Marriette and her parents spent the evening reminiscing about Pierre and hearing stories about her time in Africa. Gil and Françoise knew Marriette would be returning to McGill to begin her degree in clinical psychology. It was a comfort for them to know their daughter would be nearby for the next four or five years. In a few days, Marriette planned to drive north to McGill to officially report to the anthropology department and collect the rest of her belongings. She needed to complete writing her master's thesis before beginning the next program in September.

After dinner, the three walked to Pierre's gravesite. The cemetery was located on a steep hillside near the river. They walked along the cement sidewalks cracked and displaced by elm tree roots and frost heaves. Dozens of new American flags, replenished recently for Memorial Day, marked the resting places of veterans fallen in conflicts since the birth of the nation.

When they arrived at the gravesite there was a surprise. Someone had visited Pierre's gravestone and left an offering of respect. A Special Forces flash pin was present on the flat granite marker next to Pierre's name. A more remarkable memorial was erected beside it: thrust vertically into the earth, supported by its attached bayonet, was an old M1 Garand rifle. A steel helmet covered the end of the gun stock.

The new memorial was striking and personal, relative to the subtle black granite rectangle embedded horizontally at their feet. At that moment, Marriette thought her brother's death ambiguous. How did she really know her brother was dead? She had not attended a funeral nor viewed his body. Neither had her parents. Perhaps some unknown's body came back with Pierre's dog tags. The possibility that her brother might make himself disappear for a conceived higher cause was not out of the question for her. Pierre bought into the SF motto, totally. He lived to 'free the oppressed'. It said so on the flash pin centered on the unit crest on the Green Beret he had worn as if it was his skin. Somehow, it was comforting to think Pierre might still be alive and on some strange day materialize for a moment and then be gone again. Until that moment, as long as she needed to, Marriette would tell him her story over and over again. She sensed the telling would make her feel safe and whole. There was no one else she could tell.

Very early the next morning, Marriette returned alone to Pierre's gravesite. She knelt on the wet grass in front of the memorial. The M1 and helmet were still in place. It was raining lightly. She pulled the dog tags out from inside her jersey making them visible. Ignoring the now steady rain, Marriette wasn't going to leave until she told Pierre the story of the tragedy and tragedies averted. The skills her brother taught her had saved her life.

The early morning rain fell harder into the mountain valley and soon she was soaked. Soft rain poured over her head and into her eyes. Marriette removed a knife from its sheath and made a deep slit into the loam next to the new stone marker. Chiseled into the granite it read,

Pierre Andre LaFleur, SFC
5th Special Forces Group
'De Opresso Liber'
6 June 1944 - March 1972
United States Army
'Born On D-Day'

Marriette took out a brass rifle ammunition casing from her jeans pocket and pushed it into the earth as far as she could, tamping the earth firm with the tang of the knife.

Passing overhead, a Green Mountain cloudburst produced a deluge of rainfall limiting visibility, creating spontaneous rivulets which sped downhill merging among the gravestones and pouring over the sidewalks. Near the bottom of the hill at the edge of the cemetery, there converged an uninterrupted sheet of water breaking like waves against the uphill surfaces of the headstones, rushing across the street and down the embankment as a cascade, racing into the river. The deafening crack of a nearby lightning strike and ensuing claps of thunder echoed across the mountainsides, rolling throughout the valley.

Marriette stood up, her arms outstretched, her open palms gesturing toward the grave, the knife still in her left hand. Through the low-pitched roar of torrential rain pounding the earth, she looked up into the downpour, shouting at the sky.

"Merci, Pierre. Je t'aime mon frère." (Thank you, Pierre. I love you, my brother.)

Suddenly, a car door slammed. Her father's station wagon was on the cart path nearby. Through the downpour, Gil hustled toward Marriette with a blanket.

"Chéri, Marriette!"

"C'est bon papa. Je t'aime." (It's OK, daddy. I love you.)

"Je t'aime aussi ma fille." (I love you my daughter.) "Nous rentrerons a la maison maintenant." (We will go home now.)

Gil wrapped his daughter in the blanket and guided her back to the car. She put the knife back into its sheath, handing it to her father. It was Pierre's knife. Soaking wet, she curled up against her father sobbing into his shoulder as he drove home. Gil wondered what had moved Marriette to come here alone in the storm, but sensed she was doing what she needed to do. The rain disguised his own tears, shed both for the loss of his son and the joyful long-awaited presence of his daughter. He kissed her forehead as she nestled beside him.

"I'll be okay now, Daddy. Don't worry about me. I can come home now."

– Chapter 2 –

Back to McGill
Thursday, July 6, 1972   Montreal, Quebec

Just six days after her return from Africa, Marriette drove north across the Canadien border in a '69 Chevelle Super Sport that Pierre had purchased while home on leave in the spring of 1970. It had been stored in the garage behind the bakery and now the Chevelle belonged to her. It was nothing like the old Volkswagen bug she sold prior to leaving for Africa. As she cruised along, Marriette reflected on how much her life had changed. Two weeks ago, she was walking barefoot in the dust on another continent, today she was driving the interstate at 70 miles an hour with plenty of speed to spare.

There was a list of things that Marriette planned to accomplish when she arrived in Montreal. She needed to find an apartment. Waiting for her at the anthropology department was the other trunk to unpack which held her belongings, including several plant presses filled with botanical specimens.

The purpose of her travel to Africa had been to investigate the natural sources of medicinal remedies used by the tribe she resided with. This was as an extension of her pharmacology degree as a masters in anthropology. The foray also presented an opportunity for something adventurous. It turned out to be that and much more.

Three months prior to leaving Africa, Marriette and several tribe members had experienced a traumatic event. Coincidentally, it happened around the same time that her brother was killed in Vietnam. Within days of the incident, Marriette began experiencing nightmares and having intrusive, persistent recollections. At their worst, the flashbacks made her feel like it was actually happening again. Initially she tried to avoid thinking about the incident and made a point of distracting herself.

She soon discovered that it would be tough to avoid her thoughts. In the closely knit tribal community, individuals approached her wanting to hear the details of what had happened. They didn't avoid asking questions as would have been the case in her culture. As a result, she found herself retelling her story many times over.

In time, Marriette recognized that it was somehow helpful to talk about this traumatic event. It was painful, especially at first, when it seemed she was telling the story and reliving the incident for weeks on end. These conversations led her to examine the incident each time in detail as she recounted it. She eventually discovered that how she perceived the images and feelings evoked by the memory mattered. She began to redefine the memories as just thoughts appearing in her stream of consciousness. She found she could remove herself from them. Her symptoms had improved somewhat since the event. However, now, with the loss of her brother, the intrusive thoughts of her trauma in Africa returned.

There was another problem. As Marriette was no longer in Africa, she couldn't tell anyone about what happened due to the circumstances of the incident. That was out of the question, at the present. She had counted on being able to tell her brother as he was the only one she knew who would understand. The best she could do was speak to him at his gravesite, and in doing so, she found a modicum of peace.

As Marriette pondered this on her drive to McGill, she wondered if it might be beneficial to listen to herself talk through the incident. When she arrived in Montreal, she went to a department store and bought a cassette recorder. That afternoon, after checking into a downtown hotel, she recorded the same story she had told her brother with as much deliberate and painful detail as possible.

She planned to listen to it at least once a day and later evaluate and make notations on the frequency and subjective quality of her intrusive thoughts. How many times per day, per week, would these intrusions occur, and would her response improve over time as she attempted to reframe her thoughts?

Her first stop when she arrived on campus had been the psychology department library where she spent several hours looking through journals searching for articles concerning the treatment of traumatic stress. She found little that didn't emphasize the approach of traditional psychoanalysis which was subjective in nature and the focus of early 20th century psychology.

There were, however, a few journal articles and a textbook authored by Aaron Beck, a research-oriented psychiatrist at the University of Pennsylvania. He believed that delving into the murky unconscious of the distant past through traditional psychoanalysis had little to do with current anxieties, particularly when history of trauma was well defined and recent. He designed treatment methods and tests to demonstrate whether his approach worked. This was his point of difference. In the developing science of psychology, this was a new and evidence-based approach to understanding human behavior; it immediately appealed to Marriette.

****

The next morning, as Marriette sat in the student union cafeteria scanning through the Montreal Gazette, a grad student walking by recognized her.

"Marriette! You're back!"

She stood up and gave him a hug. "Hi, Gary."

"I haven't seen you in a while, Marriette. Where have you been?"

Gary McDonald was beginning his PhD program in the Botany Department at the same time Marriette was getting ready to leave for Africa. He had helped her prepare for the collecting of the plant specimens she needed for her thesis.

Gesturing to a friend with him, he said, "This is my housemate. James Roy. Meet Marriette LaFleur."

"Ravi de vous recontrer, James." (Nice to meet you, James.)

"Bonne aprés-midi, Marriette." (Good afternoon, Marriette.)

Gary, a native of Iowa, responded in jest, "It looks like I'm the odd man out here!"

"I assumed they spoke French in Des Moines. Sounds French to me," returned James, playfully.

Gary continued with a sales pitch to Marriette. "We just rented a three-bedroom house west of here on upper Belmont Avenue. It's about a 10-minute drive. Have you found a place yet? We have another bedroom available with its own bath. Interested?"

"Well, no, I haven't, and yes, I am interested. As it turns out, Gary, that was my project for this afternoon," Marriette emphasized, pointing to Montreal newspapers opened in front of her on the cafeteria table.

"So. I'm glad you happened by! When can I look at it? And is there a place to park off the street?"

"There's a two-car garage in the back and it's an extra five dollars a month for a spot. So that's 60 CD a month. It's a pretty clean place. The landlord only rents to graduate students. $35 CD for your part of the damage fees. Utilities included. Private families on either side of us."

"That sounds pretty good. I would like a spot in the garage."

"For that old Volkswagen bug?" Gary laughed.

"Oh, that's gone," Marriette answered. "I have my brother's '69 Chevelle SS. It's a long story."

She paused, subtly remarking off the cuff, "I have lots of long stories these days."

"Gosh, this is terrific, Marriette. Here's the address."

Gary ripped a page from his spiral notebook, wrote down the address, and handed it to her.

He continued, "We'll be back there by one. Can you come over then? I think your problem is solved. You can go right to the sports page now."

"I'll be there. Thanks, Gary. Bonjour, James."

"Bonjour, Marriette. See you soon," returned James.

Later, as Marriette approached the house, she immediately felt comfortable with the neighborhood. There were huge elm trees on both sides of the street, and it seemed quiet. She turned into the driveway and parked in front of the garage next to a yellow truck. James came out the back door to greet her.

"Bienvenue."

"Bienvenue, Marriette," James returned the greeting.

"I like it all, so far."

"Come in."

James led the way as they toured the kitchen and other ground floor rooms. "There's a laundry in the basement. Gary's and my bedrooms are on the first floor."

They went upstairs to what may have been an attic at one time. Now it was a large bedroom with an attached bath.

"I'll take it, James, if that's OK. It's better than I hoped for."

"OK!"

They went back downstairs into the kitchen and out the back door. Standing next to her car, James commented, "So, Gary told me a little bit about you. Considering your academic background, the SS 396 doesn't seem to fit in. It's beautiful. An L78. This was ordered special."

"As I mentioned, it was my brother's. It is pretty nice. It's fast. Well, very fast and it's paid for! Maybe I'll sell it and get something more practical. What's your story, James?"

"I have a semester left to get my education teaching certificate. I should be through by the end of January. I plan to teach English, French, and writing. I've considered going another three years to get my doctorate, but I haven't decided yet. I'm kind of behind my peers."

"Me, too. I'll be 30 this September."

"Really! I turn 30 in a couple of weeks."

"What have you been doing all these years, Marriette?" James inquired.

"Well, in addition to the African trip . . . I assume Gary mentioned that to you . . . my family has a bakery in Montpelier, and I worked there for five years after high school before coming here. And you?"

"After high school in Sherbrooke, I continued in Junior Hockey. Made it onto the Blackhawks for parts of two years."

"Nice!"

"Yeah, but it was clear I wasn't going to make a reasonable living and remain healthy for very long, so I applied to McGill."

"That's an interesting start. You do look like a big winger."

"Good guess. I was."

James had been immersed in the Canadian hockey culture. Despite it being over, he had no regrets. Nearing thirty, he was more comfortable writing and wanted a future in teaching.

Feeling comfortable with James, Marriette extended an invitation, "James. I have to go buy a bed. Would you like to come with me? We can talk some more."

"Sure, let's go. Shouldn't we take my truck?"

"Great idea. Thanks."

They got into the pickup and James backed out of the driveway and onto Belmont Ave.

"Marriette. I like how you addressed me in French. Might we continue that?"

"Ce me va. J'aime cette id'ee." ("It suits me. I like that idea.")

James Roy was about 6' 2", attractive and looked as though he could still play left wing for some team. He spoke in a quiet and deliberate tone, which was a manner very similar to the woman sitting on the bench-seat beside him. James and Marriette returned to the apartment around five p.m. with the furniture. She went right back out to purchase some linens so she could spend her first night at the new place.

While she was gone, Gary and James had an opportunity to talk. Gary asked James what he thought of their new roommate.

James responded, "I know this sounds ridiculous, eh? Guys say stuff like this all the time but… I think I'm going to marry this girl, someday. I just feel it."

"How about that?" Gary replied. "Marriette's pretty sharp. I'd say, don't expect to lead the way very often. That girl has a lot of drive."

"I like that," James replied. "Thanks for the intro, Gary. I'll take it from here. Ha! You can count on being my best man."

"I'm going to hold you to it."

Marriette was happy with how the day developed. She had accomplished much of what was on her list. She loved the apartment. She was already friends with Gary and, although she had only spent the afternoon with James, she liked him a lot and felt comfortable around him. What a pleasant surprise it was.

– Chapter 3 –

The Summer with James
Friday, August 4, 1972   Montreal, Quebec

Once Marriette had moved in, the list of tasks she needed to accomplish grew each day. She drove back and forth from Montreal to Montpelier several times, gathering furnishings and household necessities for her new living space.

For her studies, she began writing her master's thesis and worked with Gary McDonald to identify the plants she had collected in Africa. This segment was completed by mid-July and Gary left at that time to visit his parents in Iowa. While Marriette had been on site in Africa, she neatly organized her notes concerning the preparation of the plants and their medicinal uses by the native people. Now, she needed to reorganize that information into thesis format, which she planned to complete by mid-August.

Both James and Marriette carried a light academic load that summer, with James teaching two summer courses which would be over by the first of August. Being at home more, the two frequently found themselves in each other's presence, and discovered they enjoyed each other's company. Living in the same house was working out well.

On Marriette's last trip to her parents' place to pick up her belongings, James accompanied her, taking his yellow truck. Françoise and Gil were pleased to meet the handsome young Canadien who grew up just across the border in Sherbrooke. Gil was impressed that James had played for the Blackhawks even if it wasn't for long and was for an American team. With James's sharing the Canadien heritage, the four conversed naturally in French during the visit. Marriette's parents were hopeful when they met James. With their daughter soon turning 30, she was getting late of the marrying age for those times. With Pierre gone, Marriette was their sole chance of expanding their family.

****

Just after midnight on August 4th, James was still awake when he heard a scream coming from upstairs. He and Marriette had been talking until she went to bed around eleven. James had stayed up, finishing some school work in his room downstairs. Pausing long enough to realize what he heard,

James scrambled out of his room, ran down the hall, and up the stairs. Standing in front of Marriette's closed door, he noticed a light in the space beneath it.

"Marriette? Marriette! What's going on? Are you OK?"

She had heard him running up the stairs. "It's OK. Come in, James."

James entered the dimly lit bedroom. Marriette was sitting on the edge of her bed, brushing her hair away from her face. She was breathing heavily trying to compose herself as James sat down beside her.

"Nightmare?" he gently inquired.

"Yes," Marriette responded, looking into his eyes. She tried to speak but couldn't, still shaking. James moved closer and put his arm around her.

"Marriette. What can I do for you?"

"I'll be OK. Please stay with me for a few minutes. This hasn't happened in a while."

James softly replied in response, "That implies it has occurred before."

"Not since I was in Africa."

"Something happened there," James declared.

"Yes, something happened."

James chose not to pursue the matter further as Marriette stood up.

"I'm just going into the bathroom to wash my face with some cold water. Please stay, OK?"

"I'll be right here," James reassured.

While Marriette was in the bathroom, James looked around and noticed how all the things they moved from her family home had been thoughtfully arranged. Marriette returned and sat on the edge of the bed next to him.

"I'm sorry, James. Living in Africa for two years provided a lifetime of wonderful memories . . . but there were also some significant negatives that I'm still dealing with. Perhaps I can talk to you about it, someday, when I'm ready. That is, if you are interested."

"Of course I am, Marriette, when you are comfortable."

"I also haven't told you my brother was killed in Vietnam five months ago . . . which is why I have his Chevelle. The first I learned of his death was upon arriving home at the end of June. What was that . . . five weeks ago?"

James again put his arm around Marriette's shoulder, kissing her hair.

"I'm sorry, Marriette," he said quietly.

She turned and hugged him, holding onto him as she spoke.

"I've known you for less than a month, James, and already I feel very comfortable around you. It's been so nice talking and doing things together since I moved in. I guess I needed that more than I realized. A nice surprise."

"I think it's a fine start to a friendship. I'm comfortable, too."

Marriette lifted her head from his shoulder, and smiled sweetly.

"I have a thought," James added. "We both have some time left before school begins again. Let's drive up to the Gaspé and see some beautiful places together. We could leave in the morning. I'd like to get to know you better and I want you to get to know me. To be clear, I have no expectations of intimacy. The only thing I would hope for is that we are comfortable together. Let's just enjoy life for a few days or whatever makes sense, and then we'll come home."

"Home?" Marriette interjected.

"You're home right now, aren't you? This feels like home to me."

"Can we really leave tomorrow?"

"As far as I'm concerned. First, though, we should get some sleep. Leave your door open. Mine will be open as well, so call me if you need me."

James had moved from the bed and stood in her doorway.

"Thank you, James. I'll try not to wake you up anymore."

"Good night, Marriette," James whispered, as he blew her a kiss.

"Good night, James," Marriette responded, forming a kiss on her lips.

Marriette fell asleep with James on her mind. She woke up at seven feeling rested and went straight into the shower. After packing a couple of days' worth of clothes and necessities, she went downstairs. James's door was open, and she heard the shower running. When the water stopped, she called to him from the kitchen.

"Good morning, James. Do you still want to go?"

Wrapped in a towel, James stuck his head around the door and answered, "Good morning, Marriette. Yes. Let's have a little breakfast and get out of here. Are you making coffee, by chance?"

"Yes. I'm getting the coffee started and I'm excited about our trip."

"I am, too. I'll be right there. Breakfast here and lunch in Quebec City."

In half an hour they were finished with breakfast and loading equipment into his F-100 pickup.

"So, what do we have here?" asked Marriette, pointing to the back of the truck.

"That's a tent . . . Then, there's a couple of air mattresses, sleeping bags, matches, a flashlight, fishing gear, a carboy of fresh water, toilet paper, a little shovel, some cooking stuff, and the cooler. We need to get some ice, wine, and beer. And anything else we can think of, just in case we find ourselves in the middle of nowhere, which is kind of where we're going. We'll see."

"When did you do all this?"

"When I left you last night."

"Wow! Looks like we're ready."

Just before climbing into the truck, Marriette walked up to James and wrapped her arms around him.

"Thank you for taking care of me last night. I'm really glad I wasn't alone."
"I'm happy you weren't either," James responded, with a gentle squeeze.

****

As they were driving to Quebec City, James broached the topic of relationships.

"I would like to say something about where I am in life," James began. "I'm not a kid any longer. Twenty years of playing hockey at one level or another was more than enough. In the end it didn't make sense to continue. I love what I do now. I love to read and write, and I want to continue living in an academic environment. It's time for me to get serious about the future . . . I'm looking for that special relationship, not in playing games."

Folding her legs beneath her to face James, Marriette replied, "I very much want that special relationship, too. Maybe this is it. Maybe it isn't. James, I promise you that whatever I say, I mean. I will always be honest about what I'm thinking and what I'm comfortable with. That's hard to do… sometimes…telling the truth…and may be hard to hear. In the course of an explanation, I always hope to get it right, but if I'm misunderstood, I would like that second chance to explain myself again."

"Yes, exactly," James agreed.

"James, I don't have any skeletons in my closet. I've had a pretty stress-free life until recently, but I'm discovering how to recover from that. I believe I may be onto a new approach regarding therapy for people who have experienced extreme stress. The incident I have yet to tell you about may have delivered my PhD thesis right into my hands."

"Really? You seem pretty sure of yourself."

"Well, enough to push me forward, certainly. People who have experienced traumatic events are left with impressive images and feelings of those events, whatever they may be. Maybe some folks are more susceptible than others. Some may recover sooner and some not at all ... I've got a notion that the longer they carry those unexamined memories, the more the pathology accumulates and affects their lives.

"Although I haven't done an exhaustive literature search so far, I'm not impressed with current therapy methods, so I hope to develop a more effective approach. James, some of what I'm saying may sound disjointed and even enigmatic, but I'm hopeful you'll understand later."

"I'm listening to you, Marriette. Of course, I'm puzzled. It's obvious that your mind has been occupied looking for answers. You must have your reasons for not yet explaining what happened in Africa."

"I do. Please bear with me. What I confide to you will be told in total confidence. It's still very raw. There was a tragic event involving me and several of the tribe members. McGill University is not aware of any of this and I want to keep it that way."

Marriette nervously ran her hand through her hair, rubbing the back of her neck. "There are a lot of issues I still need to work out. I guess I demonstrated that last night."

Marriette leaned forward and adjusted the little triangular window on the door, directing a stream of cool air into the cab of the truck.

"James, I can't tell you the details of the situation just yet. I cannot tell anyone. There had been the factor of my physical safety. Simply getting out of Africa eliminated that concern. As you can see, I'm physically fine."

"OK. I'm following you."

Marriette placed a blanket behind her and propped herself up against the door, facing James.

"Thank you, James. I promise not to monopolize our entire afternoon with all this, but I should like to provide some history as I begin to tell you what the last two years were like."

"Sure, Marriette."

"A few years ago, my brother, Pierre, told me war stories including some of the horrific events he had experienced, including combat losses of soldiers he worked closely with . . . his team members.

"I was curious about all of this. I would ask him questions, trying to under-stand how soldiers coped with the loss of people they were close to or how killing was part of their job. He accepted that I was naturally intrigued and was happy to answer my questions. He said that in the years he had been in the Special Forces, those who could not process loss and fear washed out. That is, they transferred to another part of the Army or might be clas-sified as medically unfit for assignment and, to make matters worse, any behavior suggesting being unable to take the stress was often stigmatized.

"It seemed to me as though some minds were more adept at processing extremely stressful trauma while others were not. My brother said that it wasn't predictable. You could never tell by looking at someone, who could handle it and who could not . . . until they were challenged. He didn't let on what might be going on in his mind either and denied any problems."

Marriette gathered up her long hair, which was caught in the turbulence of wind blowing into the cab.

"Do you remember my telling you about the unique memorial that was left at my brother's grave site?"

"Yes, the rifle and the helmet."

"Yes," Marriette continued, "that impressed me. I believe it was put there by Pete Long . . . he's a reclusive guy who has always been around town . . . a World War II combat vet. Always wears an OD green patrol hat. He's a gunsmith and has a small engine repair business. Pete also operates a shooting range a couple of miles outside of town. I plan to visit him soon.

"My brother and he were very good friends. Pete's life has been a social disaster. He married right after the war and had a child, but his wife left him and took the child with her. He had been abusive, and a local church assisted in her getting out of town. Pete somehow managed to get a college degree in Illinois, off the G.I. Bill, before moving to Vermont. Don't know what . . . sociology, philosophy, or history, maybe. Pierre said he reads a lot.

"Pete remarried a year after his wife left and that marriage fell apart as well in just a matter of months. Pete's a recovering alcoholic, but still a chain smoker. My brother remained close to him from high school on. When Pierre came home on leave, he always went to see Pete, and all Pierre ever said to me was that he and Pete had things in common.

"I'm curious to know what happened to Pete and if he suffers from combat events or their sequelae. I went with my brother to Pete's range several times to fire their military weapons and such, so Pete does know who I am."

"You don't strike me as a gun enthusiast," James remarked, his eyebrows raised in surprise.

"Hardly. Before I went to Africa, my brother informed me that it was potentially dangerous there. He suggested that he give me some survival training. At the time, I couldn't imagine why, but I followed through because he was insistent. Unrelenting even. As it turned out, he was right."

"Jesus! Marriette, this is getting interesting."

"Weapons have their place. If you feel unsafe and threatened, it feels better to be armed. Now, I wouldn't have said that prior to the incident in Africa. While we are out onto the Gaspé, we're in bear country . . . so we take all the usual precautions. But, in addition to that, I'm carrying a .45 caliber pistol in my backpack for no purpose other than our protection. I admit I would not have considered this a few months ago. Maybe this is a temporary feeling I have or maybe I'm taking a reasonable precaution."

"Well, I can't argue with you. It's something I wouldn't have thought of either, but it doesn't freak me out. I go deer and moose hunting with my father nearly every fall."

Looking puzzled, James added, "I'm not accustomed to a pretty girl packing a .45, though. Where did it come from?"

"It belonged to my brother, of course. By the way, Pierre wasn't for or against the war in Vietnam. He just thrived doing what he did. He was a warrior, and he apparently handled the stress well . . . the thrill of the risk. Who knows, actually. He told me that most of his group expected to die, sooner or later, an occupational hazard. Pierre just couldn't stop . . . addiction of sorts.

"As for me, I'm against the war. It's just politics . . . nothing new . . . the protection of American business interests. The despicable politicians who are responsible for this war are among the worst of humanity. As usual, a lot of young kids die or their lives are destroyed, misled into thinking they're doing something wonderful for their country. With their draft, in peacetime none the less, the young and inexperienced in life, the poor, the uneducated who don't have a choice, are taken away, like slaves, tricked or forced into serving the needs of business."

James smirked at that notion. "Yes. Just more of the same. So glad that I'm Canadien."

Emphatically, Marriette replied, "I was born in Montreal. I have dual citizenship. Always will. So, I can always go back home."

James acknowledged the statement with a subtle tilt of his head. Conversation made the long drive pass quickly. They arrived at noon as planned in Quebec City.

Wandering downtown, James parked his truck in front of a restaurant that had an enticing outdoor patio. Once seated on the sunny patio at the café, they absorbed the character of the city and province. This was their culture. They ordered their meals and a bottle of red wine.

It amused Marriette that, on the drive up, they had sometimes spoken in English and sometimes in French. As they were eating lunch, she thought about this, paused, and looked up at James, smiling, maintaining her directed gaze until he responded.

"Marriette?" he asked.

As she poured more burgundy into each of their glasses, she suggested, "I propose that, when we are alone together, we always speak in our native tongue, if you will. It is so personal."

"Yes. That was actually on my mind earlier."

James waited a moment before raising his glass in a toast.

"Then, pour toujours ('for always'), if I may be so bold."

Marriette touched her glass to his.

"Then, pour toujours if I may be so bold," Marriette replied.

As they looked into each other's eyes. James rocked out of his bent wire chair and leaned across the table. Marriette responded in kind as they shared a gentle kiss on the lips.

"Our first kiss," she said.

"To our first kiss," James responded as they touched their glasses and sipped more of the red French wine.

– Chapter 4 –

The Camping Trip
Saturday, August 5, 1972   Gaspé Peninsula

Marriette took the wheel of the pickup as they left Quebec City. They drove another three hours to the Gaspé Peninsula, and followed the north road hugging the coastline. As they drove, the Gulf of St. Lawrence widened until land was no longer visible to the north. Instead, mile after mile opened spectacular views of the ocean on their left and a low growing coniferous forest to their right.

By mid-afternoon, Marriette and James discovered a gravel road that led to a stony beach and a large freshwater stream emptying into the Atlantic. Driving further over the rocky surface, they parked the truck on a level camping spot, proximate to the river with the bed of the pickup facing toward the ocean.

It was a remarkable location that they were eager to explore. They began with the sandy ocean beach, then moved on to the rushing stream emerging from the forest. They walked along the rocky riverbed upstream, following it under the highway bridge that crossed the road high above them. Under the bridge, in partial shade, a wide basin had formed. Marriette discovered Rainbow and Brook trout swimming deep in the crystalline pool. She called out to James, who was a few steps behind her, "Look at this! We may have something else besides bread and cheese for supper."

Crouching on her knees, Marriette peered into the deep pool studying the activity of the fish as James approached behind her.

"You have fishing equipment, James?" she asked, her face still next to the water. James knelt beside her on the smooth round rocks.

"Yes, I do. I've a fly rod for each of us."

She looked up at him, smiling.

"Really? You are so well-prepared."

Marriette stood up surveying the surroundings. "James, look at this beautiful land. This is our country! Oh, Canada! Africa is beautiful too, but it's so good to be home!"

"It is magnificent," James agreed.

"So beautiful James," she repeated, her arms outstretched, turning full circle.

Putting down her backpack, Marriette glanced over at James with a playful grin.

"I have to jump in. It won't scare the fish away."

"It might be a little cold," James cautioned, having no pressing interest in entering the cold stream. "You brought a swimsuit?"

"Sure, the one I always wear under my clothes. You don't mind, do you?"

"Well, ah . . . I guess we're getting to know each other," James responded sheepishly. "Do you expect me to come in, too?"

"Damn right I do, James Roy!"

James laughed from the surprise of Marriette's sudden inclination and potential for his embarrassment.

"James. I've been running around literally half naked for the last year. I guess I'll just have to get used to wearing clothes again."

Soon she was wearing only her brother's dog tags. James struggled to remove his jeans while maintaining his balance among the rocks. Marriette dove deep into the pool, screaming as she emerged on the other side. James grimaced as he walked in up to his chest and ducked under the surface. Springing back up, he exclaimed, "Damn! Cold enough for you?"

"I'll bet the ocean is even colder, Jamie."

Marriette dove under the water again surfacing in front of him. Moving closer, she pressed against his warm body and kissed him. Wrapping his arms around her, they kissed again.

"Nice second kiss, I'd say," murmured James.

"Yes, it was, Jamie," Marriette replied, with a smile.

They emerged from the pool sharing a towel and scrambled naked over the rocks back to the truck, happy with the way the day was unfolding. Dropping the tailgate, James fastened the chain supporting it. They sat together warming in the last rays of direct sun, gazing out onto the Atlantic.

The road over the bridge behind them coursed quickly uphill and disappeared at the top of a cliff to their right. The face of the rocky cliff was occupied by thousands of breeding gannets. More of the birds could be seen feeding far out to the horizon, diving with aerodynamic perfection below the surface and re-emerging, gullet full to shuttle back to their nests.

Marriette and James sat shoulder to shoulder holding hands. Powerful feelings of hope and expectation were washing over them. Both wondered if life had ever been any better than this.

Taking stock of their supplies, they inflated the air mattresses and unrolled the sleeping bags. James assembled the fly rods and chose a deep water fly to attach to each leader. Marriette was engaged in simple and comfortable tasks from her past, eliminating another wrinkle in her process of coming home again.

They carried their fly rods back to the deep pool, wading into the stream on opposite sides to make their casts. James glanced over at Marriette, who was standing in the rushing water up to her knees in her T-shirt and under-wear, making deft loops and laying the sinking line strategically over the surface. She was a lovely, tall Canadienne girl with long, pretty legs. Her chestnut brown hair was still wet from the swim and glistened in the bright afternoon sun.

The clarity of the water made it easy to see a trout pursue the fly and snap it into its mouth. Within a few minutes, they had a two- and a three-pound Brook trout to prepare for dinner.

After gathering driftwood from the ocean side beach, James started a fire and cleaned the trout while Marriette gathered blackberries that grew in abundance closer to the road. It proved to be a great dessert following Brook trout sautéed with red seaweed, cheese, baguettes, and cold Molson.

As the sun set on the hill behind them and the air became chilly, they kept the fire going. A long plank found among driftwood was placed on flatter stones to become their seat near the warmth of the campfire.

Marriette felt it was time to continue with her African story. She explained to James that she was the last graduate student to live with the tribe. The university had maintained a presence at this location in Ghana beginning in 1940, and the once primitive tribe had dramatically changed in those three decades. The student who left the year prior had been tasked with an exit study evaluating the creeping effects of civilization on the tribe. A striking example was that many of the tribe members now spoke the languages of the ever-present McGill students.

Marriette revealed there was one particular young man who spoke English and French fluently and could read and write at the level of a high school graduate or better. Although there was no designated chief for the tribe, this man, at 32, assumed most of the leadership responsibilities. He was born during the first year the university established its presence. He had, from one perspective, benefited greatly from growing up in that unusual academic environment. He desired and expected to learn new things as each new student arrived.

"As time went on, I came to know this man well. His name was Havra and he was tall and handsome and as well-spoken as you or I. As someone who had been provided with a private education, if you will, he came to realize he could go nowhere with it. Havra confided to me that during his twenties, he had considered returning to Canada with one of the students. Perhaps it might have been arranged, but, in the end, he felt responsible for his community and never left."

"Do you think he could have become a freshman in English at McGill?" James inquired, drawing a humorous parallel to his situation a few years previous.

"Probably. Maybe after a year of prep school."

"Impressive."

Marriette went on, "At the beginning of my second year there, I realized I wasn't integrating enough. Despite everyone being friendly, I distinctly felt my status as an outsider. I wanted to do better and thought I should try to assimilate. So, the first thing I did was adopt their female manner of dress. This meant wearing only a goat-skin skirt and applying a buttery orange soil stain to protect my skin from the sun and insects. I attempted to engage in everything they did, yet maintain just enough distance to be able to write about it."

"So, that explains your 'half naked for a year's comment. Havra is just about our age. Is that what you said?"

"That's right, James. Well, Havra is two years older. I was with him just about every day for some sort of educational lesson. I brought books with me especially for Havra on the direction of the students preceding me.

"As I mentioned before, we gradually became close friends. Although the tribal culture was polygamous, he had just one wife and one child, a son.

"As I participated more fully in tribal community life, I was perceived as an eligible unmarried female, however, much older by their standards since they customarily married early. To shorten a longer story for now, Havra requested I marry him, and I accepted. I went through a number of marriage rituals. I even have a tattoo souvenir from one of them. The marriage was, however, appropriately symbolic."

"Wait. Rituals? Marriage? Souvenir?"

"Yes, James. An honorary marriage. I'll explain. I know it must sound strange."

As he listened, James reached for another piece of wood, placing it on the fire in front of them. Looking over at Marriette, he kissed her on her cheek.

"OK, I'm with you."

Referring again to her souvenir comment Marriette said, "It's right here," touching the lower part of the zipper on her jeans.

"Yes, right here," she repeated with a barely perceptible shake of her head, connoting some disbelief and minor embarrassment.

James responded with a puzzled smile and a friendly roll of his eyes.

Continuing with her story Marriette explained, "Although I had anticipated a wedding night consummation, it never came to pass. That was not Havra's intention. He merely wished to protect me from the advances of other males in his tribe and neighboring ones. As it happened, it was never a concern. I was treated with respect by everyone. It seemed like a comfortable and safe place to be.

"Then, three months before I returned home, an incident occurred that changed everyone's life. Again, please James, bear with me about sharing those details for now. They will come."

Marriette stood up from their makeshift bench next to the fire to stretch before climbing onto the pickup bed. She settled prone on a sleeping bag, resting her chin in her hands as she looked into the fire.

"While a small group of us were about a day and a half trek away from the village, we were attacked by non-Africans. Havra's sixteen-year-old son was shot dead. I was nearly killed. No one else was physically hurt. The decisive action of one of the tribesmen and myself neutralized the attackers. It was a terrifying moment."

"Marriette!" James exclaimed. Astonished, he turned toward her, focusing on every nuance of her expression. He immediately moved up into the truck bed to lay beside her, propped up on an elbow. "Neutralized? What?"

"Yes, please, James. Be patient for now. I will explain when I am able. Well, we brought the young man's body back to the village. You can imagine the emotional climate. During the ensuing weeks . . . especially the first . . . things were tense in anticipation of something else happening. It never did. Funeral rituals lasted for weeks. I slept fitfully and my nightmares began. I was plagued with intrusive thoughts and flashbacks.

"Those of us who witnessed the attack spoke frequently about what had happened. I began to realize this made me feel better ... my nightmares began to diminish in intensity ... and talking seemed to have the same positive effect on the others, as well."

Stopping to catch her breath, Marriette took a sip from the can of Molson beside her and handed it to James. She remained silent, listening to the waves crashing along the beach in the dark. As each wave broke, the sound could be heard moving from left to right until replaced by the sound of the next breaker.

Ending the silence, James inquired, "How are you doing, Marriette?"

"I'm OK. There's just a little more I need to say. It's very important, and that will suffice for tonight. I'm looking forward to being close to you and falling asleep under the stars."

"Yes, sweet Marriette."

She smiled back in response.

"During the three months prior to leaving Africa, I spent considerably more time with Havra. I came to know him as a man thoroughly in tune with nature and more a part of it than I can ever fully explain. Yet because of his experience with the graduate students, he also became a man of civilization. An amazing conundrum.

"Havra sensed an end, as it traditionally existed, coming to their tribal community. Civilization was fast encroaching. After the tragic event, he began the process of discussing the future of their community with the elders of both his tribe and neighboring ones. In my last few weeks there, he revealed he had future plans to leave and make a new life in civilization. Havra knew he already had many of the necessary tools. He believed his language and literacy skills would find him work and I helped to prepare him the best I could."

James rolled onto his back gazing up at the stars. "Geez, Marriette. I know you're not getting into the specific details, but listening to what you've said so far ... Damn. What an amazing story you're telling me."

"There's more to be told," Marriette added, as she turned to face James. "Havra admitted he had never been as close to a graduate student as he was to me. Over those two years our relationship had developed naturally, apart from the ceremonial marriage. Then, there was also the tragic loss of his son. We talked about this extensively. It was painful for both of us in different ways. Although he was analytic about his own culture and tribal beliefs, he was not unaffected spiritually by them.

"According to their tradition, when a member of the community died, although there was no longer the presence of a living body, there remained a strong sense of the deceased's spirit. This connection ran deeply throughout the community and generated a great reverence for their Ancestors. Even for me, Havra's son had more of a 'soul' presence than would have been felt in our culture. In addition was the belief of reincarnation into another generation. The respected deceased was never far away."

Marriette and James repositioned themselves to lean against the cab staring out at the dark ocean. After pausing for a moment, she established eye contact with James.

"James, I fell in love with Havra. He is someone I will never forget. I have no idea what will become of him. I don't believe I could find him even if I wanted to, but if anyone can make their way in that situation, he will. He is driven and resourceful. When I think about it, it's disconcerting, but I try to put it in its proper place."

"I understand. This is tough, Marriette. And you were there just weeks ago."

"Two weeks before the driver arrived to pick me up to begin my journey home, Havra and I hiked to a mountain river where the tribe would go to bathe. It was a beautiful sanctuary. I had been there with him and the others many times before. However, that day we were alone. We made love for the first time – and did so again back at the village. Those will always be beautiful memories."

Marriette continued to maintain her eye contact with James.

"I hope you have had memories as beautiful with women you have cared for in the past. It's part of a good life if one is so fortunate."

"Of course. I understand completely," James replied. "There have been beautiful moments for me as well."

Marriette reached for his hand, holding it firmly in hers. "James, I have a concern. In this new situation we find ourselves, it is imperative that I am direct and honest with you."

In the light of the fire, James read the worried expression on her face. He felt her becoming close to him, yet detected her sense of possibly losing, with her next utterance, what was growing between them, which was still so fragile.

"James," she said, looking directly into his eyes, hoping for an understanding response, "I missed my period in June. It may easily be attributed to stress, but I also missed it in July. Maybe that's stress, too. My physiology was not regular while I was in Africa, so there are many factors. I would say I'm due anytime, but if nothing happens by next week, I plan to get a pregnancy test.

"I'm not quite sure how to say this, but I need to be very clear. My relationship with Havra was not casual. Although I never anticipated its development, if I am pregnant, that is not casual either."

"Marriette, I'm listening carefully. Your sharing this tells me who you are, does it not?" James held her close. The unexpected revelation concerned him immediately, but he chose not to react to it. Wiping a tear away from her cheek he kissed her. She snuggled into his shoulder.

"My turn for a brief story, OK?"

"OK, Jamie."

"Just two years ago, I also was in a serious relationship. We miscalculated and René became pregnant. We hadn't spoken about marriage a lot, but were a couple and understood we were heading in that direction. What I'm saying is that our relationship was not at all casual either. I loved her.

"René decided she wanted an abortion. Her decision was a shock to me. I assumed we would marry, and I disagreed with her. I was extremely disappointed, well, devastated might be a better word, about losing her, not understanding her as I imagined I had, and, worst of all, the loss of a child I was responsible for. But, you know . . . ultimately it was her right to make that choice. It was not the path I wanted for us as a couple. For me, in that instance, abortion was not an option, but I couldn't convince her otherwise. She did what she needed to do. I did as well and ended the relationship. It was painful for both of us."

"Oh, Jamie, I'm so sorry."

"So, my position is: if the will and conditions are there to raise a child, then that is what should happen. That's just me."

"I couldn't have stated it any better, Jamie."

"Marriette, of course, I recognize your situation adds concern to our relationship. You know that. I know that. But you are responding to your predicament as I believe I would, and I respect that."

James realized there was much for him to figure out and make sense of, but for the moment, he would remain hopeful and support her. He touched his hand to her cheek, directing his eyes into hers. "In the time we've known each other, I've come to feel ours is a relationship I need and wish to grow.

There is however, a lot more for us to consider, but I believe we should thoughtfully move ahead with our friendship. Do you agree?"

"I do, Jamie."

Marriette was relieved with his response, although she had braced herself for one less promising. With a soft sigh, Marriette posed a request. "I would like to go down to the stream and at least throw some water on my face. Would you come with me, please, Jamie?"

James answered, "Great, let's go. I'd like to clean up before bed, too. I may just go back in again."

James understood the reality that a child, who wasn't his, would carry into their relationship and hoped he would be up to the task. As he wasn't about to discard the promising relationship they were growing, James committed to proceed; to making it work.

Hand in hand, they made their way back to the pool below the bridge, their eyes now accustomed to the dark. The half-moon and bright star light illuminated the field of rocks, helping them to choose stepping stones to the water. Their reactive vocalizations upon reentering the cold water echoed along the river's canyon.

After bathing in starlight, they dried off and hiked back to the truck. Marriette piled the last of the wood onto the fire before climbing into the truck bed beside James. They lay together looking up at the sky, searching for satellites and shooting stars.

James turned toward Marriette, sensing her reluctance to approach. He kissed her gently on the lips. She reached up pulling him closer, returning the kiss. It was their mutual desire to secure a bond. They made love that night hoping this memorable day marked the start of a lifelong loving commitment.

– Chapter 5 –

A Baby and a Promise
Friday, August 25, 1972   Montreal, Quebec

James returned to the house on Belmont after a 50-minute workout at a local ice rink. It was a surface he had skated on many times during his early hockey career. Although he no longer had an interest in playing professionally, he coached youth hockey skills in exchange for ice time.

As James removed his equipment bag from the bed of his truck, he heard Marriette's Chevelle approaching. A moment later, the Malibu blue Super Sport turned into the driveway and parked beside him.

James called over, "Hi, Baby."

"Hi, Sweetie. Just getting back, eh?"

"It's a pretty hot day, and no air conditioning in my vehicle! The showers at the rink are just too gross to use. What do you have there?"

Marriette removed a package from the bag she was carrying and held it up in front of him.

"It's a home pregnancy test. Now to take it. Here I go…"

Unable to hide her nervousness, Marriette felt as if she were taking the ultimate test, with results that could instantly change the course of her life.

"Here WE go," James corrected, as he put his arms around her waist and kissed her. "Maybe I need to say this again for my own sake, to make sure you've understood. Whatever the result, I want to continue growing our relationship. If it's positive, we're still in this together."

Marriette threw her arms around his neck and jumped up, wrapping her legs around his waist. "I love you, too. I'm a very lucky girl."

They walked back inside, and James showered. As he emerged from the shower, Marriette called to him from the bedroom they now shared upstairs. They had turned his downstairs bedroom into an office for both of them.

"Jamie. Come out when you're ready. I've got it all set up!"

James opened the bathroom door wrapped in a towel. "So, how accurate is this test?" James inquired.

"I hope it's accurate and tells us today. The results of the hCG I had drawn won't be available for a week, but I don't want to wait that long."

James looked at the contents of the kit as he held the packaging in his hand.

"It's like a little laboratory, Sweetie. Can people really do this? The 'Predictor', they call it."

After following the directions together, they stared at the apparatus as a conclusive red ring slowly became visible in the mirror device of the kit.

"There it is, Jamie. I have a baby inside me. I guess I already knew it. They're getting larger," she said, cupping the underside of her breasts. Marriette then lay back on their bed, looking up at James.

"You sure you can do this, Jamie?"

He lay down on top of her and kissed her, whispering in her ear, "I'm sure I love you and want our relationship to thrive. There are challenges ahead and I don't know what we will encounter. I don't have all the answers, but we should try to find them together. I promise you, Marriette, I will try. I love you that much," James answered.

"I love you, Jamie. I know this won't be easy. I'm hopeful, Jamie. I am. Maybe one day, one fine day, we'll have a baby of our own. I'd like that."

"I'd like that, too."

Marriette had feared she would have to go this alone. Now, she sensed she had a partner. They both supported and encouraged the notion that everything in their lives was open for discussion and compromise. She was a lucky girl.

They made love late that afternoon, falling asleep in each other's arms, and were surprised when they awoke just as the sun was going down.

"Jamie. Jamie. Wake up. Looks like we took a long nap."

"What day is this?" remarked James, orienting himself. Marriette rolled onto her side facing him.

"I have a thought. If the hCG is also positive, I'm going to buy a house for us to live in."

James sat straight up, squinting at her.

"Buy a house. What? Really?"

"Yes. Really. My brother, as he would say, 'squared me away'. Where do you want to live?"

"Wait. Wait. I'm still not sure what day it is. How about this? Let's get dressed and walk downtown and get a pizza or something and talk more."

"Yes. That's a great idea!"

Later that week, when James was leaving for the university, he found Gary, alone in the kitchen eating breakfast.

"So, James, my friend," Gary remarked, remembering James's earlier comment about his future with Marriette, "it appears as though you were right."

"I believe I am," James nodded. "I do believe I am."

– Chapter 6 –

Sneaky Pete's
Tuesday, August 29, 1972   Montpelier, Vermont

Marriette headed north on Portal Road looking for the entrance to Pete Long's shooting range, locally known as 'Sneaky Pete's'. She spotted the sign that Pete hand carved years ago. The paint had peeled, and the sign board was split, but it still served as a marker.

Marriette visited Pete with her brother a few weeks prior to leaving for Africa. Pierre had surprised her with a return home from Minnesota. He probably knew he was going to reenlist but he didn't mention it to anyone in the family during the visit.

The range was located a half mile into the woods off Portal Road. Marriette parked her Chevelle across from the range office in front of the barn with its rusty metal roof. The back of the office was attached to Pete's compact two-bedroom house. Marriette knew Pete was home when she saw his truck, parked next to his living quarters. The truck was only a few years old and had once been Pierre's. She suspected her brother had given the truck to Pete, since it was in remarkably better condition than the house, the barn, and nearly everything else Pete owned.

Noticing the door to the range office was open, Marriette walked in and found Pete standing behind the counter, loading cartridges. Above his head was a five-foot-long quarter board carved with 'Screaming Eagles' in bright yellow enamel on a glossy black field. To the right was the iconic white eagle head and shoulder tab of the 101st Airborne Infantry carved into the pine plank. Pete looked up at Marriette recognizing her immediately.

He said simply, "I miss Pierre."

Pete was not nearly as tall as Marriette's 5' 10½". Looking older than his 48 years, Pete was thin and wiry from his chain smoking and poor efforts at nutrition. However, to his credit, he was still on the wagon after 12 years without alcohol.

He was wearing a khaki-colored Dickies work shirt. The long sleeves had been crudely removed at the elbows as if, on a hot day, they wouldn't stay rolled up and it pissed him off so much, he cut them off with the first pair of scissors he encountered. His graying hair was covered with a squared off, olive drab Ranger patrol hat.

"Hi, Pete."

"Greetings, Marriette," Pete responded, remaining behind the workbench. "Welcome back. I'm sorry about your brother. I suppose it was the first thing you heard."

"Yeah, it was. Pierre promised me he wouldn't go back in, but I kinda felt he would."

Pete shrugged his shoulders. He probably knew what Pierre had planned.

Marriette continued, "He couldn't be sane otherwise. I understood that about my brother."

"Yeah," Pete replied in his gravelly voice as he continued his work assembling the cartridges on the press.

"Pete, my parents and I appreciate your thoughtful memorial very much. It would have meant a lot to Pierre. You already know that."

"Yeah."

Pete was naturally introverted. All the bad things that had happened to him in his life, putting him where he was, only increased his reluctance to converse. Marriette assumed her brother had been one of the very few people who Pete felt comfortable around. She wondered if she could ever get Pete to talk about his wartime experiences and she suspected his exposure to combat accounted for much of his post war misfortune.

With his attention fixed on his task, he managed to say, "What can I do for you, Marriette? Do you want to shoot?"

"Maybe. I have something to show you, Pete."

Pete stopped what he was doing and looked up.

"What is it?"

"Can you come out to my car? It's in the trunk."

With a subtle nod, Pete came out from behind the counter. They walked out onto the gravel parking area and over to the barn, where Marriette opened the trunk of the Chevelle. Inside, she had placed one of the steamer trunks her brother had given her. It was the one that arrived on the carousel when her father picked her up in Montreal. She had been relieved to see it, because the missing one at that time was less critical.

Marriette opened the steamer trunk which appeared empty. Picking up the small piece of bent coat hanger she purposely left inside, she pushed the hooked end into one of the corners, lifting up the floor of the trunk to expose a hidden compartment.

****

There was a history to these false bottom trunks. Pierre had requested a craftsman in Vietnam create the two identical trunks, so he could smuggle weapons and other materials back into the U.S. He wasn't necessarily good with following rules. He was precise and unwavering with military orders, but other than that, Pierre felt he could do whatever he wanted.

Before returning to Minnesota, Pierre had given his sister the two trunks to use for her trip to Africa. At that time, he demonstrated how to remove the floor in the first trunk. The hidden compartment was empty. He then asked her to open the floor of the second. She smirked at him thinking the request to demonstrate something so simple wasn't necessary. He motioned for her to do so, anyway. When she removed the cover, there in front of her was $75,000 in neatly bound, circulated $50 bills. Pierre told her whoever had the money previously didn't need it anymore, and that it came from somewhere in Eastern Europe.

"Spoils," her brother had remarked. Pierre was happy he could pay for her education and more, but Marriette couldn't help but feel shocked. She demanded to know if he was in trouble, which he denied. The money was legal and untraceable. Pierre recommended she use discretion in spending it, giving her specific directions in that regard.

****

Now with Pete looking over Marriette's shoulder, she lifted the cover to the hidden compartment. Lying snuggly in its shaped packing was a Kalashnikov assault rifle and two 20- and one 30-round magazines of ammunition.

"Where did this come from?" Pete wanted to know.

"It was in the trunk. What can you tell me about this rifle?"

Pete reached in and removed the rifle from its casing, looking at Marriette with narrowed eyes and furrowed brow.

"AKM. It's European, not Chinese," Pete replied, emphasizing the word European with much surprise.

Pete squinted, looking further at the receiver for identification marks. He opened and checked the chamber.

"Probably Soviet or made in one of those satellite countries. Let's take it inside and have a look. That okay with you?"

"Sure. I was hoping you would," Marriette answered.

They walked back into the range office. Pete took the weapon to the work bench, cleaned off an area, and laid some shop towels down to field strip the rifle.

"So, you found this in your brother's stuff?"

Marriette repeated, "It was in his trunk."

To fill in conversation, which would otherwise be uneasy for him, Pete explained, in detail, what he was doing as he disassembled each part of the AKM before cleaning it. He checked each component for wear or defects, concluded it was in good working condition, applied some oil and grease, and, with great care, reassembled the weapon.

"Get me one of those clips . . . would you, Marriette?"

"Will do."

Marriette ran out to her brother's Chevelle and grabbed the magazines from the trunk. Pete removed each cartridge from one of the magazines to examine them. He reloaded them and then checked to see if the clip fit into the weapon well.

"Can you tell anything from the ammo, Pete?"

"Not sure. Don't think it's from Vietnam. Makes sense it's European since the Kalashnikov is. Noticed two of the clips are full . . . only two rounds left in this twenty rounder . . . you see that?"

"Ah . . . yeah, I guess," Marriette responded, surprised by Pete's thorough and unexpected observation. "Do you want to fire it?"

"Yeah. Do you?" inquired Pete.

Marriette was trying to build a rapport with Pete. She wasn't really sure if she wanted to fire the AKM again. An intrusive memory began to emerge, but she pushed it away.

"You know how?" Pete asked.

"Yes, I do. Pierre taught me well," she answered, with the faintest of a grin.

"Well, come on then."

Stepping outside, they walked under the cover of the range. No one else was around. Pete looked at Marriette trying to figure her out as he handed her the rifle and the curved 30-round magazine. She held the weapon in her hands, reacquainting herself with its feel. Pressing on the retainer, she inserted the ammunition clip and checked the safety.

"What target am I using?"

"Why don't you start with that closer one," directed Pete, pointing to a human-shaped target 25 yards away.

"OK...but wait a minute, Pete. There's something I need to do first. I'll be right back."

Marriette put the weapon down and ran back to the car to get her brother's beret. As she returned to the firing platform, she adjusted it on her head.

"I've got to do it this way . . . just this time. I'm wearing Pierre's dog tags until I don't feel I need to. You know?" She took in a deep breath and tapped her chest causing an audible clink of the stamped steel tags.

"Yeah."

Marriette picked up the AKM again, facing it downrange, dropping the safety and verifying semi-automatic. She pressed the gunstock into her shoulder while leaning forward and fired off a round hitting low on the target. She adjusted and fired three more rounds into the chest as she fought off flashback thoughts. Deciding to let them come, she sighted the next farther target, hitting it squarely in the chest. She looked at Pete quickly before taking aim again and firing a short burst.

Marriette now found herself back in the event. Rather than push the memory away, she would just deal with it. She fired another burst with dead reckoning, all into the closer target. She then placed the weapon back on safety and put it down on the bench. Wiping a tear away from her left eye, she removed the beret, placing it beside the weapon.

"Go ahead, Pete. Finish the clip. Here's another, if you want."

"That was pretty good. Solid." Pete remarked. "I guess you are your brother's sister."

He patted Marriette on her back. It was a lot for him to do, but he wanted to show his respect and affection.

"Thanks," Pete said. He meant it as thanks for coming, thanks for sharing this with me, thanks for reminding me of your brother. The death of Pierre was another substantial loss in Pete's disturbed life.

"Yeah. Let me just finish up what you've got," he continued, sighting in on the next distant target. Pete finished the clip and inserted the other magazine, measuring the accuracy of the weapon. He then removed the empty clip, checked the chamber, and placed a small piece of plastic into the barrel, sticking it out as he closed the bolt.

"Thanks, Pete. I have to go now."

"You're welcome anytime, Marriette. Will you come back?"

"Sure. I'd like to fire this again. Is there 7.62 available?"

"You're right!" Pete exclaimed, surprised by Marriette's knowledge of the appropriate ammunition. "I'll see what I can do."

"Let me leave you twenty bucks for that."

"Yeah. Thanks. Why don't you come over next time you come home?"

"I'll make a point to do that. Thanks, Pete."

They walked back to her car and Marriette placed the Kalashnikov back into its case, securing it beneath the false bottom. She looked up at Pete as she closed the Chevelle's trunk.

"You didn't see that, Pete."

"I didn't see that, Marriette."

She got in behind the wheel of her brother's Chevy. As she fired up the 396 and turned out of the parking lot, she called out, "See you next time, Pete."
"See you next time, Marriette."

Pete walked slowly back to his office pondering what more there might be to Marriette's mysterious visit.

– Chapter 7 –

The Official Word
Thursday, September 21, 1972   Montreal, Quebec

James and Marriette agreed to meet in the student union at noon, as the results of her hCG would be available that morning. Before she arrived at the psychology department, Marriette stopped in the health clinic, picked up the sealed envelope containing the pregnancy exam results, and put it unopened into her backpack.

Fall had come to Quebec, and it was a chilly walk to the student union with the temperature in the mid-40s. Marriette went into the lounge area and settled on one of the couches, waiting for James to arrive. Taking the envelope out of her backpack, she placed it centered on the low table in front of the couch.

As James came through the main entrance, she realized what a thrill it was to see the man she loved suddenly appear in public. She hoped the feeling would never change.

"Hi, Jamie."

"Hey, beautiful girl. What's that?" he asked, pointing to the envelope on the table, knowing full well what it was. They sat down quietly together on the couch staring at the envelope in anticipation.

Affectionately they put their foreheads together, and exchanged a kiss reinforcing their commitment.

"Don't you think we should open it now?" James inquired.

"OK," Marriette agreed as she tore open the end of the envelope, pulling out the folded lab report.

"Confirmation, my Jamie!"

"New chapter Marriette, here we go."

"This is for real, Jamie. I can't imagine doing this alone. I love you so much."

"I love you, too, my Marriette."

They lay back together on the couch as James quietly held her.

– Chapter 8 –

The Art of Therapy: Pete's Painting
Monday, September 25, 1972   Montpelier, Vermont

Marriette traveled home to Vermont on Sunday to visit her parents. She estimated she was three months pregnant, but wasn't ready to inform them about the child developing inside of her. She assumed they wouldn't notice as her appearance hadn't yet significantly changed.

Her first appointment with her new obstetrician was scheduled for Thursday. Perhaps, if everything appeared normal, she would return in a few weeks to tell her parents. Much of the drive from Montreal was spent rehearsing the conversation she would have with them. James had offered to accompany her when she decided to tell her parents. His support meant more than she could have ever hoped for.

Marriette wanted to visit Pete Long again, but was unable to reach him by phone on Monday morning. She decided to drive to the range early that afternoon anyway. Marriette eased the Chevelle along Pete's rough dirt road and parked next to the barn.

With the barn door partially open, the early afternoon sun was angled such that it illuminated what appeared to be a large mural or painting on the far interior wall. It drew her attention enough that she wanted to ask Pete about it at some point. It was someone's artwork, indistinct at its distance, but fascinating.

Marriette walked over to the range office with her rifle slung over her shoulder. Pete was inside eating his lunch.

"Hi, Pete."

"G'd afta'noon, Marriette," Pete responded with a mouthful of submarine sandwich.

"Sorry, Pete. I tried to call a couple of times this morning. Thought I'd take a chance."

"Yeah. I guess I wasn't near the phone. That's OK. It's good to see you. Do you want a Pepsi? That's all I've got."

"Sure."

Marriette placed her AKM on the workbench next to Pete.

"Just take one out of the fridge," Pete said, pointing to the corner of the office.

She opened the door of the old refrigerator. Except for a jar of French's yellow mustard, it was full of cans and bottles of Pepsi Cola. Flicked bottle caps that had missed their mark of the trashcan in the corner were scattered nearby on the shop floor. Marriette sat on the other chair behind the workbench. She pulled the ring tab off the can and placed it over her little finger.

"What have you been doing up there in Montreal?" Pete queried.

"I'm in school."

"Still?"

"Yep. Going for my Ph.D. in clinical psychology."

"You're gonna to be a shrink or something?" Still munching on his sandwich, a piece of shredded lettuce hung precariously from the edge of Pete's mouth.

"Probably research."

"Yeah. So, what's that mean? I mean, what are you interested in?"

"Do you really want to know?"

"Yeah."

"Be glad to explain if you want. It might hit close to home, Pete . . . but it's what I'm interested in, anyway."

"OK. Let's see what you mean by that."

Marriette toyed with the aluminum ring tab she now had placed over the fourth finger of her left hand. Holding her hand out in front of her, she imagined how a gold ring might look on her finger.

"There are things I'd talked about with my brother, and then something pretty bad happened to me in Africa, which is still bothering me. All of these things have caused me to think about what might help people get better when they experience bad things."

"What happened to you? If the question isn't indiscreet."

Marriette shifted her focus to Pete while taking the ring tab from her finger and putting it on the bench top.

"No. But maybe the answer is. I can't tell you right now, Pete, but I promise I will someday. There are some things I need to work out first."

Marriette leaned forward in her chair getting closer to him, gesturing to the AKM with the can of Pepsi she held in her hand. Changing her tone, she looked directly at him.

"But it has everything to do with that Kalashnikov. That's between you and me, Pete. I mean it."

"Yeah? Holy shit! Really?"

He removed his patrol hat, brushing his fingers through his graying hair before replacing the cap.

"Yeah, really. On both counts. OK?"

"OK, Marriette."

"You ready for this, Pete?" Marriette asked, as she removed a barrette from her jean pocket and secured her long brunette hair back at the nape of her neck.

He nodded.

"I'm interested in finding out how soldiers recover from seeing awful things that happen to their buddies or to them . . . or from being scared out of their fucking minds . . . or from doing awful things to other people whether they wanted to or not. The kind of stuff that gets into your brain, causing emotional problems and making life thereafter difficult forever."

Pete rocked further back in his chair, his eyes opened wider than their usual narrowed appearance.

"Pierre said he saw a lot of it in regular troops in Vietnam and in some of the SF, as well. There are a lot of G.I.s who washed out because of the stresses of combat. A lot of those guys coming back from 'Nam are showing up at clinics with problems. I'm not sure they're being treated effectively, if at all . . . certainly not by the military. I wonder how many even seek treatment. I mean medically. It's bad enough just coming home from this for-shit war. These guys aren't treated as heroes like you guys were . . . but it isn't just combat stress in Vietnam. It's in every war."

"Yeah . . . Yeah . . .," Pete mumbled, nodding his head as he took another bite of the sub, not volunteering anything else. Rocking back in his chair again, he stared up at the Airborne tab above him. He still didn't say anything.

"Since this bad thing happened to me," Marriette continued, "I was counting on talking it through with Pierre . . . you know?"

"Yeah."

"Well, anyway, Pete, that's what I'm really interested in. I want to help these guys and I hope to help myself. I believe I have some new ideas and I want to develop and test them. If you ever feel comfortable telling me your thoughts or your stories, I'd like to hear them."

Taking in a deep breath, Pete pursed his lips. "Yeah . . . Maybe."

Marriette sensed she had said enough on the subject for the moment.

"May I fire my rifle? That is, if you have any ammunition."

"Yeah. You bet. I have a couple hundred rounds and I can load more. Let's see what we can do. I'm going to get out the M-16 Pierre gave to me and . . . hmm . . . the STG-44 that I brought back in '45."

"OK, Pete."

Marriette understood. Pete bringing out the STG meant it was a special occasion, like opening the really nice bottle of wine.

The thoughts and act involved in firing the AK again didn't bother her as much this time. She hadn't experienced another nightmare since July. Her intrusive thoughts had occurred less often as well, and it made a big difference being back and safe in her part of North America.

Marriette realized that, through practice, she could be in better control of her thoughts. She had narrated a detailed account of her traumatic experience onto a cassette tape and listened to it daily. As she had predicted, it had been extremely difficult at first, but now, it was tolerable. She discovered that by revisiting the images, however frightening and horrible, they would pass through her mind as only thoughts, observed, separate from past reality. And, of course, there was the support of James.

Pete and Marriette spent the better part of the next hour taking turns firing the weapons. He provided her with instruction on sighting targets at distance. Her marksmanship improved and Pete was feeling more comfortable around her.

After leaving the range they stood together at the workbench in the office, disassembling, cleaning, and reassembling the weapons. Pete enjoyed watching her deftly handle the parts and reassemble the AKM without a struggle. It was a clear suggestion of her brother.

While they were working on the weapons, Marriette told Pete about her new boyfriend who was a local guy from Sherbrooke. She said having James in her life was just what she needed now. She mentioned that spending time with Pete at the range felt good and shared that Pierre had always referred to Pete with fondness and respect.

When they had finished, Pete walked Marriette back to her Chevelle. The fall afternoons were noticeably cooler. There had been a hard frost a few nights earlier and the big maple tree next to the barn was emblazoned with red and orange foliage. Marriette decided to take a chance and ask about the painting.

"Hey, Pete. Couldn't help but notice the artwork inside the barn."

Marriette caught a perceptible pause in his attention as he considered her observation.

She quickly added, "The door was open. I couldn't help but notice. Looks interesting, you know?"

Pete stared silently in the direction of the barn before replying, "All right ... I'll show you."

He pushed the barn door open, along its trolley, the rest of the way, flooding the interior with afternoon sunlight. Marriette followed him inside.

Shoulder to shoulder, they stood in front of an 8' x 4' abstract expressionist painting. Pete walked up to it, brushing cobwebs away from one of the corners. He had recently moved it from where it was stored in the barn and had fastened it to frame members along the barn wall.

The painting was a well composed composition of light and dark shapes, with colors of olive greens, reds, and brown reds on an almost black background. It was illuminated with flashes of whites and orange yellows. Some of the shapes suggested an arrangement of human forms.

With his back to Marriette, Pete looked at the painting for a while before speaking.

"I started this early one morning, all of a sudden ... before dawn ... had a nightmare and couldn't sleep, anyway. I knew what it was about. Familiar, you know ... so ... I got up and got out some colored pencils and drew a sketch of what I was feeling in my head. First thing, in the morning, I went downtown to the hardware store as soon as it opened and bought a sheet of plywood and the paint I needed to make my sketch larger. I had to do it. I couldn't not do it."

Reaching and running his palm over the work's textured surface, Pete noted, "This has been stored in the back for maybe ... I don't know ... fifteen years? After I heard about Pierre ... couldn't have been but a few days ... bad days, you know ... I had a bad nightmare again ... hadn't done so in years. So, I dragged the painting out, washed off the dust and hung it up."

Pete continued gazing at the painting, without further comment. In a gentle voice, Marriette said, "Pete. It strikes me as a well done painting. Nightmares?"

Pete turned to face Marriette, "I'm only telling you this because you brought it up already. Yeah. Nightmares related to the stuff I saw in Europe in '44 and '45. Turned out, that shit fucked with me all my life."

Carefully choosing her words, Marriette asked, "So, what was the painting about, Pete? What compelled you to do this?"

"I don't know . . . just something I found myself doing. I closed the range . . . hung a rope across my road with a closed sign on it. I spent three days working on this. All the while I was painting, I kept seeing and feeling the stuff that had happened. It was so clear. I was all worked up as I painted it. I just kept at it until it was done."

Gesturing to the painting, Pete continued, "It fucking wore me out . . . but when it was done . . . yeah . . . when it was done, I felt different . . . I don't know . . . better? That's why I dragged it out again."

Marriette walked up close to the painting to examine its landscape and feel its thick enameled surface with her fingertips. By doing so, she hoped Pete would continue to speak his mind without having her riveted attention directed on him.

"I find it very beautiful, Pete."

"It wasn't beautiful at all," he responded, quickly, almost tersely.

Marriette turned around, her rifle still slung over her shoulder, looking at him to make sure he understood her.

"No. I didn't mean it that way. Pete . . . it's beautiful because it came from within you . . . a very important part of you. And yes, it is beautifully painted and . . . yes, Pete . . . the depth of the emotions behind it . . . driving it, are significant . . . aren't they?"

"I don't know what to say about that," Pete responded, looking away from her.

"Pete. Please. Maybe someday, if you want to talk about this beautiful painting, I would like to hear its stories. I believe it might be good for you to tell someone. Just a hunch."

"Yeah. Maybe . . . maybe. I'll see."

Marriette knew that was enough for now. Maybe too much. It was time for her to leave for home. They walked out of the barn and over to the

Chevelle. Pete opened the door for her. Before she got in, she gave him a hug and thanked him.

After Marriette drove off, Pete walked back into the barn and stared at his painting. He walked over and touched it.

Resting his forehead against its painted surface, he grasped the side of the painting's edge to steady himself.

– Chapter 9 –

Suffering in Silence: No One Ever Talked
Monday, October 9, 1972   Montpelier, Vermont

It was early in the morning when Pete Long walked into LaFleur's Bakery. Recognizing Marriette's mother behind the counter, he walked over to where she was working and stood in front of her in silence until she looked up.

If Pete had visited the bakery before, Françoise LaFleur did not remember the occasion. She remembered only vague details about Pete from the little her son had mentioned. She knew that Pierre and he had been close friends and that Pete's welfare was important to him.

Pete was nervous and ill at ease speaking to Françoise. He awkwardly offered his condolences. The words he chose came across as ungainly, a social formality but, Françoise could see that it was difficult for Pete to speak even those few words without giving his true feelings away.

Without giving Françoise time to respond, Pete moved on to ask when Marriette would be home again and requested that Marriette contact him. He handed Françoise his phone number, previously scribbled on a scrap of paper. Pete explained he had some information for Marriette regarding 'a school project' she was working on.

Throughout their conversation, it was clear Pete remained uncomfortable and inclined to not stay any longer than necessary. Françoise put a couple of warm baguettes into their sleeves, offered them to Pete, and expressed gratitude for his kind memorial at Pierre's gravesite. Surprised with the gift and her reference to the memorial, Pete thanked Françoise and promptly left.

As he walked out the door, Françoise sensed the pain that Pete must be feeling. It was not far removed from her own. Through the storefront window she watched as Pete got into the familiar pickup once owned by Pierre and drove away. After informing her husband about Pete's visit, she went upstairs to call Marriette.

****

Marriette arrived home that weekend and called Pete to schedule a visit. During their brief phone conversation, Pete sounded anxious and she wondered if he might cancel their meeting at the last minute. To her surprise, he didn't. Pete was outside, waiting for her when Marriette drove onto his property and parked next to the barn.

Pete greeted Marriette as he pulled the garage door open along its squeaky trolley and they went inside. A fire was going in the wood stove. It felt warm inside compared to the chill in the early fall air. Midafternoon light filtered through the dusty transom sashes, laden with cobwebs, illuminating the dried and curled maple leaves that had blown into the barn and scattered over the worn wooden floor. A string of incandescent bulbs, which hung from the rafters, cast a warm light on the painting.

Marriette stepped closer to the painting to examine it again before sitting on a large section of maple trunk that Pete had rolled into the barn. She took a tape recorder from her bag and placed it on the barn floor beside her before she spoke.

"Pete. This is a cassette recorder. It's part of my research project. I discovered that in talking about the trauma I experienced, and then listening to my recording, I could redefine the disturbing images and feelings that I carry. It was difficult at first. I plan to test this approach as part of my thesis.

"Listening to your own account of your traumatic experiences may be beneficial. I'm hoping you'll let me record what you have to say, but I don't want it to disturb you. I understand this meeting is probably difficult enough for you. My intention is to leave the recorder here . . . with you. No one will ever hear it but you . . . if you should choose to do so. You can either forget it's there or tell me to put it away."

"Yeah. It's OK. I want to go with what you're thinking. I'll ignore it, for now."

With Pete's blessing, Marriette turned on the tape recorder.

Facing the painting, his back toward Marriette, Pete swept his hand over its surface and began, "I've been thinking about what you said last time you were here. Took it to heart," he emphasized, tapping his chest with his palm. "You are the one I want to hear why I made this painting out of the blue."

As he continued speaking, he examined the confluence of shapes and colors from one end to the other without turning around.

"Except for your brother, I've never told anyone this stuff . . . but I never really told Pierre how it all made me feel. All the stuff he did . . . never seemed to affect him . . . not so it showed anyway. Maybe it did. I suspect so. He just wasn't telling."

Pete then sat down on the other section of tree trunk with his painting now a backdrop. Opening a can of Pepsi, he took a long swig before beginning again, taking deep breaths in between statements as he relived the events of his past.

"You weren't supposed to talk about the stuff you saw ... or ... did. It's not as though there was a rule. Nobody said not to ... just nobody ever did ... and you never ever talked about how it made you feel or what it did to you later. Not if you were a man, you didn't. Maybe it just hurt too goddam much to listen to yourself speaking those words you heard in your head.

"When you got home, life was different. Of course, it was. You wanted it to be ... we were all desperate for peace ... but now the stuff you did and the way you thought about it, well ... you couldn't think about it in the same way anymore. One day, killing got you a medal in Europe, next day ... in America ... you'd be in prison. All that stuff had to be stored away in the vault up here," Pete said, tapping his skull with his index finger. "Big adjustment, you know?"

"So, Pete, you vets never talked about your experiences together when you got back to the States?" Marriette inquired.

"Negative on that. Everyone I knew ... who saw action, had problems. People don't become alcoholics for no good reason, Marriette ... but nobody talked ... not to me anyway. Years later, I understood that I wasn't the only one who felt like this."

Pete sat, hunched over with his elbows resting on his knees, his hands clasped, talking to the floor, only occasionally looking up at Marriette.

"Nobody, like nobody, really knows what happens ... you know what I hate?"

Momentarily, becoming animated, Pete raised his voice, "Know what ... I hate fucking John Fucking Wayne and his goddam fucking phony movies. He wouldn't have lasted 30 seconds out there. Just a bunch of insipid lies ...pabulum. I don't understand it. People my age think he's such a fucking hero. Yeah, but you know ... that's because none of the combat GIs ever said anything. They just got angry and drank a lot. Nobody wanted to connect the bad behavior ... the depression ... chain smoking ... and heavy drinking to their combat experience.

"You understand, Marriette? No spontaneous public outcry back then ... or now, for that matter ... recognizing that combat exposure had caused this epidemic. Sure, everybody was happy when the war was over, but they didn't know about this hidden price. Why couldn't our generation figure this out?

If anyone ever made a movie about how things really are in combat, then everyone in the audience would puke up all their goddam soda and shitty buttered popcorn."

Pete hadn't waited around to ease into his story. He proceeded as she had hoped. It was clear he'd been thinking this over since the last time they spoke. Pete closed his eyes and shook his head, realizing he was losing control and needed to check his anger.

"Let me point my compass in a different direction for a few. I've got a little story for you, I mean, before I get to the bigger stories.

There was a guy from Montpelier who used to come to the range once in a while, but then moved away to a town in southern New Hampshire. I think he had relatives up here because he used to come back every so often and we'd get talking a bit. He mentioned that once in a while he'd run into this tall, thin guy at the Cornish, New Hampshire post office ... he was a World War II vet that maybe reminded him of me. He pretty much said as much. The vet has a reputation about town for being a recluse. Except for necessities, he rarely goes into town, just stays on his fenced-off property. Apparently, only talks to people he thinks he can trust."

Marriette immediately thought Pete was talking about himself. Giving herself away with her puzzled expression, Pete quickly added,

"No, it wasn't me. Sure sounds like it though, so far. Ever heard of J.D. Salinger?"

"A Catcher in the Rye."

"Did you ever read it, Marriette?"

"Sure did. Maybe in the 10th or the 11th grade. Pierre had read it and relayed a hilarious passage about some guy in prep school who mischievously farted during a formal school assembly."

"Oh, yeah, 'goddam Marsalla'."

"So, then I read it, Pete. Even though I'm a girl, I couldn't help but identify with 'old' Holden. He was filled with the angst of alienation, I'd say ... having a difficult time making the transition from childhood innocence to an adult world he was discovering was greatly bullshit. I do remember carrying around the paperback with the carousel horse on the cover for a long time. I thought then that I'd discovered something on the grand order of a Bible and kept it close to me.

"That's interesting, Marriette. I can see that. I read the book as the result of hearing about Salinger from that guy. It then occurred to me I had actually met Salinger in France on the seventh or eighth of June 1944."

"Really? You did?"

"Yeah, honestly did. I briefly passed through an Army Intelligence post on my way back to England. Tell you about that later. Although we actually spoke, I don't remember about what. We just happened to be in the same place, same room because we shared the same Intelligence MOS . . . and he also spoke French and German."

"Small world, Pete."

"Yeah, I guess. Again, as the result of that conversation with the guy from Montpelier, I made every effort to find out as much as I could about Salinger. Well, as it turns out, there's a damn good reason why he has a reputation for being so strange . . . you know . . . called strange, because he has routinely perturbed and frustrated reporters and the like, by refusing their goddam interviews. He's turned away millions of Hollywood dollars, insisting that his "Catcher in the Rye" will never be made into their goddam movie.

So, this is what happened to J.D. Salinger in Europe. First of all, he too survived coming ashore at Utah Beach on 6 June, the second wave. I ran into him a day or two after that. From there, he was at the liberation of Paris and then actually met up with Hemingway there."

"That's incredible Pete, I mean, during the war and all. Not that Hemingway hadn't been there before."

"I know . . . but then, Salinger found himself at the Battle of the Bulge and then in the Hentgen Forest . . . the longest battle the Americans were involved in during the entire war. Intense fighting. Heavy casualties. After that was over, he found himself in southern Germany at the liberation of the Dachau concentration camps."

"Damn, Pete! How much can anyone take?

"And being in CIOS, Salinger's job was to thoroughly examine what had been going on at Dachau. You had to be there. Even the pictures released since don't give you the scope of the horror. Try to imagine the load he carried. Christ! He even checked himself into a psych ward for a while before leaving Europe. Maybe that got him some rest, at least . . . not much else, I'll bet."

"And you know, Marriette, during all that time, all . . . that . . . time, he was carrying the stories of Holden Caulfield, writing and rewriting them, whether he ran across a typewriter somewhere or scribbled something, ducked down in a foxhole, freezing in the snow."

At this point, Marriette was unable to fight back tears, turning away from Pete. He got up and walked over – putting an arm around her.

"No wonder he wants to hide away. He can't talk about it, so he wrote this novel and all the rest," Pete whispered close to Marriette's ear, then returned to his log seat.

"Oh, Pete. Nobody understands, not really understands, not unless they were there."

"Yeah . . . yeah. You know . . . Salinger hasn't released much else since '63 or so, but I'll bet you he's been writing stuff all the time though. That's what writers do, right?

"Marriette, you've discovered that talking about, or writing about what happened to you seems to be helpful. What if Salinger has been writing all along and is writing, at this very minute as we sit here, about all those experiences and how they made him feel. Maybe he's been writing one great American novel after another . . . but, you know, when he's through with one, when he feels what he needs to feel and writes it all down, he could fucking chuck it into his wood stove and start over again . . . keeping it all to himself, no evidence, no more questioning. Maybe that's how it helps him. I'd like to think so."

Pete stood up again and wandered around the barn in silence, looking outside, then touching the painting once more before sitting back down.

"It's heavy, this stuff I've been carrying . . . all the stuff we all carried. It has done nothing but fuck me up for 30 years . . . and the stuff I fucked up, just added to the mess. One bad thing piled on top of the rest of it. Thirty years of life after coming home and I have precious little to show for it."

Pete stared at the floor, nervously moving some dirt around with the sole of his shoe. His breathing was accentuated; he didn't look up, but continued on in a quiet tone.

"I had a wife . . . and a baby son, Marriette. I was so angry. Short fuse. Jumpy. I'd wake her up screaming with my nightmares, soaking wet with sweat. She'd get on me about my moods and my drinking. She didn't understand . . . but I didn't try to explain it to her, either. I hit her. Slapped her around. I didn't mean to. I hated myself for it.

"I remember an early weekend afternoon. My wife had a friend over. She had a baby in her arms, too. I was on the couch, drunk already... out of it. I looked up at them and my tears just kept flowing. I hated how I was. I hated how I was! I couldn't have them see me . . . so I rolled over and faced the back of the couch, pretending to be asleep."

Pete got up, walking quickly over to the window, to look out at the afternoon sky, remaining there for a full minute before speaking again, his back to Marriette.

"I came home from work one day in '47 and my wife and son were gone. Nobody knew anything . . . and, if they did, they weren't going to tell me . . . the asshole . . . Nobody knew what I was going through. I didn't really know myself."

Returning to the log seat, Pete took a long drink of Pepsi.

"She was right to leave me," he said, looking at the barn floor. "I wasn't fit to be with. My son would be almost 28 years old now. I thought he might come looking for me one day. Hasn't happened."

Pete waited a moment before returning his gaze toward Marriette.

"Look, Marriette, I know you're just starting to work on this, but I'm hoping you can help me get some of this off my back. Maybe it's too late."

Pete exhaled forcefully and stood to put another log into the wood stove then sat back down.

"I hear you, Pete," Marriette answered. "I promise I'll do what I can for you and all the brothers in arms . . . and maybe for a whole lot of other people, as well . . . that remains to be seen."

Pete listened to her response with his eyes closed and chin in his hand. He finished the can of soda and opened another, remaining silent for another moment.

"Thank you, Marriette, I've nothing to lose. Just nothing to lose anymore. You ready for another story?"

"Yes, I am, Pete."

– Chapter 10 –

The Specialist
Saturday, October 14, 1972   Montpelier, Vermont

Pete paced around in front of his painting, nervously kicking at the leaves on the barn floor.

"OK, Marriette. So, when I graduated high school in 1943, some friends and I decided we'd volunteer . . . been talking about it since Pearl Harbor. We'd seen a movie short at the old Egyptian Theater in DeKalb about the Army Airborne, imagining we'd be the stuff of heroes. I guess when you grow up surrounded by cornfields and not much else, you're itching to do something exciting. I was just 18, proud and brave. I got caught up in it and of course we all wanted to go kill some Nazis. How bad could it be?"

"You make it sound like a rather casual decision."

"Well, we were kids, right? Not well informed, looking back. Never thought much about it. What did we really know about life? Who did?

"Three of us went off to induction and basic together, right in Illinois. When I got there, they somehow figured out my family name hadn't always been Long. It was Langer. My father changed it when they emigrated from Düsseldorf in the 1890s. Speaking English as our main language was a priority to my parents, but we did speak German around the house. The Army really liked that I spoke fluent German and it made me of particular use to them.

"I was immediately separated from my buddies and sent to Fort Bragg and the 82nd. I was given an MOS in intelligence. I went to the Parachute Infantry School and Ranger training at Bragg and then on to Fort Benning in Georgia for Pathfinder and sniper training."

"Wow! They were really investing a lot in you. Lot of training, huh?"

"Geez, there's more. After that, I spent two months outside of Boston at Fort Devens where they held regular army German prisoners and then down to Alva, Texas, which was a special high security segregation camp for Nazis and Gestapo types. I dressed like a civilian in both places. I was assigned various jobs that allowed me to talk with the prisoners, studying dialects and learning other idiosyncrasies of German nationals. The Army Intelligence wanted me trained to be very comfortable speaking German like Germans. There were others going through the same training . . . even had a language coach. After a while, we were sent back to the 82nd.

I thought we'd be on the next ship heading for England. Turns out they *flew* us German-speaking specialists directly over to England.

"From there we went to a British parachute unit for some specific orienteering. We practiced some night jumps in England to see how good we were at finding our checkpoint without being detected. Exciting. I was learning a lot. I felt important. Finally, three of us got an assignment."

"When was this, Pete? I'm confused on the dates," Marriette inquired.

"This was in March or early April 1944 . . . about two months before D-Day. Our first mission was to deliver currency and gold bullion to the French underground. We made the jump from a stolen German transport aircraft, a JU-252, around two in the morning. We all landed safely and found the French waiting for us. We snuck into town and went to a house where we met our contact and delivered the goods. We then changed into French civilian clothes, carrying only our revolvers. Before dawn, one of the Resistance led us back to a point on the Channel. A fishing boat . . . really the British Navy . . . was waiting for us. We transferred to a Brit Navy vessel about ten miles out at sea . . . something like a PT boat . . . and were back in England by noon. I guess it went about as well as it could. Soon thereafter, we were sent on a similar mission into Belgium near the French border."

Opening another can of Pepsi, Pete returned to the log across from Marriette.

"The next mission after that was much different. The Allied Command wanted to assassinate a German general who was located at a command post just inside the Belgium French border. This regular Army general really wasn't the problem, just a target. If the mission went as planned, the Allied intelligence folks figured it would create confusion. The plan was designed to make it look like the Gestapo, without warning, got rid of a high-ranking regular army officer . . . implying a direct order from Berlin."

"The Gestapo was the secret police, right, Pete?" Marriette asked. "Basically, the Nazis?"

"Yeah. That's exactly right, Marriette. They were in charge. The German division headquarters was located in a countryside mansion and monitored by the French underground. The plan was to eliminate the General sometime during the third week of May. There were only two of us involved this time . . . me and another G.I. . . . although he probably wasn't a real G.I. I'd never met him before, but he spoke contemporary German. He was well over six feet and . . . I should add, an impressive and imposing 'Aryan spec-imen' . . . maybe in his late thirties. Perfect for the job . . . as if he'd made hits for various employers, many times before. He never said much other than what pertained to our mission.

"For this guy, Intelligence had acquired a Gestapo Feldgrau Oberfuhrer uniform with a couple of oak leaf clusters on the epaulettes; enough rank to get unquestioned attention. Everyone was terrified of those Berlin mother-fuckers. My uniform was that of an enlisted Waffen SS soldier, which was tailored for me. Didn't look too new. Didn't look too old. Just what a body-guard and driver would wear.

"We knew the layout of the building and general daily activities ahead of time. Luck had to be on our side. We had practiced the exercise in England with German dialect experts. The French underground acquired a typical vehicle for our use. When I first saw it for real, it looked just like the one the Brits had for practice.

"Sometime into the third week of May, conditions were right, so we made our way by submarine to the French coast during the night where we were met by the Resistance to guide us to the safe house. We had carried our uniforms and specialized equipment. I was issued a StG-44 Sturmgewehr, the world's first assault rifle, just like the one you and I fired the other day. Elegant and disposable. That design led to the AK, you know?"

Pete looked up at Marriette and winked, acknowledging the weaponry connection in their backgrounds.

"Uh-huh," she answered.

"We went over the plan with the Resistance. They had photos of the exterior. After a good night's sleep, we went over the plan again. Later that afternoon the mission vehicle arrived for us . . . flags on the front."

"Gee, Pete. Weren't you really scared?" Marriette asked, hanging on his every word.

"Didn't really think that way at all," Pete answered. "Practice, practice, practice. Drill after drill. It became ingrained with an acquired confidence. We made our way to the mansion. Seeing a Gestapo vehicle arrive suddenly . . . which I guess wasn't out of the question . . . got everybody's attention and intimidated the hell out of them. They waved us right through the guard station. I barely slowed down. At the mansion, I turned the vehicle around and parked it. The tall guy got out with his briefcase and walked up the front stairs and into the mansion with me close behind him.

"We behaved like we owned the place. He informed the guard that he was here to see General Krause or whatever his name was. We then walked directly into the outside office. A startled female secretary stood up, saying nothing as we passed. The guard outside the inner office quickly opened the General's door, letting the Gestapo Colonel inside, then closing the door behind him. I stood in front of the office door at parade rest, stone-faced, blocking the entry, my machine gun over my shoulder, above communicating with anyone not of our special status.

"A muffled verbal exchange was heard from inside the room. The Gestapo officer sounded terse and brief. What was supposed to happen, did. The tall guy's satchel briefcase was created so he could put his hand through the side where his finger could immediately pull the trigger mechanism. Catching the distracted general unaware, he fired one silenced round into the general's head. Krause never got out of his chair. The Gestapo officer kept barking at the dead general for effect. He opened the door and immediately slammed it behind him. We marched out as quickly as we went in, got into the vehicle, and headed to the guard gate. I saluted as we sped through. As soon as we were out of sight, I really took off. We ditched the vehicle where we were told and moved into the hedgerows. We met up again with the Resistance and disappeared into a hidden tunnel. We removed our German uniforms and put on French civilian stuff. After dark, we left for the coast and got onto another fishing boat. This happened about ten days before D-Day."

Pete stopped to take another swig of Pepsi.

"That's quite a start, Pete. And you haven't even fired a shot yet."

"Yeah, that's true, but things changed real fast. It's not as though I got much of a break after that adventure. I had a few days off but couldn't leave post. They gave me a promotion to E-6. Got a few 'atta boys' from the Colonel, but that was it. Thought I'd never see the guy who shot the general again, but I did . . . later."

"Really?"

"Yup. Then I was temporarily assigned to the 101st . . . 502nd PIR . . . to do a pathfinder mission just after midnight . . . before the D-day invasion. I was one of the paratroopers in a C-47, part of a huge early formation heading to France. We were tasked to set up radar equipment . . . a transponder . . . 'Eureka', it was called . . . to help guide future aircraft missions.

"Bad news. Our plane was hit right at the coast. The whole starboard wing was set on fire. The plane began losing altitude fast and we were still a few miles out from the DZ near the town of Carentan. We weren't going to make it there. The red light was still on. We had to get out no matter where we were. I was at the front of the stick with the other radar guys. We pushed some equipment out first and jumped after it. Must've been about 400 feet. I heard the plane crash about the same time I hit the top of a building right after my chute opened . . . landed on top of a church. I slid down the slate roof, but my chute got hung up when I was about 10 feet off the ground. The transponder crate dangling from me hit so hard it broke open scattering its parts everywhere. I cut myself loose and fell the rest of the way. There was a lot of gunfire . . . not real close . . . pretty much all German. I was OK. I got rid of all the extra gear and started looking around for the guy who jumped out ahead of me. Turned out he was just letting himself down out of a tree a couple hundred feet away. I remember his name . . . Kevin Youngs . . . a New York guy."

"Missing the DZ really screws things up, I guess," Marriette observed.

"You bet. About half made it out from the other side of the plane and lived. Didn't meet up with them until the next morning. Most on our side crashed with the plane or else didn't have enough altitude to open their chutes."

"Wow!"

"Yeah . . . so fast. One moment the aircraft is flying along full of GIs and then a minute later, a handful of us are the only ones alive.

"So, there didn't seem to be anyone else around. Most of the shooting was coming from the southwest. We could hear dozens of C-47s overhead and chutes opening with shouts and screams from American paratroopers . . . more jumping early from other doomed aircraft."

"Shit, Pete. I can't imagine. How did you ever do this?"

"I was very well-trained. Kind of took it in stride. Regular grunts though, most of them just folded. Scared useless. Not so much the Airborne. Different training than the young untrained guys that landed on the beach . . . poor bastards.

"We wouldn't have done that . . . that was total suicide."

"Yeah," Marriette acknowledged, with a shiver.

"Anyway. Youngs and I had missed the drop zone . . . the Eureka was demolished. Our primary mission was over. I thought the only thing we could do now was wait 'til dawn. There wasn't any fighting going on in our immediate area and no civilians around either. Youngs and I climbed into the cellar of a building and hid out there.

"We found some wine and opened some C-rations. We felt pretty secure and actually got a few hours of sleep . . . woke up around 5 in the morning hearing heavy gunfire coming from the coast. The sun was just coming up, so we headed outside. There was still no one around.

"I discovered my rifle wasn't working from the damage of my rough landing. As we moved further out, we found several dead American paratroopers scattered about, their parachutes never fully deployed. Then we ran across a couple of dead German soldiers. One of them had a StG-44. My lucky day. Best weapon of the war. I removed the soldier's LBE with its ammunition, exchanging it for mine.

"It was about that time we began to hear American voices and headed in their direction. They were from another company of the 101st. This part of the town being secure, they were on patrol looking to recover the dead and wounded. Some of us headed further toward where the firefight had occurred the night before. I remember assuming that German troops could still be around. In the distance, along the coast, explosions could be heard in all directions. D-Day was underway."

– Chapter 11 –

The Indelible Face in the Mirror
Saturday, October 14, 1972   Montpelier, Vermont

"We pushed ahead maybe five or ten blocks . . . finding cover . . . leapfrogging along a narrow street through the town. There were six of us moving toward the gunfire several hundred yards away. Although it sounded like they were American weapons, I was wary of German stragglers.

"Across the street I noticed Sgt. Youngs move into a door jamb to light a cigarette. Just as he paused with the flame to his face, a round hit him in the chest. He fell dead. The sniper then fired at one of the guys further ahead, wounding him. I moved to better cover. The sniper fired again in a different direction. I could see him, but my StG was useless at this range, so I grabbed the carbine out of the hands of the guy next to me. I had no idea what condition his sights were in, but I was now in a decent position for a shot. I got off three quick rounds, one slightly lower each time. We heard the sniper scream. He was no longer visible.

"I took off running in the direction of the building the sniper was in. Just as I moved inside the open door, two German soldiers were running down the stairs in front of me. They weren't ready. I was. I shot both of them. I didn't stop. I wanted to find the sniper. All I could think was he'd killed Kevin Youngs and I was going to make sure he was dead. I stepped over the bodies of the two fallen in the stairwell and ran up two more flights going toward the room where I thought the sniper might be. He was there on the floor, lying beneath the window with his scoped rifle next to him. He was barely alive . . . shallow short breaths . . . his helmet was off. I had hit him twice."

Studying Pete as he sat on the maple log across from her, Marriette observed a distant stare occupying his expression. He appeared fully transported back to the traumatic event.

"I was standing directly over him. Damn . . . face . . . like looking in a mirror, you know. I . . . I can still see . . . that face. He never gets older."

Pete glanced in Marriette's direction, his expression foreign and disturbing, like a ghost looking through her.

"I stood over him hearing myself breathe. Hearing him breathe. Catching my breath. He was dying . . . suffering," Pete gulped and looked to the floor.

"I shot him again . . . just once, to end it. His fresh blood streamed from the new wound, spreading to the edge of the darker blood, pooling around his body on the polished wood floor.

"I knelt down beside him and looked at him again. I saw only me . . . still do . . . still do . . . ah, shit."

Pete turned away from Marriette, covering his face with his hands, quiet for a long moment. With a deep sigh, he turned back, quickly wiping the tears flooding his eyes and continued, "I looked at his ID. He was 20 . . . a month older than me . . . another German guy . . . just like me. Wilhelm Millar. We were both just boys."

"You remember his name, Pete?"

Pete answered slowly, as if called back from this distant time and place.

"Ah . . . yeah, I do . . . of course, I do . . . always will. It was like a dream . . . hazy . . . unreal. Looking around me, I realized I was in a kid's bedroom. Everything seemed in place. It was clean and neat. You know, some toys in front of an armoire. A rocking horse in the corner. The bed was made without a wrinkle, but now the clean white comforter was splattered with Wilhelm Millar's blood. The rest of the house was wrecked and burnt. Its family had long since left."

Pete stood up, walking around the barn as he spoke. He paused to look at his painting again and nervously ran his hand clear across its rippled surface, from one side to the other.

"I heard one of the other GIs coming up the stairs looking for me. I grabbed the sniper's rifle along with the ammunition beside it. I left the room and ran down the stairs before the other guy made it up there. There were now more Americans outside of the building. They were loading the bodies onto a 'deuce-and-a-half'.

"We continued to move in the direction we'd been traveling. The area was secure. The sounds of war could still be heard in the distance. I turned down a street onto a square or commons where there were lots of large trees . . . blasted apart, you know . . . what was left of them and taller buildings. There was a group of GIs trying to figure out how to cut down a dozen or so dead or wounded paratroopers still suspended in their harnesses, caught in the trees or parts of buildings. Those were just the ones we could see. There were lots more. During the night jump, fires had illuminated some paratroopers as they drifted down . . . making them easy targets. Some of them parachuted helplessly, falling into the flames of burning buildings."

"Damn, Pete, that's horrible. It's all horrible."

"There's more . . . always more," Pete said, looking directly at Marriette.

"I was looking for familiars in my company or at least someone I could report to and try to get back to where I was supposed to be. As we walked, we came upon what was left of another paratrooper. His chute had snagged on the steeple of a church and then in the branches of a destroyed tree, leaving him hanging over a plaza, right at the entrance to the church. I couldn't tell what happened. He might've been involved in some sort of explosion as he descended. His body, that is, what was left of his body was still in the chute harness, just hanging there, swaying in the breeze coming off the channel. The paratrooper's legs and hips were missing, and his guts were hanging from what was left of his midsection. The drained blood had created a swirled geometric pattern on the tile surface of the plaza directly below him . . . you know . . . in front of the Lord's House . . . yeah . . . that's another image I've never been able to get out of my mind."

Marriette looked at Pete, her hand covering her mouth. Looking back at her with affection and empathy, Pete went on to say, "Strange how the mind works, Marriette. Sometime later that image became paired with another of mine.

"I thought back to a winter day when I was just a kid in northern Illinois. Maybe I was 10 or 12. It was snowing hard. No wind. I was outside with my .22 rifle. I had callously shot at a starling in a tree . . . a bad shot. I thought I missed him because he flew about 20 feet to another tree and perched on a branch higher up.

"But he was still alive. Blood dripped down from him onto the snow at my feet. I still can see those bright red pools staining the stark white snow. His entrails were hanging out of his belly, dripping blood . . . making a clotted icicle. The snow coming down accumulated on the bird's shoulders. He was shivering. It was so quiet . . . so goddam quiet. There was nothing to distract me from what I'd done. I was so ashamed. I fumbled around trying to load another cartridge into my single shot rifle. It took another two shots before I was able to put him out of his misery. I felt sick walking home in the snow. I vowed I would never hunt anything again unless I planned to eat it. Turned out, I never hunted again 'til I found myself in France."

"That's a pretty chilling account, Pete," Marriette responded. "Powerful imagery."

"I most always see those images together . . . so much so, I'm kind of used to them – usually. They've worn themselves out. Maybe it's so long ago now, I've come to believe that those images aren't quite real anymore. Stuff of dreams, maybe. Now it doesn't have the sting it used to years ago. It doesn't beat me senseless like it did. I think creating this painting somehow helped me. I cried a lot of the time I was painting . . . I . . . I did, Marriette. I don't know why, but those dream images got turned into this," Pete said, raising his arm over his head, motioning behind him.

Marriette was drawn into the trauma of Pete's imagery, gritting her teeth, trying to conceal her emotions.

"You never told this to anyone, huh, Pete?"

"Not even to your brother, not like this. No one," Pete answered. "It all kind of swirls around in my head when it comes up. Early on, hell . . . for years, I pushed it away or drank it stupid."

"Yeah."

"Think the only reason I could finally trade the booze for Pepsi is because I got tired of it all being there. It couldn't kill me anymore . . . felt like it already had by then, but that took better than 20 years. War put me in a place I shouldn't have been. Young guys get caught up in all that saber rattlin' fervor. Different with this 'Nam war . . . but then again, still the same."

"How are you doing with all this, Pete?"

"I'm okay, Marriette. I'm glad you're here now to listen, but I believe I needed someone to tell this to when I returned from Europe in '46 . . . yeah . . . me and everyone else so involved. If somehow we'd known to talk to each other . . ."

"I believe you're right about that, Pete, on both counts."

"If you can stay a while longer, I'll finish up the war part."

"Sure I can . . . but I don't want to rush you. I can come back, you know."

"I'm okay for now . . . and I want you to come back. There's just one more thing at the end that's pretty significant. As far as the rest of 6 June 1944, not much more happened around me."

"Did you know that June 6 was Pierre's birth date?" Marriette inquired.

"Yeah. I knew that. I killed the German boy, Wilhelm Millar, just about the same time Pierre came into the world. Crazy isn't it? Pretty . . . fucking . . . crazy."

– Chapter 12 –

How I Helped Put a Man on the Moon
Saturday, October 14, 1972   Montpelier, Vermont

Pete got up to refill the Franklin stove with split maple. He seemed more at ease now as he continued sharing his saga.

"The local command was in the process of sending me back to England. I was really the property of the intelligence service. I had no idea what I'd be doing next.

"Well . . . still in France on June 7th . . . early in the morning, I stepped into a hole, when I was coming back from the latrine, and broke my goddam ankle. The medics put me in a splint. On the 8th, I was sent back to England where my leg was put into a cast.

"After a couple weeks of crutching around the hospital, CIOS sent me to a prisoner of war camp in England to interview German soldiers and learn what I could from them. These prisoners weren't Nazis, just regular army guys. Once they figured out that no one was going to harm them, a lot of them started to talk. Many were disillusioned and wanted to go home to a safe place. They were separated from the people they loved, yet felt there might not be a home to go home to . . . a whole lot of regret and sadness, I'll tell you.

"I was surprised that so many wanted to help us out. They knew their side wasn't going to win. Most of the information they provided was outdated. Occasionally, someone knew about the location of something of interest, like a storage depot or a concealed manufacturing plant. One guy was hoping he'd get transferred to one of the POW camps in the States. He had relatives in Wisconsin and had never been there. He confessed he was forced into a situation he had never remotely believed in. The last thing he wanted was to go back to Germany.

"I started the interview work in England, but as the war progressed, I was transferred to areas occupied by the Allied Command to do the same thing. I had a tip leading to a place in Bavaria. We were guided to a cave-like underground storage area . . . a really big garage . . . a bunker. There we discovered a room where they'd been storing . . . I don't know . . . piles of emaciated bodies of slave labor victims. Probably had been working there. You know.

"You've seen those pictures. It was just before VE Day. The place housed rocket engines and related parts. Those rockets, let me tell you, made a lot of people real happy. Kind of paid for all my training, huh?"

"Yeah, Pete. Guess so," Marriette nodded.

"I remained stationed in Europe after VE day. Intelligence had developed a crucial program to obtain and sequester German scientists, mathematicians, technicians, preparing to move them to the U.S. There was a rush to find these folks before the Russians did.

There was one particular scientist who had been captured by the Russians and was detained in the state of Thuringia. After 1 July in '45, this was a town located in the Soviet occupied zone – East Germany. The CIOS really wanted this guy back. So, I got a call, as did the tall German guy . . . you remember . . . the guy I thought I'd never see again. He must've been comfortable working with me. The two of us were briefed. CIOS knew the scientist was being held in an apartment in the town of Meinengen and we had to act fast. We had no problem crossing the new border established by the Soviet troops. Early on the Soviets were accustomed to seeing farmers move their equipment through these checkpoints. That's how we got in . . . moving potatoes in a horse drawn cart. We abandoned the farm equipment and changed into city clothes.

"We located the apartment building and monitored activity from a room across the street. Later that day, we recognized the scientist leave the building accompanied by a Russian guard. They entered a store under our window and left with papers and beer.

"Our plan was to wait for the right opportunity to overtake them while away from the apartment . . . but things didn't happen that way.

"Late that afternoon, two guards left the building again with the scientist. We followed them to the railroad station where they bought tickets just as it was beginning to get dark. We followed them onto the train and observed them enter a private compartment. The train was empty, so we concealed ourselves in a nearby cabin. Eventually, the scientist left with one of the guards to go to the bathroom. His guard squeezed in with him . . . taking no chances.

"As soon as he did, I burst into their passenger compartment and killed the other guard. I opened the window and threw the Russian out into the night, then hid behind the door.

"I was confident the tall German guy knew what to do. Sure enough. As the scientist came back through the door, I shoved him down onto the seat and held a gun on him. The tall guy pushed the other guard into the cabin behind him. He was already dead; the next body hit the tracks.

"The three of us got off the train at the next station to reverse direction. The scientist explained that he had been taken from his family in Munich and was forced to head east to the Soviet sector. So, the Russians actually stole him from us and we were stealing him back. Important scientist, I guess."

"Hey, Pete, maybe you helped put a man on the moon?"

Pete thought for a minute and smiled for the first time that afternoon. "Maybe you're right.

"So, we boarded the next train back to where we had started. When we reached our destination, we got off and disappeared into the night. I guided us back into the Western sector without a hitch. Our orders were to stay with our rescued scientist all the way to the command in London. We turned the scientist over at the headquarters directorate as planned, then spent the rest of the day being debriefed.

"As we were about to leave the building, the tall German guy handed me a small satchel. In German . . . we always spoke in German . . . he thanked me, saying he hoped we would work together again someday. I felt that he respected me. I was surprised because we had communicated so little. He went out the main door, down the steps . . . disappearing into the crowd. I never did see him again. I doubt if he was really military, probably freelance . . . private contractor . . . bounty hunter . . . who knows . . . but very good at what he did.

"CIOS put me up in a hotel. When I arrived, I opened the satchel. It contained $15,000 American cash along with a note suggesting I buy myself a nice house when I got home.

"I stayed on for a couple more months interviewing prisoners. CIOS wanted me to stay on as a civilian, but I sensed I had pushed my luck far enough."

Pete sat on the log with his chin resting on the back of his hand, pondering his next thought.

"As far as physical scars, I had none. Just the broken ankle. It never did bother me again . . . but since it was an injury, the VA sent me 14 bucks a month, every month and still does . . . it's up to 41 bucks a month now."

Marriette acknowledged his sarcasm with a smile.

"Marriette, my injuries were all in my brain. I didn't expect that. I thought I was home free. War was over. There would be nothing now but good times. Peace, finally. Well, I was wrong. Pretty damn wrong. When you kill another human being or witness violent death ... it changes you ... it does ... just does. Spellbound by the injuries of our mind, we become prisoners of our distorted realities."

"Yes, Pete, that's it," Marriette whispered. "Well, put."

"What I'd done was not supposed to have happened. Sneaky ... sneaky stuff ... much of it against the Geneva conventions. I never received any decorations, Marriette, only fuel for my memories and nightmares."

"Your story is incredible. You've been through a lot. I'm moved ... more than I can express. Thank you, Pete."

Marriette took in a deep breath blowing it out forcefully. Pete's story had been more than she had ever imagined.

"I should get going. James will be wondering where I am. I'll be wondering about you, too, Pete."

She looked up at him with great respect and sympathy.

"Thanks," Pete replied. "It was war's traumatic stressors that led to everything else. That's what troubles me the most. I'm going to listen to the tape. We'll see what it does for me.

"Look, Marriette. If there's any way I can do it, I'd like to help these Vietnam guys. I'm realizing how important this is ... and for me, too ... what else is there, now? You know what I mean?"

"I hear you loud and clear, Pete."

As Marriette headed home, she reflected on the weight of Pete's last remarks. Helping his brothers might save his life, too. She would try to help him find that path, one step at a time.

– Chapter 13 –

A Gift for Mom and Dad
Sunday, October 15, 1972   US Route 89 NB

Marriette dropped James off at the Montpelier Public Library, before heading over to her parents' home to announce the news of her pregnancy. She had arranged to spend the first part of the visit alone with her parents. James would later join them. The plan was to have Sunday dinner and return to Canada before dark. By late afternoon, the couple was on their way back to Montreal.

As had become customary when driving somewhere of distance, Marriette placed their folded coats behind her, propping herself up against the door to face James as he drove. As soon as she was settled James inquired,

"So, Marriette, how did it go when you broke the news?"

"I guess it went okay, Jamie . . . obviously a shock to them . . . but they listened patiently to my story . . . and reacted as I expected, with an abundance of reasonable questions. I have to believe they have a lot of mixed feelings concerning my carrying this baby. I know my parents want to support me, but that doesn't mean they won't spend the rest of the evening and next few days wringing their hands while mulling this matter over.

"Living in a relatively liberal state and an even more liberal town has, over the years, tempered their Catholic upbringing. But, still, it's a lot for them to digest."

"Of course. It's been a tough couple of years for them," James responded. "My parents wanted assurance that I knew what I was doing, but there wasn't an answer I could give them that would totally allay their concerns.

"Expressing my love for you . . . and willingness to take this chance . . . works for me, but it leaves them, I'm sure, with reasonable doubt. Don't get me wrong, they're supportive of me . . . and, I hope, us . . . but nonetheless, they must have some misgivings."

"Are you changing your mind, Jamie?"

"No, of course not, Marriette. Please, I haven't changed my mind . . . but I can't help but recognize the concerns of my parents. I am their child."

"Just as important to me as this child, is that someday we have a child of our own. I know you suggested this right away . . . but I'll have to admit . . . I do need that balance."

"Yes, Jamie. I feel exactly the same way. Believe me, it is just as important to me, too, my darling."

Marriette released her seatbelt, moving into the middle of the cab to kiss Jamie on his cheek and snuggle against him.

"Thank you for coming with me, Jamie. I feel it made a big difference. I think Mom and Dad trust you."

"I believe I fielded their questions pretty well. I did my best, Marriette."

"You absolutely did. In their eyes, you are a fine, handsome, educated Canadien boy . . . brought up in a good Catholic home and, of course, as far as my father is concerned, a hockey player forever, even though you didn't play for his beloved Canadiens. At least, you played in the Forum a couple of times, no?"

James chuckled at her long description.

"And you are all those things and much more," Marriette added, softly.

She leaned closer and whispered, "I love you, James Roy."

"I love you, beautiful Marriette. What are you doing tomorrow? Any free time?"

"What are you thinking, handsome?"

"I was thinking maybe we should go look for an engagement ring. Would you wear one?"

"Yes, of course!"

She turned to kiss him, biting his earlobe playfully.

– Chapter 14 –

A Goodbye to McGill
Friday, November 3, 1972   McGill University, Montreal, Quebec

By the end of October, Marriette had completed her PhD thesis proposal. The document introduced the purpose of her study, methods for discovery, and her system for evaluating her findings. She discovered there was little present in the literature concerning the treatment of what was referred to at the time as combat stress. The standard methods for treatment appeared to be lacking in efficacy.

Marriette's personal experience with stress-related trauma, along with Pete's history and her conversations with her brother, provided the impetus for her to move in a direction she felt was missing in her profession.

Marriette set off to the psychology building, prepared to discuss the proposal with her advisor prior to officially submitting it to the department. As she headed down the corridor to the department office, she encountered her professor coming in the opposite direction. Lyle Morrison was in his mid-fifties with long gray hair fastened back in a short ponytail, just touching the shoulders of his tweed jacket. He was familiar with Marriette's background at McGill, including her trip to Africa.

As an applicant, Marriette's diverse background was unique for one seeking a degree as a clinical psychologist. Plus, she was older than her peers. Professor Morrison appreciated this fact . . . rather than viewing it as a detriment. He greeted her as she approached the door to the office.

"Good afternoon, Ms. LaFleur."

"Bonne aprés-midi, Professeur Morrison."

"Do you need to speak with me?" he inquired.

"I would like to, if you have a few minutes."

"Sure, come into my office," Morrison answered.

They entered the main office and proceeded down the hallway to his private office. Closing the door behind them, the professor offered Marriette a chair across from his desk. The fading afternoon light filtered in through the Venetian blinds, looking as though it might snow before the day was over.

Morrison glanced at the bound proposal Marriette placed on the edge of his desk.

"What's this, Marriette? It seems a bit early for a thesis proposal. I don't recall discussing this in much detail with you. Am I right?"

Marriette reached over and picked it up, handing it to him with an air of confidence and conviction.

"I wanted to get this going sooner rather than later, Professor. The topic is something that occupies my mind constantly. I look at this proposal as being fairly complete."

Arranging his long hair over the back of his chair, Morrison swiveled around, putting his feet up on the edge of his desk. Leaning back, he held the proposal in his hands and commenced to flip through its contents. He then looked up, gazing at Marriette over the top of his glasses, commenting, "Marriette, rather than sit here for the next 10 minutes staring at me, give me about that much time to look this over. It's obvious you're focused on this approach. Come back in, ah ... 15 minutes ... and just come in. I'd like to see what you have here," Morrison said as he refocused on the proposal.

Marriette acknowledged the request, getting up from her chair. As she opened the door to leave, he called back to her. "Can you make it a half an hour? Give me 30 minutes," he said, without taking his eyes from the document.

Stopping off at a restroom, Marriette stood in front of the mirror, brushing her hair as she turned sideways, profiling her torso. She placed her hands on her belly smoothing the sweater to feel the novel change in her anatomy. The baby she was carrying was starting to show.

Walking around the building, Marriette wondered what might happen with her proposal. She wasn't sure what to make of Professor Morrison's reaction, but something had his attention. She looked out the hallway window, standing in front of a radiator, warming her belly. A light snow was falling, and the walkway lamps of the central campus were coming on.

A half hour later, Marriette returned to the psychology department and walked into Morrison's office. He was busy writing notes on a pad next to her proposal as she sat down. He looked over at her, apparently pleased with what he was thinking.

"This is very well prepared," he said, pointing to the thesis proposal. "I like what you're thinking, Marriette, and I have an idea. Let's see what you think of it. You wouldn't happen to know Jonathan Richter, at UVM, would you? He's a friend and colleague."

Marriette shook her head no in response, anticipating an explanation.

"He's a research-oriented clinical psychologist. I'd like you to speak to him. And take this with you," he added, waving her proposal in the air. "I just spoke with Jon. He'd like to meet you. I really like your proposal, Marriette. It seems ready to go the way it is. I'll look closer but ... and ... this is a good 'but'. I just don't see you doing this research here. Where will all your CRS patients come from? This is Canada. We don't do war," he chuckled with sarcasm.

"And there's a Veterans Administration hospital in northern Vermont. According to Richter, the VA doesn't know what to do with the influx of Vietnam vets appearing with combat-related symptoms. There is your laboratory, Marriette! Perfect! Even after a 10-minute conversation, Jon thinks you're a fit. He'll arrange a transfer right away, if you want."

Morrison fumbled through his Rolodex and scribbled down Jonathan Richter's phone number on a 3 x 5 card.

"Can you call him in the morning?" he asked, as he handed the proposal back to her.

Astonished, Marriette exclaimed, "Yes! I'll call him first thing. Thank you so much, Professor Morrison. This is really what I want to pursue!"

Marriette jumped out of her seat and reached across the desk, shaking his hand with both of hers.

"He hasn't even met me yet. How did this happen so fast?"

"I told him he would regret it if he didn't get you over to his place. I believe the time is right for something like this."

"Oh, my, I can't get too excited!"

"I'm excited for you. All you have to do now, is move to another country!"

"Ha! The sovereign state of Vermont! Je vous remercie, Professeur! (Thank you, Professor!) Vous êtes incroyable! Merci'!" (You are amazing! Thank you!)

– Chapter 15 –

The Phoenix
Saturday, December 9, 1972   East Montpelier, Vermont

Marriette and Pete continued to meet throughout the fall. She pursued her novel therapy approach during the sessions with him. He was becoming more comfortable with Marriette and indicated that her techniques seemed beneficial. It was clear that Pete was changing, emerging from his shell, and presenting himself in a different light.

As Marriette prepared to begin at her new position at the University of Vermont, she and Pete discussed a program designed to address returning veterans who had combat stress symptoms. Pete was eager to participate and requested reading materials from her. He also began visiting the University libraries.

In early December, she felt ready to tell him her African story.

Marriette and Pete sat near the woodstove in Pete's living room. It was the first time she had been inside his house. The room was clean and tidy with the obvious additions of a new couch, easy chair, and carpet. Several filled bookcases lined the walls with more books stacked up on the floor.

"Sure are a lot of books in here," she observed, with undisguised surprise.

"Yeah. I read a lot. No TV. No reception here, anyway. Probably not missing much."

"You're probably right," Marriette agreed, getting comfortable on the tan corduroy sofa.

"Pete, my visit today isn't a therapy session for you, but maybe for me. I have a promise to keep. It's time for me to tell you my story … the story I couldn't tell you last August. I've been able to sort things out now to an extent. Keep in mind, please … there's a lot to this. I've only shared parts of it with my parents. When I finish telling you, only you and James will know the whole story. No one else can ever know … and I'd like to leave it that way, please."

"Of course, Marriette. I respect your wishes."

She paused a moment before deliberately exhaling. "It still hurts that I wasn't able to tell Pierre."

"Yes, Marriette...Pierre," he sighed. "I need to get a Pepsi. You want one? This bad habit will be the next to go."

"No thanks. Geez, Pete. I noticed there aren't ashtrays anywhere. You quit?"

"Yeah. Smells a lot better in here, too...don't you think? Just wood smoke. I decided I had enough of tobacco. Just something else pushing my brain around. Fuck that shit. Pepsi's next."

"Good for you, Pete. Just quit, huh?"

"The last pack of Camels was the last pack of anything. Yeah, as I crumpled up that last pack, I told tobacco to get the fuck out of my life! Done! I'm going to try to make something good out of the rest of my life. I want to help these young guys coming back, Marriette. I feel I can do it. It's what I think about."

Walking over to Marriette, Pete kissed her on the forehead. "Thank you for helping me, Marriette."

She looked up at him with tears welling up. "Wonderful, Pete. That makes me so happy."

Pete went back to his chair and sat down with the bottle of soda in his hand.

"First of all, I need to tell you about the baby I'm carrying," Marriette began.

Responding quickly to his inquisitive expression, she continued, "Yes, I'm going to have a baby, Pete. You'll need to listen to the whole story to make sense of it all. Please be patient. It was a little tough for my parents at first, but they're on board, now. With the loss of Pierre, they're happy James is in my life. They know he's special. They needed some hope too. For me, life would be impossibly difficult without him.

Marriette leaned toward Pete, her expression seeking his understanding. "The baby I'm carrying is not James'. During the two years I spent in Africa, I developed a deep friendship with an African man which, near the end, became intimate. The baby was not planned. I knew I was pregnant in September. There was never a moment's thought in my mind that I would not raise this child. James has offered me his full support. The situation is obviously a challenge for us as a couple, but we both want it to work."

Smoothing her hands over her belly, Marriette added, "Will this child ever meet his or her biological father? Considering the circumstances, it is unlikely."

Pete made several trips to add logs to the fire as Marriette completed telling her story. He then got up from his chair and walked over to where she was sitting. Getting down on one knee, he moved closer.

"I'm speechless, Marriette. Pierre prepared you well. I'm amazed at what you've gone through. I remember your comment about having your PhD thesis delivered into your hands. Now, I understand your resolve."

Glancing at the newly evident curvature of Marriette's belly, Pete added, "This child has an amazing mother. I'm with you, too. If it's my place, I'd say I'm very proud of you."

"Thank you, Pete. Your support means a lot to me," she said as she hugged and kissed him on the cheek. "It's getting late. Would you see me out to my new truck?"

"Sure. New truck?"

"Yes. Pierre bought me a new truck with a plow. That should keep me out of trouble. I stored the Chevelle in my parents' garage for the winter. Pierre is buying us a house, as well."

"He was pretty good to me, too," Pete acknowledged.

It was already getting dark at four o'clock as they walked out into the cold.

"Call me, Pete. Maybe we can meet in town sometime. James and I would like to take you out to dinner around the holidays."

"I'd like that. I'm looking forward to meeting James."

"Good. We'll be moving into my parents' house next weekend. Thanks again."

"My best to James and your parents. You're an inspiration, Marriette."

"Thanks, Pete. You inspire me, too … as well."

– Chapter 16 –

Getting off the Bus
Thursday, March 29, 1973   Montpelier, Vermont

A fading orange glow outlined the mountain peaks west of the river valley. Without the direct rays of the sun, the late March air soon turned chilly. Pete left the IGA carrying a bag full of groceries in each arm. Although life was changing for Pete, he still preferred to shop in the evening when he would have the place to himself.

Pete placed one of the bags on the hood of his pickup to open the passenger side door, and then loaded both bags onto the floor.

Spring peepers were calling from a vernal pond down a short embankment at the edge of the parking lot. He leaned on the hood of his truck, taking a moment to enjoy the amphibian chorus. Walking to the front of the truck, he sat down on the cement barrier anchored in the asphalt at the end of the parking lot. With the water's edge nearby, the high-pitched din of the peepers was uncomfortably loud – however, the chorus intrigued him. The hollow in the landscape had created the pond, concentrating the sounds of thousands of peepers into a level of distortion. Pete remained there for a few minutes, focusing his attention on the springtime phenomena isolating the calls of nearby individual frogs. Eventually the cold cement seat distracted his attention from the cacophony, and he stood up and climbed inside the truck to begin the drive back to his home east of Montpelier.

As Pete drove out of the parking lot, a vehicle in the distance turned onto the main street, squealing its tires, and disappearing as the road curved outside of town. About a mile further down the road, along a straight stretch, Pete caught up to the red tail lights of the same vehicle. In the dark, he watched the lights move erratically from one side of the road to the other in front of him. As Pete closed the distance, the pickup swerved right, onto the shoulder, kicking up dust into Pete's headlight beams. The vehicle then arced across the pavement, leaving the road and bouncing into a field to Pete's left. In the soft dirt, the truck came to an abrupt stop. It idled there with its headlights illuminating the edge of the spruce forest.

Pete pulled over onto the gravel along the road's edge. Reaching into the glove compartment, he grabbed a flashlight and got out of his truck. He rocked the bench seat forward to remove his automatic pistol and magazine of ammunition hidden under the rug. Pete loaded the weapon and put it in the pocket of his canvas coat.

The Vermont woods were dark and quiet with the temperature hovering in the 30s. The highway was empty. Pete made his way across the road, through the field, focusing his flashlight on the back of the truck cab. As he got closer, he recognized a familiar sticker adhered to the truck's rear window. It read "101st Airborne Division" in yellow and white letters with the white eagle head displayed at one end.

The driver's side door was partially open. An olive and black jungle boot with a blue-jeaned leg protruded along the rocker panel. Pete directed his flashlight beam into the cab and found a young man in an OD green cold weather coat slumped across the bench seat. The driver looked about 20 - apparently a Vietnam veteran. He didn't appear to be injured. He didn't react to the light shining on him, but his chest rose and fell normally, as he breathed.

As Pete fully opened the door, the dome light came on and he smelled the scent of booze permeating the cab. At this point in his life, the odor literally disgusted him. He turned off the ignition and addressed the young man, "Hey, Airborne! What's going on?"

The boy reacted to the flashlight in his face by tightly closing his eyes. He reached up to cover his eyes with one hand and rubbed his forehead. Remaining on the seat in a state of semi-consciousness, he called out, "I'm sorry. I'm sorry. I didn't mean to do that. I'm so sorry."

The boy then pulled his other hand out from beneath him, using both hands to cover his face. He began to cry, repeating his apology.

"Come on, Airborne," Pete said. "You don't have to be sorry to me. I'm just here to rescue you. You ran off the road. You're drunk, I'd say. You hearing me yet, Airborne?"

The boy mumbled back, "Aw, shit. Where . . . am I? You an MP? I mean . . . I dunno."

"No. You're lucky. It's just old Pete. Can you sit up, Airborne? C'mon now."

Pete reached over, grasping the left sleeve of the boy's coat near the eagle patch to help pull him up.

The boy looked up at Pete.

"Sir?" he slurred.

"No. Pete."

"Pete?"

"Yeah, Airborne."

"I doan feel so good, Pete. Help me outta here, will ya?"

Pete eased him out of the truck. As soon as the boy touched the ground, he turned away, putting his hands onto his knees, and threw up.

Too much of what was going on reminded Pete of himself in similar days. The boy then leaned against the truck fender, recovering. Telling him to stay there, Pete trotted back across the highway and grabbed a shop rag from his truck, wetting it in the brook beside the road. He took a Pepsi from his bag of groceries and returned to the boy's pickup.

"Here you go, Airborne," Pete instructed, popping open the can. "Clean yourself up, Airborne. Here's a Pepsi. Wash your mouth out. Let's get it together, Airborne."

The boy looked up at the older man with the Ranger patrol hat on his head.

"Thanks. Why are you calling me Airborne so much?" he asked, taking a mouthful of Pepsi, swishing it around and spitting it out.

"I served in the 101st a few years back. You back from 'Nam?"

"Yeah. Since February 5th. Hasn't gone well at all."

"What's your name, Airborne?"

"Will Mueller."

"Where you going, Will Mueller?"

"I dunno. Really don't."

"You have family in town?"

"I can't go back there, now."

"You have no place to stay, I take it?"

"Yeah. You're right."

"You're a vet. I'm a vet. Either you can stay here and sleep it off in your truck until the cops find you, or you can come home with me and sleep it off on my couch. We can talk about it in the morning. What do you think, Airborne?"

"I'll go with you, Pete. Thanks."

Putting his arm around Will, they made their way through the field, across the highway, and into Pete's truck.

"OK, Will. You stay here. I'm going to move your pick-up right behind mine. We'll come get it in the morning. I'll leave a note for 'Johnny Law'. Airborne?"

"All the way."

Will was asleep by the time Pete returned. He threw the boy's duffel in the truck bed and drove the three miles to his home.

The boy slept until nine the next morning and awoke to find Pete sitting in his easy chair next to the couch.

"Good morning to you, Airborne. Do you know where you are?"

The boy propped himself up on the couch, swung his feet around and put them on the floor. He rubbed his eyes.

"Pete's place, I take it. Good morning. Thank you," Will replied, still chagrined at his predicament.

Will Mueller was about Pete's height and almost as wiry. He had light brown hair and bright blue eyes. There was a cut over his left eye, which still had thick black sutures in it. A torn pocket hung from the front of his green plaid flannel shirt, along with patches of dried vomit from the night before.

"Your eyes open enough so you can see this, Airborne?"

Will was more sleepy than hung over as Pete handed him a framed picture. Pete had an agenda and wasn't going to wait any longer to get into it.

The boy answered, "I'm thinking this must be you getting ready for a jump."

"Care to guess when that was?"

"I'm guessing World War II."

"Yeah. That was in England, late in the afternoon of June 5, 1944. That night, I landed on top of a church in France way before dawn on D-Day."

"Wow, Pete!"

Will stared at the black and white photograph, showing four members of the 101st, including Pete. They had Mohawks and were in war paint, helping each other prepare their parachutes alongside the fuselage of a C-47.

"Screaming Eagles," the boy remarked, identifying the patch on the paratroopers' left shoulders.

"How old are you, Will?"

"I'll be 21 in October."

"I was just 20 in that picture. How are you feeling this morning?"

"I'll be OK."

"Let me help you along a little bit, Airborne. You had some problems last night?"

"Yeah."

"Maybe we should talk about that later. You've been drinking a lot since you came back?"

"Ah, yeah."

"Did you drink a lot before you left?"

"Uh-uh. I mean, no, sir."

"I take it maybe you're not particularly happy these days. Is that true?"

"Yeah."

Is anyone helping you with what's going on in your life? Does anyone out there understand how you're feeling right now?"

"No. They make it worse," Will answered tersely, with a scowl.

"Are you doing anything that might get you in big trouble? You need to be straight with me, Airborne. When I first found you off the road last night, you were apologizing to someone. You were upset and crying about it."

Will was beginning to feel cornered and looked abashed.

"Why are you asking me about all this? Maybe I can take care of myself."

"Are you sure you can? Really? I'm not getting down on you, Will. I'm on your side. You'll see."

Will didn't answer.

"Were you directly involved in combat?"

"Geez! I guess the fuck!"

"Roger that, Airborne. I've been there, too. We haven't even talked about what you came back from. Not many guys – probably no one – returns from combat completely sane. Even if they never got a physical scratch . . . they're still wounded. You hear that? They're wounded. Their minds . . . their brains are wounded."

Finding it hard to listen, Will turned away to look out the window.

Pete went on, "We come back scared, disoriented, feeling guilty, angry . . . for any number of reasons. We feel misunderstood. Hell . . . we don't even understand ourselves! Combat fucks with the brain of a grunt. Our injured minds may never again be the same. Injured minds need to heal, too. You get home and everybody expects you to magically change back to who you were the day you left, like on the day . . . when you got . . . ON . . . the bus."

The boy turned back to face Pete. "Yeah. They do. They all expected me to be the same."

Pete continued, "Combat vets don't want to admit they're in trouble when they get . . . OFF . . . that bus. The best thing you can do, if you hear me, Airborne, is to admit you have problems. Then maybe something can be done about it . . . but . . . if you don't do something about it now, it's going to wreck your life, for sure. I can promise you. No one ever had this talk with me, Will. For a very long time, after I got home in '46, my life was totally screwed up. That's a long fuckin' time ago, Airborne."

Pete now had Will's attention. The boy stood with his arms folded tightly across his chest. Even though he looked like a deer in headlights, Will could acknowledge he was finally safe in the presence of someone who understood his plight.

"Listen, Will. Here's a checklist. These are things I did or things that happened to me after I returned. See how many might apply to you. I was jumpy. I jumped at anything. I had nightmares, bad thoughts . . . had no control over them. Noises bothered me. Silence bothered me. Lights bothered me. Darkness bothered me. Smells bothered me. Words bothered me.

"I was drinking because I felt bad . . . drinking to change what my brain was doing to me. Lots of drinking. I was into alcohol for 20 years. I only stopped because my nightmares and bad thoughts must have worn themselves out. Other drugs? If they'd been available, I would've taken them, too. How about this? Loneliness and more loneliness. I couldn't keep a job. I was homeless off and on . . . getting into fights . . . angry at everybody . . . anybody. I hit my wife one too many times. She left with our infant son. I never saw them again, Airborne. I never saw or heard a word of my son . . . my boy, again! Never! That . . . right there . . . is a very heavy load to carry."

Pete grit his teeth as he spoke. Stunned, Will stood staring at Pete.

"One more question, Airborne . . . then I'm going to make us a really good Vermont breakfast. Do you think you need some help with what's going on in your life right now?"

Will flopped down on the couch and bent over, looking at the floor.

"Yeah. I've got no idea where I'm going. No plan. No job. Nobody understands.

My mother is angry and really doesn't have a clue. Sometimes it seems as though the people who really cared about me are either dead or still back 'in country'. Back here? Everybody knows, this is nowhere ... too!"

Pete walked over to Will and patted him on the back. Even Pete was surprised at what he found himself doing. He had talked to this young man more in a few hours than he had with anyone in months.

"OK. Let's take a break. Time for breakfast. While I'm doing that, you shower up. You have any clean clothes left in your duffel?"

"No, Pete."

"I'm going to loan you a pair of clean pants and a shirt. Let's throw your stuff in the washer. After breakfast we'll go get your truck."

As Pete guided Will through his compact house, giving him the things he needed, he finished up his message, "Combat soldiers are used to getting orders. Someone is always telling you what to do and when to do it. That structure is necessary in war. Stuff you do gets drilled into you. You don't even have to think. Your brain already knows what to do ... you know?"

"Yeah, you're right."

"The moment you get out, all that structure is gone. You're on your own. You don't get the chance to come back a little at a time. You just get dumped. You get ... off ... that bus and you're lost. The people who sent you home are done with you ... and they don't give a rat's ass, either. Different fucking planet! Right? And nobody understands. Am I right, Airborne?"

"Big time, Pete!"

"I'm going to give you a little direction, Will, until you can take care of yourself. You can call them orders if you want, except, you don't have to do any of it. You can leave anytime you want to. It's going to be up to you."

Pete reached out putting both hands on Will's shoulders, leaving no doubt of the boy's need to focus. "Listen up, Airborne. I want YOU to start all over again. Let's pretend that when you woke up this morning, you were just getting ... OFF ... that bus.

"Instead of people throwing shit at you, I'm the first one you see. I'm the ONLY one you see, Will. And you and I are going to bring you home easy. Just a little bit at a time. You are starting over, now! Forget everything else that has happened since February. Fucking forget it! ALL of it. It doesn't count. Start over!" Pete barked.

Will stood in the doorway of the bathroom holding the supplies in his arms.

"Thanks, Pete." Will sniffed and swallowed hard. He felt like he had gotten really lucky. Almost as a whisper, he asked, "Why . . . are you doing this?"

"That's simple," Pete answered softly, "I don't want you to end up like me. It's just that simple, Airborne. Just that fucking simple. It's a brand new day, Will. Time to start over. Airborne?"

"Airborne!"

– Chapter 17 –

Compassion and Courage
Friday, March 30, 1973   East Montpelier, Vermont

After breakfast, Pete took Will over to the range office and started a fire in the woodstove to take the edge off the early morning chill.

"You couldn't see it in the dark last night, but as you can see, I operate a firing range. There won't be anybody here today. I put a closed sign across the gate out front. Tomorrow it will be busy, though. It might be a tough place for you . . . gunfire. Do you have any thoughts on that right now?"

The boy looked bewildered.

"I don't know. It wasn't on my mind . . . didn't expect that."

"Okay," Pete responded, "We'll get back to that later. I needed to let you know. I'm thinking maybe we'll get out of here early tomorrow. I've got someone else to man the range. We'll go fly fishing for supper."

"That sounds great."

"How are you feeling right now, Will? Are you on board with the idea that you're going to ease into your coming home?"

"I think so, Pete. You know, I'm really not sure of anything, to tell you the truth. But I don't feel unsafe."

"What do you mean by that?"

"I mean, I feel safe here because I'm not going to run into anyone who doesn't understand."

"So, you get the feeling most of the folks you've come across since coming home expect you to be the same as you were the day you left? Is that what you mean?"

"Yeah."

"Well then, why aren't you the same? Why is that? What makes you different now from when you got on that bus a little over two years ago?"

"They don't understand."

"They don't understand what? What's to understand?"

"What are you trying to get at, Pete?"

"Aren't you the same person who got . . . onto . . . that bus? I'll bet you kind of look the same."

Will shook his head at Pete while anxiously looking around the room. Uneasy. Maybe looking for a way to escape, although not sure he wanted to.

"Easy, Airborne. We need to work through this slowly."

"No. I'm not the same, not the same at all . . . I want to be, but I'm not sure where that person is. So, I'm standing here in Vermont. I know my feet are on Vermont soil . . . I'm glad of that . . . but my mind isn't here. It's . . . still over there . . . you know . . . over THERE. That's how I feel."

"It's completely normal to feel that way, Airborne. Don't feel guilty about it. Most of the people here have never seen what you've seen . . . done what you've done. Only those who have served in combat can understand how you're feeling right now. No one else ever can."

Will paced nervously around the small area in front of the workbench, before transfixing on Pete's screaming eagle carving on the wall.

Pete went on, "In order for you to live here again and live sanely, Will . . . you have to put all that 'in country' stuff into its proper place. You have to find your way back home, Will, back to normal. You can't stay over there. It will destroy you."

"I've got so much stuff racing through my mind, Pete . . . it's hard to stay focused on what you're telling me. My thoughts are constantly being interrupted . . . can't control it."

"How do you mean, Will?"

Suddenly feeling overwhelmed, Will pulled up a chair and dropped onto it. He put his hands up to his face, his elbows resting on his knees. Frowning, he began to describe what he was experiencing.

"It felt like this even over there . . . so much crap flying around in my head. I'm scared of things that don't even exist here. Bad thoughts race through my mind. I don't want to see them . . . but they come anyway. I'm afraid of what my brain keeps showing me. You know? It's hard to push them away. Getting drunk helps. I know that's not good. If I'm asleep, they go away at first... but then, there they are again, in my dreams . . . just like it's real."

"You were yelling something in the middle of the night, Will. I thought to wake you up, but you calmed down right away. Do you remember that?"

"No, Pete. Not this time, anyway."

"Are there certain images you see over and over again, like movies your brain is constantly running? Stuff that happened over there?"

"Yeah."

"For now, you're part of those movies," Pete replied. "I'm hoping to help you learn to watch with less and less reaction, watching the movie, without being in the movie. That's the trick."

"I don't understand, Pete."

"I know. We're going to figure it out together."

"OK."

"I've now realized it's important you start dealing with these issues early. You do that by talking about them . . . maybe writing about them . . . again and again. I'll help you, Will, and I know of others who will, as well. The memories stored in your brain need to be reprocessed. I know it sounds like a lot, Airborne, but it's going to be alright."

"I hope so, Pete. It's wearing me out."

"Airborne, is there anything you've done that might get you into trouble? What was that apology talk about when you were passed out in the truck?"

Will stood up from where he was sitting and walked around the range office, looking away from Pete, his hands clasped behind him at his waist.

"I was at my mother's house last night. My high school girlfriend, Jane, was there. She and I kept in touch while I was in 'Nam . . . wrote letters and all. Of course, my letters never said anything about what was actually going on. I wrote back as much as I could in the beginning. The longer I was there, the less I returned letters . . . hers kept coming . . . mine slowed down. It felt like back home didn't really exist any longer. It faded away. It became somebody else's life . . . not mine. I got numb to it."

Will continued pacing up and down the floor in front of the workshop desk, stopping occasionally to look out the window.

"Of course, I kept track of when my time would be up there. But my thoughts went from always thinking about going home to more about leaving Vietnam . . . but in my mind . . . I knew I could never leave, even though I might physically be someplace else. I could never go home again . . . couldn't. After a while, I thought I'd never leave alive anyway."

Pete rocked back in his chair behind the workbench with his feet crossed, resting on the bench top.

"What do you feel like now, Will?"

"I feel like I'm not really here. It's true, Pete. I don't feel like the same me who should be home in Vermont."

"I understand, Will. It's early. Let's begin to change that feeling today. So, what happened last night at your mother's house?" Pete inquired.

"I'd been drinking. My mother and girlfriend started getting on me again about still not having a job, drinking too much and . . . basically not being who they wanted me to be. Guess that sums it up."

Will paused, looking over at Pete.

"You wouldn't have something to drink, would you, Pete? I mean . . . I'm just thirsty."

"What I've got here is Pepsi. Pepsi and well water . . . tea and coffee, if you want it," Pete answered, pointing to the refrigerator in the corner. Will walked over and opened the door.

"That's a lot of Pepsi," Will remarked, looking at the packed shelves. He opened a can, took a few swallows, and leaned back against the refrigerator door.

"So, I was drunk. Jane really started in on me. She just couldn't take it any longer . . . end of her rope. She was yelling and crying at the same time. Maybe she was thinking she had been waiting for the old Will Mueller to return, and after that long wait, when she might have found some good guy, well . . . then, all she got was this strange, angry asshole. I imagine that's what she was getting at. Jane walked right up to me . . . got in my face. She was shaking . . . screaming, 'You're not my Will . . . I hate you . . . get out of my life.' So, I slapped her. I didn't punch her. It was a bad scene. Jane fell to the floor crying. My mother began to cry and yell at me. That's when I ran off. Then you found me."

"That's a tough one," Pete squinted, nodding his head. Will went back to his chair, turned it around and straddled it, folding his arms on the backrest.

"It's not like I don't remember how things were with Jane and me before. I remember those days like it was some kind of yesterday. We had plans . . . I remember that, but now I just can't get myself back there. I want to, Pete . . . I do . . . I do . . . just too much shit in the way."

"Your father?" Pete inquired.

"He left my mother when I was eight or something. Haven't seen him since. Hasn't been in my life. Mom raised me and my brother."

"Tell me about your brother, Will."

"Roger is my older brother. He's in the Army in Germany. He's been in for three years and getting out in five months. Doesn't look like he'll ever go to Vietnam."

"How's he doing?"

"When Roger came home on leave last fall, he didn't act up, which everyone pointed out to me . . . how 'the same' he is and I'm not. So they think there's something wrong with me. Well, they're right. There is."

"I see," Pete remarked. "So, what do you think you need to do about last night's fiasco? I mean, do you think your mother is worried about you?"

"Sure, she is . . . but . . . I think driving back there and just apologizing isn't going to be enough. I've been apologizing a lot . . . you know, lots of empty promises."

Trying to encourage Will, Pete suggested, "You've got to do something soon . . . to let her know you're okay and not just wandering around . . . sleeping in the woods and drinking."

"Maybe I should write a letter and let her know I'm in a safe place until I can get it together again."

"That sounds outstanding, Airborne. Also, I'd say no more booze . . . not a drop, until it doesn't have any kind of grip on you. Be warned, Airborne . . . there is never booze of any kind on this property. No weed, either . . . nothing. I've even given up Pepsi. I'm addicted to that, too! The stuff in the refrigerator is all yours," Pete said, waving the back of his hand dismissively at the refrigerator.

Pete got up from his chair and walked over to the boy.

"Can we agree to that? And, Will, we can't lie to each other . . . about anything. The fastest road to getting back includes telling the truth. I have to trust you. You have to trust me. Do you agree with all these things?"

"Yeah. I agree, Pete. I know I can't go on like I have."

"If you think you're having trouble with any of it, being tempted, you need to be honest with me."

"OK."

"How about this, Will. Take a while, don't rush . . . think about what you want to write to your mother. I'll look it over if you'd like . . . don't have to. Then I'll take it over to her later on."

"What's our plan here, Pete? Am I staying with you for a while? I can pay for rent and food."

"If we can stick to our plan, you're welcome to stay until you're on your feet again. I have plenty of work around here. There's the repair shop. It's getting time to gather and split wood for next winter. That'll keep you busy and will help me out a lot. Splitting logs is good exercise and really good for sorting things out," Pete added, pointing to his head. "Can you handle it?"

"You bet, Pete. Thanks."

"Patience, Will. One day, maybe one hour at a time, my boy."

– Chapter 18 –

Pete's New Clothes
Friday, March 30, 1973   Montpelier, Vermont

Early spring sunlight flooded into the second floor living room of the LaFleurs' home, where Marriette and James had been living since just before Christmas. Françoise was cooking in the kitchen, Gil and James were working down in the bakery, and Harris, the couple's two-week-old son, was asleep in his crib as Marriette folded diapers.

Later in April, Marriette, James, and Harris planned to move into their new home near the university in Burlington. Gil and Françoise loved having their new family close at hand and were in no hurry to see them move out. The upper level of the LaFleur home had two bedrooms with a bath, the perfect apartment for the young family.

Harris was born early on the morning of Sunday, March 11, but not as anticipated. James and Marriette had been visiting friends in Montreal when their son arrived two weeks ahead of his due date. He was a healthy and visibly beautiful blend of his parents' genes. Gil and Françoise drove up to the Montreal General Hospital the same day James's parents arrived from Sherbrooke. The grandfathers were ecstatic to learn their grandson was, perchance, Canadien.

Françoise was still in the kitchen when the phone rang.

"Bonjour.

"Hello. This is Pete Long."

"Hello, Pete. This is Françoise speaking."

"Good afternoon, Françoise. Congratulations on your grandson," Pete offered with a new enthusiasm in his voice noticed and welcomed by everyone.

"He's beautiful, Pete. We hope you can meet him sometime soon."

"Yes. Soon, I hope. I look forward to the occasion. I would like to speak with Marriette, if she's available."

"She is. I will get her for you. Nice to hear your voice, Pete."

"Thank you, Françoise."

Marriette overheard her mother's conversation on the kitchen phone. Anticipating the transfer, she got up from the stack of diapers to sit on the sunny end of the sofa, putting her feet up on the coffee table.

"Hey, Pete. You'll have to meet our Harris soon. He's a big boy."

"Greetings, Marriette. Yes, I'm looking forward to it. I'm happy you're home as I have something important to talk to you about. Is there any chance you might get away for an hour or so? I'll come into town."

"Sure, Pete. I need to feed Harris first. How about in an hour?"

"Great! Will you meet me in front of E.B. White's?"

"You mean the men's clothing store?"

"Yeah."

"Of course, Pete. I'll meet you in front of the store in about an hour."

"Thanks. Thanks, so much, Marriette. See you soon."

"Bye, Pete."

Marriette drove downtown and parked behind Pete's truck in front of E.B. White's. Before she could get out, Pete jumped out of his truck and went around to the passenger side of Marriette's Chevy and climbed in.

"Ok, Pete, what's this all about?" Marriette grinned. "Men's store?"

"I'll get to that in a minute," Pete returned the smile.

"Here's what's going on. Thursday night, while driving home, I found this young boy who had driven off the side of the road. He was OK, but drunk. Turns out, he's a local kid . . . he'll be 21 in October. Spent the last 12 months in Vietnam. Messed up, big time. Combat stress. He's back in the states in a physical sense, but his brain is still trapped in Vietnam. He had no place to go. Already heading in the wrong direction. I sort of caught him as he was falling. He's a good kid. Seems smart. As I told him, he just needs to come home easy. He's had nothing but problems since getting off the bus from Hanscom Field in early February. No one understands his predicament. His name is Will Mueller."

"My goodness, Pete . . . that's Mary Beth Mueller's son. Will Mueller. Hmmm, did I work with him? No . . . must have been his older brother, Roger, who worked in the bakery a summer or two when he was in high school. What are you thinking about Will?"

"I told him he needed to start over slowly and that I would help him come back home. I'm committed to doing this. Marriette, I feel it's what I want to do. I've cleaned up my act. Now I feel I can help these kids."

"I know, Pete. I believe you can."

"For now, Will is going to stay with me. We've set up an agreement. I think he understands its importance. He knows where I came from and the trouble I've had. I think it's impressed him. I'm going to give it a try, Marriette."

"Wow, Pete, good for you! I think you're on the right track. Is there anything I can do to help?"

"Yes, there is. I would like to communicate regularly with you, to get your input . . . depending on how things go. Right now, the boy needs structure. He needs his days scheduled. That's the environment he came from and there's none of that here for him. It's too extreme a shift, considering where he's been . . . what he's done. He found himself back in Vermont only a week after leaving Southeast Asia. Can you believe it?"

"Mindless and cruel."

"With all those images and thoughts swirling around in his head, it's hard for him to make good decisions, Marriette. He needs an anchor right now. I'm going to keep a close eye on him. It will be a day-to-day project."

"He's one lucky kid, Pete. Have you spoken to him about his trauma history, yet?"

"I'm just beginning to. I have a pretty good idea of what's happened in the last year or so. I wanted to make sure he felt safe first."

"Perfect."

"Damn. The government just discards these kids by the thousands. Motherfuckers! Just like they always have. Nothing ever changes."

"Are you planning to take an inventory of what's bothering him specifically?" Marriette inquired.

"Yes. Just as you've described to me. I'm using that approach."

"This sounds really good, Pete. Let's talk a few times a week, if you can. I want to hear how you're doing. We're kind of working out this treatment program together, aren't we?"

"Guess so," Pete answered. "I'll proceed thoughtfully."

"Great. Now, what about the men's store? What's the angle? I see you have a haircut . . . shaved off the beard? Looks nice, Pete."

"Thanks. There's something I have to do today. I asked the boy to write a letter to his mother. I've decided to hand-deliver it and am prepared to talk to her. She really has no idea what her son has been through. He hasn't said anything of substance to her. She and his high school girlfriend expected back the same person he was the day he left. It will be a while before Will is even close to being that person again. I'll try to explain it to her. I thought I should look nice, you know, presentable."

"Of course."

"Would you help me pick out some clothes? I have no idea what to wear."

"Pete. That's so sweet you'd ask me. Sure, let's go inside and square you away."

"Great. Thanks, Marriette . . . guess it's part of starting over."

– Chapter 19 –

Reconsideration and Forgiveness
Friday, March 30, 1973   Montpelier, Vermont

Pete left White's men's store around 4:30, dressed in khakis, a light blue collared shirt, and navy sweater. The new shoes weren't particularly comfortable, but would serve the purpose.

Pete placed his new sport coat on the truck seat beside him, thinking he'd save it for another day. He drove a little further along Main Street down a few blocks to Ellis Road, and parked in front of the Mueller home.

The house was a neat little bungalow set off the road with a large sugar maple centered on the front lawn. The snow in the yard from the storms of early March had melted, except for mounds accumulated along the edges of the house where it had slid off the green metal roof.

Pete walked up to the front door holding an envelope containing Will's letter. He caught a glimpse of Will's mother passing by the front window as he approached. He stood under the overhang, took a deep breath, and knocked on the door.

Mary Beth Mueller, a diminutive woman in her forties with short graying hair, opened the door – holding it open with an extended arm.

"How may I help you?" she inquired.

"Mrs. Mueller, I'm Peter Long. I live just outside of town. I'm here to let you know your son, Will, is OK."

"Will! Where is he?" she asked in a desperate voice.

"He's fine, Ma'am. Will was driving in front of me last night when his truck went off the road. He wasn't hurt but he was drunk, as you know. Will stayed at my place last night. He asked me to give you this letter," Pete said, as he handed her the envelope.

Mary Beth didn't invite him in, but chose to hold the storm door ajar using her shoulder and one foot outside the door on the stoop. Opening the envelope, she read the letter in silence.

Mom,

Pete Long helped me out last night. If he hasn't saved my life, he at least got to me before the cops did. Pete is a vet, too. He's been through some real bad stuff, like me. I'm really sorry for all the trouble I've caused since I came home. Pete says I'm not really home yet and that's what it feels like to me. Please, let him explain to you what's going on. Please. I love you, Mom. I'm sick that I hit Jane. I'm so sorry. I don't know if she will ever forgive me. Please be patient.

Will

Pete never took his eyes from Mary Beth as she read the note. Looking up, she stared at Pete gratefully, making him feel uncomfortable.

Finally, she spoke, "Please, come in, Mr. Long."

Gesturing toward the couch, Mary Beth said, "Please, have a seat. I was planning to call the state police and report Will as missing if I hadn't heard anything by tonight. What can you tell me? I'm at a loss. This has been an awful two months. What's going on with my child? We don't seem to know him anymore."

She continued to stand, almost hovering over Pete.

"Ma'am," Pete responded, "your child was sent into hell for a year. You probably didn't expect that. He certainly didn't. If parents really knew what would happen, I doubt many would ever let their kids out of their sight."

Shaking her head in disbelief, Mary Beth responded, "Will never said anything akin to that in his letters to either one of us."

"I'm not surprised," Pete replied. "It's hard to talk about . . . and he didn't want to worry you . . . terrify you, would be a better way to say it."

Looking puzzled, Mary Beth asked, "My older son, Roger, is in the Army in Europe. He's been home twice on leave. It was wonderful having him home, but what has happened to Will?"

"Was Will ever a problem before he went into the Army? Did he drink? Smoke marijuana?"

"No, neither."

"That doesn't surprise me," Pete responded. "What's Roger's job in the Army?"

"He's a kind of veterinarian, I think."

"Ahhh . . . he's a vet tech," Pete clarified. "Do you know what veterinari-ans do in the army? It seems strange. At one time, the Army had hundreds of veterinarians. Back then, there were horses and mules. That was before they had tanks and trucks. Now veterinarians are mostly food inspectors. Roger probably helps to inspect food. His job keeps him away from the realities of the war. If he's smart, he's probably on leave touring all those beautiful places in Europe."

"Well, he is."

"Will said that his brother is getting out in five months. If Roger 're-ups', he'll probably be sent to Southeast Asia to make up for his easy tour in Europe. I hope he's wise enough to come back and go to school and maybe become a real veterinarian. Does that make any sense, Mrs. Mueller?"

"Yes."

Mary Beth finally sat down in a chair across from Pete, nervously biting a fingernail.

"Mrs. Mueller, Will has had a totally different experience. An experience he couldn't get away from. An experience he had no control over. I'm just beginning to hear the details, but get the general idea. As I explain this to you, Mrs. Mueller, try to imagine how you might feel coming away from this kind of experience."

Mary Beth repositioned herself on the chair, grasping a pillow to her chest.

"Will was involved in heavy combat. For the 12 months he was in Vietnam, he spent a lot of time being scared. Scared he might not live a second longer. Scared out of his mind for days on end, moment to moment, minute by minute, hour by hour. The alternative was being so numb to everything; he didn't know or care where he was . . . just wandering and responding to commands.

"He and his brothers found themselves in triple canopy jungle. Dark, thick, hot, and wet. Too hot to wear protective equipment. Too wet to ever get dry. Days with little or no sleep. Day after day, Mrs. Mueller . . . and many dark nights lying wet and uncomfortable from not moving . . . just waiting for something bad to happen . . . and sometimes it did.

"Will's duty was to hunt and kill human beings who were his own age . . . his 'defined enemies'. After a firefight, he had to search their lifeless bodies to gather intelligence. Even if the enemy had buried their dead, Will's patrol might dig up the bodies to search them. Most times, there was little of use discovered. Instead, he found pictures of their families, their girlfriends, their parents, or their pets. He watched these Vietnamese kids die because the Army couldn't evacuate them and, of course, he saw his friends die or get wounded.

"When the firefight was over, they cried or were numbed emotionless as they collected their dead brothers or parts of their bodies to put into bags and throw onto a helicopter. Combat is the stuff of insanity and there was no uncomplicated escape from it."

As Pete kept firm eye contact with Will's mother, he pushed on.

"You can't imagine such horror, can you? Unless one has been there … no one can."

Mary Beth didn't move or speak as she held her son's letter tightly in her hand, pressed to her cheek.

"Mrs. Mueller, Will never got a physical scratch to report. He was very lucky in that regard. His brain, however, is wounded. Brains can't process this stress. In this combat environment, you understand very quickly you aren't fighting for your country, whether it's legit or some phony trumped up cause. You're fighting for your brothers in arms, fighting just to stay alive one more day."

Pete's eye contact had wandered away from Mary Beth. When he looked up again, she was expressionless. Tears tracked down her face, dripping from her chin onto the carpet.

Pete offered a compassionate glance, but went on.

"Mrs. Mueller, this is why Will didn't continue to write as much as he had at first. He felt hopeless. He was well aware of the number of days before he would leave Vietnam, but he came to believe only his body would be returning and he would be lucky if that happened. Now, Will's feet are back on the ground in Vermont, but his brain has been traumatized. He needs to come home slowly. He must reorganize his mind and try to put his traumatic experience into its proper perspective . . . as best he can. This will be a very difficult task for him, but he will have help. For most vets, this often is not the case. I can help him and people at the VA I know can as well. You'll have your boy back someday, but not anytime soon. At least, he can come back home.

"Here's yet another insult. When I got home from Europe in '45, people were happy to see us. When Will got off the bus in Kenmore Square, there weren't the crowds of protesters . . . not like just a few years ago. But some guy noticed his uniform, walked up to him, spit on him, and ran away. Will was astonished. He soon realized he'd come home to yet another war, a war that wasn't what I experienced. I'll bet Will never told you about that either, did he?"

"No. He didn't."

The information Pete was revealing shocked Mary Beth. She was full of regret that she had unknowingly treated her son so poorly and felt guilty that she had ever let him go in the first place. She also felt betrayed by the notion that it was his duty to serve his God and his Country.

Pete suddenly realized his presentation had bordered on the excessive, but he also felt it was an honest dose of reality. Giving Mary Beth an apologetic glance, he gently said, "I hope you can begin to understand Will's recent behavior. Damaged minds need time and help to heal. Give him time, Mrs. Mueller. Forgive him. He needs your support."

"Thank you," she whispered. "Please let me know what I can do to help."

"Yes, of course. Will you be alright?" Pete asked, as he stood up to leave, feeling his question a poor attempt at concern and consolation.

Mary Beth walked up to Pete and hugged him, then burst into tears, openly crying on his shoulder.

Pete stood motionless at first, unsure how to respond. He then put his arms around her and held her. It had been a long time since he had held a woman in this way. After Mary Beth calmed, she quickly pulled away.

"I'm so sorry, Mr. Long."

"Call me, Pete."

"Sorry, Pete. I'm so upset with everything, especially myself. I had no idea," she sighed.

"Thank you for what you're doing," she whispered, as she took one of Pete's hands and squeezed it with both of hers.

"May I talk with Will? Do you think he'll talk to me?"

"Of course, Ma'am."

"Mary Beth, please."

"Mary Beth. I'll ask him to call you tomorrow. Don't get into specifics with him… please. Keep the conversation within the United States."

"I will. I promise."

"I know I frightened you, but it's imperative I tell you the truth about what has been going on, so you might begin to understand.

"It's approaching dinner time, Mary Beth. I'd like to tell you what the plan is going forward to help Will. I can call you tomorrow . . . or . . . can I invite you to join me at the Westside Café, now?" Pete inquired, surprising even himself at his request. "I've overwhelmed you with so much negative information. I'd like to provide you with the positive, as well. Your choice."

Without hesitation, Mary Beth answered, "Just a minute, Pete. I'll get my coat."

– Chapter 20 –

A Change of Mind
Tuesday, April 17, 1973   Montpelier, Vermont

After three weeks, Will was feeling comfortable with the routine at Pete's place and adhered to their agreement. He checked in with his mother at least once a week and kept the conversation simple. There were mutual apologies and an understanding to look for better days ahead.

Marriette and Pete agreed to meet regularly. At least once a week, Pete would travel to the University to meet with her, not only to discuss his experience helping Will, but also to familiarize himself with the program Marriette was developing.

Back in the woods of East Montpelier, Pete's operation of a rifle range proved to be a problem for Will, as few sounds could be so disturbing. They had talked about the range early on. Just like all the other things, it would have to be dealt with. It was a sporting range, not the war in Vietnam, but sounded like it.

Pete arranged for a friend to cover operating hours, affording an opportunity for the two of them to do things off the property. On good weather days, Pete and Will wandered through the Green Mountains, hiking and talking or fly fishing along the swollen springtime brooks and streams. These activities allowed the mind to wander to both the good and bad. Pete was always available to monitor where Will's mind might find itself.

Much of the wood needed for the next winter's heat was felled, cut and split by Will, then stacked under the overhang at the back of the house. Another project on the property involved Pete and Will removing worn shingles from the house, replacing them with new white cedar.

Along with being a gunsmith, Pete was also in the business of maintaining chainsaws for local logging companies. When Will wasn't doing other chores, Pete taught him how to repair small gas engines. This kept Will productive as he was guided through the recovery process.

Pete ensured there were opportunities for Will to talk about his experiences. The sessions had their painful moments, which later triggered nightmares. Will's screaming would awaken Pete. He would get up, turn on more lights, and check on the boy. There were also episodes when Will, half asleep, was found wandering through the house looking for a safe place to hide from whatever was hunting him. If Will was able to talk about the dream, right then, they would. Sometimes he didn't wake up completely, so Pete just held him for a while and got him back into bed.

Pete developed a knack for easing Will through the rough days and nights. As he recalled the origins of his own trauma, he realized what had been missing for him when he returned from Europe in '46.

The mission was to gradually bring Will's mind back home from Vietnam. Pete introduced Will to the notion that war shouldn't be thought of in the realm of normal human experience. Although war is ubiquitous, there are few who can participate directly and then step away from its insanity and violence without sustaining damage to their minds.

Pete advanced the idea that trauma could be diminished by identifying the problems early. By successfully addressing combat-acquired issues, the accumulated secondary effects such as addictions, arrests, bad relationships, poor parenting, and the like might never come to pass.

He counseled Will to begin separating the images and feelings of his experience "in country" from the reality of the present. Pete's barn became his clinic, at least his primary one. Mountain overlooks and large flat rocks near trout streams served as pretty good ones, as well.

He and Will met daily on the tree trunk sections in the barn with a pot of tea between them; no booze, no tobacco, and no more Pepsi for Pete. The war-inspired painting loomed on the wall behind them and a fire in the Franklin stove took the damp chill off the early spring evenings.

Pete often began their session by reminding Will that the process of healing and recovery was a long one and that he would need patience and dedication.

"Consider your flashbacks and memories as dreams," Pete suggested. "When you had a bad dream before 'Nam', you knew it wasn't real, right? You were in those dreams, however routine or bizarrely inexplicable they were…and they seemed of no conscious consequence at the time, right?"

"That's right," Will agreed.

"Of course, your experiences in 'Nam weren't dreams. I'm not saying that … but they are now just thoughts, images and feelings that continue to exist in your brain, even though Vietnam is 8,500 miles away from here. Their impact, compared to your dreams, is overwhelming by comparison, but again… they are just the raw material of memory, stored in your brain.

"Considering those images as unprocessed memories, Will . . . how would you want to . . . let's say . . . repackage them? Remember, they are just thoughts. We are going to slowly pick those thoughts apart and weaken their effect on you. You'll learn how to separate those thoughts and images from who you are. You don't have to believe your thoughts, Will . . . do you understand, you don't have to believe them."

Pete asked Will to make a list of excruciating images and feelings to be reprocessed one event at a time. The plan was to alter each one's relevance and impact and to separate them from reality.

There was one event that Will was not able to speak about. Pete acknowledged Will's reluctance, but asked circuitous questions.

"Without actually telling me about the event, can you tell me why it's so hard to talk about it?"

Will remained silent, reliving something. Pete drew him back.

"Will. Come back to the barn. Focus on the mug of tea in your hands. Listen to what I'm saying now, okay?"

"Okay."

"Let's try this. Where does the responsibility lie? Simple question . . . did you volunteer to join the military?"

"No. I was drafted," Will answered.

"Okay. Your enlistment was coerced. If someone doesn't go, they threaten to throw the teenager in prison."

"I could have tried getting into college. I didn't do that."

"You were barely 18. That's why they target teenagers. Teenagers haven't seen enough of life to understand the value of their own," Pete emphasized.

"For instance, being able to ask questions like . . . what's going on here? Is the situation in Vietnam, a place halfway around the world, such that I should risk my life . . . my body, my intact mind for it? Are those I care about at risk? Is the security of my country really at risk? Is there any evidence to support this demand on me? Did you ask yourself those questions, Will?"

"I never thought to," admitted Will.

"Of course not. You didn't know who you were. You still don't know who you are . . . just yet. That will come. It will be possible now. Do you know what I mean by 'finding out who you are'?"

"I think I know what you're driving at, Pete. I want some peace. I feel like my brain has been taken over. I can't know who I am until I get through this."

"Yes, you're right," Pete replied. "Of course, you want peace. We need to slowly work on changing your mind, every day until that happens. It can happen, if you really want it to."

"So, for me to recover, I need to think about all this stuff in a different way. How do I do that, Pete?"

"It is changing your thoughts . . . and particularly how you frame them . . . that changes your mind." Pete continued with his lesson, "Let's look more at the responsibility for actions taken. You were drafted. Those who volunteered were sold on an idea of duty and love of country, like an old car sold with a cheap new paint job and a worn-out transmission full of sawdust . . . deception and lies."

Will grinned at the analogy.

"Who is benefiting from this war?" Pete asked. Is the world any safer from Communism? Whatever that bullshit really means. The U.S. military certainly hasn't helped the people of Vietnam. The Vietnamese had their own civil war going on for chrissakes! In the long run, the only ones benefiting from this war are those whose sons were never sent there, those who are profiting from the largesse of the military industrial complex. Fogarty had it right!"

"I heard that song a lot in country," Will acknowledged.

"The war is finally winding down, my boy. Those bastards would have kept it going if things hadn't gotten so fucked up here stateside in the last few years. It seems like the riots with American cities burning, the assassinations, and war protests were worse for business than the war in Vietnam was good for it.

"The civilian leadership of this fiasco was not even 'in country' and had no functional conception of what was taking place over in Southeast Asia or how it affected its participants. Maybe they did know and just didn't give a shit. I could believe that. Fuckin' MacNamara . . . unconscious piece of shit . . . he should've stuck with making Fords. What if Kennedy, MacNamara, Johnson, and the rest of them assholes could have been there to step over the young bodies of American dead and wounded, not to mention the Vietnamese people, day . . . after . . . day . . . after . . . day . . . or to personally deliver the news to the parents of the fallen that their teenager was dead. I bet those fuckers would have changed their minds damn fast. How much inhumanity can anyone stand? Too much money to be made at the expense of the young, the poor, and the ignorant. Same as it ever was. Same as it ever was! Unconscious, self-serving monsters, every fuckin' one of them. Your captors!"

"Geez, Pete. Wow! I hadn't seen it that way... kind of assumed I could trust the President and all that...didn't give it any thought. It didn't take long for pretty much everybody over there to realize that everything going on 'in country' was bullshit," Will observed.

Changing the subject, Will admitted, "Pete, it's so hard not to feel I should have handled myself differently. I'm really ashamed of some stuff. I hear what you're saying about responsibility. It makes sense, but I'm just not there yet. It isn't like I can turn a switch in my head and feel good instantly. If I think about what happened too much, I wish I had been KIA'd."

"Yeah. I understand. Do you feel like that now, Will? Did you ever feel so bad you might take your own life?"

"Not now, Pete! No, not now... pretty much because you pulled me off the road. If it wasn't for you, I think I could have headed in that direction. Thanks, Pete. As bad as this crap is, I feel there are a lot of reasons to live, now."

"That's a really good sign, Will."

"Yeah."

"Will, please hear me again. Nothing you did in Vietnam was of your own accord. Insanity was all around you. You just became a part of it. You are very young and inexperienced in life. Add five or ten more years of life experience and damn few guys would even go. Do you think you could have walked away then from stuff which strikes you now as wrong?"

"No. Not really . . . not until the end of the tour."

"No? How come? You don't have to answer that question right now but I want you to think about it."

"No, I can answer now," Will responded.

"Okay."

"Once we were in the thick of things, our reactions were just raw. We weren't fighting for the folks back home, anymore. Shit no! We were just trying to stay alive another minute more. Not much thinking. Just reaction. Yeah, Pete. I saw crazy things. Bad stuff. Crazy things here . . . not crazy there."

"I understand," Pete acknowledged. "Although the military is a structured environment, under combat conditions in 'Nam, insanity flourished, maybe more than in other wars, maybe not. There was no national commitment to the war in Vietnam. It wasn't like World War II where America was really threatened by Nazi Germany. Then, our soldiers and all the people back home were indeed real heroes. It was a full-blown national effort that involved all Americans, military or not. Can you begin to understand the huge difference in the mindset here ... considering those very different circumstances?"

"I can ... but even knowing something to be true, when I really stop to think about framing the wars in that way, it still has to compete with my deep feelings. It's my struggle apart from anyone else's experience," Will replied.

Throughout April and into May, in small increments, Will began to relate the experiences that disturbed him. Pete encouraged him to write about these experiences, suggesting, "Write about it as an observer, Will, maybe as a writer of fiction. Try to remove yourself from what you are writing."

There was one incident Will still wasn't able to discuss. He told Pete there was an event that was, to him, so bad it was unthinkable. Will tried to push it out of his mind constantly, but it kept returning, haunting him, day and night. Pete encouraged Will to talk about it when he was ready.

"I'm afraid there's not much progress with that yet, Pete."

"There can be, Will, in time."

Sensing the enormity of the circumstance, Pete reiterated, "I want to remind you of something I mentioned several weeks ago now. Please remember, Will, that in war, soldiers find themselves doing things they would never consider under normal circumstances. You get a free pass on that. I had to realize this, too. It took me decades. No help."

"Thanks, Pete."

"And you never have to talk to anyone about it ever again, if you don't want to, but you need to talk to yourself about it. Watch the movie, but don't be in the movie. Watch it separately. Work on being the observer. Always keep that in mind."

"Okay, Pete. I'm trying my best."

– Chapter 21 –

Another Chance
Wednesday, May 16, 1973   Lake Groton, Groton, Vermont

Early Wednesday morning, Pete and Will drove to Lake Groton to fish. The sun was coming up over the lake and visible only as a bright white disk burning in the dense fog. At midweek, it was quiet with no one else around. A mist hung above the surface, limiting visibility to less than 50 yards. While carrying the boat from the pickup bed to the water's edge, the sound of a simple tap of the aluminum hull traveled far into the distance.

With all their gear on board, Will pushed the boat out from shore and jumped in. Pete sat at the stern, preparing bait on the lines while Will rowed out across the placid water. Mayflies swarmed above the surface of the lake, lighting along the gunwales. Loons called around them, startled as the boat approached in the fog. Their skipping departure could be heard, but not witnessed.

Although the early morning silence begged not be broken, a hollow clunk sounded with each stroke as the oars shifted position in the oarlocks. It was not a time for talking. A few hundred yards offshore, Will stopped rowing. Soon the ripples of motion faded away and the boat sat stationary on a liquid mirror. The men dropped lines deep into the mountain lake. Not more than 15 minutes had passed before Pete, and then Will, had a keeper Rainbow in the cooler.

As Will lowered his line back into the depths of the lake, he felt a firm tug at the tip of his pole. He opened the bale, allowing the fish to run with the bait, and watched carefully as the departure of the line slowed. He set the hook and the fish ran with the line again. Will attempted to reel against the loosened drag, but the line was stripping quickly. As he cautiously provided tension, he looked up at Pete commenting, "I think this is a pretty good fish."

"Maybe. It won't stop taking line, will it?" Pete replied, studying the line leaving the spool.

"What do you think she is, Pete? A big brown … maybe a lake trout?"

"Don't know, Will. I guess a Brown. She's sure taking a lot of line," Pete remarked, as the two watched the line rapidly emptying from the spinning reel.

"Spool is getting low," Will cautioned.

"Yeah," nodded the older man.

"10-pound test?" Will asked.

"Ten," Pete answered. As the bottom of the spool started to peek through, Will groaned, "I have to tighten the drag."

The spool's ratcheting clicks slowed, but the big fish persisted. Will stopped the drag entirely. The tip of the light rod was severely bent as the fish pulled the boat along. When Will angled the rod to allow for spring against the force of the big trout, the fiberglass fractured at the ferrules.

"Holy shit, Pete! Now what?"

"Scoot all the way up front and hand line her," Pete instructed, urging Will to move quickly with a backhand wave.

Will put the rod down. Holding onto the line he knelt on the floor at the bow, hanging over the nose, gently playing the line in his hands.

"Like ice fishing, Pete."

"Yeah, except your fish is pulling us across the lake!"

Another five minutes passed before the boat sat motionless. Will began bringing in the line, hand over hand, giving and taking as the fish demanded. Pete picked up the broken rod, reeling in the line accumulated on the bottom of the boat.

Staring at his hands while working the line, Will's mind wandered back to memories of ice fishing with friends only a few years before. Suddenly, his mind shifted into a fog of intrusive thoughts, sensing trip wire in his hands, setting a booby trap at a defensive perimeter deep in the jungle. It was night and he was impossibly tired. Fears of attack and lying in the wet earth came over him. His hands stopped moving. Although the boy's back faced him, Pete sensed Will's sudden absence. He shifted to the middle seat enough to glimpse Will's vacant expression.

"Hey, Will. You still here with me and that big trout?"

Startled, Will turned around quickly to look at Pete, his brow covered in sweat.

"Come back here, Will. Back to the pond. You have a fish to bring in."

Pete leaned forward, giving Will reassuring pats on his back. Will caught his breath and re-oriented himself.

"Okay, Pete."

Another 10 or 15 minutes passed before the fish ceased pulling on the line. The big trout was tired. Will steadily brought his catch closer to the surface.

"She's a big fish, Pete. I've never felt anything like this before."

Will worked his way back to the middle of the boat as both men looked over the gunwale to catch the first glimpse of the trout. She turned again, ran deep, and then came back to the boat. Her large shadow darted past them, disappearing again. The next pass provided a view of her long and speckled body.

"Oh, my gosh!" Pete exclaimed. "Did you see the white on the fins? This is a really big Brook trout! She's got to be a record fish."

The trout again passed from under the boat.

"Wow! Look at that, Pete. What a beautiful fish. Can she even fit in the net?"

"We'll see."

Pete reached around to get the net, which was sized for a much smaller fish. The weary trout surfaced, resting on her side as Will reached forward, grasping the line, inches from the fish's mouth. Two deteriorating hooks adorned her lower jaw with short pieces of frayed monofilament streaming from them. Pete guided the net over the fish's head. Barely two-thirds of the trout could fit into its enclosure. As Pete lifted the trout from the water, Will began to choke up.

"No, Pete. I need to let her go. I can't kill her."

"Really?"

"Look at her, Pete. She's survived so long. She shouldn't be our supper . . . not anyone's. I don't want to be the one to end her life. Tiring her out was bad enough."

Looking up at Pete, Will shrugged. "Can't do it, Pete."

Pete nodded with approval as he returned the trout to the surface next to the boat. "I understand, Will, I really do. It's okay. Let her go."

Will reached into the tackle box for pliers. He parted the netting and cut the shafts of all three hooks piercing her craggy jaw. Pete backed the net away from the exhausted fish. Her spotted blue brown back glistened in the morning sun. Will reached into the water lightly grasping the fish's tail, moving it for her. She rested for only a moment longer. With a flick of her tail, revealing her scarlet belly and white edged fins, she disappeared into the cold deep water.

"Are you okay, Will?"

"Yes, Pete. I feel much better, actually. Can't tell you why. I just do."

"I'm glad, son."

– Chapter 22 –

The Illusory Thinker of Thoughts
Thursday, June 14, 1973   Montpelier, Vermont

Behind Pete's house, a path led through a spruce and balsam fir forest to a stream. When winter's snowfall was heavy, the stream became a powerful torrent with the spring thaw, eroding the banks, especially at its curve at the end of the path. Years earlier, Pete had built a bridge across the stream. The very next winter produced a record spring flood that destroyed it. Only the old pilings remained, rotting on the far side of the bank.

At the end of each spring runoff, branches would settle in the stream, snagged among giant boulders, collecting debris. The flow of water then diverted onto a flat sandy stretch across from the big bend in the stream.

It wasn't long after Will moved in with Pete that he discovered the stream, only a three-minute walk from the house. As spring progressed, he observed new vegetation appearing on the forest floor. In early May, Will's attention was captured by the emergence of painted trilliums. Their showy white and red blossoms stood out among the relative abundance of burgundy wake robins.

One morning, as he walked the path, he found his thoughts wander back into the jungle of Vietnam. As a distraction, Will knelt in the damp moss and conifer needle debris to examine the trilliums, focusing on a single flower. He studied the veins coursing across the three white petals with their crimson interiors, and the shape of the six stamens arranged in the middle. Will observed how the flower was centered among three large green leaves, crisp in their newness. He watched tiny ants deep at the base of the pistil, climbing the pale green stamens to the yellow pollen-laden anthers at their tips. Conscious of nothing else, Will recognized that he was observing his thoughts emerge, then pass into memory, without judgment or reaction, only perception, just knowing. Absent was the cognition of trillium or moss or pollen, only the anonymous sensation of wet, cool, color, smooth, rough, and scent.

He continued down the path and looked around for a place to climb down the embankment to the stream. The springtime runoff was complete. Using the flatter rocks as stepping stones, he crossed to the other side of the brook, surveying the area. The morning sun penetrated the tops of the trees.

He heard the raspy call of a Scarlet Tanager and then got a glimpse of the flash of red orange as it flew to a position higher overhead.

Will waded into the rushing water, tugging at tangled branches caught among the rocks. He threw them up onto the bank into a pile, tidying the confusion created by the flood. They would serve as more kindling to be cut up for firewood. The leaves restrained by the seasonal dam were set free to continue their passage downstream. Just above the bend in the water, a natural accumulation of boulders created a pool where the water calmed, forming a cascade as the elevation changed. Will sat down on one of the boulders with his rubber boots in the water, observing the current as it fell over the rocks. Resting his elbows on his knees with chin in hands, he stared at the little waterfall at arm's length, concentrating on the subtle change in sounds it created.

Will visited this place often. He was reminded of Pete's words about thoughts just being thoughts. Will began to allow thoughts of his unmentionable experiences come into consciousness, as if he were seated in a theater with others around him, just watching light on a wall. He watched the event unwind, frame by frame, recognizing it as only thoughts with its strong emotions streaming by him rather than within him. He tried to observe without reaction, staying out of the movie, remaining the neutral observer. The background sound of falling water helped to calm him.

As time went on, Will began to put his experiences into perspective and better assess responsibility. He repeated this contemplative process, hours at a time, day after day, until cognitive reassessment tidied the formerly entangled framework of his thoughts. In general, things were changing for the better.

One morning in June as Will returned from the brook, he stepped into Pete's workshop. Pete was busy repairing a saw motor, so Will stood quietly in front of him until he looked up.

"Will, my boy … what's up?" Pete inquired.

"Pete. Do you have time for a session out in the barn? I've something to tell you."

Pete stood up from his workspace. "Of course. Let's see what you have."

They walked out together over the crumbled granite driveway to the barn. Will pulled open the door, allowing the morning sunlight to spill into Pete's clinic. Pete sat on his log putting his feet up on the log between them. Will chose to pace the floor as he spoke.

"Pete, I've been thinking about all the things you've said about thoughts and thinking and owning those thoughts. I've also been reading a book you have in the living room on meditation. Not sure I understand a lot of it, but I did pick up on concentrating on something simple that would focus my attention. I've been practicing it a lot... actually... down at the stream."

"Great!"

"Anyway, I'm learning how to separate my thoughts from who I am... who I want to be. I think I have a method to moving on. I want to tell you now about the stuff I haven't been able to. It's not easy. It probably never will be."

"Sounds good, Will."

As Will continued his pacing, he looked up at the ceiling, then out the barn door onto the late spring morning, searching his thoughts for a place to begin telling his story, kicking the dirt around on the barn floor.

"We were out on patrol. We hadn't been back to base for a couple of days. The usual shit. No sleep, not much to eat. Nobody can think straight like that. We were chasing down a bunch of VC and thought they were hiding in this village. The area around it had been bombed pretty heavily. We took some KIA earlier that morning... my brothers... including this great guy, Sgt. Earle, who had been there the longest. Losing him made us crazy angry to get these VC.

"The lieutenant ordered us to go into the huts and tear the place up... pretty much kill any male or anyone who might offer resistance. Thinking back, it seemed like the order could've been interpreted as killing anybody still alive. Depending upon who was holding the weapon, that's what happened.

"I can't say I wasn't part of that mindset... at least at first. I went into one hut to hunt around, but no one was there. It felt like I was in somebody's home... not just some gook hut. Pictures. Photographs of the family, I guess. Some toys on the floor. It threw me off.

"I heard gunfire coming from the next hut and a lot of screaming, so I ran in that direction to see what was going on... sounded like children... When I went through the doorway, I saw Corporal Smith. He had a girl down on the floor, raping her. Two little kids were climbing on his back, trying to stop him. The young girl trapped beneath him was screaming and crying.

"As he shoved one of the kids away, he looked up at me... annoyed... I said something like, 'what are you doing, Smith?' He then said something like, 'kill these little bastards, I'm busy.'

"I didn't hesitate ... never thought it through ... all I could see was him raping my girlfriend ... Jane. That's what I saw. I swear it. I rushed up and threw the little girl who was pulling at his collar off his back. Smith was still going at it. I kicked Smith off the girl with my boot. He rolled onto his back and looked at me like I was totally crazy for stopping him. I raised my 16 and put a round through his head.

"Then, I looked down at the girl and realized she wasn't Jane at all. I was so sure at the time. I froze for a moment ... looked over at Smith's body to convince myself I had really shot him. His eyes were still fixed in that pissed off surprised expression.

"The young girl looked up at me as though she thought she was getting the next bullet. I just bowed and shook my head 'no'. I gestured for the other little girls to go to her. They might've been five or six years old. One of them had an infant rolled up in a blanket in her arms. I'm guessing it was the father's body I noticed lying in a pool of his own blood, just inside the door.

"I actually pulled up Smith's trousers and left the hut like I didn't know anything. No one had seen me. It really didn't hit me that I had killed one of us ... not until later, anyway. When our group got back together and Smith didn't show up, I said nothing. When one of the other guys found him, we evacuated his body along with the others killed and injured that day. No one seemed interested in figuring out what had happened. Turned out, that was the end of it."

Pete didn't move other than to nod.

"Pete, you know, over these past few days I've been thinking about why I killed Smith. I cried a lot about it down at the stream. Maybe if Smith had never gone to Vietnam, he might've been a saint ... or, then again ... maybe a loser, anyway. How would you know? We were all just trapped, weren't we?"

"Yes, you were, Will."

"Also, it's about how we all acted as a group. When we were on patrol, alert and afraid, we were functioning like one big angry scared animal. An animal roaming around with an insane mind. Maybe that's how we stayed safe. There was no Will Mueller or anybody else ... just the animal. When things calmed down, the animal mostly disappeared. Somebody like Smith didn't get that. In the short time he was there, he did things that were dangerous for the animal. The Lieutenant was always getting on his case. So was Sergeant Earle ... we called him 'Duke'. When Duke was killed that day, the animal got even crazier.

"So, we gathered up our KIA and guys being evacuated with wounds. I remember listening to the Huey approach. At that very moment, I understood why I hated the war and hated being there. I knew we had been bullshitted. That's when it became clear in my mind.

"I wasn't the only one thinking this way. When our group went out again on the next patrol, Lieutenant had this plan not to engage. Like never. We faked everything we could. Went on like that for months. They knew what we were doing. They didn't care, either. Guess it was late in the war. Everybody knew this was nowhere. Shit, do you think the guys in helicopters wanted to come out and get killed for nothing? Lieutenant would tell the pilot to just take us someplace safe. Safe for us ... safe for them. Yeah ... we went out into the jungle and hid. So fuckin' crazy, Pete. The only person I knew for sure I killed in Vietnam, was ... you know, an American."

Will sat down on his log, taking in a long breath and exhaling hard as he looked over at Pete with deep sadness in his eyes.

"How you doing, Will?" Pete asked.

"I'm OK. I'm making my way through it, Pete."

Will got up, turning in the direction of the barn door. He took a few steps before glancing back at Pete.

"Hey, Pete. I'm going to get some water and split wood for a while," he said, shaking his head from mental exhaustion.

"Thanks for everything Pete. I couldn't have done this without you."

Pete stood up from his log and walked over to Will, hugging him, "Good, very good. Changing your brain takes attention and effort. What your mind is, your life becomes. You're on the right path, Will, my boy."

"Yeah. I like that, Pete. What your mind is, your life becomes."

Pausing a moment, Will asked, "What about all the other vets?"

"Yeah, I know, what about all the others?" echoed Pete.

After the boy left, Pete leaned against the door frame, looking out across the driveway toward the forest and mountains in the distance. Will was coming along and, yes, Pete did wonder about all the others, all of them.

He walked back into the shop to resume his repair work. As lunchtime approached, Pete walked behind the house where Will was still splitting wood. On his way, he stopped at the well and pumped cups of cold spring water.

When Will heard the well handle clanking, he stopped and watched Pete walk in his direction.

"Hey, Pete. That's just what I need. Thanks!" he said, acknowledging the cold metal cups in Pete's grip as he handed one to him. Will put down the splitting maul and put a foot up on the chopping block, resting on a bended knee.

"This is a morning where I'm spilling stuff, Pete. Splitting wood is a great activity for thinking things through."

"Anything else come to mind, Will?"

"Yeah … after the incident I was telling you about, a lot of stuff changed for me. A light went on," Will emphasized, flicking an imaginary light switch on a wall in front of him. "From that point on, I made an effort to keep my thoughts anchored within me."

"As I flew back to base that day, shoulder to shoulder with my brothers, my mind drifted off to a memory. I grew up going to church on Sundays. My mother insisted. I never made much sense of it. She was just trying to do the right thing for me. It's what everybody else did. I really tried to believe it. Didn't make a lick of sense most times . . . an aggravation, really. It wasn't how I wanted to spend Sunday mornings. I would've rather gone fishing or something like that. I thought it all harmless. I'm thinking now … it isn't."

"I agree," Pete nodded.

"So, on the helicopter ride out of the boonies, I'm thinking and trying to square what I knew about religion with what I'd just been through. I thought about how 'God' was supposed to be all knowing, all powerful, and loved us all. The ultimate conundrum … I looked up that word.

"So how could this old guy in the sky allow those little girls to see their big sister beaten, raped, and her husband killed in front of them and live such a miserable life that they, in no way, brought on themselves? Was it 'God working in strange ways', again? I was convinced it was just bullshit. The greatest bullshit story ever told.

"And then I started singing right there in the packed helicopter that Christmas song, of all things, about Santa Claus. Soldiers were lying packed in tight on the helicopter floor, wounded in many ways, hoping to make it back before they got worse. Hoping to be wounded just enough so they could get the fuck out of the country."

Suddenly, Will began singing, "'He knows when you are sleeping. He knows when you're awake. He knows if you've been bad or good, so be good for goodness sake.' and, you know … all the rest."

"I watched as Vietnam passed underneath me out the open door of the chopper. I couldn't get this crazy song out of my head. Like, typical of the craziness, several of the other guys joined in with me. Crazy bastards, shouting over the noise of the helicopter engines and blades, whoop-whooping, and the occasional machine gun fire from the gunner in the other door. We must've sung it several times before I fell asleep. I was changing my mind, Pete … changing my mind. They wasted my time and attention. There is no god. There doesn't have to be. At least, not the one I was taught about."

****

By late July, Will's recovery had made considerable progress. He began feeling as though he was finally home. Not that he didn't have his moments, but now he knew how to handle them better.

Pete had introduced Will to Marriette. She and Will met several times throughout the late spring and summer. The sessions with Marriette reinforced and augmented what Pete was teaching him.

A pilot program was underway at UVM by June. Veterans were referred to Marriette's clinic. Soon Pete joined her, interviewing clients and advising them – using treatment plans with the protocol being developed. Will split time living between his mom's and Pete's place.

In early August, Will returned from town one afternoon, excited with news for Pete.

"Guess what, Pete? I'm going to college in September. I'm all signed up at UVM. I've got the G.I. Bill working for me. I'm going to study psychology."

"Wow!"

Pete jumped up from his workbench and shook the boy's hand, then wrapped his arms around him.

"Great! You've come a long way. Airborne! I'm so proud of you."

"Airborne, Pete! I'm just so damn lucky you found me that night," Will said, still holding onto his mentor. "I've become fascinated with how the mind works, Pete. I want to learn more. I'd like to hang out with you and Marriette at school. When I mentioned it to her, she said it would be instructive for me to be part of the research project while I'm an undergrad. Marriette helped me choose my classes and wrote an awesome recommendation. She even hand delivered it to the department head! Then we went over to admissions and squared away the G.I. Bill paperwork. She's amazing."

"Yes," Pete agreed. "Marriette is going places. Follow her lead."

"I need to help my brothers, now," Will said. "It's my duty. I'm excited."

"I am, too! Finally... I am, too!" Pete replied.

Jennifer Taylor

PART 2

– Chapter 23 –

Young Alice: Pennsylvania Farmstead
July 1950   Riverdale, Pennsylvania

Eight-year-old Alice Stevensen bumped along the gravelly road as she pedaled her rusty red Columbia bicycle from her home near the village to her grandparent's house out beyond Burton Williams' dairy farm. The route was bound by a river basin forest on one side and hayfield after hayfield on the other. The road was little traveled, but when a car passed, she slowed her peddling, wincing until the cloud of dust settled behind her.

The grass close to the road remained uncut, as the farmer avoided the shallow drainage ditch separating the right-of-way from the hayfields. The margin, dense with timothy grass overgrowth, milkweed, asters, and Queen Anne's lace, hosted an abundance of butterflies and other interesting insects for her to observe and collect. Come evening, the fields were noisy with crickets, and a cacophony of katydids called from the adjacent woods.

On hot summer mornings, Alice would bring the gauze butterfly net that her grandmother had helped her make. In the wire basket attached to her handlebars, she carried a collection jar of whatever insects she had collected, along with an oak tag accordion file of sheet music.

After her piano lesson with Grandma Stevensen, the insects trapped in the Mason jar, now no longer among the living, would be soft and ready to be arranged in the display boxes her grandfather had crafted for her.

One of her favorite insects was a striking female Promethea moth that Alice had discovered dead beneath the porch light at home. Another was a giant, bottle green dragonfly with iridescent blue spots on its wings. These were hard to catch, but Alice found this one stuck, undamaged, on the radiator of her father's '49 Plymouth. She referred to the big-eyed, lacy-winged insect as a B-36, this name eponymous with the huge bombers she viewed rising from behind the high hills across the river, departing Olmstead Air Force Base where her dad worked.

Never wanting to leave for very long, Riverdale, Pennsylvania, was always home to Alice.

****

1968 Riverdale, Pennsylvania
The Handful

Eighteen years later, Alice, her husband Harlan Taylor, and their four-year-old daughter, Jennifer, moved into their new four-bedroom ranch. The house was built in the woods near the same old gravely country road of Alice's childhood. The road was recently paved and not far from the river that ran through the town.

Alice Stevensen and Harlan Taylor first met at a country and western night club in downtown Nashville in the winter of '61, during their sophomore year at Vanderbilt. They caught each other's attention one Saturday evening as Alice sat at a nearby table while Harlan was performing. Alice was an attractive girl with long honey colored hair, much taller than her contemporaries, and a pianist with a beautiful voice. When Harlan stood up from his pedal steel guitar, revealing his lanky six-foot-three frame, an exchange of lingering glances prompted him to visit her table after the set. He was enthralled at meeting a pretty girl, his age, who was also a musician. This would be the first evening of their future partnership.

Alice had attended Vandy to pursue her dual degrees in music and psychology, while Harlan was raised near Nashville, the Smoky Mountains being the ancestral home of the Taylor clan since the 1700s. He would graduate from the University of Tennessee Dental School in June of '68. With their schooling complete, Alice convinced Harlan to move back to her native eastern Pennsylvania town. To begin their new life, Harlan opened a practice in the village.

One month after the Taylors arrived, Bill and Doris Plimpton moved into the house next door. The Plimptons had three children, a daughter, Lisa, (11), and two sons, Lincoln (7), and Randal (4).

Bill Plimpton, a general practice attorney, maintained an office in town, however he conducted much of his business from their home and, therefore, was usually around. Doris was a full-time mother.

Separating the neighbor's properties was a hundred-foot swath of partially landscaped beech and maple woods. There were lots of trees to climb, including a giant beech with an old tire swing hanging from a branch high up. A path soon developed, worn in by the back-and-forth travel of Jenny and Randy between their two homes. From the Taylors, the trail led directly to a basketball court that Bill had constructed after they moved in.

He had played basketball at nearby University of Pennsylvania and the game remained a passion.

Initially, it was Bill and his daughter, Lisa, who played on the court. The ambient sounds heard coming from the Plimpton yard were the rhythmic slap of the ball against the painted asphalt and the vibration of its impact on the plywood backboards.

As Jen was the Taylors' only child, the Plimpton children soon grew to be like brothers and sister to her.

When Randy was visiting at the Taylors' home, he basked in the musical environment surrounding him there. Harlan was a fourth-generation Tennessee fiddler. From the Plimpton home, Harlan could often be heard playing and singing some country tune in his backyard. There might be the trill of mandolins or the pluck and strum of a banjo. Often, Alice would join him. Jenny quickly demonstrated her talent in the family's relationship with music as well.

For Jen, the Plimpton home emanated the culture of athletic games and competition, especially basketball. Although Randy and Jenny were only four at the time, Bill gently introduced them to the game he loved.

When Jen turned six, she eagerly participated in Plimpton family pickup games, which included the older brother, Lincoln, nicknamed Linc, and his sister, whose name had shortened to Leese.

Jen's thick light brown hair now nearly reached her waist. Most of the time her hair was gathered up into what became her signature ponytail, which danced behind her as she played. When she was tired, she pulled her ponytail around to her cheek, like a cherished blanket, and fell asleep.

Jen was considerably taller than Randy by the time they reached the age of seven. Randy wasn't as interested in sports as his siblings were and hadn't the physical presence of the other three children. From Jen's perspective, he was gentler in nature. She was protective of him. When Randy showed an interest in the Taylors' musical sessions, Alice provided him with piano lessons while Harlan introduced the boy to guitar. Alice's mentorship and calming presence became Randy's shelter from the raucous and constant competitive atmosphere surrounding his siblings, and Bill, for that matter. As Randy's musical skills grew, he began to join in the Taylor family sessions. Music became an important part of his life. He spent much of his childhood at the Taylor home and Jen seemed to spend a similar amount of time at the Plimptons'.

****

Friday, September 28, 1973 a.m.
Geo. A. Hershey Elementary School

One early autumn morning during recess, fourth grader Jen noticed an older boy hit Randy with a stick. Randy fell to the ground, holding his leg and crying. The same boy, with a history of playground bullying, stood over him, wielding the stick, threatening to strike again.

Jen charged across the playground toward both boys yelling "Stop!" as she ran. Children were gathering around to watch the commotion. As Jen leaned over to help Randy up, the boy threw the stick at her, like a spear, striking her boney upper cheek and splitting her skin.

Stunned, Jen reached up to feel the gap in her skin as warm blood spilled through her fingers. It had been bad enough that it was one of those days when a school event made wearing a dress imperative. Now this happened. Later that afternoon, Jen was supposed to play the piano to accompany the third and fourth grade classes, singing songs in the autumn music pageant.

She glared at the big sixth-grader as blood trickled down her face onto her pink dress. The older boy froze in place, wide-eyed, realizing what he had just done. In an instant, Jen pounced on him, knocking him to the ground, pinning him there. She pummeled the boy's face as she straddled his chest in her petticoat dress, throwing focused lefts until two teachers arrived and struggled to pull her off.

The older boy was bawling, his face covered in their blood. Jen was mad. She tore herself away from the clutch of one of the teachers as the other attended to the boy. Both were yelling at Jen, who looked as though she wasn't through and just might go after the boy again.

Pasquale Camilio, the elementary school principal, trotted across the playground from the school building making his way through the assemblage of children, toward the center where the combatants and two teachers were. He approached Jen, kneeling down in front of her, placing himself between Jen and the older boy. Her face was smeared with blood and dirt, coagulated drips of crimson accumulated under her chin and on the palm of her hand which was pressed firmly to her cheek. Her new pink dress was bloodied and covered in playground dirt and fragments of dried maple leaves. The tip of her ponytail looked like a paintbrush dipped in sandy carmine paint. Jen was still glaring ominously at the 'big kid'. She continued to hold onto her cheek, scowling, narrow-eyed, gritting her teeth so hard that her breathing was almost a growl.

Principal Camilio knew Jen was not a troublemaker and was shocked to see her in such condition. He patiently waited for her explanation, only wanting to take care of her. As he peered over the top of his wire rim glasses, his soft eyes and gentle smile never changed as he quietly spoke to her.

"Jenny? Look at me, Jenny."

She relinquished her attention on the bully. "Yes, Mr. Camilio."

"Jenny, we need to take care of your cheek."

The principal pulled out the starched white handkerchief that he always kept folded up in a special way in the lapel pocket of his tweed blazer. Coaxing Jen's hand away from the wound, he placed the handkerchief over it, holding it there for a moment.

"There, that's better, Jenny. Now, let's go back to my office. I'll call your Mom and maybe she can meet us at the hospital. I think you're going to need a couple of stitches to close that cut. Don't worry, Jenny, everything will be okay. Please wait right here for me. I need to see how Danny is first," he calmly assured her, with a smile.

Jen took in a deep breath. Knowing Mr. Camilio was not her enemy, she smiled back and thought to thank him. After checking on the other child with the same kindness, the principal directed one of the teachers help the boy to the nurse's office.

When Jen and the principal arrived back at his office, she took a seat in the chair next to his roll top desk. Mr. Camilio sat down in his wooden armchair, and rolled closer to Jen. He cleaned the blood from her face and hands and wrapped rolled gauze around Jen's head, snugly securing his handkerchief to the wound beneath her eye.

"Now, Jenny. Please, tell me what happened."

Jen leaned back in the big oak chair while keeping pressure on her cheek using her left hand. The once shiny, black, patent leather Mary Janes, now scuffed and dusty, didn't quite reach the floor. Jen scowled as she recalled the incident looking directly at Mr. Camilio. Pointing out the tall office window in the direction of the playground, she explained, "I was over there … by the big chain fence. I saw Randy lying on the ground. He was crying. The big kid hit Randy! He was standing over him with a long stick … like this."

Jen held her right hand up in the air as if brandishing a fly rod.

"I ran to help Randy... he's like my little brother. Next thing, I got hit! That big kid... Danny White... he's a bully... all I know is he threw the stick at me! My face was bleeding a lot... so, I beat him up."

With Riverdale being a small town, within the half hour, the sixth-grade boy with a bloody nose, missing two front teeth, and the fourth-grade girl in the bloodied pink dress, with a bandage wrapped under her eyes and around her head, were in the same emergency room. Danny went home, but Jen insisted on returning to school to play the piano, as planned. Alice took her daughter home, cleaned her up, and headed back to the school auditorium just in time for the two o'clock concert.

Happy to be back in her jeans, Jen performed, wearing a bandage taped to her swollen, sutured cheek. A couple of blue Band-Aids, with bright yellow stars, covered the knuckles on her left hand. Alice had cut a long ribbon from the ruined crinkly chiffon pink dress and fashioned a bow with long streamers to adorn Jen's ponytail for the concert.

Despite the earlier turmoil, Jen wasn't about to miss this opportunity. She carried herself as though she relished the idea of establishing a distinct contrast between the unfortunate morning incident on the school playground and her artistic contribution in the afternoon. Just as she had watched her parents play in Nashville clubs many times, she felt the school was her club. This was her time. This was her place.

After the concert was over, Principal Camilio checked to see how Jen was feeling. Alice was speaking with some of the other mothers when she heard the piano being played again. She looked up to see her daughter and Mr. Camilio sitting together on the piano bench. Jen had taken the principal's hand, as he had taken hers earlier that morning, and invited him to sit beside her. She purposely brought along other music sheet with the plan to thank Mr. Camilio for his care and kindness by singing him a song her mother had been teaching her. As she began to play, she signaled to her mother to approach the piano to add harmony. The remaining folks in the small auditorium gathered closer to the piano as Jen sang Carole King's, "You've Got a Friend" to the school principal. Charmed, Mr. Camilio thanked her, nodding his approval with the same soft eyes and gentle voice.

Later when he returned to his office, the principal noticed blood stains on the floor and the oak chair next to his desk. As he walked to the janitor's closet to get a wet mop and bucket, he pondered how such a talented little girl with such a sweet voice could be such a terror.

After meeting with Danny White and his parents regarding the incident, Principal Camilio suspended the boy for three days while Jen was suspended for one day for the use of, what amounted to, excessive force.

Bill and Doris Plimpton thanked Jen for coming to Randy's aid. When Jen saw Linc the next evening, the first thing he said to her was, "You'll do anything to get out of wearing a dress, wouldn't ya?"

Typical of Bill Plimpton's style of mentoring, he discussed the incident with Jen – asking her to consider the measure of her response. The incident was not taken lightly by anyone. It was part of Jen's learning to control, and use wisely, her emerging fierce and unrelenting competitive nature. Jen always looked to 'Coach' Bill for guidance. She would never want to disappoint him. As far as she was concerned, his word was as 'gold' as was her mother's. Bill Plimpton would always be her other dad, next door.

– Chapter 24 –

The Tiger with a Ponytail
October 1973   Riverdale, Pennsylvania

When Linc Plimpton was in the seventh grade, and Jen in the fourth, she had a crush on him. Although Linc was much taller now, when he wasn't looking, she would tackle him anyway, knocking him onto the rug to tickle him. He would end up pinning her down and tickling her breathless which, of course, was exactly what she wanted.

When Jen was over at the Plimpton home watching TV, she would inevitably jump up onto the couch to sit right beside him, getting as close as she possibly could. Being three years older, it mostly annoyed Linc and he would protest that she was crowding him out. Jen would always deny it, claiming she was there first. She would then get close up, into Linc's face, and try to stare him down with her big brown eyes or whack him playfully with the end of her ponytail. Linc admired his 'cool little sister' next door, so he usually put up with it.

Jen also loved to compete with Linc and did so fearlessly. She wasn't afraid to play hard, and constantly challenged him, often being knocked to the pavement. As the result of her aggressive play, Jen wound up with her share of skinned knees and bruises, but that never made her cry. Of all four children, Jen was the athlete – her ball handling and shooting skills constantly improving. She made basketball moves no one expected of someone her age. Bill would often remark, shaking his head, "You can't teach that!"

When Linc stole the ball and got around her, she would get mad, but she kept coming back. She soon figured out how to steal the ball from Linc, then trash talk him and laugh at his remarks, making it more difficult for him to keep up his defense.

Yet, sometimes, when she got overly frustrated, Jen would throw the ball into the woods, and storm into the house, only to return five minutes later, eating a banana, and wait on the edge of the court for Bill to invite her back into the game. When she became too revved up, 'Coach' Plimpton would take her aside, sit her on his knee, wrapping his arms tightly around her until she calmed down. He would then explain how she might use her competitive spirit more effectively rather than throwing punches at Linc and chucking the ball into the woods. Young Jen was known as a 'handful' and Coach Bill's 'work in progress'. Unable to sit still for very long, she had only two speeds, full speed or fast asleep.

Alice and Harlan were quite happy to bring up a little girl who was not content to dress up and play with dolls. They encouraged Jen to become whoever she would mature into and provided her with many opportunities to follow her own personality.

Great Granpappy Taylor once said of little Jen, in his Tennessee mountain way, "Mmm, doggies, Harlan . . . you's growin' somethin' wild and unruly."

A relative once gave a doll to Jen for Christmas when she was in the second grade. After the holiday, she took the doll to school and traded it for a harmonica. When Jen returned home from school that day, she surprised her mother by playing the new instrument.

"Jenny," Alice inquired, "what are you going to say to your Aunt Gladys about the doll should she visit us?"

"I'll play her a nice song," Jenny answered. "Better than looking at some plastic girl in a dress! Dad will teach me how."

The Taylor household provided constant opportunities to play and appreciate music. As an infant, Jen would sit in her mother's lap as Alice played the piano and sang to her. When Alice gave voice and piano lessons to clients in their home, Jen was always nearby.

The big music room at the back of the house was filled with acoustic and electric guitars, banjos, mandolins, two pianos, a Hammond organ, a concertina, a basic drum kit and recording equipment. Jen learned to play the piano, followed by the guitar. Harlan purchased a small fiddle for her. She quickly learned how to play by mimicking her dad. By the time Jen was nine, she played the piano, banjo, fiddle, harmonica, and guitar well enough to accompany her parents.

This was what they did in the Taylor household, and Jen loved all of it. The family often traveled to Nashville throughout the year to play with friends living there. Those folks had children who played instruments as well. She also accompanied her parents when they performed in country and western clubs in Nashville. Jen would tell her parents that she wanted to be the best and she practiced hard to achieve it. The young girl was mesmerized by the style and talents of the performers and asked her parents when she might have her chance on stage.

An opportunity to do just that arose when the "Hee Haw" TV show ran a talent contest searching for children who played country music to be featured on the program. Jen had visited the Grand Ole Opry with her parents and watched the weekly TV program, so the chance to be on television excited her. Jen confidently told her parents, "I can do that!"

Harlan and his daughter began to practice a song that had been recorded by one of the stars of the show, Buck Owens. The Taylors worked together on an arrangement of Owens' "I've Got a Tiger by the Tail." After completing a reel-to-reel tape and an 8mm movie, they sent off the material to the production crew at "Hee Haw".

On a very memorable day in Jen's young life, a large manila envelope arrived in the mail inviting them to appear on the show. Apparently, she had been expecting the invitation. Harlan would later tell the story that after a lot of hootin' and hollerin' on Jen's part, the nine-year-old declared with nonchalance, "What took them so long? I thought it would never get here!"

The Taylor family then traveled to Tennessee, prepared for the taping of an episode of "Hee Haw" at the WLAC studios in downtown Nashville. Bill, Linc, and Randy Plimpton flew to Nashville to join the live audience for the taping. When the Taylors met with Buck Owens and the production crew, Buck was amazed at her abilities.

As Jen was not timid around adults, and often outspoken, she made it clear that she didn't like the dress the costume crew wanted her to wear. She did like, however, the new cowboy boots and fancy embroidered shirt they offered as an alternative.

She knew how she wanted to play the song, and, despite Mr. Owens' initial suggestions, he found himself amused at having to bargain with this determined little girl with a long ponytail.

"I think we should play it this way, Mr. Buck," she insisted.

"All right, Jenny. That'll work," Buck finally agreed, nodding at the piano phrase she wanted to play. "But . . . we will need to compromise on some things, okay?"

"Yes, Mr. Buck," Jen answered, as he sat down on the piano bench next to her grinning. The cameras had already begun running as he turned toward Jen.

"Here's what I'd like to propose Miss Jenny. I'd like to give you a special nickname. It's seems apt that you're singing this song with me. So, Jenny?"

"Yes, Mr. Buck?"

"I feel as though I've got a tiger by the tail, right here and now! How 'bout if I call you Tiger from now on?"

Looking up at him, beaming, she thought about the suggestion.

"I think I like that . . . Yeah! I like that a lot, Mr. Buck!"

The song was taped with Buck on rhythm guitar, Harlan on pedal steel, and young Jen on the piano singing high harmony with lead guitarist, Don Rich, plus the rest of the Buckaroos. It was finished in three takes. Buck was pleased and so was Tiger.

When they finished the song and Jen stood up from the piano bench, Buck hugged her and announced directly into the camera, "From now on, as far as I'm concerned, the world is dealing with Tiger Taylor!"

The special moment made the cut and was included in the program when it aired on television two months later. Most of Riverdale had watched the show and throughout the rest of Jen's childhood the nickname stuck like glue. Without even trying, she lived up to it.

The experience further boosted Jen's confidence. Alice and Harlan recognized that it was a fine accomplishment to perform well on national TV, but they emphasized that the experience was only one small part of her life. Their daughter was reminded to always remain humble as there were many other things to accomplish.

– Chapter 25 –

The Boy's Club: No Girls Allowed
Friday, September 19, 1975   Riverdale, Pennsylvania

Tiger Taylor played in the Riverdale basketball youth league for four years. Bill Plimpton usually attended most of her games. If he was late, she would watch from the court for 'Coach' to appear in the stands. When she caught sight of him, she always picked it up another notch.

Sometimes, Tiger became frustrated with how the others on the team played. Bill always made a point to step in to discuss the issue and provide his perspective. He wanted to help her understand that even though it could be frustrating, there had to be a plan to make it work as a team. He reminded Jen that basketball was a team sport, and the goal was to win, but she couldn't accomplish it alone. There were no other choices.

"You should lead the way," he would tell her, and Tiger bought into it. From that time forward, with Bill's help, she played to make her team better. During her last two years of youth basketball, she led the entire league in scoring with her teams finishing first.

When Tiger attended Lisa's high school basketball games with Bill, he continued to instruct her about the game as they sat together high up in the stands watching the team play. Jen admired everything about Lisa. She watched as Lisa excelled on her high school basketball team and knew that Lisa was also good at her studies in school. Realizing the importance of good grades, she focused her competitiveness on getting As. Throughout life, she would always remember Bill's words, "Get out in front of them . . . and don't let them catch up."

Tiger continued her objection to wearing dresses throughout grade school until one evening in May, during Lisa's junior year. A boy in a tuxedo arrived at the Plimpton door to take Lisa to the prom. Jen happened to be sitting in the living room when Lisa walked down the stairs in her gown and was presented an orchid from her date. Tiger had never seen such a fancy dress on someone she knew. She also noticed the way Lisa had her long hair styled up on top of her head. At that moment, Tiger reconsidered her reluctance to wear "all that girl stuff."

Later that evening when nine-year-old Tiger was getting ready for bed, she called for her mother to come into the master bathroom to show her how Lisa had put her long hair up. Standing on a stool, in a T-shirt and underwear in front of the large mirror, she attempted to arrange her long ponytail in a swirl. Alice stepped in and deftly fixed her daughter's hair to Jen's approval.

Examining her new hairstyle, Tiger exclaimed, "I like it!" She then held her hands high on her chest and asked her mother, "When do I get breasts like you and Lisa? Her fancy dress showed her, you know . . . ah."

"Cleavage?" Alice grinned.

"Yeah, that's the word . . . cleavage!" Tiger confirmed, turning toward her mother.

"In a few years," Alice responded. "We're going to talk about that soon, but not tonight."

"Do you think I'll look good with breasts, 'M'?" Tiger queried, still holding her hands on her chest.

"Yes, Jenny, darling. You're already a beautiful young girl. That's enough of that for now. It's time for bed."

Tiger shook out the new hairdo and held onto her ponytail as she ran off to her bedroom. After seeing Lisa in the gown, young Jen made some exceptions to her 'no dresses' rule.

****

A picture hung in the Plimpton home of Tiger on one of the youth teams Bill had coached. Standing in the first row on the end, she had one hand placed on her hip and the team basketball squeezed between her other arm and waist, her big ponytail flipped over a shoulder in front of her. There was a confidence in her stance and a look in her eye focused on a horizon well beyond the camera - a look that was not present in her teammates.

****

Prior to the start of basketball season, when Tiger was 11, an unexpected letter arrived in the mail. Alice opened the envelope and read the letter aloud as Harlan peered over his wife's shoulder. It was from a Mr. Ralph Litterer, the individual in charge of recreational activities in the town. The letter stated that a recent decision had been rendered prohibiting girls from playing on the youth basketball teams. The ruling was effective immediately and meant the end to their daughter's participation in the league.

Calling Tiger into the room, Alice re-read the letter to her. Tiger stood in disbelief at the significance of the document.

Squinting her eyes, she asked her mother, "Is this for real?"

"I have to say it is, Jen."

"Why?" Tiger exclaimed.

"Jenny, we're going to look into this," Harlan interjected. "This isn't fair."

Tiger looked at both parents for an immediate answer.

"It's Friday night," Alice went on. "There's nothing we can do for now except consider this and be prepared to challenge it."

Tiger clenched her teeth, motioning to her mother with an open hand to give her the letter. Taking it she ran out the door.

It was pouring rain outside as she splashed along the path in the near dark among the great beeches, across the basketball court, to the Plimptons'. She ran into the breezeway and opened the kitchen door.

Linc was standing in the kitchen as the soggy 11-year-old stepped inside.

"What's going on, Tiger?" Linc asked. "You been crying?"

"No! It's raining outside!" she blurted out, wiping her face off with the back of her wet forearm.

"Well, you're upset about something, for sure." Linc turned as he threw her a dish towel to dry off.

"Is Coach around, Linky?"

Just as she was finishing her sentence, Bill Plimpton walked in from the other room. Tiger looked up at him with a sad and frightened face, summoning all her strength not to burst into tears. Saying nothing, Tiger held out the damp letter at arm's length. Bill took it from her and sat his six-foot-five frame down at the kitchen table, not taking his eyes from the letter.

Tiger waited impatiently, as Bill quietly examined the contents of the letter. He glanced up at the ceiling nodding his head, doing that funny thing he always did with his lips when he was pondering what he would say next.

The kitchen filled with the rest of the Plimpton family. After a knock on the back door, Alice and Harlan entered as well. Bill motioned for Tiger to sit down across from him at the kitchen table.

"Tiger, I'd like you to calm down and listen as I read this letter to everyone. We are going to address this issue."

"OK, Coach," Tiger replied, as she referred to Bill whenever he directed instructions her way. Without taking her eyes off his, she reached around, wrapping her wet ponytail in the dish towel, squeezing rainwater from it.

September 17, 1975

Dear Mr. Taylor,

I regret to inform you that the Riverdale Youth Basketball League will, beginning this coming season, limit enrollment to boys. The decision was reached by a consensus of the coaches of the youth league, this office, and the superintendent of elementary schools, Gertrude Anthony. It was determined that, in the interest of safety and to meet the requirements of our insurance policy, this action will be taken immediately. I am personally sorry to deliver this news to you.

Sincerely, Ralph T. Litterer

All eyes in the kitchen focused on Bill, waiting for his response. Tiger clenched her teeth again so firmly that the facial muscles of her jaw were bulging.

Not able to help himself, Linc yelled out, "This isn't fair! It's wrong! I know what's going on here. She's a girl and she's the best player in the league! Those idiot coaches are sick of having Tiger wiping up the floor with their sons."

Red in the face, Tiger barked out, "Assholes!"

"Jennifer! No!" Alice retorted, surprised at hearing her daughter's playground language for the first time.

The older Lisa nodded in affirmation at her brother's assessment and Tiger's response. Bill put the letter down in front of him and looked up at everyone.

"Woah! Everyone settle down. Please. This action deserves a thoughtful response on our part." Looking up at Jen's parents, he asked, "Do you agree?" directing his question primarily to Alice, Harlan, and his wife, Doris. The three nodded in affirmation.

"I'd like to point out," Harlan added, "that this change in policy is not just about Jen, although she is currently the only girl in the league. It concerns all young girls, as the door was also open to them ... and the Town's argument only reinforces discriminatory thoughts to the young boys who will then play without the girls. Our endeavor should be to keep the door open and argue against this stultifying attitude."

"Yes. Well stated, Doc," Bill agreed.

Tiger cut in. "Dad? What did you say? 'Stull . . .'?"

"Stultify. To frustrate, hinder, impede, suppress, smother," Alice clarified. "What we're feeling right now, Jen."

"I don't like that feeling," Tiger grumbled. Tiger knew her mother was serious anytime she referred to her as Jen or, worse, Jennifer.

"Tiger," Bill continued, "if your parents agree, I'd like to represent you. I will gladly volunteer my legal services. I want to represent you and all the girls who decide to play basketball in Riverdale. We will consider a thoughtful plan to reverse this decision. Our emotions of anger and frustration can be let out in private, but those reactions, if vented beyond this kitchen, will get us absolutely nowhere.

"We have the whole weekend to think about how to constructively address this issue. Let's get back together Sunday afternoon. I will outline my approach to all of you then."

Smiling sweetly, Tiger looked over at Bill, relieved. "Thanks, Coach."

– Chapter 26 –

Here in Pennsylvania: Feathered Canyons Everywhere
Saturday, September 20, 1975
Riverdale State Forest, Kittany Ridge, Pennsylvania

The next morning, Alice asked her daughter if she'd like to hike in the State Forest, a favorite location throughout the seasons for Taylor outings. Not only were the views of the Delaware River Valley beautiful, but there was a special place in the mountains where they often stopped to play music. This time, however, Doc Harlan would not be joining them, as he was seeing patients. Alice was forthcoming with Jen, citing the hike as an opportunity to discuss the situation from the evening before.

Alice and Jen began their climb into the hills above Riverdale. The late summer was well into its transition to autumn with the morning starting off chilly, but comfortable for hiking. During the school week, Jen often felt there wasn't enough time to spend with her mom the way she wished she could. The outings into the mountains of Kittany Ridge were special when her dad was along, but it just felt different, special, when it was her and her mom.

Both carried special backpacks that Alice had designed; each backpack held a small Gibson six string, water bottle, and their lunch. Once out of the valley and well up into the hills, they left the main trail. Jen and her mother climbed down onto a large rocky gorge where they watched the water rush among the rocks, falling into a deep pool just below them. Tilted conifers hung precariously at the edges of the rock face and colors in the deciduous trees were changing to red and orange. Basins of water had collected in depressions in the flat rock from the heavy rain that had fallen the evening before. A catbird dropped down from a nearby tree to drink from one of the pools, while noisy jays, busy with the new crop of acorns, cawed and whistled from surrounding oak trees.

Putting their gear down on the rock, they walked to the very edge of the gorge, then lay on their bellies beside each other, as they watched the torrents flow among the rocks 30 feet below, dropping still further into the pool. Jen threw a stick upstream, following its descent, languishing in the 'eddies' before being caught up in the main current and disappearing into the waterfall.

Moving back to a flatter expanse of rock, Alice sat with her arms wrapped around bent knees. Jen sprawled out on the rock, warmed by the morning sun, and looked up at her mother.

Alice was a tall, beautiful woman. She wore her light brown hair parted down the middle, always falling free across the tops of her shoulders. Her nose was densely freckled across its bridge, the freckles becoming lightly scattered over her cheeks. This distinctive pattern was now developing on her daughter's face. As Jen grew older, she had begun to recognize their resemblance and was enamored with it.

Alice's singing voice, as well as her speaking manner, was soft and expressive, while it was already apparent, in contrast, that Jen's voice was powerful with an extended octave range.

The events of the previous day were very much on Tiger's mind as she began the conversation, "Mom, what do you think will happen? Do you think I'll get to play like last year?"

"I'd rather not guess, Jenny, but I'm hopeful. How we proceed will be up to Bill. He knows the law regarding this situation. I'm confident he's constructing a formidable case this weekend. We're fortunate to live next door to Bill and grateful he's such an influential person in your life. Dad and I can't teach you everything. It's important to know adults who can also be mentors – in addition to your parents. Dad and I admire him very much. Bill's like a second dad for you."

"Yeah. Dad number two . . . '2Dad'. I like that, 'M'! You know, it's funny. It seems I talk with Coach Bill more than I do with Daddy. It's more like how you and I talk, but different. I love Dad. He's always showing me new stuff, but it's just different. I need them both . . . and Lisa, Linc, and Randy are more like cousins than my real cousins are."

"I know what you mean, Jenny. They're more like your siblings. You're all together so much . . . which is beautiful."

Jen sat up and looked directly at her mother.

"So, Mom. What do you think those coaches are up to? Is Linc right?"

"Yes, Jenny. He probably is . . . but first let's try to look at the bigger picture and help put this situation into perspective."

"Okay, 'M'."

"There's a lot of luck involved in living one's life. Plenty of girls your age in this world don't have a place to live, are hungry, or are in constant danger from circumstances beyond their control. We're very fortunate to live where we do and have those opportunities afforded us. It's just luck. Let's keep this perspective. What's happening with the basketball program is, for the moment, a big deal to us, but in the larger view, it is trivial. Keep in mind that we hope life gets better for everyone and we should try to do our part."

"Mom, would you say you've had a better life than Grandma and maybe her life was better than her mother's?"

As Alice pondered Jen's question, she reached over, unzipped the backpacks, and removed the guitars, handing one to her daughter.

"I'd say in general, if we're speaking about women, opportunities have improved, but we have yet a long way to go."

"What do you mean?" Jen asked, busy tuning her guitar to her mother's.

"Well, let's look at it this way. Since the beginning of civilization and even before that, the role of women was mostly limited to bearing and rearing children. Men were in control of everything else. Until somewhat recently, only 50 years ago, women didn't even have the right to vote in this country . . . our country. White men made the rules and the laws. They still do. I believe there are only 15 members of the Congress who are female. That's 15 out of 92. When might it be half-and-half? Who knows?"

As Alice finished tuning her guitar, she sat cross legged, leaning her forearms on its body.

"In today's modern world, we should have a clear path to equal opportunities. That's what the feminist movement and Equal Rights Amendment are seeking to ensure. There needs to be a fair balance, which doesn't exist yet.

Women and men are different in many ways, but they have much in common, as well.

"Darling, let's take a little break from this and play some tunes."

"I'm ready, 'M'."

Mother and daughter stood up with their guitars strapped over their shoulders and walked along the ridge of the little canyon. Stopping to face each other, they took separate parts and began playing Kate Wolf's "Here in California." It was a song they had practiced together throughout the summer. Jen had previously thought casually about the lyrics, however today, here in the little canyon, the song's message of a mother's words to her daughter spoke to Jen. After playing a prolonged instrumental introduction of contrapuntal musical phrases, they began to harmonize.

Alice's velvet voice was as clear as a bell.

"When I was young . . . my mama told me . . ."

Taking turns with lead and harmony, they smiled at each other as they recognized the echo of their music along the walls of the chasm. 'Natural reverb', as Harlan would say. It was an enchanting way to spend a September morning. Alice and Jen were a beautiful team.

Hikers across the gorge stopped to sit on the rocks as they listened to mother and daughter sing two more verses. Jen moved to stand behind her mother, leaning firmly against Alice's back as they continued to play and sing. Jen wondered how life could get any better, as they finished the song with an extended instrumental exchange, listening to their guitar's filling the little canyon.

After finishing, they sat down on the rocks and unpacked their lunch. A short while later, Alice spoke again. She had a mother's agenda to share with her daughter this day.

"Jenny, I believe when you get to be my age things will be much better, however, there will most likely continue to be a struggle for power. Men have always had power and only the more enlightened men are willing to share it. What you're experiencing now, with this basketball ruling, is sexual discrimination against women. It's ingrained within our culture. Men and, yes, women, too, carry on with business as usual. With every generation however, things do improve, but only because those who seek a better way push it ahead."

"I guess it's kind of tough out there," Jen observed.

"Well, yes, it can be tough and unfair out there . . . but there can also be much beauty and happiness. We should try to find the good and the beauty and act thoughtfully to correct the injustices, to move our culture in the direction of well-being for all."

Jen loved these special moments with her mom. She lay back down again, resting her head against Alice's thigh, guitar across her chest, quietly picking as Alice explained it all. "This is your first battle, Tiger," Alice counseled. "And it won't be your last, by any means. As a woman, you'll always be second in line unless you strive . . . sometimes demand, to be first. That's how it is. You can either accept it as is . . . or do something to change it."

"What can I do now, Mom?"

"We'll come up with a plan. You may need to speak up and help defend, not just yourself, but other girls who will come after you and want to play basketball in Riverdale."

"I can do that. So, those coaches have a problem with girls?" Jen asked.

"Darling, it's hard to get people to change. Most folks don't often think critically about how they behave or how they really feel about things. They go on with their lives as they always have, influenced by the people they keep company with, their parents, their education, and the personality they're born with.

"They're really not trying to be mean and I don't think that's the case with these coaches either. They're just doing what they were taught, what they are used to and feel comfortable with. There doesn't seem to be any deep thought process, self-examination or reflection, which…," Alice paused for emphasis, "… I would point out, is important for every one of us to do. But eventually change creeps into their lives a little at a time, until one day it's there and they aren't even aware that it happened."

"Everything seems to take a long time. Is that it?" Jen pondered.

"Yes. It does," Alice answered.

"How do I fit into this? I was just playing basketball."

"Well, of course, you're not the problem, darling. The problem is with them. It's hard to do, but try not to take it personally. You do, however, have to defend yourself. The coaches are not used to seeing a beautiful girl with your physical skills and competitive drive, allowing you to dominate their league… their league! It frightens and intimidates them."

"Mom, if I was just another boy playing, the coaches not having me on their team would be disappointed, but they would recognize that there was a better player out there who they just didn't have … but when that player happens to be a girl, it's different."

Alice was pleased with her daughter's quick assessment.

"Yes, Tiger. You nailed it. It doesn't fit into the model of how they view life. It's a threat to their rigid, but accepted expectations. They have no thoughtful awareness of other ideas. Many of the men are insecure and afraid of losing the control they feel from being in charge and winning games, even if they're winning by commanding children."

"I get it, Mom. Linky found out my coach voted for the girls to play. Is he thoughtful of other ideas?"

"Yes. Good point, Tiger. We don't know how the coach really feels, but he probably enjoys having a winning team."

"Yeah."

"Hopefully, we can begin to change their minds in addition to winning the legal battle here."

"Yes, 'M'."

"By the way, referring to them as assholes doesn't help the problem, Jenny."

"Sorry, Mom. I was mad."

"No need to be sorry, darling. I was angry, too . . . but we do need to channel that kind of energy into a positive effort to win this case. That's what we want, right?"

"Right," Jen agreed.

"Here's a good example of how you might accomplish what you want. If you had a coach right in front of you and you called him a jerk or worse, wouldn't you just alienate him even more?"

"Yes, 'M'."

"But if you could thoughtfully find a way to help him understand something in a new way, I'd say you're more likely to get closer to where you want to go. Which choice is better? Give this idea some thought."

"Sure. I can see that, Mom," Jen nodded.

"There's some good news," Alice continued, "which should help Bill get the change we need. In 1972, the United States Congress passed a law. It's called . . ."

"Title IX!" Jen cut in. "I remember you said it would be important. Lisa mentioned it last night."

"Yes. It's a civil rights statute. Civil law concerns legal relations between people. This law ensures that no American citizen can be discriminated against, on the basis of their sex, in any scholastic activity funded by the United States government. Public school is so funded. Ask Bill to explain this to you. I suspect when he presents this information to the administrators, it will expunge any case the Town of Riverdale has to discriminate against elementary school girls. Frankly, I'm surprised it got this far."

"I'll bet Coach Bill has it figured out, 'M'."

"I'm confident he has, Jenny. Just one more thing and then let's get back to enjoying this beautiful day and playing some more tunes."

"Okay, I'm getting pretty full of information," Jen replied.

"Yes, my darling. I've given you a lot to think about. Every day you become less a little girl and more a woman. Be kind about what you say and how you approach others. Blow off steam in private. If there is a basketball season for you this year, Tiger, you can channel frustration in your determination as you play ... and if there is no basketball season, we'll find something else to do."

"Thanks, Mom. Will do. I love you so much, 'M'."

"I love you, too, Jenny. So much!"

Alice and Jen laid back on the smooth flat rock, quiet for a moment. Alice closed her eyes, resting her guitar at her side, her hands folded across her chest. Jen fashioned a pillow from her jacket alongside her mother's head so she could lay opposite, temple to temple, avoiding the right-handedness of their instruments from coming in contact with each other.

Jen looked up into the bright blue midday sky and quietly picked on her Gibson as she surveyed the rows of puffy white cumulus clouds billowing high overhead, forever changing shapes in the stratospheric winds.

"'M'?" she asked, nudging her head against her mother's.

"Yes, Jenny?" Alice answered, her eyes still closed.

"Look at the clouds, 'M'."

"They are beautiful, my darling," Alice replied, glancing above her.

"Feathered canyons everywhere ... do you see them, Mom? Is this what Joni had in mind?"

"I would say so. Ice cream castles, too," Alice added, rolling onto her side, propping up onto an elbow to face her daughter.

"I think that means ... with canyons above us and the little canyon below us ... we should play 'Clouds'," Tiger suggested.

"Yes, perfect! One more song before we go."

"We have to go?"

"We should get back soon, darling. Dad will be returning from the office."

Jen began to play her guitar accompaniment, stopping long enough to stand and stroll nearer the canyon's edge, repeating the beginning phrases, waiting for Alice to join her.

"You sing and I'll play the lead, Mom."

"You are loving the guitar lately aren't you, dear, and getting very good. Dad is amazed."

"I think I love it best, 'M'."

Alice joined her daughter and began to sing the first verse as Jen's accompaniment cycled around.

"Rows and flows of angel's hair and ice cream castles in the air ... and feathered canyons everywhere ... I've looked at clouds that way ..."

– Chapter 27 –

A Quiet Recovery: A Gentle Stare
September 1975   Riverdale, Pennsylvania

Riverdale was not a large town, but rather a picturesque suburban village located about an hour outside of Philadelphia. The town was so small it didn't have a mayor and one could easily speak to someone in town hall the same day and get an immediate response.

Early on Monday morning, Bill Plimpton placed a call to the superintendent of schools, requesting to meet with him the next day. After informing the superintendent that he would be representing Jennifer S. Taylor and her parents, he summarized the issue and requested that the elementary school assistant superintendent be in attendance as well.

The following afternoon, the three met in Superintendent Harold Wilson's office. A man in his forties, he had taught school in Riverdale and other local towns after graduating from college. Elementary assistant superintendent Gertrude Anthony had worked in the local school system since graduating from normal school in the thirties.

Bill opened the meeting by explaining he was not there to represent just Jennifer Taylor, but all the girls currently in the school system – and the ones yet to arrive. He proceeded to read the essentials of Title IX. Miss Anthony was not yet aware of Title IX, but Superintendent Wilson was familiar with the law. What Wilson was not aware of, however, was the recent directive issued by the recreation committee. With pursed lips, he nodded in agreement as Attorney Plimpton read through a summary of the statute. Bill went on to address the claim, cited in the letter to the Taylors, that the exclusion of girls from the team reflected insurance issues. He demonstrated why the claim was inaccurate and probably fallacious.

Bill argued the case that girls and boys playing ball together should be seen as a positive. At such an early stage in development, it was important for girls and boys to gain the experience of interacting equally in all circumstances. If coached competently, the team would benefit from learning both teamwork and respect.

To further bolster his argument, he suggested that the blatant discriminatory practice was a hot topic and something the media would eagerly take up, as would the newly formed National Organization of Women. Jennifer Taylor might just be the young and eloquent poster girl they were seeking.

To soften his argument, Bill emphasized the challenge was to make the school system better for everyone and suggested that a small community such as theirs should handle the issue in a friendly and co-operative manner.

After Attorney Plimpton completed his presentation and was preparing to leave, Mr. Wilson reached across the conference table and shook his hand.

"I agree, Bill. I'll take care of this today. Please inform your client she will play this fall … and … I'll give you a call later this afternoon," Wilson added.

"Thank you, Hal. Good day, Miss Anthony."

As he stood to leave, Bill asked if either of them knew of Jennifer Taylor.

Miss Anthony responded she did not. Superintendent Wilson was a dental patient of Dr. Taylor's and knew Jen came from a family of musicians. He also remembered that she was first in points in the entire youth league during last year's basketball season. As Bill left the room, Wilson called after him.

"Why do they call her 'Tiger'?"

Turning, Bill answered, "I've lived next door to Jenny Taylor for six years. She's an amazing kid. A sweet, smart, talented, competitive, but tenacious kid," he said, with a smile. "Very tenacious."

Later in the week, after the basketball controversy was resolved, Hal Wilson discussed the salient issues with all the coaches and the town agreed to post a public notice, encouraging girls to sign up for the new youth basketball season.

****

The following Saturday afternoon, as Jen and her parents were shopping in a local department store, Jen went off alone to explore. As she walked down the sports equipment aisle, she encountered Jim Langston, one of the coaches who had signed on with the ruling to omit girls from the youth basketball teams. Jen knew that he recognized her, but she introduced herself anyway.

"Hi, Coach. I'm Jenny Taylor."

"Hi, Tiger," he responded, sheepishly.

"Do you have a minute, Coach?"

Langston was trapped. He had his two four-year-old twin girls with him, one in each hand.

"Are these your girls, Coach?"

"Yes. This is Janet and this is . . ." he paused, ". . . Jennifer."

Tiger scrunched down beside the toddlers, bringing her long ponytail around in front.

"Hi, Janet. Hi, Jenny." Pointing to herself, she added, "My name is Jenny, too!"

The younger Jen reached out to touch Tiger's ponytail hanging over her shoulder. Tiger handed it to her as if it was a pet.

"That's my flag!" Tiger remarked, tilting her head. "Do you like it?" The child's eyes lit up, bright with connection.

Tiger then stood up, grinning at Langston. At the end of the aisle Harlan and Alice paused, observing their daughter involved in conversation with Jim Langston. As Harlan began to move in their direction, Alice grabbed him by the sleeve, pulling him back.

"She's fine, honey. Let's leave her alone. Why don't we go down the next aisle, maybe we can hear their conversation."

Wanting to make a point, Tiger picked up a basketball off the shelf and spun it in her hands, balancing it on her fingertips high up in front of her. The coach watched as though hypnotized. As the ball began to slow, she stopped it and stuck under her arm as she continued.

"You like sports, right, Coach? Do you have any boys, yet?"

"Of course, Tiger. And, ah . . . no, not yet anyway."

"You know, Coach, boys and girls are the same in a lot of ways. Some need sports, some don't. Some of us need sports a lot . . . just like you and me, Coach."

Tiger kept firm eye contact with him until he flinched.

"Well, I gotta go, Coach. Nice to meet your kids. See you later."

As she left, she waved to the two little girls.

"Bye, Jan. Bye, Jenny."

The younger Jen, wide-eyed and smiling, waved back.

Either trying to be friendly or attempting to mend the fence, Langston called out to her as she was leaving.

"Hey, Tiger. Maybe I'll pick you in the draft next week?"

Turning around, Tiger walked backwards, as she answered,

"Yeah. Maybe. If you're lucky, Coach." She waved bye at him.

– Chapter 28 –

It's Not Even My Birthday
Saturday, March 25, 1978
Grand Ole' Opry House   Nashville, Tennessee

A man dressed in a dark gray business suit, carrying a guitar case, stopped briefly to speak to a passerby in the backstage hallway of the Grand Ole' Opry House who pointed him in the direction of one of the practice rooms. He walked further, peering into a plate glass window of the equipment filled room.

Thirteen-year-old Jen Taylor was seated on a folding chair playing her mother's 12-string Martin, singing to herself in an otherwise empty room. A half an hour earlier, she and her mother had finished a set in the Saturday matinee. Alice briefly left to place a call to Harlan, who was back at home in Pennsylvania.

The man knocked on the door before partially entering.

"Jen? Good afternoon. May I come in?"

Jen thought he looked familiar, especially when she recognized the logo on his identification badge.

"Yes, please do."

The man placed a guitar case on the floor near one of the empty chairs and introduced himself.

"My name is Philip Church, Jen. I represent the Gibson musical instrument company. I was hoping you might have a moment to speak with me."

With a curious expression, Jen answered, her hand outstretched, pointing to a nearby chair. "Oh, I do. Please, sit down, Mr. Church."

Her parents had spoken with company representatives occasionally, but this was a first for her.

"Please call me Phil. I just spoke with your mother down the hall. She asked me to tell you that your dad is doing fine. She should be back in just a few minutes. I wondered why your dad wasn't here, and she explained what had happened."

"I talked with my dad this morning. He sounded a little groggy, but doing better. Thursday night . . . we were planning on leaving Friday morning . . .

Dad said he was feeling awful and ended up going to the emergency room. A few hours later he had his appendix out. My parents considered canceling but, then we agreed that Mom and I could do this together."

"I'm sorry your dad couldn't be here, but your set today was just wonderful."

"Other folks said it was pretty good, too," Jen responded. "I hope so. I wasn't sure. I'll listen to the tape later. Mom and I play together all the time anyway, so we were just doing what we usually do."

"Jen, your voice is really developing. Quite the range. Powerful. A lot of people are taking notice ... And your guitar skills are remarkable for someone your age."

"Thank you. It was different for us to play without Dad. Just as soon he'd been here, though."

"Of course, and I look forward to seeing The Taylors performing again.

"Jen, I have to run. I have a meeting in an hour at one of the downtown hotels, but before I leave, I'd like to present you with a little gift from Gibson."

"Really?"

"Yes, really."

Phil leaned over in his chair, tipping the guitar case on its back, releasing the clasps on its sides. Lifting the lid revealed a customized 12-string Gibson acoustic guitar, fit snugly onto a bed of emerald green fake fur. He reached in, picked it up, and handed it to her.

"For me? This is beautiful, Phil!"

Jen returned her mother's guitar into its case as she accepted Phil's gift. Turning the guitar over in her hands, she examined every aspect of it.

"Yes, Jen, it's all yours," he nodded, tossing a couple of his business cards into the bottom of the empty guitar case.

"We think you're going places Jen Taylor and hope you will stay in touch. Gibson would like to follow what you're doing."

Getting up from his chair, he extended his hand to Jen as she stood and shook it firmly.

"Thank you so much, Phil. I appreciate your encouragement. It means a lot to me."

"Stay in touch?"

"I sure will."

Mr. Church opened the door and waved goodbye. Jen found herself standing there in amazement, staring at the door for several moments before sitting back down to tune the new guitar. She had just begun to play as Alice opened the door and leaned inside the room.

"Hi, my darling. I see that Mr. Church found you."

"He did, 'M'. How's Dad. Is he okay? Did you tell him about our set?"

Still leaning inside the door, Alice answered, "Dad is doing just fine. He's sad he's not here. I told him you'd call him in a little while."

"Yeah, I'll go right now."

As Jen began to get up, her mother gestured her to wait.

"Yes, Tiger, give Dad a call a little later, but right now, there's someone here who would like to speak with you. I'm going to give Grandpa Taylor a call."

A tall thin man with wavy hair moved past Alice through the doorway. Recognizing him, Jen's eyes grew big with excitement.

"Good afternoon, Jen. Happy to meet you. I'm Roger McGuinn."

"Yes, you are! I'm Jen Taylor," she responded, nervously. "You're playing tonight. Mom and I are going to stick around and watch you, of course. We can't wait!"

"Great. I'm looking forward to it, too . . . but I wanted to stop by to tell you how much I love your voice and the way you play . . . the two of you were fantastic together this afternoon."

"Why, thank you. Thank you, Mr. McGuinn."

"Please, Jen. Roger."

"Okay, Roger. I'm down south now, so I'm trying to act more polite."

"What do you have here?" Roger inquired, as he sat down on the chair beside Jen in front of the open guitar case. "I see your mom's 12-string, but what's with the new Gibson? Fancy!"

"I can't believe it, but this nice man from Gibson, Phil Church, just gave it to me. I mean, only 20 minutes ago. It's not even my birthday!"

"Nice guitar. Well, this is the music industry, Jen. Gibson thinks you show promise . . . and I agree with them . . . so they're keeping an eye on you. That's pretty neat for a . . . I won't even guess, how old are you, Jen?"

"I'll be 14 in July."

"Well, I am impressed. Keep working your craft."

"It's what I love to do, Roger. I'm a pretty lucky kid."

"And you've got great parents."

"That's for sure. Just wish Dad was here with us, though."

"Your mom told me about his operation. Please say hello to him for me."

"I will for sure!!!"

"Your mom refers to you as 'Tiger'?"

"Sometimes."

"Where did you get that nickname? I don't know many girls named Tiger."

"Buck Owens gave it to me when I played on Hee Haw. I think I was about nine."

"No kidding. Buck. He's a wonderful guy. You'll have to tell me about it sometime, Tiger . . . but right now I'd like to extend an invitation."

Jen leaned closer as if he were about to reveal a secret.

"What are you thinking, Roger?"

"Would you like to join me on stage tonight? I think we should do a song or two together. I know the guys in the band are totally cool with it, and its fine with you mother, if you're okay with it."

Jen jumped out of her chair.

"I'd love to! You bet. That would be totally great."

"You wouldn't be nervous?"

"Nervous? About what? I've already been out there today. Mom and I threw that set together. Only one practice. But we do play together all the time, anyway. Actually, it wasn't that tough. As my coach next door says, 'if you get an opportunity to shine, take it!'"

"Great! I think I'm getting the 'Tiger' thing now." Roger removed a folded sheet of paper from his shirt pocket, opened it and handed it to Jen.

"Here's the set list. Do you have any preferences?"

"All acoustic, right?"

"Yeah."

Jen held onto her ponytail as she scanned the list thoughtfully.

"How can we not do "My Back Pages" together?"

"All right. Let's do that one. Might as well get started now. Which guitar you want to use, Jen?"

"I think I'd better stick with my mom's since I'm so familiar with it. Barely touched the new one yet."

"Tiger, I think you should play the new one. Do you know why?"

"Not really."

"If Phil is in the audience tonight and I can't imagine he wouldn't be . . . along with all the other reps . . . he'd really like to see the Gibson being played. I don't go on until eight o'clock, so there's lots of time to practice."

"You're right. I get it. Let's get started."

For a few moments Alice observed their interaction through the corridor window outside, then thought it better not to interrupt the two musicians.

****

7:55 p.m.   Grand Ole' Opry Media Center

Harlan Taylor searched for his phone among the tangled bedcovers, picking up on the third ring.

"Hi, honey," he mumbled from his hospital bed, wincing as he propped himself up on the pillows.

"Hi, my Tennessee man."

"I wish your Tennessee man was in Tennessee with his two girls' right about now."

"How are you getting along tonight, darling?"

"I'm okay. A little groggy from the pain meds, I guess."

"Well, I'm sitting in a corner of the media room . . . looking at three monitors of the stage. We have a surprise for you."

"What's that, honey?"

"Roger McGuinn is scheduled to go on a little after eight and our daughter will be joining him."

"No kidding! How did that happen? Golly, Alice, I can't believe I'm going to miss this."

"The video tape will be available later. I'm staying right here with you to describe the play-by-play, hoping you can hear some of it. Best we can do tonight, sweetheart."

"Is Jenny okay with it?"

"Are you kidding me? She can't wait to get out there. She and Roger practiced close to an hour this afternoon. He made a tape for her to follow. She's going to play on an acoustic version of "My Back Pages" and an alternate lead for the solo. Jen's already developed it and set to go. She was in practice with them to work out her fiddle parts and then her harmonies on "Knocking On Heaven's Door". I think that's the encore. I had to remind her to eat something."

"Our little girl is having quite the day!"

"Kind of a Nashville coming out party. Seems like it anyway. A lot of backstage buzz, Harlan."

"Boy-oh-boy, how about that, Alice!"

****

At a little after eight, as the lights came up on stage, Roger McGuinn and his band members walked on to much applause and performed the first songs of the evening. As the third number was being introduced, Jen quietly entered the relatively dark edge of the stage and stood near the back of the group with her fiddle. As soon as she appeared, the front rows of the audience recognized her and began to applaud.

Grinning broadly at the impromptu interruption, Roger turned and extended his hand in Jen's direction.

"Well, I thought we could just sneak her in here. Guess not. Jen Taylor will be joining us for a couple of songs . . . Jenny Taylor, Nashville!"

Applause spread again throughout the auditorium as the youngster returned a wave. After a song playing fiddle, she moved back off stage as the band proceeded with their program. Alice continued to watch the monitors, anticipating her daughter's return. As she was explaining the scene to Harlan, one of the screens showed Jen coming back onto the stage carrying her 12-string and moving up to the front.

"Now she's walking up front, next to Roger," Alice reported to Harlan. "I think this might be "Back Pages". She has the new Gibson. I think she likes it . . . nice narrow neck."

Alice went on to describe how Jen's voice blended flawlessly with the harmonies of the refrain, followed by her singing a solo second verse, then yielding another wave of applause from the Opry crowd. When Roger went into the bridging solo, Alice held the phone up to the speaker, hoping Harlan might be able to hear the counter solo his daughter was so beautifully weaving into the instrumental bridge.

Harlan lay back in his hospital bed, his phone propped up against his ear with a collection of pillows, thoroughly immersed in the moment. His abdomen felt heavy and sore, but his heart was incredibly light and filled with joy. His daughter was becoming a woman and a professional entertainer.

On an overcast Saturday in March of '78, young Jen Taylor left an impression on the Music City. The following morning, the reviews in the Nashville papers proclaimed a new C&W star had been born. Jen went on to attract the attention of the music industry and musicians across the spectrum – from those entering the wave of popularity to classic performers. Tiger would take the lead. It was her future that was ahead.

– Chapter 29 –

Swimming Angry
Friday, May 21, 1982
University of Pennsylvania, Philadelphia, Pennsylvania

The starting gun fired. Jen broke the pool surface first – with a clean start. With not 25 yards to the first turn of the 100-yard freestyle, she rotated side to side, following the long black line at the bottom of the pool, coaching herself through the race.

"Reach. Pull . . . a breath . . . Nobody around . . . Gold . . . Gold! Nobody . . . Quick turn. Pick it up! Gold . . . Gold! Nobody . . . Pick it up! Gold. Gold! Quick turn! Go! Gold . . . Pick it up! Quick turn! Pick it up! Go. Go! Pick it up! Pick it up! Pick it up! Go, Go! Hard! HARD! Quick! QUICK!"

With a touch of the contact pad, Jen popped up out of the water, landing her forearms on the edge of the pool. The other lanes were finishing. Her teammates were excited and cheering, but she didn't notice. As she caught her breath, she leapt from the pool and ran towards the locker room, unaware of the poolside commotion she had just caused. Someone remarked, "What's wrong with her? She's crying."

Opening her locker, Jen peeled off her tank suit, and quickly dried off. She put on her sweatpants and jacket and was tying a shoe when the varsity coach came into the room. "Tiger, what are you doing?"

Jen didn't reply.

"I thought you were sick or something. I came as soon as I could. Are you sick?"

"No. Not like you mean," she muttered, putting her other foot up on the bench, tying the lace.

"You're leaving? What's going on, Tiger?"

Looking up at Coach Murphy, Jen shook her head, "Yeah, you're right, Coach, I'm leaving. I can't do this anymore."

"You're kidding me, Taylor! You're walking out? Really? Do you know . . ."

"I'm done!" Jen tersely cut her off.

As Jen zipped her jacket, she spotted an empty cardboard box in the corner of the room. She strode over to get it, as Coach Murphy continued talking, then dumped the contents of her locker into it along with her backpack.

Looking closely at Jen, the swim coach realized she had been crying.

The coach softened her tone, "Tiger, will you please stay and tell me what's going on here?"

"No. I just can't do it anymore. That's … that's how I feel right now, anyway," Jen fired back, quickly wiping under her eyes, then shaking her head in almost a shiver. She grabbed the box and stormed out the locker room door without another word, leaving her coach clueless to explanation.

It was the end of Jen's freshman year – and the end of the women's swim team season at the University of Pennsylvania. Time trials had been held throughout the morning and the races had significant bearing on who would make next year's squad.

The year before, Jen had been recruited by numerous schools, especially on the East Coast, reflecting her national rankings and two Mid-Atlantic high school records. Every scout who had followed Jen Taylor during high school had returned to their institution reporting her high skill level and fierce competitiveness. With that reputation, the coaches at Penn had expected much more from Jen. However, her season proved to be relatively unremarkable, not living up to that of the athlete they had hoped for. Her strong skill set and competitiveness were frequently absent during the season; she was often moody with little to say.

Jen walked out of the arena into the late morning sun, moving at a brisk pace along the sidewalk in the direction of her dorm. Despite the Taylor home being only a 65-minute drive away, she had decided to live in a dormitory her freshman year. She didn't want to live at her parents' house and she also didn't want to be a great distance away from the Plimpton family.

Bill Plimpton was still enroute to U Penn. He was aware of the time trials as Jen had discussed them with him during a phone conversation the evening before. He wanted to be at poolside, but a late change in schedule necessitated his being in court early that morning. He especially wanted to be there because he knew it was going to be a rough day for her.

Today was the one-year anniversary of Alice Taylor's sudden death. It had been a very painful year for Jen. To distract from her grief, Jen decided to start her freshman year at the University of Pennsylvania early, during the summer semester - only two months after Alice's death. Jen had planned to do the same thing again this summer, welcoming the distraction a full schedule would provide.

The intimate pattern of the Taylors' lives changed abruptly with Alice's death. In an instant, it all vanished. There was no 'Taylors' without Alice. Music became unbearable for Jen apart from her mother. Harlan was devastated as well and took a different and singular path. Although he had not typically been inclined to express his emotions outwardly, now, with the death of his partner, he immersed himself in his music, and, for the first time, began composing songs. Consistent with his private demeanor, it was difficult for Harlan to offer emotional support to his daughter. He was always available for everything else but, for as long as Jen could remember, her emotional needs had been met by her mother and her 'other dad', Bill Plimpton.

* * * * * * * *

Bill arrived on campus, driving along the road toward the swim complex. Slowing down, looking for a curbside parking spot, he noticed a tall girl with a long ponytail approach, carrying a large box in front of her. Pulling over, he got out of the car and called to her.

"Tiger!"

She had already walked past, but upon recognizing his voice, spun around on her heels. Jen hadn't counted on seeing him until early afternoon. Dropping the box, she ran into his arms sobbing, sobbing so hard that it was difficult for her to breathe. Eventually, she was able to speak between chopped up phrases and uneven breaths.

"I'm so glad ... you're here, 2Dad. I feel ... feel so awful. I can't ... help it."

Bill held onto Jen tightly, clasping his big hand against her head resting on his shoulder, until she settled down. He took Jen to his car and got her inside. Picking up the box he placed it on the back seat. He continued driving in the direction of the swim stadium and pulled into the parking lot. With a nod over his shoulder, referring to the box she was carrying, he asked, "What's going on, Jenny?"

Jen looked over at Bill with a bewildered expression, her eyes were red and swollen. She addressed him quietly, in a defeated tone.

"I did my hundred. Waiting around for my heat, I started getting angry. By the time I got out of the pool ... I lost it ... just really lost it. I went into the locker room and left."

"Does anyone know you left?"

"Yeah. Coach Murf' came into the locker room as I was packing up. I told her I didn't want to do this anymore."

Jen thought for a long moment.

"I'm not really sure of that … I don't know … probably not going to make the team, anyway. It wasn't much of a year, ya know? I can tell … they're disappointed in me."

"Jenny, what can I do for you?"

"I guess I don't want to be alone … mostly, I just want to go home."

"We will, Jenny. I would like to talk to Coach Murphy first. Would that be okay with you? I know what to say."

"Oh, would you? I was really upset. I'm sorry," Jen answered with regret in her expression.

Bill leaned across the console, patted her shoulder, then kissed the top of her head.

"Jenny. I'll take care of this. Stay right here. I'll be back in a few minutes and then we'll find a place for lunch. Are you hungry?"

"I'm starving!"

"That's my Tiger. I'll be right back."

Bill entered the Sheerr Pool Complex and hustled down the stairs. The trials were on break for the morning. Walking into the pool arena he sought the attention of the coach, who appeared to recognize him. Although Bill had attended every home meet and made several of the away trips, they hadn't formally met.

"Good morning, Coach Murphy."

"Mr. Taylor. Good morning. So glad you're here. I was hoping to get a hold of you."

"I'm not Dr. Taylor, but please let me introduce myself. My name is Bill Plimpton, Jen's next-door neighbor. Our families are very close. Without exaggeration, Jen has spent half of her life in our home. I consider her my other daughter."

The coach extended her hand in greeting.

"Mr. Plimpton, excuse me, I just assumed … Very nice to meet you. Please come into my office so we can talk. Do you happen to know where Tiger is?"

"Yes, she's in the car, waiting for me."

Perplexed, the coach sat down behind her desk, motioning to Bill to take a seat. Nervously rubbing the back of her neck, she began, "Jen left crying, and saying she couldn't do this anymore! What's going on, Mr. Plimpton?"

"Coach," Bill explained, "today is the one-year anniversary of Jen's mother's sudden and unexpected death. Alice Taylor was only 39. Jen and her mom were extremely close. It's been a very difficult year for her."

"Good lord! I didn't know any of this."

"Jen has sensed the disappointment of the coaching staff. She knows she hasn't been the swimmer you recruited. Well, I guess she hasn't been, but now you know the reason. I know Jen wants to swim, but today was just an extremely bad day in a bad year. I hope you can understand."

"I had no idea, Mr. Plimpton ... no idea at all."

"Bill, please."

"Bill, she never mentioned any of this to me or to any of the other coaches, as far as I know."

"I'm not surprised. Jen has gone into a shell."

"Please, there's no problem here. Ask Jen to come and see me when she's ready. I hope she'll want to return next season. Did she tell you she broke the school freestyle 100 record today? She demolished it! Nobody's been close in twelve years."

"No. I don't think she knows. Right now, Jen just wants to go home. She doesn't know what she wants. She's all over the place. This isn't the Jen Taylor I know, I can assure you! Somehow, she's kept her marks up and stuck with the swimming to the extent that she has. But she's only just beginning to address her mother's death. Slow process."

"I understand."

"What do you know about Jen, Coach?"

"Not much, really. She doesn't talk to anyone. Doesn't hang out with her teammates. Practice, meets . . . rarely communicates. I learned she lifts weights with the men's team. She's on and she's off. When she's on ... she's focused and can intimidate everyone. Fierce. Then, suddenly, she's barely there. Well ... it all makes sense now. Sad."

"I think I've seen you at almost all of the home meets, Bill."

"And as many of the away ones as I can manage," he added.

"Yes. Sometimes a young man comes and sits with Jen in the stands after practice. I've seen them hugging. Doesn't seem like a boyfriend though."

"That's my son, Randy. He's a freshman here, too. They grew up together, like brother and sister. Randy was very close to Alice as well."

Coach Murphy was still holding Jen's file in front of her, which prompted another question from Bill.

What else do you know about Jen?"

The coach glanced down again at the file.

"As far as personal stuff, not much, let's see here . . . QPR 3.2, first two semesters . . . it says . . . she plays the piano."

"That's true. The piano, guitar, fiddle, banjo, pedal steel, mandolin . . . and just about any other musical instrument a country and western musician might play. Great voice, too. She grew up playing and singing with her parents. No siblings. She found brothers and a sister at our house . . . my kids.

"The weekend before Alice died, the Taylors performed in Nashville. It's something the family did regularly, especially in the last few years. They were well-known in the Nashville music scene. A few winters ago, before Jen turned 17, Capitol Records approached the family with a lucrative contract for Jen. Alice and Harlan decided to hold off on the contract until after she finished high school.

"Although Jen had been accepted at Penn, the morning her mother died, she left for school expecting to have a career in music. By that evening, all such thoughts were lost to her..."

Astonished, Coach Murphy shook her head, "How sad. Never a word from her about any of this."

"Maybe breaking the 100 record today is an indication of her killer competitiveness returning," Bill suggested. "Actually, I believe Tiger's better in the 200. I know that remains to be seen. Right now, my main concern is taking care of her."

"I understand. I'm so glad we had a chance to talk, Bill. May I have a contact number?"

"Of course. Here's my business card. I would like to say a word about Jen's dad, Harlan. He loves his daughter and is very proud of her but he has also been struggling with his loss as well."

"Thanks Bill. Again, please ask Jen to come by when she's ready."

"Good day, Coach Murphy."

When Bill returned to his car, Jen had moved it under a tree for shade and was fast asleep on the front seat. He drove out of the parking lot and was nearly in town when she awoke. Jen stretched and yawned before looking over at Bill.

"Hi, 2Dad. Guess I dozed off."

"How are you, honey? Still hungry?"

"Yes. May we go down to O'Toole's Pub?"

"Right away."

"I'm so glad you're here."

Bill smiled affectionately and said, "Did you know you broke a 12-year-old school record in the hundred today?"

"Huh?"

"Yeah."

Jen sat straight up, glancing over at Bill again.

"No shit! Really?"

"Really, Tiger. Coach used the term 'demolished it'."

"Yeah? I wasn't in the best lane, but I never saw anybody."

"Sorry I missed it. Almost made it."

"That's okay. I feel much better with you here now . . . just want to go home and see everyone. That's all I want right now. Glad to get out of school, too."

Bill drove into the parking lot behind O'Toole's. They entered through the dark brown rustic door in the back, proceeding to the bar and took seats at the far end.

Jen immediately asked, "Is Randy home?"

"He came home last night."

"Is my dad at home?"

"No, Tiger. He's still in Nashville this week."

Jen blew out a big sigh. "I talked to him last week. Our conversations are still difficult. He doesn't know what to say. It makes me sad. I know he's suffering, too... but he won't talk about it. I'll call him tonight. Dad did write a song, though, about his feelings for Mom. He didn't come out and say it, but I know that's what the song's about. Looks like a new C & W guy, Dwight Yoakam, is going to record it."

"Really! That sounds like a big deal."

"It is."

"Good for Harlan. Maybe that's how he gets through all this."

"I hope so. I feel he's drifted away from me. I don't mean to say it's permanent, but it's sure a loss for now. I try to keep him close. I would feel very lonely without my family next-door."

"Your dad will come around, Jenny. It's just his way. He's trying to grapple his way through this. He loves you. Better days will come, you'll see."

"I know he does. Yeah, better days ... soon, I hope."

Bill reached over with a napkin to dab the tears running down Jen's cheeks.

Feeling the reassurance of Bill's presence, Jen buried her face in his shoulder crying softly. After a short while she sat back in her bar stool and threw her head back, looking up at the ceiling. She took in a deep breath and smiled. "I love you, 2Dad."

"I love you, too, Tiger."

"I'll be okay ... just glad we're heading home. I need a little break. Oh, yeah ... by the way ... did I tell you anything about my meeting with the psychologist?"

"You haven't said anything. When was it, last week?"

Twisting up a corner of her lip, Jen quietly reflected on the encounter.

"Yeah, it was. I really didn't get much out of the meeting. She gave me another appointment date, but I canceled the next day. I wasn't comfortable with her. She didn't have any clear suggestions. Can you believe that? She listened without saying much for the entire 50 minutes. Gave me a bunch of pamphlets and a suggestion for a book to read. Geez, I thought she was kind of weird. That's the last thing I want."

"You did the right thing. Maybe you can try again with another therapist. Tiger, what's that on your sweatshirt?"

"Where?"

Bill reached over pulling off a long piece of dried banana skin stamen stuck to the sleeve of her fleece jacket.

"Sure. What else?" Jen laughed.

Jen looked deep into the mirror behind the bar with her chin in her hands, then swiveled on her bar stool to face Bill.

"I need to pick a major, pretty soon. I was thinking medical. Maybe psychology. Maybe a combination. I'd rather build the pre-med base. I got organic chem out of the way already."

"That sounds solid, Tiger."

"I wish I understood why I've been struggling so this last year. It feels like torture. Now I know what other people go through. Aghh! Maybe I should've gone to see a psychologist sooner. You're right, though, probably just got the wrong person. Maybe I'll try again."

"Good idea."

"I've also discovered something about swimming."

"What's that?"

"I kind of noticed it in high school . . . but it's more obvious now. It seems like it's a way to clear my head of everything distracting . . . at least for 45 minutes or so. When I'm doing a long swim, I concentrate on what every part of my body is doing. I can identify where everything is and whether it feels equally the same on both sides of me . . . the moving water should feel the same . . . and the bubbles should sound the same. The best part is . . . the new part is . . . I'm at peace. I like it."

"Interesting. I think you've discovered something. Very important for you . . . a meditation . . . and sounds like it might make your swimming mechanics even better."

"On another note . . . I really enjoyed my introductory psychology class. Maybe because I really liked the professor, too. I aced her class."

"Did you happen to have a chance to talk to her about how you're feeling; what's going on in your life?"

"I did a little . . . and a week ago Prof. McTague stopped me in the corridor and handed me a pamphlet she had recently received in the mail about a conference being held in Chicago next month. She highlighted a research clinical psychologist from Brown University who's giving a series of lectures on therapies to treat traumatic stress, including grief therapy. The psychologist is well known for having developed a new, more effective approach during the late 70s. A big deal. I'm thinking I'd like to go."

"That's sounds like a great idea. Maybe we'll work on setting that up this weekend."

Jen removed a pamphlet from her backpack and handed it to Bill. Unfolding it, he scanned the schedule then read aloud, "Marriette Roy, PhD."

"Her last name's pronounced 'Oo-Ah'. French."

"Okay. Like the new Canadian's goalie, Patrick 'Oo-Ah'."

"Yes, Wah," Jen chuckled.

"Marriette LaFleur Roy, PhD." Bill continued. "Recent developments in the treatment of traumatic stress related disorders', June 10th and 11th. University of Chicago."

"What do you think?"

"I like it! You should definitely attend this one. Gotta keep moving forward, Tiger," Bill encouraged.

"2Dad. I'm so unsettled. I feel so empty. Such a huge chunk of me is missing. I'm not even sure who I am anymore," she sighed, pausing between sentences. "So strange. I feel like I'm starting over. I just haven't gotten very far in a year."

Bill turned to face Jen, "I'd like to point out, you've accomplished a lot at school this year ... but you need to take time to heal. So much has changed in your life and in your dad's. It's been a shock to your sense of well-being. Your life will need redefining. Stabilization. There's a lot to figure out here, Jenny. Just try to move in that direction a little each day."

Once again, Jen looked deep into the mirror behind the bar, as though seeing a different version of herself. "It was all there ... just the way I wanted it ... we wanted it ... and it all disappeared in an instant ... I kept thinking there was some mistake, that it would all come back ... yeah ... all my expectations ... all I assumed was so permanent wasn't at all ... it wasn't."

Jen paused, nervously tapping the bottom of her glass against the bar top, "So, I guess I'm avoiding the remnants. It's why I still can't deal with the music right now. I know I need to get back into the things I love; to create some sense of normalcy. I can't always be afraid ... I'm just not ready."

"Maybe we should try to explore some of those things this weekend," Bill suggested. "Just a little bit, Tiger. Perhaps you, Randy, and I can take a walk up to the little canyon or at least in that direction. It would be good for him too. Maybe begin to welcome back some of those precious memories. We can work on that together."

"I know. You're right. We will, I promise," Jen agreed.

"I spoke with your dad when he was home last week. Did he say anything to you about his moving back to Nashville?"

"Yeah. Dad's seriously considering it," Jen answered. "I'll bet it's a done deal."

"He admitted it was difficult to stay in the house. Same as you feel, Jenny. I wouldn't be surprised if he sold the house and started a practice in Nashville."

"I think you might be right," Jen replied. "He is back and forth from Tennessee a lot. I get it. I can never live in that house again. Never."

"You'll always have your home next door, Tiger. We aren't going anywhere."

"Yes, 2Dad. That's home for me, now. That is home."

– Chapter 30 –

My New Passion
August 1982   Eastern Pennsylvania

In August of '82, Doris Plimpton noticed a local realtor pounding in a home-for-sale sign in at the end of the Taylor's driveway. Bill's suspicion that Harlan would move to the Nashville area proved accurate. The following day, Harlan arrived with a moving company, packed up, said his good-byes and moved to a quiet town along the Tennessee River between Clarksville and the city limits of Nashville.

Returning to Tennessee was what Harlan seemed to need. Pennsylvania was beautiful, but it wasn't really home for him. For 20 years, the Taylor family had traveled back and forth between Riverdale and the Music City.

But now, Harlan couldn't remain in the house where Alice died any more than his daughter could. Turning his practice over to a young dentist from Pittsburgh, he joined a dental group in Nashville. Over the course of the next year, however, his participation in the new practice waned. He no longer had the heart for dentistry. With some early success, he began to make his living in the musical tradition of the generations of Taylors before him.

Harlan Taylor was a private man in many ways and not one to display his feelings outright. He kept his anguish over Alice's death to himself, but Jen felt her father's chronic stoicism was a ruse of sorts. For years, Jen had recognized that her dad's emotions would creep to the surface and escape while playing his music. That's all it took.

Now, back in Tennessee, Harlan channeled his hidden elegiac laments into the music he wrote. He began to sell his sentiments as country songs. In the first few years after Alice was gone, he attempted to coax his daughter to return to the music scene with him but found her to be deaf to the consideration. Harlan confided to close friends that he wished his daughter would record his songs rather than other country and western stars, but Jen had now moved in an entirely new direction.

After the summer of '82, Jen moved out of the dormitory and in with the Plimptons. The Taylors' home was sold in October. The once well-worn path connecting the two homes was now overgrown with encroaching thorny brambles and adventitious shoots emerging from the expanding grove of beech trees.

Jen was disconsolate with feelings of powerlessness after Alice's death - so different from being able to control outcomes in the past with her sheer grit and intelligence.

Jen remained on the swim team for another season, breaking her own record in the 100 and then the 200 freestyle in official meets at the University of Pennsylvania. Bill had been right. Her 200 performance at Yale established an enduring conference record.

During Jen's last year at Penn, she did little else but study, devoting the time to finishing school in three years. Her QPR climbed. She spent little time socializing. It was school and home, home and school, trying to distract from thoughts too painful to revisit. She dated a young man on the men's swim team for a short time; a curiosity at first, but it ran its course and ended.

For the fall semester, Jen was granted an independent study program at the University of Michigan, Ann Arbor. Her trauma, along with a lasting impression after attending the lectures of Marriette Roy in Chicago, led her to focus her attention on the treatment of post-traumatic stress disorders.

An academic connection between colleagues at U Penn and Ann Arbor provided Jen with an opportunity to explore research in this discipline. The research program at Ann Arbor so inspired her, that she quickly immersed herself in the task at hand. Jen was moved by the stories of patients she helped interview, mostly aging young men who had been victims of combat stress from their war experience in Vietnam. She found that they were helped by the program at the Veterans Administration hospital, the institution that worked in partnership with the University of Michigan. The faculty was impressed with Jen's dedication and ability. They invited her to apply to their graduate program for the following fall.

****

Ann Arbor, Michigan   1984

In the fall of 1984, Jen and Randy Plimpton drove a U-Haul truck packed with her belongings, along with a Toyota Corolla in tow, from Pennsylvania to Ann Arbor. This marked the first time she lived away from home by herself. As Randy pulled away from the curb, heading back to Riverdale, she knew she was really alone. She hurried to get a telephone line installed.

During the next few weeks, she placed many calls to her father in Tennessee, but daily calls to 2Dad in Pennsylvania.

The tincture of time had begun to provide healing and understanding. Jen discovered new ways to think about her mother and how to diminish anxiety-producing thoughts, replacing them with thoughts of loving solace.

Jen began to practice the piano regularly again. But she avoided music that the family had covered together; especially those songs she played with her mother. Jen realized, sometime late in the second year after Alice's death, that her mother would not wish her daughter to abandon music.

As Jen began the fall semester, among the required graduate courses were three in statistical analysis – taught by a post-doc fellow named Dennis Walker. He had just completed his doctorate in theoretical mathematics and was beginning a postdoctoral two-year program. Dennis was originally from the coast of Rhode Island. His parents lived in the small town of Denessen, about 45 minutes outside of Providence where he had attended public schools. Although a good looking young man of medium build and height, he was quiet, shy, and uncomfortable around girls growing up, so dates in high school had been awkward, few, and far between.

Dennis's parents met during World War II while working at the Fore River Shipyard in Quincy, Massachusetts. His father, a steamfitter, and his mother, a machine parts inspector, began noticing each other at the end of shifts, as they walked back to the lot where their vehicles were parked. Conversations struck up and a romantic relationship ensued. They married in 1948 and moved to Rhode Island.

Dennis's father, Ned, continued his work as a union steamfitter, traveling throughout New England to construction sites. His mother, Glenice, found employment as an inspector in a machine shop in Providence. In 1956 their first and only child, Dennis, was born.

Ned was a talented man and jack of all trades, an engineer at heart. He built, wired, and plumbed the additions to their home. Behind their house, in the barn, he repaired their cars, and built a riding lawn mower that converted into a snow blower. He also crafted a large wooden boat for lobstering. He designed and fabricated a power plant for the boat from an old Cadillac car engine and made a trailer to haul around the wooden boat. It seemed like there wasn't anything he couldn't do. Ned passed on his skills to his son, being a good and patient teacher.

While in middle school, Dennis discovered his talent in mathematics.

The string of 800s on his SATs in high school came as no surprise. Given a choice between MIT and the University of Chicago for college, Dennis chose the Windy City.

****

As Jen proceeded through the statistics class with Dennis as her instructor, she needed help in designing the metrics specific to the requirements of her research discipline. Dennis offered his assistance and they began to meet regularly.

Dennis was eight years Jen's senior, a kind, soft spoken, and patient young man. Each time they met, both learned something new and interesting about the other. Jen began to feel comfortable around Dennis. Nearing completion of his education, he was following a well contemplated path and seemed grounded. Jen was attracted to those qualities, which she felt were absent in herself.

After their first couple of meetings, Dennis began to look forward to the next, sensing that she enjoyed his company, too. It was a new experience for the young mathematician, as Jen was strikingly beautiful as well as intelligent. He perceived himself as being way out of her league.

When she informed him of her academic direction, Dennis admired her dedication. Jen shared her feelings and involvement with the veterans she was interviewing. Although he didn't fully understand their problems, he was impressed with her resolve to help them.

It took Dennis four weeks before summoning the courage to ask Jen out on a date which was simply to meet for coffee after one of their sessions. Jen had been waiting patiently for the invitation and, had another week slipped by, she was prepared to ask him herself.

As time went on, they shared their histories. Both were only children. Dennis learned that Jen's mother had died suddenly three years earlier and that she had experienced much uncertainty during that time – and was still feeling unsettled. Dennis seemed so stable in comparison. He was quickly becoming a source of reliable support that might be the safe harbor in which to anchor herself. By fall, they were dating regularly. There was the first kiss, then later, they made love. As a potential partner, Dennis now offered the grounding previously provided by her mother and Bill, which would again allow her to run free, at full speed, to accomplish what she needed.

Dennis considered himself lucky beyond imagination. He, quite frankly, found it difficult to believe Jen continued to be interested. As they spent more and more time together, he began to sense how comfortable she was becoming with him.

When Dennis learned of Jen's imperative swim workouts and regular trips to the gym for strength training, he attempted to improve upon his own attention to fitness, or to at least make a decent showing. The exercise made him feel good about himself in a new way.

He also became aware that Jen regularly practiced the piano and was puzzled that she mentioned little about her family's long history and deep involvement with music. One afternoon, Dennis asked if he might accompany her to watch her practice. She agreed. When she sang to him, he was entranced.

Later that afternoon, after leaving the practice room, the couple passed a group of Michigan students setting up their band instruments in a larger practice room. A guitarist was experimenting with the lead part to a song they were working on. Hearing one of the phrases caught Jen's attention. She approached the musician, vocalizing something Dennis couldn't hear from where he was standing. He watched in utter amazement as the musician smiled and handed Jen his guitar. She placed the strap over her shoulder, then tuned the guitar, and got back the feel of the Rickenbacker 12 string. It was just like her 370-12, still back at home in her bedroom closet at the Plimptons.

A moment later, Jen cued the drummer and jumped into Dylan's "My Back Pages", singing the first verse. As she continued to play, the others picked up on what she was doing and joined in. Playing the instrumental bridge, she glanced over at Dennis and winked, apparently feeling comfortable with this little foray back into music, yet still not elaborating.

Dennis was also in constant awe of Jen's high energy level, knowing he could never keep up with her whirlwind pace. He was industrious and got the work done, but then he usually wanted to relax, which meant being quiet, reading, or perhaps watching a baseball game on TV. If Jen fell into an easy chair, it might last for five minutes; then she was onto something else, rarely sitting still.

When Dennis's lease ended in January of '86, he moved into Jen's apartment and the two settled into a comfortable routine. As their relationship continued to develop, Dennis addressed the topic of children. He felt it was important to discuss early on. Having grown up without siblings, something in him longed to be a father. He wanted to have children.

Although Jen was an only child as well, she had never felt like one. The constant presence of Lisa, Linc, and Randy filled that vacuum for her, but she recognized the difference in their childhoods and understood Dennis's position. A week later, after their intimacy, during a quiet moment in the dark, she whispered, "I would love to have children with you." Dennis acknowledged the moment silently with a tear tracking down his cheek, detected only as a salty dampness where she rested her lips.

On a gentle afternoon in August of 1986, when the coastal winds of late summer had changed harkening the oncoming of autumn, Jen and Dennis were married on the beach of Narragansett Bay, just across the road from the Walker home in Rhode Island. The ceremony was small and included Glenice and Ned Walker, Harlan Taylor, and the Plimpton family. After the ceremony, the wedding party walked up the beach road to an area along the marsh at the edge of the river. The Walkers announced to the thrilled couple that this parcel of land was to be their wedding gift. They then walked along a new path to where Ned had cut a partially cleared house lot. Ned and Glenice asked everyone to sit on the felled logs that Ned had arranged in a semi-circle. Harlan opened a guitar case which was hidden behind some cleared brush. He performed a song he had written as a gift for the couple, a wedding song, along with its rights. Little did they know that the composition would go on to be performed at thousands of weddings well into the future.

Jen and Dennis's son, Scott Taylor, was born in September 1987, followed by Carolyn Alice in November 1988. While she was completing her degree, Dennis took a temporary teaching position. Jen was granted her PhD in clinical psychology in January 1989. Dennis accepted a position at Brown University to begin in September of 1991. After maintaining a research program at the VA in Ann Arbor, Jen then transferred to a similar position at the VA in Providence, Rhode Island.

– Chapter 31 –

It's Just Another Day
Monday, October 5, 1992
Veterans Administration Hospital   Providence, Rhode Island

Monday morning at 8 a.m., the clinic workday began at the Rhode Island Veterans Administration (VA) Medical Center. An attendant knocked on the door before directing a young Marine officer into the room. Dusty venetian blinds partially blocked out the bright morning sunlight that spilled over the walls painted Government hospital light green, now grimy with age and yellowed from cigarette smoke of its former occupants.

The Marine, in khaki dress uniform, hat in hand, sat down on a bench-like chair constructed of a gray painted steel and aluminum construction, matching the desk and all the other furniture in the room. Although George Bush was now president, a framed photograph of a grinning Ronald Regan still hung on the wall behind the soldier.

A young woman, dressed in a dark gray business suit, rose from behind her desk and offered a hand in greeting.

"Good morning, Cpt. White. I'm Dr. Walker. Jennifer Walker."

"Good morning, Ma'am."

The Captain sat down, nervously scanning the room as he slapped the seat cushion beside him, "Not much of a couch for a psychiatrist's office."

As Jen sat back down at her desk, the chair's rusting springs squeaked, "I'm a clinical psychologist, Cpt. White. I agree, the decor certainly leaves a lot to be desired. I'm trying to ignore it."

He seemed to be testing her. She felt quite confident he knew the difference, but his questioning continued along in a similar vein.

"First patient?" asked Cpt. White.

"Yes, first patient of the day," she answered.

"No, I actually meant first patient. I'm confused. Someone out there told me you just started."

"Yes, Captain, this is my first day here at the Rhode Island VA Hospital. And, indeed, you are my first patient at this facility, but not my very first patient.

If it's helpful, you are my 800th and something military patient I've seen since starting to investigate and treat military trauma related stress. My husband and I recently relocated here from the University of Michigan. That's where we attended school. I treated patients at the VA at Ann Arbor."

The soldier took a deep breath before asking the next question. Jen waited patiently, wanting him to find his own way to become comfortable.

"I thought about this meeting all the way up here on the plane. How do you listen to this stuff? All this horror, all these unspeakable accounts, without letting it get to you?"

Surprised by his question, Jen put a finger to her chin, while glancing up at the somewhat askew picture of Reagan.

"Well . . . Yes. You're right, it does affect us all. This is my fourth year of treating military patients. I've had to find a way to protect myself pretty quickly. The way it works for me is not far removed from the treatment plan provided to our patients. I've discovered how to remove myself from my thoughts. After my first two months of treating veterans, I was essentially in the grip of the traumatic stress disorders of others. I had to take a break from my practice. If you can't figure out a way to ameliorate that, you change your specialty really fast. So, enough about me, if that explanation is sufficient, Cpt. White."

"Thank you, Ma'am. It is."

"Cpt. White. Are you here because you want to be or because you were you ordered here?"

"Actually, Ma'am, I specifically requested to see you. I wasn't getting anywhere at Walter Reed. You were cited as one of the authors of this treatment program. I asked a lot of questions . . . read what I could."

"That's good. Are you feeling as though you might be comfortable talking to me?" she inquired, hoping he was getting over his initial nervousness, trying to impress the pretty girl, or whatever other reason might have been behind his initial presentation.

"So far, Ma'am."

"And are you concerned about promotion status if certain diagnoses might be established?"

White looked up at her, now making direct eye contact in a serious effort to communicate his essential concern.

"Look, what I care most about is getting well. I think I already carry the diagnosis and history of behavioral issues that will prevent me from being promoted. I can't be sure, but it's what I assume."

"What makes you say that?"

"Well, as my medical record indicates, a psychiatrist at Walter Reed diagnosed me with PTSD. I believe the diagnosis is accurate. Certainly had the right experiences to qualify on the checklist."

Jen nodded indicating support for his last statement.

"Also, I've made what's been deemed inappropriate, public statements about deployment policy. Mouthing off. It's come out with my anger. There are things I've said on base, outside of the hospital, which will affect my promotion status."

"Angry a lot, Cpt. White?"

"Yeah. Since the incident. Comes out of nowhere sometimes, easily triggered."

"Not surprising."

Cpt. White shifted sideways on the bench searching for a more comfortable way to sit on the awkward piece of furniture.

"Since I was a kid, I saw myself making a career in the military. My father was a career Marine officer. I'm not so sure I qualify any longer to follow in his footsteps. I may not even want to," White smirked, uttering a conclusion that he never would have dreamed of a year ago. Leaning forward, he rested his forearms on his knees, staring at the carpet.

"Where had you been deployed, Cpt. White?"

"I was previously stationed at the American Embassy in Beirut, the one that was overrun last year. I expect we will talk about that later."

"When you're ready."

He looked up at Jen with an expression of surprise quickly changing to disappointment. "At first, I thought I had gotten through it all right. I seemed to be okay for the first couple weeks. Then things changed."

Reaching down to his ankle, White pulled up the leg of his trousers, revealing a small single circular scar in the center of his kneecap.

"What is that?" Dr. Walker inquired, reacting to the odd location and symmetry of the wound. She got up from her chair and leaned across her desk to get a closer look.

"That's my physical trauma, Ma'am. I'll explain later."

"Okay." Jen responded, raising her eyebrows.

"I was brought back into CONUS soon thereafter for debriefing at the Pentagon. The embassy attack was a big-time incident. But just to keep me busy while the investigation was on going, some motherfucker at Walter Reed assigned me to death notification duty."

Squinting one eye, Jen understood what he meant, astonished at the inappropriate assignment.

"Here I was, back at the Pentagon, and they assigned me this job which, of course, someone has to do, but I didn't think I was the best choice to be that someone at that time."

"I agree," Jen nodded, leaning back in her old chair, which squeaked each time her weight shifted.

"So, one afternoon, after lunch, I went out on assignment with a military chaplain, as is customary. We drove up to a soldier's home in a pathetic little puke green government vehicle . . . just the two of us . . . in full dress uniform, to knock on their door and inform his parents how goddamn sorry the fucking Secretary of the Army was that their only son was dead . . . killed in action."

Gritting his teeth, White stared up at the single light in the center of the ceiling, its round translucent globe harboring a plethora of dead moths. He then closed his eyes, deliberately taking in a deep breath before continuing, "Maybe we'll talk about it more, later."

"Of course, Cpt. White. When you're ready."

"When we got back the chaplain dropped me off to report to my unit headquarters. I was extremely agitated from the experience and went inside and freaked out. I burst into this Major's office who I knew had assigned me the duty . . . dumb ass desk jockey admin type. I cussed him out good. My outburst only made me angrier. I coulda' beat the piss out of him. Someone like him has absolutely no fucking clue how things really are. He could've been working at Macy's doing the same fucking thing!"

"Sorry, Ma'am . . . anyway . . . the MPs arrived just in time. I spent the night in the brig with screaming nightmares to boot. Hey! I guess someone decided I was really crazy and got my appointment at Walter Reed moved up pretty fast."

Jen shook her head, her face scrunched up, biting her lower lip.

"You heard of anything like that before, Doc?"

"Yes. I'm afraid I have. I'm sorry. So, tell me about the nightmares, Cpt. White."

"Yeah. The recurring nightmares. Basically, a rerun of the incident. Here's what happened, Doc.

"After the embassy was overrun, three of us were captured and tortured by the insurgents. Two other Marines had been killed as the bad guys broke into the compound. One Marine was tortured to death before the two of us were rescued. The nightmare doesn't ever change much. I wake up screaming, fucking scared out of my mind all over again. I somehow push the images away when they want to show up during the day."

"When you're ready, Cpt. White," Jen interjected, "I'd like you to tell me as much as you can remember about your experience in detail, as well as about the nightmares. As we proceed through this treatment, I'd like you to keep a diary. I'll give you a list of things to record, on a daily basis. This is an important part of your treatment. Try to do your best. Write as much detail as you can remember. This is called prolonged exposure therapy and it works."

The thought of recording his experience was unsettling to White. It was exactly what he did not want to do. Jen immediately recognized this, observing his beleaguered expression.

"I know, Cpt. White, it seems counterintuitive. Just what you don't want to do, right? Yes, it is difficult, but I'll work you through it. It will help you. Well-designed studies bear this out."

Cpt. White's breathing was uneasy as he responded, with beads of perspiration forming on his brow, "Okay. Not sure I follow all you're recommending, but I'll work on it."

"Good, Captain, we will work on it together."

"So far, I feel I can talk to you. It's not you, Doc, but I feel a bit rattled right now ... just telling this much of the story. Do you think I can take a short break here? I need a smoke."

"Sure. Smoking increased?"

"Yes, Ma'am."

"Drinking?"

"Yes, Ma'am.

"Anything else, Cpt.? Other drugs?"

"Negative, Ma'am, but yet another reason I wanted to change treatment locations."

Jen stood up beside her desk, pointing toward the door, "Take five. Down the hall on the left at the exit sign. There's a porch for smokers so designated, Cpt. White."

"Thank you, Ma'am."

With one hand on the door frame preparing to leave, he smiled back over his shoulder at Jen and asked, "I want to get through this. Are you going to heal me?"

"Yes, Cpt. White, but you're going to heal yourself . . . and I'm here to help you."

"Thank you again, Ma'am."

Jen wondered if the trauma of her first patient was an indication of more of what she would hear during the rest of her day. The good news was that White had done some homework. He recognized he had problems, had already identified some, and seemed committed to seeking solutions.

– Chapter 32 –

A Quiet Evening at Home
Monday, October 5, 1992
Halsey St., Providence, Rhode Island

Jen put away her notes after seeing her last patient of the day. She walked out to the hospital parking lot and got into the 1981 Corolla her parents had given her a few months before graduation from high school. It was a five-minute drive back to the house that she and Dennis had purchased at the edge of the Brown University campus.

Dennis was beginning his first semester teaching in the mathematics department. He was happy to be back home on the Rhode Island coast. He had just picked up their five-year-old son, Scott, and four-year-old daughter, Carolyn, 'Scooter' from the university daycare as Jen walked through the door.

"Hi, Denny. Hi, Scooter."

"Mommy! You're home, FINALLY!" yelled her ever rambunctious daughter.

"Yes, Scoot . . . finally."

While Dennis was squatting down to change Carolyn's sweatshirt, Jen bent over and kissed him on the top of his head.

"Hi, Sweetie, can you check on Scott?" Dennis asked. "He just ran around the corner."

"Scotty? Scotty? Mom's home. Come see Mommy."

Jen gathered up her young son and returned to the room where Dennis was helping Carolyn.

"Oh, oh, Scotty, what's all that goo on your shirt?" Jen inquired.

"Something from art class, Mom, play-dough mixed with slime," Scott answered as Jen sniffed the front of his shirt.

"I guess, Scotty. Weird color, huh?"

"It's dog poop, Mommy!" his little sister interjected to antagonize her brother.

"No, it's not, CA-RO-LYN!" Scott barked back in reply.

"Don't call me Carolyn, dopey!"

"Stop it, you two," Dennis insisted.

Jen smiled, momentarily closing her eyes, amused at the dramatic shift from the hospital environment. It was good to be home.

"Denny, can you fix Scotty while I get changed? I'll trade you."

She picked up her daughter, cuddling her, as she headed off to their bedroom. Scooter climbed up around her mother's neck, immediately wanting to be let down into a guided somersault - something they'd practiced many times before.

"Again, Mommy!"

"Scoot! In a little minute. I need to get out of these clothes first, honey."

Jen put Carolyn down on the bedroom rug among a pile of wooden blocks while she changed out of her work clothes. Dennis walked into the room with Scott riding up around his shoulders.

"How did your first day go, Jen?"

"Okay, as first days go. Back at it. Later, after the kids are asleep tonight, I'll tell you all about it. I feel as though I need to unload."

"Ugh!" Denny sighed, with a grimace.

Dennis and Jen were now a typical busy couple starting out, juggling schedules in order to raise their children while progressing in their careers.

In grad school, Jen had authored two papers published in respected clinical psychology journals. Plus, she was a lead author of the current PTSD treatment program adopted by the U.S. government. Another co-authored paper on PTSD had recently been accepted for publication in the *Journal of Consulting and Clinical Psychology*. Jen was building a solid reputation in her field of study, already establishing the groundwork for a successful career.

Her future ambition was to apply for a position at Brown University. Jen's mentor at a distance, Marriette Roy, was an esteemed pioneer in cognitive behavioral therapy and a member of the Brown faculty. Roy was a significant source of inspiration to Jen, someone Jen had yet to meet.

Still standing in her underwear, she pondered the evening schedule. "Den, here's a deal. I'd like to run over to the swim complex and get in a good workout. I really need to clear my head. When I get back, I'll make dinner and clean up or you can make dinner and I'll take charge of the kids."

Jen had picked Carolyn up and was spinning her around in a tight circle, holding her daughter securely to her chest. From his lofty position, Scott's eyes were transfixed on both his mother's and sister's long ponytails extending centripetally as Jen spun rapidly in place.

"Okay, beautiful. Go get your swim in," Denny smiled, admiring the musculature of Jen's back. She was easily 5'10" with long muscular legs and a long waist, definitely athletically inclined.

"Will you always have muscles like that?" Dennis asked.

"Of course I will! You can, too! Muscle mass is essential for health," Jen answered as she stopped spinning, lowering her giggling daughter to the carpet. She flexed her back muscles for Dennis.

"Ha! Like those swimmer's lats? Give me 90 days with you at the pool and weight room, and you got them too!" she preached. "C'mon, Den. You only get one body and you've got to take care of it."

"Oh, gee," Dennis replied sarcastically, having heard this lecture before.

The notion of exercise had been slipping away from Dennis since they married, and even more so, with his new responsibilities at Brown. Jen often had to remind him to work out. On the other hand, she remained dedicated to fitness. Although she always turned heads, she never gave it much thought.

Jen donned her tracksuit and shoes for the quick run to the gymnasium. As soon as a lane was available, she was in the water.

The rhythm of swimming and effortless turns allowed Jen to drain the day from her mind, putting her thoughts into their proper perspective. Swimming played as much a part of her mental health as it did for her physical exercise.

There was also a peacefulness about the underwater environment. While at Penn, being attentive to the rhythmic strokes of swimming created a sanctuary to help deal with the grief of her mother's death. This mindful practice afforded a space free of unwanted images and conversations with herself.

Back at home, with dinner cleaned up, and the children asleep, Jen and Denny settled in on each end of the couch, facing each other. Two years earlier, back in Michigan, they had sat on the same couch watching CNN, when the Gulf War began. The 24th Mechanized Infantry Division had been leaving Fort Stewart, Georgia for months. Hinesville had emptied out, deployed to the Middle East.

Throughout the fall of 1990, flatcars loaded with Bradley FVs and Abrams A-1s creaked along rarely used tracks to the main line, heading up the coast to Charleston or south to Jacksonville. The distinctive hum of C-5s overhead, heavy with troops and supplies, signaled their departure from Hunter Army Airfield, one after another, well into December.

Jen and Denny watched that night as Wolf Blitzer, in Atlanta, and Peter Arnett, sequestered in a high-rise Baghdad hotel, provided a surreal play-by-play as the city was set on fire. This began decades of everyday war in the Middle East with infidel troops treading on sacred tribal wastelands, soaked in black crude. It was a war made for TV.

That evening in 1990, Jen had remarked, "It looks like I'm going to be busy for a long time," referencing her specialty in counseling psychology. In fact, it was only a matter of a year before the first influx of traumatized minds would overwhelm the treatment system.

****

"So, Jenny, my love, tell me how it went today?" Denny inquired.

"Darn glad I got that swim in, Denny honey," Jen answered as she changed position to rest her head on her husband's thigh. Looking up at the ceiling, her ankles dangling over the arm of the couch, she began to ramble.

"It's wonderful that we can help these troubled vets. They desperately need it. Many may seemingly recover, but many are unreachable, and yet so many more won't even come to these clinics. Something about their culture keeps them silent . . . as though it's their duty to suffer. We can only help them if they show up and stick with the program."

Closing his eyes, Denny was grateful it was quiet. Both children had fallen asleep at the same time. Hopefully, they would sleep all night, although, maybe not. It felt peaceful to have his wife's head resting on his leg, her long hair draped across his lap. She was thinking out loud, and he knew there was a message, so he took care to listen.

"You know, Denny, it just seems to be part of the human condition. I know things in the world are getting better . . . world wars are probably a thing of the past, but it's also hard to imagine humanity without its violent skirmishes. And along with those so-called conflicts, there's always one batch after another of young victims sucked into someone else's conquest for wealth and power. Ugh!"

Denny continued to stroke his wife's thick light brown hair. "I don't know how you do it, Jen. Most of the time I'm lost in the impersonal realm of numbers and symbols. If I didn't come up for air, I wouldn't know that any of this is going on. Can't say I don't like my approach, though."

"Ah, yes, the life of a theoretical mathematician," Jen giggled. "Did you get any chalk on your coat today?"

"Oh, stop it," Denny retorted, tapping her playfully on the head.

"Since you've asked me, Den, I'm going to give you an idea of the kind of situations that come across my desk. I promise I won't make a practice of this."

"That's good. Thanks," he grimaced, considering what might be coming.

"The first guy I saw today is a Marine captain in his early thirties. His dad was a lifer. The Captain has had a few bad months. He was at that embassy that was attacked a few months ago. Insurgents stormed in, killing two of the five Marines. The good guys killed a half dozen of the bad guys before they were killed. The insurgents tied up the other three, including my patient, the Captain, because the bad guys wanted information which the Marines had no access to.

"Well, the bad guys didn't believe the Marines, and one insurgent took an electric drill and began drilling into the knees of the first Marine. He then went down the line putting a hole in each knee. The first guy was an O-5. So, I guess, they concentrated on him, drilling more holes in him, despite the others screaming that they couldn't tell them anything. Then he drilled a couple holes in the LTC's head. When the LTC went unresponsive, the insurgent moved to the next guy and put a hole in his hand. That's when the percussion bomb went off – flooding the room with gas, gunfire and SEALs."

Holding the top of his head with both hands, squeezing both eyes shut, Dennis blurted, "Jesus H. Christ, Jen! That's enough! It makes me sick! Dammit, Jen!"

"Yeah. I know," Jen replied softly.

"How the hell do you listen to this abomination every day?"

"Well, I wouldn't say it's typical, Den. It's just more horrible than most of what I hear, which is, nonetheless, horrible."

"Really!"

Jen looked up at Dennis, who was still holding his head and covering his ears, indicating he couldn't bear to hear anything more.

"Den?"

"C'mon, no more, please? How the hell do you cope with this?"

"I'm sorry, darling. No more. But Den, this is how I cope. I have to think of all this stuff as not really real, as if they are just fictitious words to be recorded as fictitious events. As though someone is making up a story, although I assume they are not. As though I'm reading it in some novel that I didn't want to read in the first place."

Dennis looked down at his wife's face, sifting his fingers through her hair, concerned that her job was traumatizing her.

"I listen to it," Jen went on, "and then separate myself from those thoughts and emotions as they pass through my stream of consciousness. I evaluate the severity and then leave it as soon as I'm able. I don't hold on to the story. My job is to assess the impact of the event on my patient. That's all. I know it's real if I allow myself to think about it, so I don't. At the end of each day ... every day ... I close my office door and exhale, as if blowing it all out. You know, like a shortstop after making an error, turning around, facing the outfielder, and blowing it off or spitting it out to get ready for the next pitch. I close the door and leave ... it ... there! It's a ritual.

"When I get home, I immediately change my clothes and empty my mind of the day by playing piano, or, even better, by the repetition of swimming laps. Yeah, maybe the chlorine cleans up whatever's left."

"Oh, Jenny, Jenny, Jenny."

"Yep, I swam pretty fast today. Churned up the water, big time! Felt I needed to."

"Jenny. You're still so wound up. I'm keeping an eye on you."

"Thanks, Den, my love. Don't worry. I'm okay. Really. Gee, I'm still hungry. I've burned through supper already!"

"Jen, I swear you burn calories even when you're just lying around! Your head is hot."

"Matter of fact, I do. That's the big secret."

She jumped up and went into the kitchen to grab a couple of bananas, a jar of peanut butter, and a glass of water.

That night while Jen slept soundly, Denny lay awake, watching her sleep and worrying.

– Chapter 33 –

An Administrative Error
Tuesday, July 27, 1993
VA Hospital, Providence, Rhode Island

Jen sat at her desk reviewing chart notes, anticipating the arrival of her next appointment, Army First Lieutenant, Andrew Kelly. His company saw action in Iraq. Andrew had been transferred from Europe to the military hospital system in CONUS to receive psychiatric treatment for military-related stress trauma.

Several months earlier, while his company was deployed near Mosel, Iraq, a convoy was attacked, sustaining significant loss of life on a single day. Fifteen soldiers under Kelly's command were killed, with 12 others seriously injured.

The sights and outcome of the battle scene were unbearable for the First Lieutenant, traumatizing him to the point that he was deemed unfit for command. He was then admitted to the Walter Reed AMC for definitive care. Following two months of treatment, he was transferred to the Veterans Administration Hospital in Rhode Island.

Today marked the ninth therapy session with Jen as his clinical psychologist. He had made considerable progress on issues that dealt with his combat trauma. What he now struggled with was the idea of returning to active duty, along with the burden of family expectations. These concerns were the current focus of treatment.

Andrew had received no sympathy or understanding from his father, Lt. General Francis X. Kelly, who was still serving on active duty at the Department of Defense in Arlington, Virginia. Lt. General Kelly was relentless in his demand that his son return to active duty and get over "whatever it was" he imagined he suffered from.

The Kelly family history was steeped in military tradition. Like Andrew, his older brother, Francis, Jr., graduated from West Point and was currently a battalion commander in Iraq, receiving promotions ahead of his contemporaries in rank. Andrew's grandfather had retired as a flag officer, as well. A greater grandfather, Samuel Israele Harrington, was a celebrated southern general during the Civil War.

Andrew's predicament was that he did not demonstrate the same familial attributes as those of his higher-ranking relatives. During therapy, Andrew revealed that he felt alone in the world. He had married immediately upon graduation from West Point in 1992, only to divorce a year later. His mother was deceased. Kelly was under concomitant psychiatric care, but it was unclear whether he had been taking his prescribed medications. He admitted to having suicidal ideations, although no attempts had been reported. Whatever military camaraderie he had experienced was gone now that he was separated from his command for reasons considered by some as cowardly.

His father, General Kelly, had been ordered to Vietnam following his graduation from West Point in the mid-1960s. As an infantry captain he served well before being captured and surviving nearly two years of brutality in a North Vietnamese prison camp. Despite torture and near starvation, Kelly Sr. managed to escape and recover, soon returning to a combat command in country. The experience made him demand the same stalwart attitude from his sons and all those under his commands.

General Kelly concluded Andrew's diagnosis of military related post-traumatic stress disorder was ridiculous and unacceptable. He had tracked down Dr. Walker and reprimanded her for prolonging what he deemed unnecessary treatment of whatever his son thought he had. Kelly Sr. also demonstrated zero confidence in the assessment of WRAMC or respect for the treatment protocol of the VA mental health department.

Jen had experienced similar phone calls from non-collaborative, commanding personalities whose aggressive approach did not work well outside of the military chain of command. She didn't take it personally, but instead, reported the content and dismissive nature of the communication with Kelly Sr. to her medical department supervisor. And she discussed it with Andrew.

He was not surprised, admitting that being raised in this environment had made him feel powerless to reject his father's views. Jen suggested that Andrew consider the effects of chronic stress generated by his father's criticism. She also recommended that he reconsider his fitness for this type of military occupation, citing legitimate differences in his personality compared to that of his father and brother who, in contrast, had similar approaches to life and the military.

Jen sensed Andrew's growing dependency on her as his therapist and as someone he felt comfortable talking to. It was evident that he was searching for the safety of friendship, a connection now absent from anyone or anything inside the military environment.

Jen considered him a potential risk for suicide and documented such. A recent decision had been made in conjunction with the psychiatry staff, just days before, to place him on indefinite medical leave for the purpose of further treatment prior to a recommended medical discharge from the U.S. Army. Dr. Walker was planning to discuss this decision with Andrew during their next session.

As Andrew had not yet come to her door, Jen went out to the main desk after a few minutes, to see if he had registered. She learned that he had arrived only moments before but left in a frenzy after reading the contents of an envelope waiting for him on the desk.

Jen was then informed that the administrative director of the hospital had canceled Kelly's appointment due to a notification sent to his office from DOD in Washington. There lying on the reception desk were the military orders Andrew had received, left on top of an open SF65B shotgun envelope.

Jen quickly read the official documents in the envelope ordering Kelly to report to Fort Campbell for duty later that week. He had been administratively discharged from psychiatric care and reassigned to the 101st Air Assault Division in Kentucky. Understanding how this information would affect the friable personality of Andrew, she hurried to the nearby third floor window and looked down onto the parking lot, spotting Andrew approach his vehicle.

Turning back to the staff members standing at the desk, she instructed, "This isn't good. I'm going after him. Notify security. Brief the Psych Chief, now!"

– Chapter 34 –

The Right Thing to Do
Tuesday, July 27, 1993   Providence, Rhode Island

Jen ran back to her office, grabbed her car keys, and raced down the stairs to the parking lot in an attempt to stop Kelly. As he was driving away, she yelled out to him, but it was too late for him to hear her. She ran to her vehicle and sped out of the parking lot. Catching a glimpse of his car, she watched him turn onto Dean Street heading toward the highway. He drove up the ramp onto I-95 South and immediately took the exit onto I-195 East.

The time was approximately 3:30 p.m. on a cloudless summer afternoon in Providence.

Kelly appeared to be a quarter mile ahead of her in light traffic. Suddenly, just before the Gano Street exit, he slowed into the breakdown lane making a U-turn into an inactive construction site. Jen continued to follow, taking the same turn at a separation in the Jersey barrier which led onto a gravel road. He was already well along the construction road and approaching a smaller secondary bridge spanning the Providence River.

Stopping at a barrier placed across the entrance to the bridge, he got out of his car, and walked towards the bridge. Slowing down, Jen assessed the situation. If Kelly was going to jump from the bridge, he had too much of a head start. There was probably little she could do to stop him.

Jen then noticed a smaller road to her right. It was more like a cart path coursing down the hillside next to the Garden Hilton. Her old Corolla was just small enough to ease down the path and enter the hotel parking lot, then return back onto a road leading to the park at India Point. As she neared the river, she drove on the pavement leading to Brown University's boathouse.

Turning onto this road, she again had a view of the bridge. Jen watched with dismay as Kelly plunged into the water. Leaving the road, she drove along the river's edge, speeding over the grass through the park, choosing a place along the riverbank where he might be intercepted.

As she stopped her car at the edge of the river, Jen spotted him approach, bobbing in the outgoing current. Without giving a second thought, she committed to an attempt to rescue him. Kicking off her shoes, she pulled off her suit jacket and dress pants and grabbed an elastic band from the cup holder to secure her hair in a ponytail. From her gym bag in the back seat, she grabbed a pair of swim goggles, putting them on as she perched on top of the granite retaining wall. With one last glance at Kelly's position, she dove into the murky brackish water of the Providence River.

With the tide was going out, the water was cold beneath the surface and the air rancid just above. Kelly was still above water, thrashing about in the turbulence. Jen recognized that his jump, from maybe 30 feet, wasn't one that would have killed him. It was more like a poor, uncommitted attempt at suicide by someone conflicted and unsure of what he wanted to do. She would try to bring him back.

With her head down, Jen swam hard to her estimated point of intersection, about 50 yards out. When she next looked, she confirmed Kelly was still there and made course corrections, churning through the brackish water.

The bright sun shone beneath the surface water, illuminating the yellow-brown haziness and the debris passing by her. With the speed of the exiting tide in her favor, she was soon upon him.

When Kelly was within touching distance, she rode the current alongside him, yelling his name. He looked astonished at seeing Jen, as she lifted her goggles to her forehead. He attempted to scream at her, coughing and spitting the swallowed fowl river water.

"Leave me alone! Ah! I just want to die!"

Kelly was fatigued and having difficulty staying above the water. The two intermittently collided as the current maneuvered them. Jen yelled back in between waves splashing in her face, spitting and wiping her mouth.

"No, you don't, Andrew! Let me take you to shore!"

She tried to grab his shirt.

"No! No!" Kelly resisted, as Jen sensed his confusion. He didn't seem committed to living or dying.

"No, Andrew! I want to take you back with me!"

He continued to thrash about in the current, which was carrying both of them out into the Narragansett basin.

Jen again attempted to approach him and grab his collar, realizing she was running out of close land to swim to. Kelly swung recklessly at her, tearing away a piece of her blouse sleeve. He now seemed panicked and more desperate to stay afloat than resist. She tried again, pushing the turbulent water away from her face.

"Andrew," Jen implored, "Come on! I'll get you through this. I promise! Come on, Andrew!"

As he began to disappear under the surface, Jen dropped her goggles and dove underneath to retrieve him. His shadowy form thrashed about in the filtered sunlight, hazy brown and yellow against the dark depths below. The light fabric of her blouse momentarily billowed up into her face. Jen again grabbed Andrew by the collar and pulled him to the surface. Running out of landfall and now desperate for his cooperation as he continued to resist, she recognized what she had to do and yelled, "Sorry, Andrew."

Kicking higher in the water, she yanked him closer to her and punched him in the face twice, as hard as she could, stunning him. As they slipped under the water again, Jen gripped Andrew's shirt, pulled him to the surface and began the swim to shore using the strong current to assist her. Working hard to keep his head above water, she towed him across the swift moving river, angling toward the last bit of visible shoreline a hundred yards away. Beyond that, both were at the mercy of the Coast Guard, if anyone had actually notified them.

Andrew remained subdued as she kicked her way to the shallows, landing in the mudflats of low tide at Brant Point Park. As the water grew shallow, she dragged him backwards in the ooze. The 50 or so pounds he had over her hadn't been a problem in the water, but now became an arduous task, slogging through the mud, hauling his half-submerged body toward shore. Jen slipped and fell backwards, submerging herself in the thick muddy water. She dragged Andrew in as far as possible, knowing the outgoing tide would soon drain the area around them.

Breathing hard, she knelt in the shallow water and muck, supporting his head. After catching her breath, Jen bent over and spoke softly into his ear.

"Andrew … It's Dr. Walker. Andrew … You're not … you are not going back to active duty. We can stop that. Can you hear me, Andrew?" Jen stroked his head and patted his cheek.

Andrew opened his eyes and mumbled something inaudible."

"Things are going to get better now, Andrew, I promise."

Breathing deliberately, exhausted, but conscious, he whispered back again, "Thank you."

Jen attempted to sweep her hair from her eyes. Her ponytail was plastered in mud as she pulled it forward over her shoulder. She tried to wipe away some of the mud covering her face, managing only to push it around.

Seaweed clung to her blouse, which was now darkened with filtered sediment. A sleeve was ripped at the shoulder from her tussle with Andrew and her right foot ached near the heel. As sirens were heard approaching, Jen looked up to see two police officers running over the salt flats towards them. A Coast Guard helicopter approached, hovering high overhead.

"Ma'am, how are you doing here?" one of the officers asked as they arrived at the scene.

"I think we're okay," Jen answered. "EMS on the way?"

A young Rhode Island State Police officer knelt beside them. "Roger that, Ma'am," he responded, while addressing the other officer as well. "He's one lucky guy. Outstanding, Ma'am!" he remarked, referring to Kelly.

Now comfortable knowing medical help was on the way, Jen replied, "This young man is Andrew Kelly. He's a patient of mine. We're from the VA. He was having a bad day, but now he has another chance. I hope you heard that, Andrew," Jen added, looking down at him.

Blinking his eyes, Andrew offered a hint of a grateful smile to Jen. Rescue vehicles were now approaching over the rise behind them. Soon, an EMS crew arrived, lugging a stretcher and equipment across the mudflats.

Jen leaned closer to Andrew and whispered, "Andrew, I'm staying right here with you. We're going back to the hospital together. I won't leave you . . . but I need to talk to these folks who are here to help you."

After identifying herself to the EMS crew, she proceeded to contact the hospital to report the incident. Speaking to the Chief of Psychiatry, she provided a brief explanation of what had happened and that they would be back at the hospital ER within the half hour.

As Jen was discussing the matter with the police and EMS personnel, a news crew arrived from WPRO. A nicely dressed eager young female reporter holding her heels in one hand, a technician, and a cameraman trudged out across the tidal flats. The reporter began introducing a newsfeed as they waited for an explanation from Jen and the state police. Jen politely accommodated the reporter with succinct noncommittal blather, then proceeded toward the ambulance.

A medical technician handed Jen a set of clean scrubs along with a couple of containers of saline to wash the grime from her face, arms, and legs. She pulled the scrubs on over the remainder of muck and seaweed sticking to her. The technician cleaned and bandaged a laceration on her heel.

As Jen climbed into the ambulance with Andrew, the state police officer asked Jen, "Is there anything I can do for you, Ma'am?"

Jen thought a moment, diverting her attention from Andrew, who was safely being secured in the ambulance for the trip back to the VA.

"Yes, you can, come to think of it," Jen answered pointing in the general direction of where she had entered the river, "I'm parked illegally on the lawn at India Point Park," she grinned.

The officer smiled back in reply, "Don't worry, Ma'am. I'll contact the towing company and have them take your vehicle to the VA hospital. Would that be okay with you?"

"That would be great. Keys are in it," she quipped. "Thanks, so much, Troop."

Wishing to communicate his admiration, the trooper went on to say, "I was heading westbound on I-I95 when I noticed your vehicle leave the highway. Thought you were trespassing. It took me a moment to turn around and see what you were up to. I arrived just as you dove into the river. I could see the young man in the water, too. I called for support and headed in the direction to where I thought you might come on shore, if you did. I notified the Coast Guard just in case."

"Yeah, a few more minutes and I would've been looking for that helicopter. Thanks again," Jen said, as the officer shook her hand and left.

– Chapter 35 –

Just Do Your Job!
Tuesday, July 27, 1993   VA Hospital, Providence, Rhode Island

On the way to the hospital, Jen's thoughts returned to the events leading up to the rescue. Moments before leaving the office to follow Andrew, Jen had asked the clerk at the clinic desk why her patient had left. She was informed that William Alton, the administrative chief at the hospital, had delivered a sealed envelope, by hand, with instructions to deliver it to Lt. Andrew Kelly. Kelly had casually opened the inter-office envelope, not expecting what he would find. As he comprehended the nature of its contents, he dropped the letter on the desk and rushed out of the hospital.

Now, with Andrew sedated and medically stable in the emergency room, Jen focused on hunting down the administrator to demand an explanation. She rode the elevator to the eighth floor, moving quickly down the corridor into the administrative suite. Still running on an elevated level of adrenaline, Jen was agitated, wondering why Alton hadn't been in the emergency room, waiting for them upon return.

As she opened the door to the main office, Alton stood directly in front of her reaching for the door, prepared to leave for the day.

"Are you Mr. Alton?" Jen inquired, knowing full well who he was.

"Yes, I am. What is it? Who are you?"

The crisp white lab coat Jen found in the ER covered up only so much of her disheveled and muddied appearance, alarming him. He stared at her, eyes narrowed with an emergence of disdain. Jen blocked his path, her hands and hair spotted with river mud.

"What is going on here? Who are you? No ID?" he demanded, inspecting her disheveled appearance.

"Oh, c'mon, Mr. Alton. I'm Dr. Walker. Jennifer Taylor Walker. I've had a rather busy afternoon. Wouldn't you like to know why? I'm appalled that apparently you don't," Jen snapped, irked at the administrator's attitude. She picked a piece of seaweed out of her hair and flicked it in his general direction.

"Maybe another time. I'm late. I need to leave now," Alton tersely responded, attempting to move past her.

"You're kidding me! I saved your ass today along with the life of one of our patients who you dismissed."

"What?"

Alton managed to slip past her and was proceeding down the corridor in the direction of the elevator. Jen spun around, shouting after him, "What do you mean ... what? Don't give me that bullshit! You know damn well who Andrew Kelly is ... don't you!"

Alton not responding, she pursued him down the corridor, speaking loudly as she hustled behind him.

"When Lieutenant Kelly read the military orders you delivered, he bolted from the hospital and tried to kill himself. I was able to prevent it. Short of that, we would be waiting for his body to wash ashore ... somewhere!"

Finally getting his full attention, the administrator stopped and turned around. He couldn't escape and she wasn't about to let him get away. Jen stepped closer, lowering her tone of voice.

"I can tell you for certain the psychiatry department did not release him from our care."

Alton sneered back at her, "I wasn't privy to what was in that envelope. I just delivered it!"

As Jen moved closer, he backed away. She wasn't getting the response she expected and reacted vehemently.

"I don't believe you!"

Stepping closer still; nose to nose, she added, "You want to know why I smell so bad, Billy? Why I'm so all riled up! Huh?"

Alton craned his neck backwards, attempting to maintain some distance. Jen poked her finger into his sternum while emphasizing every word. "Andrew Kelly and I went for a dip in the fucking Providence River! I somehow wrestled him to shore, dragging him through the mudflats at Brant Point Park."

Alton stood there, his jaw dropped, now looking at her in shock, beginning to realize his culpability. Jen grabbed the sleeve of his suit jacket and pulled him over to the windows near the elevator peering down eight floors onto the ER parking lot.

"You see that, Billy? Those are the local news people. You'd better get your act together and think fast before they pounce on you."

Alton glanced back at her, fearful that she would turn him over to the media. Her ferocious presence intimidated him as he looked back out the window and then down at the floor. Jen's foot was bleeding through the bandage and oozing onto the carpet. He looked back up at her again.

"Don't worry about me," Jen said. "I'm saying nothing to them. This is an internal matter. You best figure out your part. Might be a good idea to drop in at the ER and see what's going on. Just do your job!" she barked at him, like a drill sergeant.

"OK, OK," he managed to say, as he let out a slow deep breath, dramatically changing his attitude.

"I should have known better. I didn't anticipate Kelly's reaction. I didn't."

Alton continued staring down at the parking lot, bewildered, as another news van drove up.

"Who issued those orders?" Jen inquired in a quieter tone. Alton turned around and sat against the windowsill ledge, now focused on the depth of the problem at hand.

"I don't really know who issued the orders, but I suspect Kelly's father had something to do with it."

"So, you knew they were coming," Jen remarked. "If you had informed us, this might never have happened. General Kelly is a bully. I suspect you've had at least one phone call from him yourself. I have."

"Yes. Several calls. I was coerced. Never imagined this would happen. How is Kelly?"

"He doesn't appear to be injured from the fall from the bridge, however he's in the ER, being evaluated."

"Bridge?"

"Yeah, bridge. He really needs our help. The recommendation for Andrew's medical discharge was finalized last Friday. I was planning to inform him of that decision this afternoon. Now we need to make sure it happens."

"Yes, of course, Dr. Walker, thank you. I'm sorry. I'm so sorry. I made a serious mistake. I did. I'm sorry."

Neither spoke on the elevator ride to the ground floor. Alton was deep in thought attempting to measure his responsibility in this unfortunate situation.

Jen returned to the ER and found Andrew still asleep in the cubicle. She was in the process of entering a note in his chart when an older driver from

Blackstone Towing walked up, smiling, dangling her Corolla keys in front of him.

"I'm kinda sure I've found who I'm lookin' for, pretty lady. Sorree. Took us a while to get here. Traffic wuz movin' laak pond watah."

He dropped the keys into her outstretched palm.

"Thenk you, Ma'am. You are vera brave. You saved a Vet today. I can 'preciate thet vera much, havin' been ther ma self," he added, tilting his head down and pointing to the front of his well-worn 24th ID Korean War ball cap. "Yer shoes, an' the rest of yer clothes is on the front seat. I don't know if there's anythin' else yer missing. We'all looked around the area pretty good. Woulda got 'em dry cleaned for ya if we had time."

"Thank you very much, sir," Jen responded, shaking his hand, grateful to have her car back.

"Oh, no, Ma'am," he grinned. "I wernt no off'cer. Ah' worked for a livin'."

Jen watched the driver as he walked away, touched by the manner of his sincere statement.

A nurse approached and tapped Jen on her shoulder, stating that Jen had been paged a few minutes earlier with a message that her husband had called. Jen sat down at an ER desk space and phoned Dennis. Just as soon as he picked up, she skipped the salutation, "Everything is okay, Denny. I'm okay! Everything is fine. Just fine. Fine."

"Jesus, Jen! What's going on?"

"Denny, really, I'm fine, and my patient is fine. There might be a bit of turmoil from this, but that's for tomorrow."

Walking toward the front of the house, while pulling the long coiled cord from the kitchen wall phone, he checked on the commotion at the front of the house. "The turmoil is going on right now, Jen. There are three news vans with bright lights set up outside our house. I told the reporters you weren't home. Sweetie, maybe you should park over on the next street and cut through the yards to come in the back door."

"Good idea. What are Scotty and Scooter up to?"

"They're both perched on the couch looking out the window. Maybe they've already been on TV."

"Cuties!"

Scott jumped from the couch and ran over to his father, excited and concerned.

"Dad! Is that Mommy? Where are you, Mommy? Dad, is Mommy coming home?"

"Mom's still at the hospital, Scotty, but she's fine. It's all right, Scott."

Scott spoke loudly in the direction of the receiver, "Mom! Come home, Mom! TV trucks are in the front yard, Mom!"

"Scott, she's okay. Mom's coming home soon."

Carolyn had wrapped herself around her father's leg, sitting on his foot as he tried to walk. Feeling ignored, she yelled, "Where's Mommy, Daddy? She needs a bath, Dad. Mom! Come home, right now, Mommy!"

"Kids, please. Mom will be home soon, Scoot. Scooter, let go of my leg, please ... Carolyn!"

"Dad!!!"

"Kiddos, go check on the TV guys again. Please let me talk to Mom. I'll be right there. Okay?"

The two ran back into the living room and onto the couch pressing their noses to the window panes.

"Kids a little excited, Den?"

"Yeah, wild! Jen? You were on TV, covered in mud, soaking wet in your underwear!"

Responding nervously, especially after hearing the commotion of the children in the background, she answered, "Yeah. I suppose. I guess that was my 15 minutes of fame that Warhol promised."

"Not funny, Jen. Are you coming home anytime soon?"

"Yes, Denny. Sorry, I'm kinda wound up. I'll come in the back door. First, I'm going to take a shower here at the hospital and find some clean scrubs to wear home. You wouldn't believe how grubby I am! I must still have a pound of mud on me. I also cut my foot which needs to be cleaned and sutured, and a really nice man just towed my car back to the hospital."

"What? Jenny! Ah! Jen."

"When things quiet down tonight, I'll tell you about it, okay? Sweetie, I'm okay. Really, I am. I did the right thing, Denny."

"Yes, honey."

"Oh, Den. Is there anything to eat at home? I'm starving!"

"Jesus, Jen!" Dennis responded, wondering how she could think about food at such a moment.

A little after 8 p.m., Dennis heard his wife come up the back stairs to the porch. Jen poked her head around the edge of the kitchen door before singing out, "Mommy's home."

"Hi, Sweetie!" Dennis called, coming from the living room. "Scooter! Scotty! Mommy's home."

Carolyn and Scott ran into the kitchen as Jen scooped Carolyn up into her arms and Scott grasped onto his mother's leg.

As Dennis kissed her, a few tears suddenly tracked down her cheeks. All at once, she felt relieved to be home with her family.

"Hi my darling. I'm so sorry, Den. It's been a tough day, 'ya know? I'm sorry," she sniffed, shrugging her shoulders as she shifted her daughter to free her head just enough to turn and kiss her husband on the lips.

"We were watching the six o'clock news. That was quite an amazing rescue," Denny remarked, looking at his wife with both love and exasperation.

"I don't know, Den," Jen responded, finally calming down.

"Mommy! Your hair is stinky. Yuck!" five-year-old Carolyn complained, as she squirmed from her mother's arms reaching for her father.

"I know, Scoot," Jen sighed. I'm going to wash it right now." Scott had already scurried back to the living room windows.

"Jen, I've saved some supper. How about if I get the kids ready for bed while you shower."

Handing Carolyn back to her father, Jen answered, "Thanks, Den. I do need to get cleaned up. Scooter, please get ready for bed with Daddy, and I'll come kiss you good night in a few minutes."

"Tell me a little story, Mommy?"

"I will, Scoot."

"Scotty," she called to the six-year-old, "Time to get cleaned up for bed. Please help Dad. I'll be there in a few minutes."

Picking up a banana from the bowl on the kitchen table, she trotted off to shower.

With the children asleep and kitchen cleaned up, the couple finally settled on top of their bed to talk about the day. The Red Sox game on TV was muted near the foot of their bed. Mo Vaughn had just hit a home run in the Bronx.

Lying on pillows stacked against the headboard, Jen recapped the afternoon.

As Dennis listened, she slowly began to slump into the pillows behind her. Somewhere during the explanation of a helicopter hovering over the mudflats, her words began to slow to one or two at a time with pauses and mumbles and audible exhales until only gentle breathing could be heard.

Dennis would have to wait for another time to finish hearing the rest of the story. He continued to lay propped up on one elbow admiring his lovely wife. She was so still now, asleep, but when awake, had boundless energy he could never keep up with. Dennis adored Jen and was very much attracted to her energy, but that energy also wore him out.

Her dedication, be it to family or anything else within her focus, was absolute. The tears shed when she came home suggested she realized she may have gone too far in taking the risk to save Andrew Kelly. Although Jen had done nothing she wasn't capable of doing, she knew her own confidence did not necessarily allay the fears of her husband.

Dennis was grateful that his wife and mother of their children was now safe in bed beside him. He covered Jen up with the quilt as he kissed her on the forehead, nuzzling his nose into her hair, before turning out the light. Sometimes Jen was a mystery to him. He loved this woman, thoroughly, but did not always understand her. Unable to fall sleep, Dennis resigned to turn on the small end table light to read. Jen didn't move all night.

– Chapter 36 –

Convergence

It hadn't taken long for Jen to alter the appearance and, more importantly, the general ambience of her office. Over the previous Christmas break, on a quiet Sunday morning, she dragged the old government furniture out of her office, leaving it stacked up next to the storage area in the basement.

The grinning Ronald Reagan had joined the stack of old furniture. The official picture was replaced with a painting given to her by her father, depicting an early morning rushing mountain stream somewhere in the Great Smoky Mountains of Tennessee. Dennis was cajoled into helping paint the office and by the end of the holiday there was a new rug on the floor, plus an appropriate couch and chair for her patients.

****

August 23, 1993 - October 7, 1995
VA Hospital, Providence, Rhode Island

The bright orange light of line three began blinking on Jen's office phone as she perused a professional journal, finishing lunch. Picking it up, she was informed by the desk clerk that she had a call coming in from someone at the Brown University Department of Psychology. The caller had a distinct French accent and, although the clerk had difficulty pronouncing the caller's name, Jen recognized immediately who was speaking.

Jen knew of Marriette LaFleur Roy through professional literature, but had yet to meet her. This woman was the significant inspiration for Jen's choice of sub-specialty. Dr. Roy was world renowned as an innovator; she had published seminal papers in the field of trauma stress research and cognitive behavior therapy. Excited about the significance of the call, Jen's hand hovered nervously over the phone for a moment before lifting the receiver.

"Good afternoon. Jen Walker speaking."

The voice on the other end responded in a deliberate speaking manner.

"Good afternoon, Jen. This is Marriette Roy."

"Yes, my goodness," Jen replied. "Thank you for calling, Marriette. I've been wanting to connect with you for the longest time. When I realized who was calling, I was thinking I should have called you by now."

"You have been in my thoughts as well, Jen, so pardon me for not contacting you before this. I've read your excellent publications and know you're hard at work at the VA. I was hoping we might get together sometime soon."

"Oh, yes! Absolutely."

"Do you live in town … nearby the University?"

"Yes," Jen answered. "We're down at the end of Halsey Street. I can see the Moses Brown track from my front windows."

"My goodness, Jen. My husband and I live in the big yellow house with the iron fence at the top of Prospect … you must be right around the corner."

"Yes, I know the house. Ha! We're neighbors!"

"When do you think we can get together? I was hoping you might give a guest lecture at Brown sometime this fall – if you're interested. And I'm also hoping there may be room for collaboration in our research."

"I would love to! I'm honored that you'd invite me, Marriette."

"Wonderful!" Marriette responded.

"Marriette, I must relate a quick personal story. In 1983, when I was in my second year of undergrad at Penn, I attended your summer lectures at the University of Chicago. It was your inspiration that led me to pursue my career direction. I am very much looking forward to finally meeting you."

"Oh, my, Jen! That is so gratifying to hear. Did we meet then?"

"No. I wanted to, but the line was very long and, as an undergrad, I felt way down on the pecking order."

"Well, there is no longer a line, so let's not delay. When are you available? Is Friday afternoon a possibility?"

Jen glanced down at her large calendar blotter on the desktop.

"Yes, I believe so. I'm off on Friday afternoon this week."

"How does three sound, here at my office?" Marriette suggested.

"I think that will work. Let me check with my husband's schedule so he can be available to watch our children. Dennis is a mathematician at Brown. I'll confirm as soon as I speak with him this afternoon."

"Good, I look forward to spending some time with you, Jen. I've heard great things . . . and I understand you are a pretty good swimmer, too."

Glancing up at the ceiling, as she rolled her eyes, Jen responded, "Oh, that! I prefer swimming inside, however."

****

Friday afternoon, Jen walked over to the psychology department at Brown University, just a short distance from her home. Walking down the long corridor of shiny linoleum, she stopped at the sign over Marriette's office door. After a quick knock she heard, "Entrez, s'il vous plait." (Please, come in.)

Smiling, Jen walked in. "Good afternoon, Marriette. That's about all the French I understand."

Marriette's back was to Jen, busy packing up boxes with her books and journals, removing them from the metal bookcase behind her desk. She turned with a handful of books in her arms.

"My apology, Jen. Sometimes, when I'm distracted, the Canadienne in me slips out."

Marriette walked around from behind her desk, casually dressed in jeans and a sweatshirt. She was tall and lean with sharp, angular facial features; her chestnut hair was fashioned in a long braid. She was just a month shy of her 51st birthday.

Face-to-face, seeing each other for the first time, Marriette spoke first.

"My goodness, Jen. Look at you. What a beautiful girl you are! Why, we're about the same height – and our long hair!"

Jen reflexively brought her ponytail around to the front of her jacket as they reached out simultaneously touching each other's hair, laughing at their spontaneous reaction.

"Thank you. Yes, Marriette, the ponytail, my flag. It's been that way since before I can remember. My mother used to say I treated it like a pet," Jen quipped.

"I feel the same way," Marriette nodded. "I had my hair cut short once in high school and regretted it. I've kept it long ever since."

"And I love the braid, Marriette. I'm so happy to finally meet you. Lots of boxes," Jen observed as she glanced around the room. "It looks like you're moving?"

"Yes, I am. I'm headed for the ground floor. One of our faculty is retiring and I'm next in line for his beautiful historic office, with its original antique furniture. I'm delighted to occupy it until it's my turn to move on."

Marriette suggested that they take their meeting outside. The women sat on a bench in the shade of an old silver maple on the quadrangle. As they comfortably conversed, they spoke about their families. Dennis taught at Brown, while Marriette's husband James taught at Moses Brown School. The Roys had two sons, Harris, a senior at Brown, and Jake, a junior at Boston University. Jen's children attended the Moses Brown School. Scott, soon to be six, was affable and easy to parent, while his younger sister, Carolyn, who had early on earned the nickname, Scooter, was a handful, constantly in motion. Jen explained that Scooter was the apple that didn't fall far from the tree.

Marriette was interested in hearing about Jen's academic past. The colleagues went on to discuss their current work and research plans for the future. Marriette invited Jen to give three lectures during the 1993 fall semester and asked if her Brown graduate students might be able to participate in studies that were ongoing at the VA. Jen enthusiastically welcomed the opportunity to collaborate.

At one point in their conversation, Jen returned to a topic she had briefly touched upon.

"Marriette, as I mentioned earlier, you were the inspiration for me to pursue my career direction. Without going into great detail, I'd like to give a further explanation. A year before I attended your lectures in Chicago, my mother died suddenly: entirely altering the direction of my life."

"Oh, my, Jen."

"During my freshman year in college, I tried everything I could to distract myself from the grief I was feeling. My life felt adrift. Somehow, I managed to keep my grades up and stay on the swim team. It was, of course, a terrible year for me, searching for answers. Your therapeutic focus offered something I could connect with, Marriette. You became my mentor at a distance."

"Thank you, Jen, for sharing that with me," Marriette offered, thoughtfully. "I completely understand. And now, here we are together, years later, about to expand upon this touching connection."

"It is quite amazing, isn't it?" Jen remarked, feeling the significance of the moment. Wondering if Marriette might have a similar story to share, she asked, "What led you to come up with your ideas? Your treatment approach was so original."

As Marriette hesitated, the atmosphere of their easy exchange seemed to momentarily fade. "Perhaps we can talk more about that someday in detail.

Briefly, there were some personal experiences, along with the surprise death of my brother in Vietnam. I began to consider the images and feelings that such experiences generate as being just thoughts. I discovered that in revisiting those thoughts, I could observe them, but not react to them. I found I didn't have to believe them and, over time, I could separate myself from them."

Although given an academically accurate summary, Jen found Marriette's explanation to be incomplete, with her core issue remaining private and protected. Marriette sensed Jen's assessment, but let it stand. There was a story to be told, but not on this day.

After hearing her second lecture in late October, Marriette was convinced that Jen was the candidate she was looking for. She invited her out to dinner and inquired if she might consider applying for a faculty position at Brown beginning the summer semester of 1995. Although two years away, Marriette wanted time to groom her for the position. It would also allow Jen adequate time to build a relationship with the psychology department. In this way, when her name came up for consideration, she would already be a familiar and qualified candidate. Although Marriette already had sufficient status to hire Jen on her own, she wanted no doubt left in anyone's mind.

The women's friendship grew rapidly: they discovered that they shared many interests. Being both colleagues and close neighbors, they found regular occasion to take long walks throughout the campus together, exchanging ideas. It soon became a rarity not to have daily contact with each other, paving the way for a future of successful professional collaboration and an enduring friendship.

****

One warm Saturday evening in the fall of 1993, the Roys invited Dennis and Jen to their home for dinner. Sitting together at a table on the enclosed piazza off the kitchen, they continued to get to know each other while they dined.

Glancing out toward the backyard, Dennis became curious at what appeared to be a fancy canoe lying across two sawhorses sitting next to an oversized double garage. He noted that a large shed had been added onto the older carriage house structure.

"That looks like quite a distinctive canoe, James," Dennis remarked, pointing in its direction.

"Thanks, Dennis." James replied with his usual enthusiasm and subtle French Canadien accent. "I build canoes from raw materials, carrying on the family tradition of my grandfather in Quebec. I have fond memories of him building those same canoes in his shop behind my grandparents' home outside of Sherbrooke, not far from my parents. I would often ride my bike over to watch him at work and listen to his stories. It's a history I hold dear – plus I enjoy working with my hands. I love the precision and patience it takes to make canoes," James added, taking a sip of his wine.

"It looks as though you've added onto the garage," Dennis commented.

"Yes. I had an addition built onto the carriage house about ten years ago to incorporate the shop. I generally sell the canoes to cover the cost of my materials or enter them in raffles to help local organizations. I made a few to raffle off for the youth hockey program while our boys played, and even a few after that. Would you be interested in seeing the shop?" James inquired, noting Dennis's rapt attention.

"Yes, very much," Dennis answered, suddenly fascinated with the craft.

After dinner, James showed Dennis the canoe in the backyard and another in its final stage of construction in the woodshop. The shop was filled with the sweet scent of fresh sawdust; shavings covered the wooden floor. An array of power and hand tools were positioned efficiently, allowing room to work on the craft.

As the two men sat on stools in the work area, conversing about the construction process, Dennis asked James, "Would you mind my watching you build one? I believe it's a craft I might be interested in pursuing. I helped my dad build a couple of small fishing boats a few years back."

"Sure, you're absolutely welcome to," James answered. "I have an order I'm planning to begin soon. I'll let you know as soon as I'm ready to start."

"Thanks, James. I'll definitely make the time."

As they left the garage, they walked through a separate bay with a covered vehicle sitting next to Marriette's Volvo.

"What do you have here, James? It looks like the shape of an old Chevelle."

"You're right!"

Reaching under the rear bumper, James freed the edge of the cover, peeling it back to reveal most of the classic muscle car.

"This is Marriette's 1969 L78 SS396. It has a little over 30,000 original miles and it's just about perfect. I keep it temperature and humidity controlled."

"Marriette's?" Dennis looked surprised, running his fingers over the shiny Malibu blue enamel.

"Well, it was her brother Pierre's. He ordered the Chevelle in '69 and drove it only a few times. Pierre was killed in Vietnam in 1972. Marriette was driving the L78 when we first met. I remember the day she pulled into the driveway ... out of nowhere, a very pretty girl in a hot car."

"That must have been quite the day for you!"

"It wasn't the most practical of cars to drive in northern Vermont, so it stayed housed in her parents' garage, well-attended by her father, until we brought it to Rhode Island. It still remains the special family car for many reasons."

"Looks like a lot of history here, James," Dennis remarked, continuing to admire the Super Sport.

Over the following 18 months, Dennis regularly walked around the corner to visit James's garage and eventually assist in building the canoes.

At first, James remarked to Marriette how quiet Dennis was, having little to say other than those things that centered around canoe building. Gradually, as they spent time together, Dennis felt more at ease around James and conversation emerged more spontaneously. Dennis displayed an instinct for the craftsmanship and devoted himself to the task. Hours passed pleasantly during those times in James's garage.

Dennis confided to James that he someday hoped to have his own place to build watercraft when he and Jen built their home on the land given to them by his parents. Seasons passed and their friendship grew – born from work and quiet conversations together in the woodshop.

****

Saturday, October 7, 1995 5:30 p.m.

Dennis left home late one afternoon for his familiar walk up the hill and around the corner to the Roy's house, planning to work with James on the canoes. As Dennis rounded the corner onto Prospect Street, his meandering thoughts snapped into sharp focus. An amorphous and frightful notion passed through him instantly.

Police cars were parked along the sidewalk and in the Roy's driveway. Dennis slowed his pace and then halted in front of the familiar pale yellow house. Marriette's car was there, but James's red truck was not. In the driveway was a Rhode Island State Police car parked behind Marriette's Volvo and a City of Providence cruiser behind that. The loud radio inside the idling vehicle was signaling codes about Route 95. A third cruiser, parked across the street, pulled away and sped off before Dennis could make inquiries.

Deciding to go no further, Dennis turned around and hurried home. As he walked in the back door of their porch, he found Jen in the kitchen crying over something on the local news. Seeing Dennis, she fell into his arms. Her face buried in his shoulder, Dennis looked over at the TV on the counter. The news video was reporting a multi-vehicle accident scene located on the sharp curve on Route I-95 Northbound. The images, taken from a helicopter hovering overhead, clearly revealed only the bed of a red pickup visible beneath an overturned trailer truck, crushed against the guard rail. He began to shake uncontrollably.

– Chapter 37 –

The Curve on I-95
Saturday, October 7, 1995, 5:30 p.m. Providence, Rhode Island

Later, much later, Marriette would recall walking into her kitchen and see something move outside her window. A police cruiser was idling there in the driveway, and then another pulled in behind it. She instinctively looked to see if James's truck was parked in front of the garage, but it was not. As she looked back out the window, an officer emerged from his vehicle, then was joined by another. The two men walked towards the back stairs. As Marriette again glanced toward the garage, searching for the red pickup truck, she realized James was late. She ran into the living room to look out the front window, thinking maybe his truck was parked in front of the house. It was not. Then, there was a knock at the kitchen door. Her heart rate soared.

A Rhode Island State Police trooper, accompanied by a City of Providence police officer, stood in the open kitchen doorway. The state trooper began to speak, his mouth moving, yet Marriette heard nothing. When she didn't respond, the trooper quietly repeated his message. This time, Marriette responded only with a nod of her head. And then, "Are you sure?" she gasped.

The officers answered in unison, "Yes, Ma'am."

One of the officers placed a clear plastic bag containing James's driver's license, his familiar wallet, and a ring of keys on the countertop. Marriette slumped onto a chair at the nearby kitchen table, asking them to repeat what she was sure she hadn't heard. Unable to move, she drifted into a fog, detaching from the surreal moment.

****

After being briefed by Dennis, Jen ran around the block toward Marriette's house, knowing she was alone.

Sprinting along the straight stretch of sidewalk, she halted at the bottom of the driveway, then moved past the two police cars, up to the back porch stairs, and directly into the kitchen.

As Jen caught her breath, the officers turned to look at her. She quickly glanced around the kitchen noticing the license, wallet, and keys on the counter. With the two officers standing over her, Marriette sat motionless at the kitchen table, life gone from her pale expression. Marriette's pleading eyes then met Jen's as though saying, 'Tell me this isn't true. Help me, Jen.'

Jen knelt beside Marriette whispering, "I'm here, Marriette. I will stay with you."

Marriette managed a weak, "Yes, please. Stay, Jen."

As Marriette continued to look into Jen's eyes, trying to grasp the situation, she asked, "What is going on? I don't understand any of this."

Resting her head on her forearms, barely able to speak, Marriette raised her head back up, watching her hands tremble. Again, in a vague and hazy manner, she repeated, "Qu' est-ce que c'est?" (What is this?) "Que se passe-t-il?" (What is going on?)

Jen gently put her arm around Marriette's shoulder, "Did the officer tell you about James?"

"He said James was killed. Is this true? Are they sure?"

Officer Kennedy Walcott knelt down beside Jen and softly repeated the tragic news to Marriette. "Yes, Professor Roy. I am sorry, Ma'am. James died in an automobile accident at around 4:30. I was there, at his side. I'm so sorry, Ma'am."

Jen kissed Marriette on the head, then directed her attention to the officer. She had recognized the state trooper when she first entered the kitchen, but before she could speak, he remarked, "Dr. Walker, we have met before."

"Yes, we have," Jen nodded, recognizing Walcott as the officer present at her side on the Providence River mud flats, two years earlier.

She stood up and momentarily stepped away from Marriette to speak with the officers, formally identifying herself and asking what needed to be done. The City police officer gestured toward the plastic bag laying on the counter.

"This contains Mr. Roy's wallet and keys removed from the steering column. His driver's license and registration are also in the bag. We removed the license from his wallet as a means of attempting identification. There is information in the outside pocket of the bag indicating where the vehicle will be stored. A family member or close friend may want to recover other personal effects which may still remain in the vehicle. Our office will gladly assist you. A phone number is included."

Jen felt her chest tighten as she processed the instructions. Trooper Walcott asked if anyone else was at home or would be coming home. Jen remembered that Jake usually came home from Bentley College almost every weekend. Harris had just begun his second year of medical school at Rutgers University. She leaned down again to Marriette, holding her close.

"Is Jake coming home tonight?"

Not answering, Marriette continued to stare out the kitchen windows, visions of her husband's face flashing through her mind. She could see the red truck backing out of the driveway. James was going on a quick errand. He said he'd be right back. She remembered throwing him a kiss. Did she say she loved him?

Jen again asked softly into her ear, "Marriette, is Jake coming home tonight?"

"Yes, Jen," Marriette finally responded. "He said he would be home by seven."

Jen glanced up at the kitchen wall clock. It was already 6:45. She turned toward Walcott.

"Would you be able to stay, Officer Walcott?"

"Yes, Ma'am, of course."

Jen closed her eyes for a moment, taking in a deep breath. The other police officer indicated he would be leaving.

Officer Walcott again motioned Jen away from Marriette to speak with her privately. He inquired if she thought Marriette might wish to identify her husband. It was not a requirement. However, he suggested that often individuals needed this personal proof for closure.

"I will discuss it later with Professor Roy."

In a hushed tone, the young state officer also informed Jen that James had sustained disfiguring head and upper extremity injuries.

"Thank you, Officer Walcott."

As the two continued conversing, Jake arrived home and had to park out on the street. Seeing the Providence police car backing out of the driveway and the state police car parked in front of it, he jumped out of his truck, and ran toward the house. Jen noticed him run past the window along the driveway, then stop, looking for his father's truck. As he climbed the back stairs, he yelled in French, "Maman! Maman!" halting at the kitchen doorway. Marriette summoned all her strength and stood with open arms, beckoning her son.

Speaking softly to him, she said, "Il y avait un accident. Ton pe're est parti . . . Il est parti." (There was an accident. Your father is gone. He is gone.)

Stepping back, Jake looked at his mother, glanced at Jen, and then over to the state police officer – searching for more positive information. He started yelling, "No! No! This can't be right." He turned and ran down the back stairs, over to the garage and into the workshop, looking for his father. Officer Walcott ran after him. Jake stopped in front of one of his father's canoes, maniacally searching in all directions. Looking up at the officer, he implored, "Is this true? You know this?"

Officer Kennedy Walcott, a rugged African American man with a kind face, removed his gray straw campaign hat, and held it across his chest. If he was older than Jake, it wasn't by much. With tears welling up in his eyes he answered, "Yes, Jake, it's true. I was there. Your father died as the result of injuries he sustained when a semi-trailer truck lost control on I-95 and rolled over, striking his truck. I'm so sorry, Jake."

"Where is my dad now?"

"Your dad was taken to Roger Williams."

Jake put his head down against the canoe's smooth surface, embracing it as he cried, speaking to his father in French. When Jake next looked up at the trooper, Walcott quietly suggested, "Jake, maybe we should go in and check on your mom. She's going to be calling your brother soon."

Officer Walcott put his arm around Jake's shoulder and helped the young man from the shop back to the house. Lawrence "Larry" MacAllister, a longtime family friend, suddenly appeared, walking up the driveway. Jake stared at him as though an apparition.

Larry was the respected headmaster at the Moses Brown School – and a close friend of James. He had known Jake and his brother, Harris, from the time they entered kindergarten. The boys were closer to Larry than any other man, except their father. He had been a hands-on mentor for both boys as they grew up in this tight academic community.

"Jake," Larry beckoned. The young man ran into his arms.

When the three men returned to the kitchen, Marriette and Jen were standing close together. Marriette was about to dial a number on the phone. As soon as her eyes met Larry's, she dropped the phone and grabbed onto him, crying softly into the shoulder of his dark blue blazer.

"Oh, Larry. I'm so glad you're here. The boys need you now. I need you."

He held Marriette's head tenderly between his hands, touching his forehead to hers as he reassured her, "I'm here, Marriette."

Marriette then broke down sobbing for the first time. Larry held her until she was able to gain some control, while Jen and Officer Walcott stood by exchanging anguished glances. Jake was still clinging to the young police officer. Marriette finally took a deep breath, sighed and looked up at him. "I need to call Harris now, Larry."

Jen handed her the receiver. "I'll dial the number for you, Marriette."

– Chapter 38 –

The Phone Call to Rutgers

Saturday, October 7, 1995, 7:30 p.m. Providence, Rhode Island

Harris Roy's cell phone was ringing while he was in the shower. His medical school classmate, Clyde Henderson, called to him from the kitchen.

"Hey, Harris. Your phone's ringing."

From inside the bathroom, Harris yelled back, "Yeah, I hear it. I'm just getting out. Would you check to see who it is? It might be Laine McGovern, my date tonight."

"Really!" Clyde exclaimed. "Lucky you!"

As Clyde walked into the bedroom, he quickly glanced the area code.

"I think it's your mother," he responded.

"Would you mind getting that? Tell her I'll be there in 30 seconds."

When Clyde answered the phone, Marriette was expecting Harris. Although she spoke in French, it was clear that she was upset. With only his elementary knowledge of French from high school, Clyde recognized something terrible must have happened. Uttering the first words that came to mind, he replied, "Un moment, Madame."

Covering the microphone, he quickly went to the bathroom door.

"Harris. It's your mom. Hurry up."

Harris, wrapped in a towel, opened the door, immediately sensing from Clyde's expression that something was terribly wrong.

Clyde handed Harris the phone and sat nearby on the arm of the couch as Harris spoke with his mother in French, attempting to decipher keywords from the conversation. "accident . . . parti . . . mort."

Harris's face went pale as he hung up, staring right through Clyde.

"My father died in a traffic accident late this afternoon. I need to get home right away. I'd better get going. It's about a five-hour drive, at best."

Clyde stood up, walked over to Harris and held onto his shoulders, focusing on his roommate's eyes.

"Har, you can't drive. It takes too long," Clyde advised, realizing the folly of Harris's snap decision.

"Go get packed. I'm going to call the airport and see if there's a flight to Providence tonight."

Harris swallowed hard, still staring at Clyde.

"Come on, Harris. Get packed. I'll drive your car up to Providence tomorrow and take care of all the shit with school, too. I've got you covered, man," Clyde said as he left to make the phone call.

Having made the arrangements, he returned to Harris's room to find him sitting on the edge of his bed with his hands on his knees, staring at the wall. Clyde gathered up his cell phone, its charger, and threw some of Harris's medical textbooks into the travel bag. He grabbed the keys to his car from the bureau top and put them in his pocket.

"Harris, listen to me, man. There's a flight to Providence at 10:30 tonight. You're on it. I told them the situation, for what it's worth. When you get in, take a taxi home. Do you have your wallet on you?"

"Yes, I do."

"You said you were going on a date with Laine tonight, right?"

"Yeah."

"I'll call her."

"Her number's on the pad next to the phone," Harris mumbled, not yet budging from where he was sitting.

"Okay," Clyde answered, as he zipped up the overnight bag. "Grab your jacket, Har. I'll drive you to the airport and get you on the plane. Call home now and let them know you're flying into Providence ... go ahead. I'm going to call Laine. I'll be right back."

Harris was a handsome young man, tall like his biological father, but broad-shouldered like his grandfather, Gil LaFleur. These influences gave him a body similar to James, the father whom he had known from infancy. Harris was also big, fast, and a great skater, as was James. He had been recruited by hockey schools including Boston College, Boston University, and his hometown team, the Providence College Friars. Harris had had enough of hockey by the end of high school, but at Brown, he skated with the Moses Brown team during practice to help his father coach – as much as his academic schedule would allow.

In manner and build, Harris's brother, Jake, was a younger version of James. Jake did accept a hockey scholarship to Boston University, playing for two years before sustaining a season-ending knee injury at the NCAA tournament in '91. That was the end of his hockey career.

Both brothers had in mind more practical career paths. At the time of their father's death, Jake was beginning his first year in the Bentley CPA program. Harris was in his second year in medical school at Rutgers.

The personalities of the two brothers were quite different. From early on, Jake was the more extroverted. He loved to talk, and everyone knew when Jake was in the room. At Moses Brown, he was one of those kids who knew everyone. Everyone liked him, occupying the rare air above the cliques.

Sharing more similarities with his mother, Harris was relatively quiet and deliberate, often seemingly deep in thought. While displaying excellent leadership qualities, he accepted but never relished being the leader. He was elected president of his junior class in high school and was voted captain of the hockey team by his teammates for two years. Never one to raise his voice, he quietly, but demonstratively, led by example.

Clyde drove Harris to the airport, seeing him through the boarding door, onto the airplane. During the short hour flight from Newark to Providence, Harris fought to clear his mind, feeling the painful reality of the situation press upon his chest. He thought about his mother and brother and what he would find when he arrived home. He knew he would be the one to hold it all together.

He tried to recall the last conversation he had with his father over the phone, only days ago ... maybe Wednesday? When did he last see him? Yes, it was Labor Day weekend. He and Jake had come home for three days. During the holiday weekend he spent time with his father in the shop behind the house. Dennis had been there on one of those occasions to work on the canoes.

Harris remembered going to the North Smithfield rink to skate with his father. It had just been the two of them on the ice surface for half an hour before Jake joined them. That was it. That was the last time they were all together. Harris momentarily lost himself in the memory.

They had skated together, passing pucks in designed plays, shooting into an empty net. The three big Canadiens shouted directives to each other, hearing the crunch and scrape of their skates over the ice, playfully checking each other, the sharp crack of the puck on sticks, the thud of their errant shots into the boards, and their laughter echoing throughout the empty rink.

In the quiet dim light on the plane, Harris huddled against the window waiting for the lights of Providence to appear, realizing life would never be the same again. It would be a different course for all of them, a future never imagined. He would grieve with his mother and brother and would help them move on, all the while cherishing and honoring, in his soul, everything about his father.

Finally arriving at T.F. Green, Harris walked through the quiet corridors of the small airport and out the front entrance where he caught a taxi. It was an approximately15-minute ride home.

As the cab approached the city on route I-95 NB, traffic slowed and moved to the extreme left of the northbound lane. A nighttime crew, with bright lights ablaze, was repairing the road surface and guard rail where I-95 swept in a sharp curve only a minute before the exit home to the east. Although he wished he hadn't seen it, he determined this must have been the place.

When Harris reached home, only his mother's car was parked in the driveway. He noticed his brother's truck parked across the street and another car that looked familiar in front of the house. As the taxi pulled away, he found himself staring into the light of the living room. No one was visible. He now wished he were somewhere else, or that there was another reason for him to be here tonight. He wanted to believe that somehow this was a mistake, but he knew it wasn't.

Harris stood on the sidewalk, alone in the darkness with travel bag in hand; it took several minutes before he could move. He contemplated how his father would want him to take responsibility for caring for the family, to be the captain. Although his mother had never been weak at heart, this might be the great exception. In that moment, he made the decision, 'I will not go back to school until my mother is safe.'

Pulling himself together, expecting his mother and his brother to be alone, he walked in the back door to find Larry MacAllister sitting at the kitchen table, waiting for him.

"Mr. Mac!"

"Harris," Larry called to him as he got up to hug him. They held each other for a long moment before Harris finally spoke, "I guess it's true."

"Yes, Harris. It is. I'm sorry."

"How are Mom and Jake?"

"They are in shock," Larry quietly answered.

"Somehow, I feel the need to be the strong one, Mr. Mac. I'm so thankful you're here. We'll need your help."

Sitting across the kitchen table from one another, Larry took one of Harris's big hands and held it in both of his to emphasize his words, "Harris. I will stay here tonight. If you need to talk, I will just be here."

"Thank you. Mr. Mac."

"I believe Jake may have gone upstairs. Your mother is in the parlor with Jen Walker."

"Okay," Harris nodded.

"Harris, if you like, tomorrow I will call the dean of the medical school and let him know what has happened."

"Please. That would help a lot."

"Of course. This is going to be a very difficult weekend."

"Thank you," Harris acknowledged, trying to concentrate through the deepening fog.

"Just one more thing, Harris. Knowing you as well as I do, I know you are committed to taking care of your mother and Jake, but please don't forget to take care of yourself. Allow yourself to feel what you need to feel. We are all here to support you."

– Chapter 39 –

The New Red Truck

October 9, 1995   Providence Police Storage Compound
Providence, Rhode Island

Sometime, amidst the fog of that first weekend after James's death, Jake and Harris made the decision to replace their father's demolished truck with a new one, the same model, with the same options, and same factory color of bright Clear-coat red. Harris and Jake sensed that something so obvious and personal, in their father's absence, might provide them with a comforting and tangible presence.

The Monday following James's death, the brothers drove with Kennedy Walcott to the Providence police storage facility. Unlocking the door in the chain link fence, Kennedy guided the men through the many rows of vehicles; stolen, abandoned, confiscated, or simply in various states of collision-induced disrepair. As they walked the main right of way, the bright afternoon sun produced a sharp glare from windshields, twisted chrome, and crumbled glass fragments densely mixed in with the gravel beneath their feet.

From time to time, as duty might require, Kennedy had occasion to visit the facility. The compound seemed yet another type of mortuary, another sad place to confront the dark cloud of disbelief, along with the painful glimpse of tragic reality when a loved one never returned home.

Although locating the red truck was their sole purpose, the search brought with it the price of frightful discovery. Their father's red truck, once whole and perfect, was now inconceivably broken and changed forever. Kennedy looked for the red vehicle, as well, but his main concern was the brothers' reactions when the vehicle suddenly appeared.

Harris methodically scanned the yard, from one side to the other. Jake walked beside his brother with head his down, watching his boots scuff through the dirt, glass, and boneyard debris. Harris pulled his brother off to the side as a city wrecker moved slowly past, hauling a demolished vehicle secured on a dolly, throwing up a cloud of dust into the sunlight.

Harris slowed his pace to study the incoming vehicle as it passed by. The collision had collapsed the driver's door, bending the frame of the sedan into the shape of a U. A portion of the door and A-pillar had been cut away to gain access to the trapped driver. A blood-smeared airbag draped over the contorted steering wheel, and a child's shoe lay on the dashboard with the child seat resting on its side, partially obscured beneath the glove box.

As the dust settled, the three young men came upon a step van, concealing James's red pickup behind it. Without a moment's hesitation, Jake rushed toward it. As he got close enough to view the inside the cab, he froze in his tracks, turned pale, and began to fall. Harris and Kennedy caught him, lowering him onto the gravel.

"Easy now, Jake," Kennedy reassured. "Take some slow deep breaths, man."

Harris positioned himself behind his brother, so that Jake could lean back against his legs. As Kennedy attended to Jake, Harris stared at his father's truck. The driver's door, facing him, was ajar. The passenger side of the vehicle was completely crushed, extending from the headlights to near the end of the bed. A portion of the driver's seatbelt had fallen outside, across the rocker panel, revealing a ragged end, cut by the emergency crew. He took in a deep breath to collect himself, inhaling the acrid odor of the mixture of fluids leaked onto the gravel from demolished vehicles. Placing his hands on his brother's shoulders, Harris leaned over Jake. "What do you think, Jake? Are you up for this? We don't have to stay."

"Yeah," Kennedy chimed in. "Both you guys can go if you need to. Just tell me what you want, and I'll get it for you."

"No. No," Jake responded, shaking his head, "I'm stayin'. We're going to do this. Just too much, too fast. But I've got to do this."

Patting the top of Jake's head, Kennedy replied, "OK, Jake, but just stay where you are a minute. Harris and I need to pry open the door. Harris, let me check it out first."

Concerned with the obvious presence of blood, Kennedy looked around the interior of the cab.

"Do you think you could help me? It's seems okay in here," he confirmed, looking over at Harris.

"Sure," Harris answered. "The morgue was worse than this."

The previous day, Harris and Kennedy had gone to the morgue at Roger Williams Hospital. Harris felt it necessary for a member of the family to close any question of uncertainty – if one should ever come up. Kennedy cautioned Harris that his father had sustained extensive head and chest trauma.

Harris stood dazed in front of his father's covered body. As a prompt, Kennedy asked Harris if there was any unique characteristic about his father's lower extremity. Harris recalled his father fracturing his right ankle a few years earlier, after an awkward fall and sliding into the boards at speed.

The morgue technician exposed James's legs below the knees. Harris placed his hand on his father's cold right leg, turning it inward, revealing the healed incision, along with a prominent screw at the distal head of the fibula. Harris bit down hard on his lower lip, closing his eyes as he nodded an affirmation of recognition.

******

And, now, a day later, Harris and Kennedy were yanking on the door, forcing it fully open. They found the driver's side was relatively intact. Jake stood and carefully made his way to where the other two were silently leaning into the cab. Realizing the brothers needed some time alone, Kennedy suggested, "I think I should give you guys a few minutes. I'll go grab some Coca-Colas and come back in a little while. That sound OK?"

"Yeah. Thanks, Kennedy. Sounds good," Harris answered breaking his silence.

The brothers stood together staring at the inside of the cab as they held their arms tightly around each other. Nothing more needed be said about where their father took his last breath.

When Kennedy returned, Jake and Harris were waiting on the opened tailgate with the bright afternoon sun in their faces. Sitting there, the brothers had sketched out a plan to replace the perfect parts on a 1996 truck with salvaged parts of their father's truck. They wanted to keep as much of their father's truck as they could, the tailgate, center console, knobs, and switches. Whatever could be salvaged, would be.

The mechanics of the collision had preserved the driver's bucket seat, so the three removed it to be stored in James's woodshop, covered over in a corner. In days to follow, Jake and Harris would alternate sitting in the seat whenever they retreated to the woodshop. They chose not to tell their mother of the new truck plan right away. When the 1996 vehicle arrived, the swaps would be made.

– Chapter 40 –

The Longest Week in a Long Time

Thursday, October 12, 1995   Providence, Rhode Island

During the days after James's death, Harris and Jake visited places where their father's presence still lingered. The brothers sat together on the players' bench in the empty hockey rink, their arms and chins resting on the dasher, staring at the fresh sheet of ice, remembering better days. At home, they walked around the woodshop amidst their dad's canoes, tools, and sawdust, immersed in an excruciating blur of mixed emotions.

Jen stayed close by, available to Marriette throughout the weekend, accompanying her on long walks, and responding as she could to her friend's needs. They would sit quietly together in the living room, sometimes conversing but often in silence. At one point, Jen asked Marriette if she might prefer to be alone, but Marriette wanted her nearby.

Filtering through the veil of fog, the brothers heard words of gentle guidance from Jen and Larry. "Take care of yourselves. Don't forget to eat. Sleep when you can. Tell each other what you need. Be angry safely. Cry when you want to. There is no timetable."

With Jen's absence during that first week, Denny's parents moved into the Walker home to help care for Scott and Scooter. With so much of Jen's attention focused on supporting Marriette, little time was left to communicate with Dennis. By mid-week Jen felt a sense of remoteness from her husband. She knew he could appear to be stoic or disinterested, but that often wasn't the case. Walking into his home office, Denny sat at his desk with his back to the door. As she approached, she expected him to turn around or at least acknowledge her presence.

"Denny, honey?"

Dennis had also been fully involved during the tragic week, caring for their family as well as helping with plans for the memorial service. When he turned around, it was evident that he was upset.

"Denny?"

Looking up at Jen with tears in his eyes, his voice quavered, "I miss him too."

Having overlooked her husband's cherished relationship with James, a wave of guilt washed over her.

"I can't believe he's gone," Denny sighed.

"Oh, Denny. I know. James was so special. I haven't been here for you, have I? I'm so sorry, honey," Jen confessed holding onto her husband.

"Den. I promise I'll be around more now. It's time to get our little family back together again. It won't be the same for a while, but I'm hoping the worst has passed."

"It will never be the same, Jenny."

"Yes, Den. It never is. I feel that, too."

– Chapter 41 –

Memorial at the Field House
Saturday, October 14, 1995
The Moses Brown School, Providence, Rhode Island

James Patrice Roy had been an educator and head hockey coach at the Moses Brown School for 15 years. From the time he and Marriette arrived in Rhode Island in 1979, he taught French and English courses, including preschool and kindergarten French.

As the result of early exposure, many of his students grew up understanding the French-Canadian hockey language. During games, strategic commands or phrases of encouragement were enthusiastically barked in French by Coach Roy. The players would then use the phrases on the ice to communicate with each other, resulting in a unique Canadien québécois atmosphere to their games.

Many of these players along with other Moses Brown students and alumni from the New England area, were expected to be in attendance at the memorial service.

James's death proved to be a significant loss for Dennis as well. The mentorship of his friend had contributed to Dennis learning a more confident way to carry himself.

Marriette requested that Jen and Dennis help oversee the memorial arrangements. The two moved forward to put together a plan. Dennis suggested that 'someone' might sing the Canadian national anthem. Without hesitation, Jen looked at her husband with her customary determination and answered, "Great idea, Denny. I will, of course." She learned the first verse of the anthem in French and planned to perform the second verse in English.

Dennis also suggested using the national flag of Québec as a centerpiece of the service. With the help of a friend, Dennis pieced together a 4' x 6' presentation flag with appliquéd fleur-de-lis of royal and white. Prior to the ceremony, the flag was hoisted to the top of the gym and placed between the American flag and the school colors.

Kennedy Walcott had kept in contact with the family, particularly Jake. When he learned of the flag ceremony, he also offered to help. Before attending the Rhode Island State Police Academy, Kennedy had served as a U.S. Marine Military Police. Familiar with flag protocol, Kennedy suggested that a colors presentation would add strength to the service. He asked members of the boys' hockey team, dressed in their uniform sweaters, to function as the color guard. Kennedy spent several evenings teaching the young hockey players the purpose of the tradition, instructing them in the ritual of lowering the flag from the rafters, receiving the flag, and folding it precisely for presentation.

On the evening before the memorial service, after the team had walked through the flag ceremony for the final time, Jen came to the rink to rehearse her songs. The team, along with the assistant hockey coach, Kennedy and Lawrence McAllister sat quietly together in the stands to watch her. The stadium was dark except for a few of the larger lights positioned over the wooden floor. Walking to the center of the basketball court in jeans and an oversized Moses Brown sweatshirt, Jen plugged in her Martin and flawlessly performed the Canadian anthem. After finishing the first verse of her next solo, she abruptly stopped as she began the second verse, stepping away from the microphone. Suddenly filled with painful memories of her own loss years ago, she turned her back to the stands and raised an arm in the air, signaling a pause. After a few moments she turned back, focusing her attention on the folded flag resting on Larry McAllister's lap. "Here we go, again," she said, starting over from the beginning, finishing strong.

******

Morning clouds filled the Providence sky on the day of the memorial service. A cold, hard rain had fallen throughout the night; a chill penetrated the autumn air. The sun was just beginning to break through the clouds as Jen left the house early with guitar case and microphone bag in hand, loading them into her Jeep. She removed the wet orange and yellow leaves from her windshield which had fallen from the maple at the edge of her driveway.

By 10 a.m. the Fieldhouse was nearly full. Many of Marriette's colleagues and other members of the academic community, including Pete Long, were in attendance. A player from the Detroit Red Wings, who had begun his hockey career at Moses Brown, was there as well. Morning sun shone through the skylights in the gymnasium ceiling, brightly illuminating the royal and white flag hanging above the crowd.

Following his eulogy, Larry MacAllister invited all attendees to come down from the bleachers to form a circle under the flag. The maple floor of the Fieldhouse slowly filled with friends and family, standing shoulder to shoulder. Harris and Jake positioned themselves on each side of their mother with their arms firmly wrapped around her waist. Her skin pale and smoky blue eyes dulled, Marriette stood tall and stoic, holding tightly onto her sons.

Standing directly across from Marriette, Jen performed the first verse of the Canadian national anthem in French. Many of the French-speaking friends joined in spontaneously. Dozens more joined in for the English verse. Marriette's father, Gil, and Patrice, James's father, stood arm in arm, singing and weeping.

When the anthem was over, Harris stepped to the center of the circle to offer his words of endearment.

"Dad was our mother's perfect partner – and our constant loving mentor and father. He provided love and support to many of you here today – and to the Moses Brown School community.

"In his absence, what we will miss ... we will never know ... but what he gave to us, is that which we will never forget. Without him, we would not be the people we are today. Without him, we will never be the same."

With Marriette and Jake at his side, Harris thanked all those in attendance for their presence and kind words. The ceremonial flag of Québec was lowered, folded by the young hockey players, and presented to Marriette by the captain of the team. Jen moved up to the microphone again to close the service, singing Rodney Crowell's "'Til I Gain Control Again".

"Just like the sun over the mountain top..."

At the end of the song, Jen quietly said into the microphone, "Thank you, James." Then, in a voice, so soft and kind, she whispered, "I love you, 'M'."

– Chapter 42 –

Among the Ancestors
Saturday, October 21, 1995
Brown University, Providence, Rhode Island

After leaving the University pool, Jen stopped at a neighborhood sandwich shop to pick up a light breakfast before heading to her office. The morning air was cold and damp with wet leaves covering the sidewalks from the wind and rain of the evening before. She ran down the steps into the basement of the psychology building, past Marriette's office, to her own office and stopped at her door to remove her keys from her backpack.

The unexpected echo of footsteps approaching down the dark hallway captured Jen's attention. She looked up to see Marriette emerge out of the shadows, looking thinner than usual. It had been two weeks since James's death.

"Marriette!" Jen called out.

With a somewhat slow affect, Marriette answered, "Good morning, Jen. I just stepped out for a walk. I called your house earlier and spoke with Dennis. He said you would be coming to the office after your swim. I was hoping we might talk."

"Of course," Jen replied. With backpack still in hand, she gave Marriette a one-armed hug and kiss on her cheek, noting Marriette's face gaunt from exhaustion. Jen had been coaxing her to eat and get more sleep, but it remained a struggle.

Entering Jen's office, Marriette immediately dropped onto the couch, took off her shoes, and put her feet up on the coffee table. After storing her backpack, Jen cleared a place on the desktop.

Using a throw pillow to re-position herself on her side, Marriette looked over at the white bag on Jen's desk.

"Jen, dear. I know that must be your breakfast. Please go ahead and eat. We can still talk, yes?"

"Yes, of course, Marriette."

Removing the breakfast sandwich from her bag, she placed it next to a glass of water that she had just poured from the dispenser under the window.

Resting her chin on her forearm, she glanced thoughtfully over at Marriette, curled up on the couch.

"Marriette. Have you had anything other than a cup of coffee this morning?"

"Not yet."

"May I please share this with you?"

Marriette flashed a disinterested look.

"English muffin, egg, a little Cheddar, Canadian bacon . . . Come on. I can only imagine how you must feel, but you just have to get some good stuff down . . . a little bit at a time. You're losing weight."

Jen removed a knife from the top desk drawer and cut the sandwich into quarters. She carried it over to the coffee table and sat down next to Marriette, putting an arm around her shoulder.

"Come on. Little bit at a time. Then we'll talk if you want. Here's some orange juice, too. Okay?"

"Okay," Marriette answered, crying softly, ignoring her tears. After she had finished the first quarter of the sandwich, Jen demonstrably pushed another quarter from the open wrapper in her direction.

"Let's try something, Marriette. You know this approach. This is what we do every day, right? Let's try it."

Marriette looked up with sad blue eyes, waiting for her suggestion. Jen pulled a piece of Kleenex from the box on the end table and gently dabbed the tears on Marriette's cheeks.

"There, Marriette. Now, close your eyes for a moment. I will, too . . . and let's imagine that James is here with us on the couch."

Marriette momentarily took in a quick breath in response to the suggestion.

"What might James say to you, knowing you're not sleeping well, knowing you're not eating. James will always be a part of your life. Isn't that true, Marriette? James is among the Ancestors now. Isn't that a beautiful concept familiar to you? Remember? You told me that about your tribal family."

"Yes, James is with the Ancestors. I will try to keep him close," Marriette sighed.

"That should be of some comfort to you," Jen added.

"Yes, my dear," Marriette nodded. "It will be . . . I'm trying to get there."

****

Earlier in the week, Marriette confided to Jen she had experienced a panic attack in the middle of the night. She awoke from a fitful sleep to the reality again that James was not there. He wasn't just off on another overnight trip with the hockey team. He would not be returning.

Marriette had gone to bed that night wearing one of James's dress shirts. She arranged the pillows on their bed, adding more from the guest bedroom to simulate James's presence against her back. Awake in the dark, she realized she could no longer detect his scent on the pillow she held close to her face. She lay there alone and afraid of the future.

It then occurred to her that James's T-shirts might still be in the laundry unwashed. She wondered if Jen or one of the boys had already washed the clothes. Marriette sat straight up and turned on the light next to her. Running out into the hallway, she hurried down the stairs through the parlor, the kitchen, and into the laundry room. She switched on the single hanging light, which cast a yellow hue on both white appliances and on the line of coats and jackets that hung along a series of hooks.

The room was the smallest in the house and nothing much had changed since the family moved into the Victorian in 1979. Boots and shoes were arranged in a row against the mopboard under the coats – most of them James's. The washer and dryer stood next to each other along the opposite wall under two ornate windows. A braided oval rug covered most of the polished fir floor.

Marriette momentarily hesitated in the doorway, then opened the wicker hamper, emptying its contents onto the rug. She checked inside the washing machine but found it empty.

Getting down on her hands and knees, Marriette desperately combed through the pile of clothes to be washed, separating out four of James's undershirts. Gathering them together in her hands, she buried her face into them, crying out in anguish. Her panicked vocalizations, traveled throughout the house, waking Jake and Harris.

Hearing their mother's cries, the brothers bolted downstairs to discover Marriette kneeling on the floor amidst the pile of family laundry, trembling. Looking up at the boys in desperation, her speech muffled by the T-shirts held to her face, she sobbed, "Dad's T-shirts. I need them with me. I can't tell Dad's pillow from mine anymore! Je ne peux pas dormir sans lui!" (I can't sleep without him!)

The boys knelt down on the rug and held their mother in their arms. Finding her so vulnerable, Jake began sobbing, too. Sensing his mother and

Jake's feelings of fear and abandonment, Harris would not allow himself an emotional outpouring. He needed to anchor his family with calmness and could hear his father's voice reminding him to "Lead the way, Harris . . . sometimes you have to lead the way."

The three of them settled on the rug together, leaning against the wall enveloped in the large shadow cast by James's coats hanging overhead. Harris and James continued to hold Marriette between them, resting their heads against their mother who still clutched her husband's undershirts to her chest. After a short while, she and Jake fell asleep.

Harris stayed awake, staring blankly into the dulled yellow light reflected from the enameled washer and dryer at his feet. Reaching up, he pulled down two of his father's coats, spreading them across the three of them. Eventually, Harris fell asleep, quietly weeping to himself. The family remained huddled together until dawn's early light poured in through the stained-glass windows above them.

****

Jen turned again toward Marriette. "What are you feeling now?" she asked.

"Sometimes it's hard to understand enough of what I'm feeling to express it. Right now, I feel so removed from what I know as a professional. I'm not much help to myself."

During the previous weeks, Marriette had repeatedly recounted to Jen her recollections of the afternoon of October 7th. The process was as predictable as was her need to tell it. She sought to recall her last conversation with James, trying to remember if she had said that she loved him before he left. She didn't kiss him goodbye as he was only going out for a short while. She was contemplating dinner. Would they go out or stay at home? Jake was due to arrive. There weren't enough ingredients in the refrigerator to make a salad. She would have to run out to the store. James and she were planning to go out Saturday night. She couldn't recall where. They had made love the previous weekend. That was the last time. She remembered watching the red truck back out of the driveway. Then, there was the state police car.

Marriette managed to eat a second, then a third piece of the sandwich. She began weeping again.

"I'm so sorry, Jen. I'm so tired. I can't sleep without feeling James next to me. We have forever fallen asleep lying against each other . . . me wrapped up in his arms . . . my Jamie."

As Jen continued to comfort her, she wondered if Marriette was taking her sleep medication. The thought also crossed her mind that she and Dennis never slept that closely. In fact, they rarely touched while sleeping.

"Are you taking the meds that Phil prescribed for you?" Jen inquired.

"No, I turned them down. I didn't think it was necessary," Marriette answered, looking away.

"Marriette, what would James want you to do? Ask him that. You're losing weight. You're exhausted. What is he saying to you, Marriette?"

Marriette closed her eyes and blew out a deep breath.

"He's saying . . . it would hurt him if I didn't take care of myself. It's just so hard, Jenny."

"Yes, 'M', it is . . . very, very hard."

Jen stood up and arranged a pillow under Marriette's head, as she laid back on the couch.

With a loving smile, Jen looked down again at her, "Marriette, just rest a bit. Keep James close. I'll be right here at my desk."

"Yes, Jenny," Marriette murmured, as she fell into a deep sleep. Jen sat back down at her desk and finished the remaining quarter sandwich while watching Marriette sleep. She got up again and unfolded the quilt draped over the back of the couch and covered her.

As Marriette slept soundly, Jen went out into the corridor and paged Phil Pontbriande, a university staff psychiatrist. He quickly returned her call. Jen then updated the psychiatrist on Marriette's current status, noting her concerns. She explained that Marriette was asleep on the couch in her office. Jen believed their colleague might now be willing to try a short-term medication.

Knowing Marriette well, Dr. Pontbriande was not surprised at Jen's assessment. After making rounds at the hospital, he said he planned to slip a script for Marriette under Jen's office door.

As the days went on, Marriette and Jen continued to spend regular time together, providing Marriette with opportunities to tell stories of her life with James again and again. Jen would come to know James better through those stories, as well as learn so much more about her friend and mentor.

The therapeutic techniques of their profession, many of which Marriette herself had researched, developed, and published, were put into practice. But ultimately, it was the ancient concept of 'Ancestral presence' that Marriette had experienced firsthand in Africa, that permitted James to drift away more naturally, completing the transition from physical to spiritual presence.

– Chapter 43 –

A Common Bond

Saturday, February 24, 1996
Brown University, Providence, Rhode Island

Marriette found herself gripped in an agitated mood throughout most of the day. Although it was late in the evening, she felt compelled to call Jen. Marriette recognized there would be days like these. They had surfaced before and would come again. No matter what she did to distract herself, it felt like a looming heaviness, and she was disappointed with her inability to shake herself free. Earlier in the day, she had had a stormy phone conversation with Jake, and immediately called him back to apologize. Jake understood, explaining that he too felt that way more often than not.

As a professional, Marriette knew angry times would be predictable. But today she felt that her anger had ambushed her. Although apologetic because of the late hour, Marriette was unable to disguise the agitation in her tone of voice.

After calming her, Jen stated she would be over in a few minutes.

"But it's so late and so cold outside, Jen," Marriette hesitated.

"Doesn't make any difference. I have some ideas," Jen insisted. "Bundle up. We're going over to the Student Union."

"What? Really? Okay. I'll get ready," Marriette agreed, second guessing her decision to have called Jen on this late winter night.

Jen hung up, went into her bedroom, and pulled her jeans on over her flannel pajamas. After giving Dennis a brief explanation, she trudged out the back door, down the snowy path to the garage.

When Jen reached her friend's house and steered to the curb, Marriette was already walking down the driveway. As she got into the Jeep, Jen could see her inquisitive expression. "I hope what I have in mind will help, Marriette. It's another step."

"Okay," Marriette replied, holding her gloved hands in front of the hot air vent on the dashboard. "It's so late, Jen. I shouldn't have called you. I'm sorry. These moods!"

"It's okay. Really it is. This is important."

As Jen drove the rough and bumpy road of accumulated unplowed ice, she explained to Marriette, "We're going over to the practice rooms where I go to play the piano and sing. You can make all the noise you want in there and no one will ever hear you."

Marriette glanced over, surprised and skeptical. Jen read her look and flashed an understanding smile.

"I realize this might not be the approach you would take, but I'm encouraging you to revisit those feelings of anger today. Let your emotions spill out. Cry, scream . . . whatever, until you're through. It worked for me, Marriette."

Marriette was uncomfortable with the idea, but politely agreed to go along with Jen's suggestion.

The women entered through the front door of the Student Union and walked down the steps to the practice room area which contained a spacious common room with comfy furniture. A television mounted on a column was still on, emitting only a scratchy hum with bright flickering lines moving across the screen. Opening a door to one of the rooms, Jen explained, "I'll be right here waiting for you, Marriette. I know . . . this probably isn't for you . . . but at any rate, please give it some thought. Give it a try."

Marriette glanced back over her shoulder at Jen, as she reluctantly entered the room. She mouthed the words, "Thank you," as she fastened the door behind her, appreciating what Jen was trying to do, and finding her effort endearing. Shaking her head while simultaneously biting her lower lip, Jen reconsidered her spontaneous late-night notion as probable folly.

A security guard, making his rounds, approached Jen and asked why she was in the building so late. Standing there in her knitted hat with winter coat open, flowered flannel pajama top down to her knees, jeans, and wet, unfastened snow boots, she presented her Brown University Faculty ID, informing the guard that she was a therapist with a grieving patient in one of the practice rooms. Perplexed, he nodded, shrugging his shoulders, and proceeded on his rounds. Feeling the exhaustion of the late hour, Jen lay down on one of the couches and promptly fell asleep.

When Marriette exited the practice room only a few minutes later, she found Jen fast asleep. Sitting on the edge of the couch beside her, she recalled how Jen had so faithfully been at her side for the last five months. For a brief moment she imagined her as her daughter. As Marriette watched Jen sleep she affectionately stroked her hair to awaken her. Jen slowly opened her eyes, surprised that she had fallen asleep.

"Thank you, Jenny," Marriette spoke lovingly. "You are so good to me. However, I wasn't able to do much screaming. It's just not a place that feels comfortable to me."

"Yes, of course. I understand," Jen replied, yawning and rubbing her eyes.

Smiling, Marriette quickly added, "I did take some time to think about the process, though. Your point is well taken, my dear. It's now in my toolbox, if you will."

"It was just an idea," Jen acknowledged, smiling back, trying to conceal another yawn. "I'm sorry. I fell asleep."

With a deep sigh, Marriette looked down again at her. "Yes. You've been doing a lot, Jenny. It's time we both get some sleep."

The women walked out into the frigid night air to the parking lot. It was shortly after 11 p.m. when they got back into Jen's Wrangler. A bright winter moon shone intermittently in the partly cloudy sky, casting long purple shadows over the snow- covered campus.

On the drive back to Marriette's house, Jen seemed uncharacteristically quiet, prompting Marriette to say something.

"Are you all right, Jenny?"

A short period of silence ensued before Jen answered.

"Marriette, I've been wanting to share something with you for weeks now. I honestly didn't know if tonight would be the right time, but maybe it is."

Again, Jen hesitated.

"What is it, dear?" Marriette gently nudged.

"Well, when we first met, I mentioned to you that my mother died when I was in high school. I didn't elaborate at the time."

Anticipating a deeply personal revelation, Marriette turned toward Jen's darkened face, briefly visible only as the Jeep passed beneath a street lamp.

"Late in my senior year … May of '82 … my mother suddenly became ill. She had experienced headaches for only a couple of days that we were aware of. She suffered a brain hemorrhage and died while my father was at work and I was at school … I found her lifeless body on the kitchen floor when I returned home from school that afternoon. My mother must have been trying to call for help. The phone receiver was on the floor next to her. She was ashen."

"Oh, Jen!" Marriette gasped in horror at such a discovery.

"Marriette, my mom was the most important person in my life. We were a set. I refused to allow myself to grieve. I pushed those feelings away with distraction, rather than trying to deal with them. At that time, I didn't know how to do that."

"Oh, Jenny!" Marriette turned in her seat, leaning closer to her.

"The first few years after her death, I spent wrapped in a fog. I was at Penn. I dealt with my anguish by trying to remain focused on my studies and swimming. At times, I thought I had my feelings under control, but they weren't at all. My approach only served to delay recovery. Recurring nightmares diminished, but never went away. I didn't recognize that my grief was an undercurrent for years. I've never told this story to anyone."

"What about your dad, Jen?"

"My father kept his suffering to himself, went into a shell, and disappeared into his music. He tried his best to comfort me, but just couldn't. A year later, Dad sold our house and moved back to Nashville. I avoided music altogether for a long time. Before the day I found my mom, I had planned to be a musician, and a performer. I wanted to make it my career. That notion vanished in an instant. Penn was only supposed to be my backup."

"You've never told me any of this, Jen. Your singing at the memorial service came as a total surprise."

Marriette focused her full attention now on Jen as the Jeep bumped and creaked along the frozen road. For the first time she was hearing the story behind Jen's path to the present.

"It sounds as though you might have been all alone in this, Jenny?"

"Fortunately, that wasn't the case. My support came from the family next door, the Plimptons. Our families had been very close. Their children became my siblings. The father, Bill, was a huge part of my life from the day they moved in. I practically lived at the Plimpton home.

"It was Mom and Bill who were my emotional guides throughout childhood. Bill became like my other dad. He understood me completely. He knew when to encourage me, when to push me ahead ... and when to rein me in. He helped me to channel my competitiveness into basketball, then swimming. He was my coach in many ways, beyond sports. A lot can be learned about life if you have a good coach. Bill was the one who supported me through the initial weeks following my mom's death, taking care of me as he always had."

"How do you feel about your dad, Jen?" Marriette inquired further.

"I love my dad. He's a kind and gentle person … but very different from Bill. Dad was a great provider and taught me just as much about playing music as Mom did … a solid source of encouragement, but Mom was the lead parent. I always wanted to be close to her.

"I guess Dad's male culture influenced him to keep his grief private. However he handled Mom's death, he did it his own way. He soon began writing country and western songs, one after the other. Unless you're familiar with that genre, you'd probably not be familiar with him. Harlan Taylor has written quite a few famous songs, for sure … but he keeps to himself … never performs in public. Guess that's where his feelings reside. We've talked in recent years about how we each handled our grief, and it has been healing for both of us. All that seems to be missing now is the music connection. I think that will come someday … don't know when, but someday."

Marriette gently held onto Jen's shoulder as Jen slowly drove along the uneven pavement, the tires crunching through the icy surface. The streets were empty on the clear and quiet night. Tiny crystals of coastal effect snow glistened in the path of the headlights.

"I'm sorry Marriette. I'm feeling guilty that I dragged you out here so late in this wicked cold. I reacted too quickly without thinking it through. Now we're out here in the cold and I'm talking about me! I'm so sorry."

"Oh, Jenny, you needn't be. Please, I feel something positive from our little excursion tonight. Sharing your story with me has found its time. And, tell me, Jenny, tell me something about your experience in the practice room and how it seemed to help you."

"Yes, the experience sure surprised me, 'M'. When Denny and I moved to Rhode Island, I began to frequent the practice rooms at the University. I wanted to bring music back into my life. A couple of years earlier, my father sent me some CDs he had converted from reel-to-reel and cassette recordings. Recordings that we had made in our studio, along with performances at clubs and concerts. Among the CDs was one of my mother and me singing a Kate Wolf song in our studio in Pennsylvania. I hadn't heard my mother's voice since her death. Feeling brave one evening, I decided to run it through the sound system in the practice room. Closing my eyes, I listened to our voices together, imagining her there in the room with me.

"It was just so beautiful that I began to cry. I then lost all control and started screaming and yelling and cursing. I was so fucking angry. I sat down on

the floor in the corner next to the piano and cried until I was exhausted."
Jen pulled the stocking cap off her head and flung it onto the dashboard.

"Later, I felt some relief. Relief? I don't know. Something like that. Sometimes,
I think some of those bad dreams, intrusive thoughts ... and such ... is our
brain reminding us of unfinished business that still needs to be attended to."

"I do think you're right, dear."

Tilting her head, Jen looked at Marriette. "I had a lot of unfinished business.
For me, it was a way to begin to heal. I continued to listen to the recordings
... and listen again ... and again, until it couldn't kill me anymore. That's
when I began to see it differently, I could embrace them. Now, I cherish
listening to my mother's voice. Those recordings are my treasures. It's all
I have 'M'."

Tears were now running down Jen's cheeks, glistening under the light of the
street lamps.

"You really haven't confided this to anyone before, have you, dear?"

"No, 'M'. Can you believe it? I really haven't."

"Oh, my, Jenny."

Staring out on the snowy landscape, Jen wiped condensation off the windshield with the back of her hand.

"It took me a long time to adjust to the new life I was living ... to find a new
wholeness. I had lost such a huge piece. My old life, which seemed so
permanent back then ... was ... gone!"

As Jen finished her last sentence, she bit down on the fingertip of her red
leather glove. She was tired, and the late-night outpouring had taken its
toll. She began to cry and pulled over to the side of the road, shutting off
the engine. She turned toward Marriette in the quiet of the Jeep cabin.

"Remember this, 'M'," she cried out, "You're not supposed to drive if you
start crying. It's dangerous!"

Gripping the steering wheel, she pressed her forehead against it, breaking
into a full sob as Marriette responded in kind. Reaching for Jen, they held
each other and wept.

– Chapter 44 –

My First Marriage

Saturday, March 9, 1996
Prospect St., Providence, Rhode Island

Snow fell, blanketing the evergreens along the far end of the driveway as Marriette pondered the day. Earlier that week, she awoke with the notion that she wanted to tell her African story to Jen.

Other than her old friend Pete, James had been the only other person to hear the entire story. Considering all that had transpired recently, along with the growing depth of their friendship, Marriette was ready to confide her secret.

It was nearly 10 a.m. as Marriette peered out the front windows, anticipating Jen's arrival. A car drove past the house in silence, traveling over several inches of new unplowed snow. Looking down the sidewalk to her right, she spotted a lone figure approaching, indistinct at first in the falling snow. She soon realized it was Jen. Marriette went to the back kitchen door to greet her.

"Good morning, Jenny. The snow is accumulating quickly!"

"Good morning 'M'. Yes, it is. I decided to walk. I needed some fresh air."

"Come in, dear."

Jen shook the snow from her hat and coat and left them on the porch divan next to her boots. She gave Marriette a hug.

"It's so pretty out there this morning. No wind. Dennis and the kids bundled up and are heading over to Moses Brown to go sledding."

"Know it well," Marriette nodded. "That's where our boys used to sled."

"They had to stop at Benny's hardware first. Scooter's been causing such a fuss over how Scotty's sled is faster than hers. He offered to trade, but Scoot was having none of that. She wants her own fast sled, faster than Scott's!"

"That Scooter is certainly coming into her own, isn't she!"

"Yeah. Look out world!" Jen acknowledged in agreement.

Marriette and Jen moved to the living room, where Jen sat in a large comfy chair, her legs tucked beneath her. Marriette lit the flame in the gas fireplace, adding an extra layer of warmth to the already cozy living room.

As Jen settled into her chair, she glanced over at the family photographs on the table beside her. One was of Marriette, James and the boys, taken on the front steps of their home. Others depicted life in this home as well as their first home in Vermont. From her chair she had a clear view of the steadily falling snow on Prospect Street through the large panes of the Victorian era windows.

"Jenny," Marriette began, interrupting Jen's gaze out the windows, "do you remember our very first meeting when you inquired about how I initially developed my treatment approach?"

"Yes, I do . . . I felt I'd unintentionally gotten too personal . . . especially considering it was our first meeting."

"Your question, Jen, was perfectly reasonable, but it took me by surprise. I wasn't ready to discuss it then, but I would like the opportunity to do so now."

With rapt attention, Jen turned toward Marriette, "I would love to hear about it, 'M'."

"Well, in 1971, I was 28 and scheduled to begin my MS/PhD program at McGill University. I somewhat impulsively postponed the program for two years, deciding instead to join a group from the anthropology department that was studying isolated primitive tribes in West Africa. Going to a strange new land intrigued me. The program had been sending graduate students to study this particular culture since before World War II. It was an opportunity to do something different. So, I lived in West Africa during my academic years of 1971 and 1972. I met James a few weeks after returning."

"How different," Jen remarked.

"Yes, I surprised even myself with the decision. The tribes were semi nomadic, living in northern Ghana. The tribe I resided with numbered about 70. They had already been substantially affected by outside culture by the year 1971. But back in 1940, when the program started, they were relatively isolated.

"I had a double undergraduate major . . . psychology and pharmacology. My plan was to focus on primitive medicine and the botanical sources of pharmaceuticals. I was interested in studying how this culture approached their medical needs with the use of endemic plants. When I arrived, there was another student from McGill living with this tribe. He stayed an additional year before leaving to return home."

"Wow! I'm not sure I could've done such an adventure," Jen exclaimed.

"Looking back, I realize I was taking quite a chance. But the University had sponsored the program for years without incident. Faculty supervisors in the region would check in regularly.

"It was also understood that the program was scheduled to end in the near future. My thesis was only approved because its premise did not depend upon how much of the tribal culture had changed due to civilization's influences – which was somewhat ironic, given the presence of the McGill students.

"Most of my first year I felt an obvious outsider, but I was able to learn their language because many of the tribe's members already spoke serviceable English and French. Their ability to learn those languages was the direct result of having been exposed, as infants and children, to the omnipresent graduate students.

"One of the young men in the tribe, just a few years older than I, was fluent in both languages. I had heard about him prior to my arrival. He had a reputation for valuing the presence of new graduate students, hoping, if not expecting, each would arrive with new books and other useful information.

"His name was Havra. He is a central figure in the story I'm about to tell you. Although his tribe had no designated chief, so to speak, Havra was generally thought of as the leader in his community. Despite learning much from him and a few of the others, I felt a frustration of not being able to get closer to the rest of the community. I needed to do something to change this. At the end of the first year, the other student returned to Montreal, leaving me alone with the tribe."

"Alone. Really," Jen mused, getting up from the chair, and taking a pillow to lie down in front of the fire. Marriette joined her, sitting down on the red and golden Heriz rug, leaning up against the front of the couch.

"One morning, before leaving my tent, I decided to dress more in keeping with the other female members of the tribe. So, I removed my typical tan safari shirt and gathered my long brown hair into a single braid which fell just below my shoulder blades. I walked over to the central gathering area where several of the women had already congregated, working and tending to the children.

"That morning, the community began to open up to me. The men had already left for the day to tend the herds. Initially, the women looked puzzled, curious about my new appearance. They had always been friendly, but as in the way one would be to an outsider. I believe my new body language and expression signaled my genuine desire to become more a part of their community.

"Tiesha, a young woman around my age, moved up closer to me. I can still picture her big smile. Placing both of her hands on my shoulders, she greeted me by name. She then circled around and stopped at my naked back, examining my braid with her long fingers. Touching it, she commented how soft it felt compared to hers. She then continued around to my front, placing her hands on my breasts and squeezing them playfully. Many of the other women my age had already experienced multiple pregnancies. I guess they were amazed that someone our age still had round breasts that defied gravity!"

"Oh, Marriette. That scene conjures up some very interesting images!"

"Oh, I know it sounds daring and way out of character for me now, but it really made sense at the time… circumstantial.

"One of the elder women stepped up with an earthen bowl. Traditionally, these people covered themselves with a thin mixture of plant oil and goat butterfat, mixed together into a fine orange clay. The combination protected their skin from dryness, heat, and insects. Every few days when the tribal members traveled to the river, or if it were the rainy season, they would wash the mixture off and then reapply it.

"The woman approached me and carefully smeared some of the mixture on my chest. I stood in amazement as several of the other women joined in to cover my upper body with the protective balm. It was exactly what my very white French Canadienne skin needed.

"The women then peered at my khaki shorts and asked if I wanted to wear the traditional wrapped goatskin skirt. I nodded in consent as I undid my belt buckle to remove my shorts. The women were curious about my underwear, as though the article of clothing seemed out of place and unnecessary. Off it came. They presented me with a goat skin skirt, which fastened around my waist with leather ties. I still have it. I'll show it to you sometime, if you'd like."

"Really? Wow! Of course I want to see it!"

"When the women finished painting the parts of my body that would be exposed to sun, they sat me down, while Tiesha, one of the tribal artisans, fashioned beads to adorn my braid as other women and children began to gather around, delighted with my transformation."

"And how did things go after that, Marriette?"

"Very well, Jen. For the next year or so, I continued that same mode of dress and made every effort to be as much like the tribe as I could – while still maintaining my position as an academic observer. I made sure I was seen going into my tent, getting out my papers, and writing."

"Curious. How did the male members of the tribe react?"

"Well, this changed my relationship in a more positive manner with several of the male members. I continued to participate in all the activities of the women, but it also improved my relationship with the medicine man, Ava, who gave me the opportunity to observe how he practiced his craft. I began to learn how herbal medicines were prepared and used to treat medical or psychological conditions.

"I also grew closer to the young tribal leader, Havra. He was a tall and handsome man. He had a wife, Seeba, who had been chosen for him at a young age by the elders. According to McGill records, Havra was 31 at the time. He and Seeba had one son, Tave, who was 16."

Marriette rose from the rug, walked over to the bookcase and picked up a framed picture. Handing it to Jen, she pointed to Havra and his wife. Marriette was also in the photo.

"Oh, look at you. Such an unusual portrait. You look so beautiful. What a treasure this is! You have a T-shirt on?"

"Yes, I knew a department advisor would soon be arriving. Ha! Removed it after he left."

"That's so funny," Jen chuckled, as she handed the picture back to her as Marriette.

"As I mentioned earlier, Havra spoke English and French fluently. He was always eager to learn from the McGill students and had many questions for me as well.

"It soon became clear that Havra was not the civilization-free tribal member that the anthropologists had once sought to study. The tribe was very quickly changing. Early on, I sensed that a part of Havra would like a chance to escape. I began to understand why McGill planned to end the program."

"Interesting. Caught in between. An anachronism," Jen observed.

"Yes. I agree," Marriette nodded, sitting cross-legged, readjusting the clasp in her hair.

"During the day, the home camp was almost entirely occupied by the women. Most of the men were away from sunrise to sunset –except for elderly men and some of the younger boys who stayed back to perform necessary duties. Males were recognized as men after their initiation at puberty. For the women, this milestone was achieved upon marriage. I became close with several of the younger women. They shielded me from the men who found me appealing, as I was now not just a white girl from Canada. However, there was never, even remotely, a threat. I always felt safe.

The women helped each other with chores and also groomed one another. It wasn't uncommon for one to attend to my hair or want to look at my white teeth or touch my perky breasts to compare theirs with mine."

"Really! As if to say, 'Oh, mine used to be like that'," Jen giggled, putting her hands up to her breasts, mimicking the tribal curiosity.

Amused, Marriette added with a wink, "Occasionally, one of the men would attempt to do the same, literally checking me out to see if I might be good marriage material. In fact, an interesting thing happened during that last year in Africa. One day, while braiding my hair and replacing some of the ornamental beads, Seeba nonchalantly informed me that Havra wished to have me as his other wife.

"The culture was polygamist. Havra was unusual in that he had only one wife.

"According to custom, it was Seeba's role to deliver the news. As you can imagine, I was completely caught off guard, but tried not to show it. I had become very sensitive to the tribal culture, especially now that I was so much more a part of their daily lives. When I reminded Seeba I would be departing later in the year, she responded that Havra was aware of it, and confirmed it did not change his request."

"Oh, my goodness, Marriette!" Jen exclaimed. "It seems like you might've gotten in over your head!"

"At the time it didn't feel that way. I had a reasonable understanding of many of the tribal rituals, including the marriage rituals. I had attended several weddings and was invited to dance with the unmarried women and wear the traditional leather headpiece, signifying my eligibility for marriage.

"Jen, I believed it to be a great opportunity to learn and experience things none of the other graduate students had. It worked out just fine, but bear in mind, these were the decisions of a much younger, more adventurous, me."

Completely absorbed in Marriette's story, Jen interjected, "This is all so fascinating, 'M'," as she moved back to the chair, draping her long legs over one of the arms.

Marriette continued, "I spoke to Havra about the, I mean, our marriage after giving a tentative 'yes' to Seeba. I felt it necessary to inform him of my non-virginal status, and I explained how our culture was different from his in that regard. He considered it, but it didn't change his mind.

"After my acceptance of the proposal, a series of tribal events commenced, which included various public celebrations and prenuptial rituals. The latter was of some concern to me, as I wanted to make sure there would be no disfiguring body changes. Again, I had developed trust, particularly with Seeba. I asked many questions, and was provided with considerable detail regarding marriage preparation, and what a bride's responsibilities were. She understood, as did the other core group of women, that I still remained a visitor studying their culture.

"Several of the women adorned me with jewelry in my new status. They were clearly delighted with the idea of a foreigner, now an accepted friend, becoming part of the tribe even though it was of an honorary status.

"With the marriage ceremony just a week away, Seeba sought me out to explain the traditional tattooing ritual to be performed by the women closest to me."

"Tattooing? No one said anything about tattooing!" Jen quipped, now totally engrossed in the story.

"That's exactly what I thought. Again, I had many questions. She explained that it would be appropriate if I had the traditional tribal tattoo placed strategically where Havra could view it prior to consummating the marriage."

"Geez, 'M'!"

"The tattoo depicted a bird of prey commonly observed in their surroundings. It also happened to be Havra's personal tattoo. He wore one on the side of his neck; it was a combination of tattoo and keloid scar. Another was located at the base of his penis. These particular tattoos were commonly worn by tribal couples representing their traditional mark of responsibility and ownership.

"Seeba explained the entire ritual to me. I felt somewhat anxious but was comfortable enough to proceed. I hadn't actually witnessed the ritual being performed. The first one would be my very own. The tribe had become my new family, so far from home. In a sense, my thesis research, while still relevant, now become secondary to the experience of living the tribal life."

"This is utterly amazing, Marriette!" Jen exclaimed, breathless.

"Early one morning, a few days before the wedding, Seeba and several other female relatives escorted me to a hut which was prepared especially for the occasion. One of the women had arrived earlier and created an incense fire, leaving the interior smelling of light smoky floral scents. Blankets and softened goatskins were stacked up on the floor, creating a soft palette.

"Seeba instructed me to remove my tribal skirt and lie down on the stack of goatskins. My tribal sisters, now positioned on their knees, encircled me. They began to sing and chant a distinct tribal song through each part of the ceremony. The intention was to welcome me as a new bride and to celebrate the time when a girl becomes a woman.

"Seeba gently cradled my head between her knees on a soft goatskin pillow. I must admit, my heart was beating rapidly. Scented butterfat oil was rubbed above my waist, on my arms, chest and shoulders. Two of the other women provided the same attention to my legs. I was never restrained at any time, only comforted."

Jen now sat on the edge of her chair. "Marriette. Do you have this recorded somewhere?"

"Yes. I kept a diary during my time there and added to it later. Early on, when I shared this story with James, he questioned whether interjecting myself into tribal life in such intimate ways might be considered inappropriate by anthropology standards. I had to agree. We decided to keep the story to ourselves. I still consider my intimate participation in the tribe as private . . . a young person's adventure."

"What an adventure!"

"I was informed earlier that the tattoo would be very small and placed on the smooth skin of my lower abdomen, a few inches above my vagina. A cleansing ritual of the inguinal area ensued, using the warmed butterfat oil.

"Tiesha, one of the tribal tattoo specialists, was responsible for performing this part of the ceremony. She moved my legs apart, bending up my knees. Two of the other women held my legs gently, but securely, while continuing to anoint them. Tiesha rubbed the oil on my lower abdomen and inner thighs, concentrating on softening the pubic hair around the area where the tattoo would be placed.

"I wasn't quite sure how to react. The touching was both anxiety provoking, yet somewhat pleasurable at the same time. I wanted to respond in a respectable way, knowing I was receiving a rare honor. Tiesha carefully shaved the well lubricated skin creating a clearing in the hair. The women gently holding me, chanted softly in unison, to help me relax into the ritual.

"I remember maintaining my focus on a dusty shaft of morning sunlight streaming in through a small opening in the hut roof, shining directly onto my prepared skin. In that dim light, I could see some of what was transpiring and the beautiful faces of those caring for me. Most of the time, however, I kept my eyes closed, or looked up at Seeba as she cradled my head. I began to feel the sensation of Tiesha drawing the image, holding my skin taut and flat.

The women started singing a different chant as Tiesha began to pierce my skin. I winced and felt myself move at first. The women continued to chant holding me firmly. Seeba offered me a goatskin chamois soaked in a wine-like fluid containing an herbal preparation to help relax me. The piercing was accomplished using sharpened, hard wooden needles. The process was moderately painful. Tears ran from my eyes, but I did not cry out.

"When the procedure was complete, Tiesha looked up at me with pride in her eyes at the accomplishment of her gift to me. I understood the ceremony was of tremendous importance to her and my sisters in the hut, all of whom wore their own tattoos. The bonding I felt for them, as they for me, at that moment was palpable.

"Seeba and Tiesha then physically changed positions. It was traditional for the primary wife to observe the artistry and cleanse the area free of blood and ink. It was also the practice for her to examine the vagina to determine if the hymen was still intact. Although Seeba already knew my condition, it was still her ritualistic duty to examine me. She carefully probed me and smiled reassuringly."

As Marriette stopped to take a deep breath, she looked over at Jen and found her sitting up, wide-eyed, biting her index finger at the knuckle.

"Geez, 'M', shouldn't Seeba have done the exam thing before the tattoo?"

"I wondered too. I can't answer that. It's just how Seeba chose to do it."

"Well, going on . . . to finalize the ritual, one of the women left the hut to seek the presence of the shaman, Ava. He played a role in the pre-nuptial ritual as well. After entering the hut, he knelt between my legs and carefully examined the tattoo. He would, of course, per protocol, report back to Havra, the husband-to-be. After consulting with Seeba, he assured everyone present that the ritual was complete and successful. The women then began chanting that the bride was ready to be married. I felt as though I was as well."

"I take it you still have your unique souvenir?"

"Yes, I still have the eagle tattoo. Now there's a souvenir! I've never explained its real origin to any of the host of gynecologists I have encountered . . .

childishness in college was my laconic response."

Astounded, Jen stared at Marriette, wide-eyed, "Marriette. What an amazing story!"

Outside, the snow continued to fall. A dark green city plow truck, with a yellow flashing light on its cab, passed by the house.

"I must say, Jen, I'm enjoying telling you this story. I haven't thought so thoroughly about my adventure in a long time. Do you have the time to stay a little bit longer, dear?" Marriette inquired.

"I think so. I'll call Dennis right now. I just bought my first cellular phone. It doesn't always work, but it's pretty reliable in our neighborhood."

Jen rose from the chair and walked over toward the windows. The snow was now falling steadily and a neighbor across the street had begun shoveling his front walk. As Jen wiped condensation along the edge of the window pane with her fingertip, Dennis's phone began to ring.

"Looks like about 10 inches out there, 'M'… still coming down. Well, he's not answering, so I'm assuming they're still out sledding. I'll try again in a little while."

After leaving a message for Dennis, Jen sat back down and Marriette picked up where she had left off with her story.

"As the day of the wedding ceremony approached, I spent more time with Seeba. She and Havra were the same age, and their 16-year-old son, Tave, was also soon to be married. The evening before the wedding, I was still unsure of what to expect about the actual consummation of the marriage.

"After the ceremony, I waited in my tent, somewhat apprehensive, but not afraid for Havra to appear. When he finally entered my tent, he lay down beside me, and took my hand into his and smiled. He revealed that he believed a consummation of this marriage was not appropriate.

Another surprise! I wasn't sure how to respond. He explained that I was essentially an honorary wife and understood my culture enough to exclude me in this way.

"Astounded, I can recall my reaction as being mixed, appreciating his thoughtfulness, yet considering our growing friendship, feeling some disappointment as well."

"Really!" Jen remarked. "Pretty handsome guy!"

"Yes, I do admit, I was curious."

"Jen, I'm going to leave the description of the wedding for another time. I want to get to the part of this story that's germane to my concerns."

Jen moved back to her armchair, clutching onto a pillow across her chest.

"One day, a small group of us set out to the west, hiking towards the hills and mountainous region. The purpose of the trip was to collect medicinal plants. After all, this was the purpose of my study. I had made the same journey several times over the course of my two years there.

"On this particular occasion, I traveled with the shaman, Ava, and Tiesha, plus three younger men. One of the young men was Tave, Havra and Seeba's son. The other two were Jema (also in his teens) and Bewa (a man in his twenties). The men established a safety perimeter several hundred yards in front of and behind us. All were armed with bows and arrows. Tiesha, Ava, and I traveled in the center, along with a mule carrying our supplies, plants, and my botanical collections in plant presses.

"We planned to be away from the village for three days: one day traveling to the mountains, one day on site, and one day to return. We weren't in anticipation of encountering anyone on the trail as we hadn't in previous excursions. Other tribes resided in the area, and communication was well established with them. The scouts were mostly there to protect us from predatory animals, although this was usually a remote possibility as well.

"As we entered into the deciduous forest, we came upon a familiar stream, which, at this time of year, was flowing full with mountain water. A large grove of trees, 10 or 15 feet high with light green compound leaves, provided shade and dappled sunlight. Taking advantage of the bathing spot, we enjoyed the beautiful setting. We camped there the first night, as we had done in the past. The following day we climbed to a higher elevation, collecting plants to take back to the village. Ava instructed us on what to collect and explained their medicinal purposes. I took individual samples of the herbaceous plants, placing them in between layers of newspaper, then into the plant press. When we completed our mission, we began our descent, spending the second night in the forest."

Marriette began to pace about the living room as she continued her story. She walked over to the windows, peering out at the snowfall, not focusing on anything in particular; her thoughts thoroughly transported back to Africa.

"We left the mountainside camp early the following morning with approximately an hour trek back to the river. We made a few stops along the way to rest, and to collect additional plants. I looked forward to bathing again in the river. The group spread out in their usual travel formation.

"Near the end of our descent, we could hear the rushing water as we approached through the dense foliage. The water, overflowing its banks, was an impressive site. The scouts closed ranks and joined us. We tied the mule up where he could feed and drink the water.

"Tiesha and I were the first ones into the stream. Eventually, everyone else joined in. I undid my braid to wash my hair, while the two of us enjoyed splashing around. Tiesha had undone her plaits during the previous river crossing, so we braided her hair more in keeping with mine. I recall the two of us resting on submerged rocks, our heads just above the water, with our long hair flowing all around us, her hair mixing with mine. It was a beautiful moment."

"I can picture that," Jen sighed. "Sounds idyllic."

"That was the good part of the day. What I'm about to tell you next, I've never told anyone, other than Pete and my dear James, but I want to tell you now, Jen, for many reasons."

"Yes, Marriette."

– Chapter 45 –

The Land Rover

Saturday, March 9, 1996
Prospect St., Providence, Rhode Island

Marriette stood in front of the fireplace, rearranging some of the framed photographs on the mantle.

"After leaving the river, our little band walked along the well-established pathway, covering another mile or so. As before, Bewa and Tave were at a distance behind us, with Jema in the lead. Ava, Tiesha, and I took turns guiding the mule along the gravel trail. The terrain was now somewhat level, dusty and rocky, with a mixture of grassland and trees. There were smooth-barked trees about 15 feet tall at most, numerous and scattered."

As Marriette continued her story, she began pacing around the living room again, then stopped nervously to straighten a cluster of paintings hanging on the wall. Jen noticed a change in Marriette's demeanor as the casual circumstances of the expedition began to shift.

"Although the sound was faint at first . . . we began to hear a vehicle coming closer and closer, making its way along the trail behind us. We couldn't get a view of it because of the dense vegetation cover. The sound was unexpected and disconcerting. The three of us stopped to listen. The vehicle seemed to stop moving somewhere nearby, although the engine could still be heard at idle.

"Then, a single report sounded from a firearm, and the shouting of foreign voices. They definitely were not native voices. I grabbed the reins of the mule and directed everyone off the trail, even though there was really nowhere to hide, especially with the mule. We heard the vehicle begin moving again . . . the typical sounds of it passing through the gears. Soon, it was nearly upon us. As the vehicle approached, we stayed off the road. In hindsight, we probably should all have scattered and hid the best we could, but there was no time."

Jen winced, tucking herself deeper into the chair, her arms wrapped around a large pillow. Marriette walked back toward the window and stared out at the snow fall.

"A tan Land Rover maneuvered around the corner at some speed, skidding to a stop near us. Two armed soldiers were seated in the vehicle, dressed in soiled, sand colored fatigues. One of them quickly dismounted and pointed his assault rifle directly at us. Both soldiers had the appearance of being Eastern Europeans, maybe Russian. They seemed to be alone. It was clear they were not Soviet military. Their uniforms were unmarked, and the only markings on their vehicle were numbers.

"I smelled alcohol on the soldier even before he spoke. I then spotted a bow and sleeve of arrows in the back of the vehicle, plainly belonging to one of our boys. That explained the gunshot. I knew we were in trouble."

"Oh, 'M'!"

Marriette sat down on the burgundy sofa, resting her elbows on her knees, staring at the coffee table. After taking in a deep breath, she slowly began again.

"It was never clear who they were … or why they were there. Mercenaries? Something to do with diamonds? Smuggling? Slavery?

"The other soldier then got out of the vehicle. He was inebriated as well. There were vodka bottles visible on the floor of the truck. They spoke in loud voices to each other, as though they were arguing, while glaring over at me more than anyone else in the group … you know, the interesting half naked white woman standing beside two black natives.

"One of them motioned for us to get on the ground. Tiesha began crying, clinging on to me. The mule had wandered off to graze. The other soldier, or whatever he was, walked over to the mule to search through the load on its back. He ripped open one of the blankets holding the plants while jostling through the other packs. Who knows what he was looking for, but he didn't find it. He rolled his eyes in caustic disappointment. I couldn't believe what was happening. He stepped back, took out his sidearm, and killed the mule with a single shot to its head.

"Before I could fathom the horror, the other one grabbed me and stood me up, pushing me further off the path, toward the woods."

"Marriette!"

"When I resisted, he pushed me so hard with the stock of his rifle that I stumbled and fell. He pulled me up by my hair and shoved me along in front of him until his final shove threw me to the ground in a small clearing. He was having a hard time standing … and his stench! I remember wondering, would I be raped or murdered? I lay on my back on the ground, propped on my elbows staring at this monster."

Jen now held the pillow so close to her face that only her eyes were visible.

"He staggered toward me, lifting my goatskin skirt with the muzzle of his weapon, pushing at the insides of my knees forcing them apart. The degenerate dropped his pants and stood over me stimulating himself until he achieved an erection, never taking his eyes from mine. He put down his AKM where he could easily pick it up again. He was so drunk…he dropped to his knees and began to move between my legs. Glaring at me, he sneered something in Russian.

"As he was just about to come down on me, I glimpsed something move in the brush behind him. I heard the swish of an arrow in the air and the thud of its shaft piercing deep in his chest. The arrow's shiny tip emerged slightly through the front of his tunic. Then came the sound of his agonized male scream, an unexpected sound for those anticipating mine instead."

Marriette now held her head in her hands looking down at the carpet. Jen sat straight up and moved over to the couch beside her, putting an arm around her.

"As he fell forward, I rolled away and scrambled for his AKM. Dropping the safety, I charged the weapon just as his comrade cut through the bushes, raising his rifle. From my position, I fired a series of bursts that exploded through his abdomen and chest. It threw him off his path into the bushes, dead instantly.

"I jumped up, still clutching the AKM by the pistol grip, my finger just off the trigger in anticipation of something else … maybe others who might come to investigate the weapons fire."

Marriette looked up as she brushed the hair away from her damp forehead with her fingertips.

"What a reversal of emotions! I now felt in control. Bewa was instantly at my side, bow in hand, with another arrow ready to fire. That's when he informed me that Tave had been murdered by the soldier at my feet. I looked down at the mercenary lying face down in the dirt, moaning, bare butt and all, the arrow shaft protruding from his back. Without a second thought, I put a round in his head, and watched a part of his skull slowly fall away."

Marriette turned toward Jen, grabbing one of her hands.

"Oh, my, Jen! It was a different reality. This … this … was not me, not the graduate student from Canada! It wasn't me!"

Jen tightened her hold on Marriette.

Shaking her head as she closed her eyes, Marriette took a deliberate breath.

"We called for Jema. I instructed Bewa to get Tave's body and bring it back, pointing in the direction where Tiesha and Ava were huddled together.

"As Bewa ran off, I slung the rifle over my shoulder and ran back to the others. When Tiesha saw me approach, she ran toward me throwing her arms around me. Ava was still shaking, but relieved to see that I was alive. I explained what had happened. That Tave was dead. I quickly took charge, assigning tasks to everyone."

Jen remained close as Marriette's breathing was uneasy, her face now covered in perspiration.

"That day, Jen, my tribal friends collided with a civilization totally foreign to them. I told them we needed to escape quickly and would take the truck. I felt sure others would follow.

"I examined the Land Rover and found the spare gas cans on the back were full. As far as I could tell, everything seemed in order. We emptied most of one of the two gas cans into the fuel tank. There was a satchel of AK ammunition magazines in the back, a few boxes of sidearm ammo, and a case of military style rations. Nothing else. I adjusted the shoulder strap on the AKM, carrying it against my back. For the next month, I always kept it with me. I slept with it."

" 'M', this is simply terrifying! Why, it's akin to what I hear from our soldiers! You've carried this with you for this long? It makes me sick for you!" Jen gasped, releasing the pillow and wrapping her arms around Marriette.

Forcing her thoughts back to the present moment, Marriette looked at Jen, "Yes, Jen. This is what led me to begin considering how one's brain could process these horrific images."

Jen released her hold on Marriette, moving further back on the couch, gazing at her colleague in admiration.

"Imagine that," Jen uttered, as tears ran freely down her cheeks. "So, this is your story."

"Yes, that is how it began, indeed," Marriette stated, wiping her own tears with her sleeve.

"Next, we dragged the bodies far off into the woods and disposed of them in a crevice among some large boulders. Covered the bodies with rocks. We left no trace. I removed their side arms, taking them with me."

Marriette moved to one corner of the couch, wrapping her arms around her knees while Jen took a similar position at the opposite end of the couch, facing Marriette.

"I remember throwing one of the mercenary's boots into the crevice on top of their bodies. For a split second, I thought how each of these killers were once some mother's young son. This was how life ended for them.

"We cleaned up any blood and tissue as best as we could. I remember picking up a piece of the mercenary's skull and angrily winging it far into the bushes, like a skipping stone. We took care to camouflage as many of the things that had been disturbed as possible. Tiesha swept away traces of our footprints with tree bows.

"These ghastly images are all still alive, if I allow myself to re-visit them. I usually don't."

Marriette stood up and walked over to the window again, to gaze out before sitting back down on the couch. Jen, moved closer and quietly asked, "How did you know what to do, 'M'? You showed such quick thinking."

"My brother, Pierre, returned from Vietnam in early 1969. He had been a Special Forces advisor. He was indefatigably dedicated to his profession, and obsessed with risk, weaponry, and survival. Pierre had the soul of a warrior. Between stints on active duty, he lived in the wilderness of Minnesota. When he learned I might be going to West Africa, he tried to talk me out of the idea. When I refused, he vehemently insisted on teaching me some survival skills. So, I stayed with my brother for two weeks that summer before I left for Africa. At first, I thought it was silly. I guess Pierre proved me wrong. Although he didn't reveal anything specific at the time, he may have been privy to information about some aberrant military goings-on in West Africa.

"Along with other survival skills, he taught me how to fire and maintain an M-16 and an AK. They were among the weapons Pierre had smuggled out of Vietnam. Just after I left for Africa in June of '71, Pierre reenlisted, rejoining his SF group. Four months prior to my returning home from Africa, Pierre was killed, most likely in Vietnam. It was the first news I received upon my arrival.

Jen gasped, "Oh, no!"

"I'm still sad that I never had the opportunity to tell my brother about what happened. It would've been so gratifying for him to know that he had saved his sister's life and the lives of her friends. Pierre was a taskmaster.

His instruction was thorough and complete. As it happened, in real life I fell into the drill."

Marriette, reached into the pocket of her cardigan sweater, "Look at this, Jen. It's one of the casings from a round I fired on that spot. I buried another in the earth beside my brother's gravestone in Montpelier."

Marriette leaned forward, pressing the piece of brass into Jen's palm. Chills ran through Jen's body as it touched her open hand.

"Oh, Marriette," Jen remarked, holding the tarnished casing in front of her, closely examining it between her thumb and forefinger.

"I went back into the woods," Marriette continued, "to find the dead mule and grabbed the plant press I brought with me, putting it into the back of the truck. We struggled to drag the mule's body further off into the woods to keep attention away from the site of the bodies.

"Our lead scout, Jema, along with Bewa's help, placed Tave's body in the back of the Land Rover. They were covered in their companion's blood. A singular wound could be seen through Tave's forehead, with a large exit wound at the rear of his skull. We carefully covered his body with goatskins. Hugging Bewa, I thanked him for taking the decisive action that saved us. I remember his eyes looking big and alert, the mindset of a warrior."

"I'm guessing that although you were on a long hike, it would be a much shorter drive back to your village. Am I right?" Jen inquired.

"If the Land Rover ran well, I thought we could get back to the tribal community by late afternoon. The terrain was such that the vehicle could run freely. I started the engine and managed to operate the complicated clutch … again, thanks to my brother."

Marriette stood up and wandered back to the front window, pushing the curtain aside with the back of her hand, to view the snowy conditions.

"Everyone got into the vehicle and was instructed to hang on. Bewa sat up front with me to navigate. If someone was coming after us, we would have to put many miles between us and them. I was ready to move … hoping we'd be lucky.

"I didn't really think much about anything else during the escape. I concentrated on Bewa's directions, keeping my eyes focused on the road conditions ahead – and the fuel and temperature gauges. We continued to drive for several hours. The sun was well beyond noon when we stopped to fill the tank with the second gas can.

"Later that afternoon, as the landscape grew more familiar, my mind wandered back to the ambush. I realized I would carry the image of that drunken bastard hovering over me for a long time. I could still feel the weight of the assault rifle in my hands. I could see the guts of the other Russian's chest jettisoned behind him. I had no doubt he would have killed me along with the others.

"However vile these men were, I had just killed two human beings within a minute of each other. As I drove, I realized that my arms, hands, and legs were splattered with the blood of Tave and the Russians. I wondered how long it would be before I would feel safe again."

Stopping momentarily to take a short break, Marriette walked out into the kitchen. Jen got up to look outside at the snowy conditions. Returning with two glasses of sparkling water and a box of Kleenex, Marriette resumed her story.

"The sun was setting as we finally drove into camp. The entire community slowly gathered around the Land Rover. Havra moved up through the throng to where I sat behind the wheel. His expression said it all. Everyone was present except his cherished son. Looking directly into my eyes, he sought an explanation not possible. Havra then saw Tave's body wrapped up in goatskins in the back of the vehicle. I opened the rear gate and he placed his head on his son's chest, as Seeba moved up beside him.

"As soon as there was an opportunity, I urged him to quickly do what was necessary. The leader in Havra took over. He instructed the tribe's people to follow my directions. We then moved Tave's body to Seeba's hut.

"I had been thinking about how to dispose of the Land Rover. It occurred to me to bury it, since there was absolutely no place to hide it. I assumed others would be looking for the missing men, and the truck would be easily visible from the air.

"I gathered some of the able-bodied men together to drive the Land Rover away from the immediate camp and bury it as quickly as possible. I directed others to clear the ground of the vehicle's tracks as we departed. The sun was beginning to set as I started up the Land Rover, loaded with the crew. We headed out about a kilometer from camp, away from any established trail, and chose a spot where we hoped the digging would be easiest. With the two entrenching tools found on the Land Rover, along with other crude digging instruments, it was slow going. Soon we found ourselves digging in the light of a half moon and starry sky. Hours later, an 8-foot-deep cavity was excavated, including a steep ramp. I had somehow managed to collapse the top of the vehicle and fold back its windshield before leaving camp. I backed the vehicle down the ramp, into the hole, and we began to carefully backfill, shoveling dirt under the vehicle to avoid air spaces. Within an hour or so the Land Rover was completely buried . . . sometimes . . . I've wondered whether it is still there.

"We arrived back in camp at the first sign of dawn. The last thing we did was to send guards out about a kilometer from camp, to provide us with early warning, should we need it. I went into my tent and fell asleep, holding my AK across my chest, until I awoke sometime in the early afternoon."

Marriette stood up again from the couch and headed back in the direction of the kitchen, looking exhausted from reliving this long held secret.

"Jenny, I need another drink of water," she voiced, wearily, "How about you?"

As Jen followed Marriette into the kitchen, her eyes lingered on the top shelf of a sideboard, covered with framed photographs. Stopping for a moment, she selected a photo of Marriette's two boys, carrying it with her. Marriette had just closed the refrigerator door and was opening a bottle of water. Choosing a lemon from a bowl, she rolled it firmly with her palm on the countertop before slicing it into quarters and squeezing the juice into each glass. As Marriette turned to hand Jen her glass, Jen held up the photograph.

"Havra is Harris's father. That's my guess."

"Yes . . . he is, Jen," Marriette sighed. "Yes, he is."

"Does Harris know?"

"Yes, he does, however, he's never heard the story I just told you. He only knows that the whereabouts of his biological father is unknown. James is the father he knew and who loved him since birth."

"Marriette," Jen quietly suggested, "You've been reliving this story for about two hours now. Don't you think it might be a good time for you to take a rest and collect your thoughts?

"I can come back later, maybe this evening, if you like. I should get back to the house anyway and check on Dennis and the kids."

"I agree, Jenny. I'd really like to finish telling you the story this weekend, if possible. You've heard most of it, already, and . . . please, I'd rather you not mention what I've told you to anyone, not even Dennis."

"Of course, 'M'. I'll call you when we've figured out a time."

"Thank you, my dear. Come now, I'll drive you home. It looks like more snow has accumulated out there."

The familiar sound of a plow's steel rollers grinding the pavement was heard as it by passed the house.

Putting on their winter garb, the women got into Marriette's Volvo and drove around the corner to Halsey Street. As Jen stepped from the car, she turned and leaned back in, "What an incredible story, 'M'. Thank you for sharing it with me. I've always admired you and your accomplishments. This only adds to those feelings . . . immeasurably. See you a little later. I love you."

"I love you too, Jenny. Yes, dear. Talk soon."

– Chapter 46 –

Escape to Civilization

March 9, 1996   Prospect St. Providence, Rhode Island

The evening sky shone bright with stars as Jen returned to Marriette's to hear the rest of her story. Scott and Scooter were sound asleep at home, with Dennis propped up on the couch, reading and watching the Bruins playing in Calgary.

The two women settled in next to each other on the living room rug, in front of the fireplace.

"When we spoke earlier, Jen, the commotion in the background was quite entertaining," Marriette commented.

"You're referring to all the shouting from Scooter?" Jen inquired.

"She certainly came through loud and clear," Marriette laughed. "'Tell Marriette I beat Scott! Tell her, Mom!' Precious."

"Scotty is such a sweet little boy. 'Let the Wookie win!' he said, 'It's easier!'" Jen chuckled. "It won't be long before Scoot does win - and without any help at all."

"Hmm. Does she happen to remind you of anyone you know, dear?"

Jen looked at Marriette and winked, nodding her head. "Yep, ponytail and all."

Marriette took a sip of her burgundy before returning to her story, "Oh my, Jen, where was I?"

"I believe you had fallen asleep with the rifle across your chest," Jen answered, reaching for her glass of wine on the coffee table.

"Yes. Sounds outside my hut must have startled me awake from a deep sleep. The heat of the day was beginning to build inside my tent. I remember momentarily feeling disoriented, thinking I was back at home in Montpelier, but then the tragedy of the previous day quickly seized my consciousness, and the tightness in my chest returned.

"When I left my tent, I noticed the usual daily activities had changed. I began searching for Havra and Seeba. I had yet to provide Havra with a full account of what had happened. I wondered how the community would react to the death of Tave. As I wandered through the village, people I now knew well, especially the women, came up to embrace and hold me, expressing their gratitude.

Changing her position, Marriette turned onto her side to face Jen, her back now toward the fire.

"I noticed many of the tribal members were involved with funeral preparations. Custom held that it was essential for the young man's body to be moved to the appropriate place ... the site where his umbilical cord and placenta had been buried 16 years earlier. There was a concern that Tave had died away from his home territory, which meant his spirit would need to be guided back to the tribal village. Although his physical remains were returned, the belief was held that his spirit still wandered, waiting to be united with the Ancestors. A cascade of cultural rituals were initiated to ensure that Tave would join the Ancestors without delay, and therefore avoid being caught in a state of metaphysical limbo. Achieving this would permit Tave's spirit to reincarnate into the life of another."

Jen moved back up onto the sofa to face Marriette.

"I imagine the rituals, these memes, must have some adaptive function," Jen reflected. "Seems as though there are many similar rituals throughout the world."

"Yes. Good point, Jen. In this particular community, not inconsistent with other African tribal cultures, existence was viewed as part of a continuum of life and death... alternate states of being. Although no longer physically present, Tave's spirit was believed to be close by. I understand now why this custom diminished the angst of sudden loss."

"Ah, yes," Jen added. "A cultural behavior evolved to mollify individual grief."

"Yes," Marriette nodded, rolling onto her back, and folding her hands across her chest.

"As I was observing the funeral preparations, Havra found me. He explained that the ritual process would obligate his presence for several days. I then provided the essentials of what had transpired the previous day. He conveyed his gratitude for my part in saving the others. However, I emphasized it was the courage and quick thinking of Bewa that made saving any of us possible.

"The funeral moved forward in a series of ceremonies in which Havra and his immediate family were involved in all stages of the process. The grieving, as well as the celebration of Tave's spirit joining the realm of the Ancestors, would continue for several months.

"One morning, a week or so after the attack, Havra came to see me in my tent. At last I felt I had the opportunity to fully explain in detail, what had happened on our return trip from the mountains. We sat together, face-to-face on the floor of my tent, as I related everything I could remember about the attack.

"After we had painfully revisited the emotions of all that had transpired, Havra confided another concern to me."

Marriette then shared with Jen, the conversation she had with Havra in March of 1972.

****

March 1972   West Ghana

"Marriette, I have been thinking deeply about what the future now holds, thinking about you, and the enduring influence the McGill graduate program has had on my life."

"Yes, Havra?"

"I have come to a place where I no longer belong in my native homeland. This realization has been growing in me for a long time. The event of last week has only accelerated this conclusion.

"Although I still consider myself an Original, I have become more a part of your Civilization, than mine. After all, I was raised to think like my North American mentors, however, I can still call upon traditional values when I find it necessary. I now feel my presence here is holding me back from what I must pursue.

"Although it has been one week, and the scouts have not seen or heard anything, this does not mean I carry no fear. More change is coming. The Others will soon be upon us. I now believe our tribe must depart from here and disperse among our related neighboring tribes to the south.

"For me, I too, must seek a new path. I need to encounter the other world and experience it for myself. I have discussed this with Seeba. She has no interest in following me, but understands my desire to do this. I cannot foretell the immediate future, yet I know I cannot remain here."

"What can I do to help you, Havra?" Marriette asked.

"I understand that in less than three months the courier will arrive to return you to your home. During the time we have left, my wish is for you to prepare me, as much as you are able, for entering the new world of Civilization. This is my voyage to the moon, yes?"

"Yes, Havra, it is. Do you have a plan?"

"My first responsibility is to settle our people. Depending upon that outcome, I plan to walk to a destination south, where the railroad reaches.

"I have an advantage in that I can speak African dialects, French, and English better than most. I'm hoping there will be value in that. My disadvantage is that I have had no direct experience with the culture of Civilization."

"Yes, you'll need to learn more about that world," Marriette offered.

"I feel as one kept," Havra explained, "one who has done wrong, a prisoner, if you will."

"A prisoner of your unique circumstances, Havra," Marriette nodded in agreement.

"But the door is now open," Havra added. "The time has come."

"That it has, Havra. I have confidence in you, that you will find your way."

Marriette reached over, taking his hand into hers. "I have come to know you well, Havra. I sense your deep commitment. Unflagging determination can make all the difference.

"I heard much about you before arriving here, Havra. Those I spoke to recognized your passion and desire to learn as much as possible about the modern world. Moving a little closer, Marriette emphasized, "Continue to seek those who can teach you ... but here is an important point. Among the tricks is learning who you can trust. Some of it will come from your intuition; some of it will be gained through experience."

"What is your understanding of intuition, Marriette?"

"Intuition is sensing that you know something, yet not knowing how you know it," Marriette answered. Tapping herself on the chest, she went on, "It's a feeling one has in the 'gut' before thinking things all the way through. But you must remember to also examine the facts. Taking your time to examine the facts is extremely important. It's easy not to.

"Mistakes will happen, Havra, but try to guard against big mistakes. When you live in an environment such as this village, where everyone is familiar with everyone else, individuals know they must be honest in dealing with each other. Good reputations work well in small groups. Bad reputations don't.

"But things will be very different once you're away from your tribal community. There will be people with whom you are unfamiliar, and, although they will look like you, they will need to earn your trust. Be careful. Don't forget this."

"I'm listening, Marriette."

"Good. We will begin to work diligently to prepare you the best we can."

Marriette leaned forward, gently kissing him on his lips. He returned her kiss. Suddenly, her tribal marriage no longer felt an ephemeral adventure in anthropology.

******

The grating sound of a snowplow interrupted the moment as it passed in front of the house. Stretching out on the rug with a pillow under her head, Marriette glanced up at the ceiling.

"It was the first time we kissed. After that, our friendship deepened. I counseled Havra with all the wisdom a 30-year-old could offer about the world Havra would encounter," Marriette recollected, smiling.

"During my last month there, we became lovers. The thought of leaving him behind filled me with a profound sense of emptiness."

"You were falling in love."

"Yes, Jenny. When I recall my last image of him disappearing into the dust of the vehicle as we drove off, I can still feel the same pang of loss."

"You must wonder whatever became of Havra."

"Yes, I do. Re-living this story brings so much of it back to consciousness."

Returning her thoughts to the present, Marriette sighed, "Oh, Jenny, I feel such an emptiness in my life, with my boys away at school and my dear James gone. I wonder… I wonder how I'm going to handle all of this."

"'M'?" Jen responded, propping herself up on her side, waiting for Marriette to turn toward her, "You and I both know this can't be rushed. You will find your way. Maybe it's time to write that book only you can write."

"Perhaps, Jenny. Perhaps you're right. Maybe."

– Chapter 47 –

A New Day is Coming

Saturday, May 25, 1996   Horseneck Beach State Park
Westport, Massachusetts

Spring had arrived after a long, cold, sad winter. The new red truck sat parked in the garage bay next to the woodshop, efficaciously a family totem. Although a sympathetic replacement, the new truck appeared identical to James's original. His original Rhode Island license plate under the tailgate read, 'QUEBEC'. Marriette was determined to take the new incarnation of James's red truck on its first field trip. Jen was to accompany her. Earlier in the month, Harris and Jake revealed their decision to re-fit their father's truck. At first, the idea disturbed Marriette. However, in recent weeks, she had become more accustomed to its presence.

She started leaving the garage door open, allowing the truck to be visible from the kitchen window. After a time, Marriette would sit in James's seat in the cab, permitting her feelings to flow forth. She began to foster a relationship with the bright red totem. Slowly, as she made thoughtful adjustments, she began to perceive it in a new light.

Marriette thought about how people visit cemeteries and stare at their loved ones' granite headstones. For her, that concept felt distant and impersonal. Instead, the truck became the intimate memorial for her and the boys. It was not unlike how she felt about her brother's Chevelle which still occupied the bay beside the red truck.

One afternoon, as Marriette sat in solitude in the cab, she recalled the concept of the Ancestors of her African family and how they viewed the spirit of a deceased loved one as living among them. Perceiving it in this way, the goodbye did not seem as permanent – not so complete.

She reflected on how the tribal community communicated openly about death, sudden or otherwise. Their rituals were dedicated to sharing their grief together. One never felt isolated, or alone, thus greatly diminishing the anxiety of separation.

The memorial service for James held similar qualities. Support had come from people who loved and cared about him and his family – all spontaneously singing the Canadien anthem together. At a most fragile moment in her life, Marriette had felt safe and comforted.

The connection between Harris and his biological father re-surfaced for her. Harris was metaphorically Tave reincarnated, and Harris's African family would have recognized him as such. Marriette considered how processing grief in this way helped to build a different future, based on a reconstructed module of relationships.

She questioned whether those ancient customs worked better than what her culture had to offer. Had modern culture's memes not evolved to mollify the hardwired presence of anxiety separation? Marriette began to examine this idea with fresh eyes. She also understood it would take time to heal, to adapt, and to recreate a new whole.

****

Dennis was getting ready to take Scott and Scooter for a visit to his parents' home on the coast, a 45-minute drive from University Hill. As Jen and Dennis secured the children into their seats, Marriette arrived driving the new red truck. Kissing everyone goodbye, Jen joined Marriette in the pickup, climbing up into the passenger's seat.

Marriette turned onto Prospect Street and drove down the hill to Main, traveling through campus until she entered I-195 East. As they crossed over into Massachusetts towards New Bedford, Marriette suggested they stop for lunch at the Roys' favorite Portuguese restaurant. Unsure of what feelings might surface there, Marriette hoped to find James's loving spirit.

Perhaps yesterday she could not have attempted this, but today she would try. On the way, Marriette discussed her ambivalent feelings of visiting the restaurant, noting she would go as far as she felt comfortable.

Slowing for the Washburn exit, Marriette turned left onto Coggeshall Street and parked the red truck in the lot across from Antonio's. Before leaving the vehicle, Jen reminded Marriette, "We will stay only as long as you want, whether it's for ten seconds or an hour. Okay?"

"Okay, thank you," Marriette answered with a deep sigh, gathering her courage.

The restaurant had just opened its doors for the day, and a handful of customers were already seated at the far left of the bar. Marriette walked directly toward the short end of the bar on the right, in front of the front windows, where she and James usually sat, preferring the cozy seats in the corner.

While they waited for lunch to arrive, Marriette inquired about the classes being covered in her absence. She then asked for an update on a paper she and Jen had co-authored, which was waiting approval for publication. This marked the first time Marriette had shown interest in life at the University.

Jen again brought up the idea that Marriette consider writing a book on traumatic stress disorder recovery for the general public, reminding Marriette that she had already been approached by publishers.

"Yes, Jen. The book idea has indeed crossed my mind lately. I was hesitant to write it previously; I was unsure of my approach. I believe I'm now ready."

Gently tapping Jen on the shoulder, Marriette inquired, "Would you consider co-authoring?"

"'M'. Of course, I'd love to. Let's do it! . . . whenever you're ready. It makes good sense."

"Well, here we are," Jen reflected, "both bearing scars of tragic circumstances in our lives. We should be able to write a book with all the authority of our experience. Considering our professions, few others would be so qualified, which is our huge point of difference."

"It is and we shall," Marriette nodded, smiling. "When I 'gain control again'."

Jen flashed a smile back, at Marriette's reference to her song sung at James's memorial.

Swiveling her barstool around, Marriette glanced out at the parked red truck, alone across the street, sparkling in the bright sunlight. After lingering a moment, she turned back to face Jen.

"Jen. I'd like to think I've thanked you already. Maybe I have, many times, I hope. I've lost track of so much in this fog. I want to be sure this time. The support you, Denny, and Larry gave us those first few weeks meant so much. I can't imagine having managed without it. It made all the difference."

Tears welling up, Marriette reached over and touched Jen's arm. "The anthem was for James. The Rodney Crowell song was for me," she added. "It was simply beautiful. And your voice, I had no idea!"

"Thank you, 'M'. It is a beautiful song." Jen responded, looking up from her lunch, long enough to capture Marriette's tender gaze.

"'M', I chose to sing that song at my mother's memorial service. I was 17. Don't know how I ever did it. I wanted to honor her in the most personal way I could muster. A lot of those same feelings came back at James's memorial service."

Marriette leaned over kissing Jen on her temple. "Oh, Jenny," Marriette sighed, briefly closing her eyes.

Feeling concerned, Jen tried to assess Marriette's emotional state. Reacting to her expression, Marriette reassured her, "Really, Jenny, I'm okay. Last night, I looked at the video recording Dennis made of the memorial service for the first time. I cried for my James, but also cried for feeling so loved."

Quietly, the bartender walked over with a box of Kleenex, placing it in front of the women with an understanding smile. Jen had begun to sense a shift in Marriette. There now appeared to be some acceptance, and the beginning of a path forward to finding a new way of life.

With leftovers packed up, they walked back across Coggeshall Street to the truck. Marriette requested that Jen drive. They passed through downtown New Bedford, encountering Route 6 before heading out onto the peninsula into Westport. The sun was bright in a cloudless sky. Springtime had arrived in New England, with deciduous foliage fully emerged. Along the road, miles of stone walls established the perimeters of hayfields. Already tall, the grass concealed the nests of newly arrived bobolinks.

At the end of the long stretch of road, they arrived at Horseneck Beach. Jen parked on a field of rounded rocks which comprised the parking area. The sound of surf could be heard as a distinct rattle of these rocks as they tumbled in with each breaking wave.

The women walked toward their left and sat atop a large granite formation that established a boundary between the rocky beach to the south and the sandy beach to the north. Looking out onto the calm Atlantic, they inhaled the salt air, expressing their welcome of spring.

Five minutes hadn't even passed before Jen, with brown eyes wide and excited, exclaimed, "I'm going in!"

"What? Jen! No! You'll freeze. And you just ate lunch!"

"No, I won't . . . and I didn't eat that much."

"So that's why you didn't finish your lunch! I should've known you had something in mind."

"Yup. I'll finish it right after my swim, I promise," Jen replied, tugging at the collar of her Brown University sweatshirt. "I even have a swimsuit on, but I'm going to put on a wetsuit over it. Don't worry. I won't be in long. It's probably freezing!"

"Oh, Jenny!"

Jen ran back to the parking area and grabbed her backpack from the bed of the truck. Returning to the rock, she pulled her wetsuit on over her swimsuit.

"Jenny. Please be careful."

"I'm fine, 'M'. I've actually done this before, right from here," she said, looking out at the ledge extending out into deep green water.

"I'll dive in here but have to come out of the water just over there on the sandy beach," Jen explained, pointing toward the shoreline to the north.

"I'm not going that far. It should be plenty. You'll be able to see me all the way, 'M'!"

Pulling up her hood, Jen carefully stuffed her ponytail inside. It was high tide and she was confident of where she was going.

Marriette stood as Jen tiptoed out to the edge of the granite ledge and dove into the clear green salt water. She swam straight out about 30 yards, turned left, and angled back in along the beach. Marriette made her way over the granite outcropping and down onto the beach carrying a towel. She continued to walk along the edge of the surf, monitoring Jen, keeping pace with her as she swam among the waves. Marriette had covered a few hundred yards when Jen finally turned toward shore.

Emerging invigorated with the last breaking wave, she ran splashing through the shallow water to where Marriette was waiting.

"Pretty cold, yes? That was more than a quick dip, my dear!" Marriette exclaimed, handing her the towel.

"Yeah, but it felt so good, I just had to keep going," Jen looked up, all smiles. "Wicked cold on my face!" she mused. "I love the salt water!" she added, pulling off her hood and shaking out her long hair in the breeze.

Marriette was entertained by Jen's constant energy, but relieved that she was back on shore again. Walking along the beach together, they returned back to the rock formation. Jen peeled off her wetsuit and went down behind the big rock to change back into dry clothes.

When she returned, Marriette was staring out at the ocean, sitting with her arms wrapped around both legs, chin on knees, her long graying hair flowing behind her in the breeze. The women sat beside each other on the ledge, facing the Atlantic.

"So, how is the day going for you, 'M'?" Jen inquired, as she opened the takeout box and began to finish her lunch.

"For whatever reason, Jenny, I'm having a good day. However, I just can't count on anything, good or bad. It is what it is. I'm slowly making my way through this maze."

"Yes, 'M'. By the way, I've noticed your hair is getting a little more peppered, Jen observed, brushing a stray strand back over Marriette's shoulder.

"Yes, I've chosen not to color it any longer," Marriette replied. "I've decided to ease into my natural grayness."

"I like that idea. It will be beautiful."

"And I'm definitely keeping it long," Marriette added. "Long hair has always been my flag."

"Me, too!" Jen nodded. "That's how we feel, isn't it? When I was a kid, I called it my 'power tail'!"

"Of course! Tiger and her Power-tail. Doesn't that just fit you!" Marriette laughed.

Jen grabbed a fistful of her wet hair and held it at length out in front of her.

"That's interesting, people used to say that, actually. It does make the swimming housekeeping more difficult, but that never bothered me. Maybe I'll let mine grow a little longer, too."

Marriette smiled at their new project. "Nice. We'll have to compare how we both look at the end of the year!"

"It's a deal!" Jen agreed.

As they sat resting on the granite ledge, a pair of hooded mergansers landed in the water directly in front of them. The women watched as the couple dove and resurfaced several times before paddling around to the other side of the big rock, out of view.

Looking over at Jen, Marriette thoughtfully remarked, "Today, I find myself pensive."

"Anything in particular?" Jen inquired.

"Well, yes, Jen, I've been thinking about the grieving process . . . trying to make sense of it."

"Oh, yeah . . . the origin of grief has yet to be adequately explained to my satisfaction," Jen interjected.

"The response to significant loss is excruciating, disorienting and exhausting," Marriette reflected. "Few can survive it alone. My goodness . . . where is the adaptive value in that maelstrom . . . what is the purpose of having to go through this?"

"Stops normal life 'on a dime', for sure," Jen commented.

"I've been doing some reading," Marriette continued. "I went to the library this week searching for articles related to grief. It's still not well understood. Some good suggestions, but not much evidence."

"Hard to investigate," Jen added.

"I agree, Jen," Marriette acknowledged. "It is suggested that grief was not shaped by natural selection directly, but thought to be the neurological byproduct of a closely related behavior, which evolved to support attachment in young offspring."

"I can't remember who at the moment," Jen noted . . . "but a researcher pointed out that the event of temporary separation is much more common in nature than a permanent separation . . . you know . . . an actual death. Makes sense though . . . reaction to any separation, to something missing . . . is a safety issue . . . it's necessary, independent of age . . . but with both behaviors neurologically related . . . we seem to get stuck with this crippling reaction to all out grief."

"Yes, stuck with it is a good way to describe it," Marriette agreed, "especially in modern culture. Generally speaking, not everything works perfectly. Humans today are still running on behavioral software, designed for other times and other conditions . . . not modernity."

"Any other thoughts?" Jen inquired, finishing her last bit of chourico and sautéed pepper sandwich.

"Well, yes, look at our cultural differences. If a typical reaction to the loss of a close family member is devastating to the point of dysfunction, that reaction, at its core, absolutely represents a safety issue. In the presence of such a reaction, it requires others to be available, to provide what is necessary for the survival of the bereaved, until the dysfunctional reaction fades."

"Right," Jen nodded in agreement.

"And this is exactly what I observed in my African family. Their social environment attended to grief on several levels, lending protection for the bereaved. In addition to the close physical proximity of the tribe members, comfort was also found in the concept of death not having permanence, a perception that the loved one was not completely gone. They believed in the presence of an ancestral spirit, with an accepted path to reincarnation. These cultural biases have been alive and present for tens of thousands of years and served, still serve, to diminish the perception of loss."

"Yes . . . of course it would change one's perception."

"As you can see, in the pre-agricultural existence of an intimate group . . . the tribe," Marriette explained, "social survival resources were already in place, which reduced anxiety. In our culture, a relative isolation is experienced with such a significant loss, for example, the loss of a child, the early loss of a parent or . . . the loss of one's spouse, with its associated dependency."

"We may not always be fully conscious of this dependency," Jen offered, "but we are very much attached to our resources."

"Yes," Marriette concurred, "attachment resources, might include a house, job, or relationship, etc. Consider the relationship to a spouse as one component of a resource module. To enter into a relationship, commitment is costly, involving a process, and time to develop trust. Trust, as a component of attachment, is a social investment that is not easily replaceable."

Jen jumped in, "Let me put all of this together. All things considered . . . a level of comfort is recognized and experienced in an intact module of our necessary resources . . . which produces a sense of well-being . . . "

"Yes, well-being!" Marriette agreed.

". . . if the module is intact, stable, and predictable . . . ," Jen went on, ". . . we are happy. If we are happy, we are doing something right . . . but . . . if we are unhappy, our brain signals sadness, stress, and depression as alarms . . . indicating that we are most likely deviating to circumstances which are less than optimal . . . call it . . . unsafe. Therefore, a diminished sense of well-being emerges . . . until something changes again, to restore it to an adaptive state, signaled once again . . . by our brain, as . . . well-being."

"Yes, that's it!" Marriette affirmed.

"Wild armchair biology!" Jen exclaimed. "I know it sounds like we're getting carried away tossing around these ideas, but it is very interesting. I think we're beginning to write our book right here at Horseneck Beach."

"Yes, Jenny, my dear," Marriette laughed. "I believe we may have just outlined a chapter. I love it! I'd say . . . more lunches at the beach!"

"I agree! I think saltwater makes everything better," Jen quipped. "And something else, so personal, 'M'," Jen added, pointing toward the parking area. "Now, I understand why the boys reconstructed the red truck. They acted on their intuition to preserve what they could of their father's essence. So very beautiful."

Audibly exhaling, Marriette looked over at the truck, closing her eyes, trying not to let her emotions drift off into sadness, still so close at hand. "Yes, it is beautiful. My boys. So, here we sit, Jenny," Marriette turned her attention back to Jen, "Two researchers of stress disorders and best of friends helping each other. Very, very special."

"Yes, 'M' . . . it certainly is."

Reaching over, Marriette put Jen's hand into hers. "Darling, something sweet you do . . . I notice you don't often call me 'Marriette' any longer, but . . . 'M'."

Jen smiled, "I didn't plan on that, but I've noticed it, too. I used to call my mom 'M'. It's come to feel right. Is that okay?"

"I'm honored, darling."

"A new day is coming, 'M'."

"I can almost see it, Jenny dear."

Havra Emerson

PART 3

– Chapter 48 –

It Was 20 Years Ago Today
Monday, June 20, 2016   Denessen, Rhode Island

Jen was at home in her office on Monday evening tying up loose ends after a long day at the University. The comfortable room took on the warmth of the setting sun that streamed through the windows. Opening an east facing window, she looked out onto the backyard where her husband was scooping leaves from the lap pool.

In 2003, she and Dennis began construction of their new home on the parcel of land given to them by Dennis's parents. The four acres of coastline woodland formed a small peninsula surrounded by salt marsh overlooking Narragansett Bay.

Their home was unique, constructed on reinforced concrete columns with the living areas raised 12 feet above ground. The second floor had a superior view of the estuary and featured a kitchen, master bedroom, and great room where Jen had positioned her grand piano in front of an array of tall windows facing the marsh. Their much-loved home was the culmination of years of dreaming and planning together.

Jen would turn 52 on her next birthday at the end of July. Twenty-five years had passed since she and Dennis arrived in Rhode Island with their two toddlers. During those years she established respect within her profession with dozens of professionally published papers, along with two commercially successful books co-authored with Marriette.

Although Marriette was a generation older than Jen, the two women maximized their synergistic relationship. Marriette was frequently the source of original thought, while Jen provided organization, energy, and the finishing touches to complete their projects. Their individual temperaments complemented each other. They appreciated an uncommon level of trust and a healthy dependency. Their shared experiences created an enduring and special bond – much like a daughter and mother.

Dennis was about to turn 60 in the fall and was now a tenured faculty member at Brown. Their daughter, Carolyn, 27, was a graduate of Brown University and their medical school. She had recently completed a residency in emergency medicine, and was working as an ER physician in Eugene, Oregon.

Their son, Scott, 29, became a golf professional. His first job was at a private course in South Carolina where he met and fell in love with the daughter of a member family. A magnificent wedding followed three years later. He now worked as head pro at a private course outside of Baltimore. With both children doing well, Denny and Jen had settled into a post-parental routine.

****

As Jen tidied up her office desktop, she picked up a package that had been delivered to her department mail earlier in the day. Opening up the box, she discovered a layer of bubble wrap placed over the covers of two books she had written with Marriette.

Jen picked up the larger of the two volumes and held it out in front of her. The idea for its distinct cover design had occurred to Marriette in the fall as she was raking up leaves in her backyard. The coarse-grained paper of the white jacket cover was finely embossed with dozens of maple leaves, captured in the helical swirl of a dust devil, scattered across the front cover, along the spine, receding onto the back. The title was printed in a large scarlet traditional serif font reading, 'LOSS & RECOVERY', the first book that they had written together – published in 2000. It was an intelligently written manuscript, guiding the reader through the trauma of personal loss onto a path of recovery.

'L & R', as the two women referred to it, sold reasonably well in its first year of publication. After the American tragedy of September 2001, it quickly became ensconced on the *New York Times* bestseller list. The book remained on the list for three consecutive years, becoming widely known and academically acclaimed. It received a National Book Club Award in 2004, making Marriette and Jen household names. 'L & R' was now in its third edition.

Sitting beside the book in the package was a well-worn, first edition of 'The Mental Game of Golf,' published in 2007. It was primarily authored by Jen and was known as 'MG2'. The cover had been drawn by a Rhode Island School of Design student. The semi-abstract image depicted a young golfing couple with Zen-like expressions, turned facing one another in profile, nose to nose. The upper hemisphere of their craniums was drawn as cartoon brains; glistening white with a uniformly shaped surface and dimpled like a golf ball.

There was an accompanying letter, tucked inside 'MG2,' sent by a prominent golfer on the PGA tour. He wrote that he had carried the book with him for years, citing it as an invaluable tool in organizing his mental game. He felt it was a contributing factor in his current success. The man had experienced the sudden loss of his father in 2004. He wrote that their book, 'L&R,' was paramount in helping him manage his grief. The letter went on to express his gratitude. Included in the package, were two autographed photos, two match-worn, autographed gloves and four tickets to the weekend rounds of the 2017 Masters Tournament, along with hotel accommodations.

He asked if Jen and Marriette would autograph the books for him, as well as a copy of a 2007 Golf Digest that was in mint condition, protected in a thick, clear vinyl sleeve. It was apparent that he was a big fan, and Jen was touched.

The request prompted Jen to glance up at the many framed photographs hanging on the wall of her office. Her eyes settled on the same *Golf Digest* cover, showing the women in profile, wearing white golf visors, facing each other, brim to brim, replicating the illustration on the 'MG2' cover. Alongside that photo was a framed issue of a *Redbook* magazine, published in February of 2002, that featured an article about the two women and their popular, 'Loss & Recovery.' The glamorous cover showed the two psychologists sitting back to back, perched on a single stool, smiling out at the studio photographer.

'MG2' had been written metaphorically about golf to address mental challenges typically present when immersed in any competitive environment that requires effective concentration and appropriate handling of moment-to-moment success and failure.

Jen's inspiration to write 'MG2' came when her son Scott discovered that the challenges he encountered playing golf were really more of a psychological nature than biomechanical. Jen drew on her own years of elite competitive swimming experience as a foundation to develop the guide.

It was an unusual package to receive on a quiet Monday evening – requests for autographs were infrequent now. After photographing the letter, books, gifts, and a photo of its sender, Jen sent the images to Marriette in an email.

'M', can you believe this was ten years ago? Looks like we're going to the Masters?!!!! Love

****

Jen and Marriette found the writing of 'LOSS & RECOVERY' a richly rewarding undertaking. It was exactly 20 years since its inception. Not only had the project deepened their relationship, it also provided a pertinent and purposeful book for the general public: one which the authors were proud of.

The promotion of the book had been a grand, but fleeting departure from their usual day-to-day business. When book sales suddenly took off in October 2001, their lives changed dramatically as the publisher's promotion schedule went into effect. For the first few months, the tour was novel and fun. Marriette and Jen met interesting people, visited new places, and found themselves in situations they had never encountered before. They appeared on the *Today Show, Good Morning America*, and *Oprah*, along with giving notable radio interviews, such as *Fresh Air*, and Diane Rheem.

Quite suddenly, people interested in seeking treatment began to call Brown University requesting appointments – despite the fact that, as researchers, neither had a autonomous private practice. Phone numbers had to be changed, and everything was now directed to Francine Burnette, their attorney and publisher.

That first year, the women found little time for privacy and, soon, Jen found the additional responsibilities difficult to manage.

For the first time in her life, the demands of raising a family, meeting expectations as an educator and researcher, along with attending to her rigorous exercise regimen, proved to be too much. She felt overextended. That led to friction with Dennis, and guilt from feeling she wasn't sufficiently available for their children.

On the other hand, Marriette's academic sabbatical happened to coincide with the year of book promotion. She had the time, and the desire, to stay busy, whereas Jen now found it necessary to significantly reduce her promotional activities. Marriette had recognized the strain on Jen early on and tried to convince her colleague to return to a more normal schedule. At first Jen resisted, believing she should carry her half of the load. Soon, however, an argument with Dennis and an introspective look in the mirror convinced Jen that a change was necessary.

The next day Jen appeared at Marriette's office. Flopping down on the couch next to Marriette's large antique desk, she finally conceded that she just couldn't keep up the pace – a difficult conclusion for Jen to admit.

Marriette rose from behind her desk and beckoned Jen to her. As the women hugged, Jen attempted to apologize. Holding Jen's face in both hands, and gathering every fragment of Jen's attention, Marriette assured her that everything would work out. They were still in it together and, for the moment, this was the path that needed to be followed. She then kissed Jen on the forehead, waiting for her agreement. Gritting her teeth, with a corner of lip curled in frustration, Jen nodded in the affirmative.

During the rest of Marriette's sabbatical year, she traveled frequently, lecturing at universities throughout North America and Europe, continuing to promote their book. Seven years had passed since James's death. Marriette, then 60, was well known, single, attractive and roaming the world. There was no shortage of interesting men hoping to date her. However, she found the dating scene uncomfortable. On only a rare occasion, did she attempt to foray into an ephemeral relationship. She found it awkward; it was still difficult to be intimate with any man other than James. Marriette understood that such relationships would be different, yet emotional redefinition was confounding to her. Now, 20 years later, the matter still remained an unattended path.

Jen packed up the contents of the package to take with her to the office, so she and Marriette could consider the request together, and thoughtfully personalize the items for the golf professional. She moved back over to the open office window and sat on the sill for a while longer, scanning the marsh aglow in the setting sun.

Denny had just settled into a chaise, watching the retractable deck move back across the length of the lap pool.

– Chapter 49 –

I Read This News Today. Oh, Boy!
Tuesday, June 28, 2016
Brown University Providence, Rhode Island

The sun was barely up when Jen walked into her office at home to gather up things necessary for work. Removing her phone from its charger, she noticed Marriette had sent a text late the evening before, after returning from a visit with Jake's family in Methuen. *Jenny. Hoping you will be at yoga class at 7. Received a disconcerting e-mail. I'm fine, but would like to talk with you about it. Love.*

Jen arrived on campus just before 7 a.m., dressed for yoga. She ran down the steps into the basement of Fulton Hall, the clinical psychology department building. After dropping things off in her office, she hustled back up to the first floor, down the empty main corridor, and out the front entrance of the building facing Atlantic Avenue. The class was just beginning to gather under the maple trees lining the edge of the soccer field.

Marriette was already there, stretching. Jen placed her yoga mat down on the grass and walked over to greet Marriette. The women hadn't spoken since the Friday past.

"Good morning, darling," Marriette greeted Jen as they hugged.

"Good morning, 'M'. I'm sorry, I left my phone in my office last night and didn't get a chance to look at it again until early this morning. What's going on?"

A young looking 74, Marriette appeared as fit in her yoga gear as she had when Jen first met her.

"I have a problem," she answered quietly. "Do you have some time for a chat later today?"

"Of course I do. Whatever is going on?"

"You'll never believe this, but someone has been digging into my past."

"Your past? What could be so problematic about that?"

As Marriette looked at Jen with a slight head tilt, Jen let out a deep breath, suddenly guessing at what might be going on.

"Digging? Could you possibly mean?"

"Yes, exactly, the Land Rover."

"The Land Rover!" Jen exclaimed, lifting her Oakleys from her eyes, inadvertently speaking louder than intended.

Marriette put a finger to her lips. "Shush, darling," she said, guiding Jen off to the side, away from the gathering class.

"I received an email from a *LeMonde* reporter which included a very detailed video recently reported on a Paris television station."

"Oh, no!"

"Yes, indeed, but I can't get into it right now. Maybe at the end of the day?"

"Yes, of course. I'll make it work."

"Do you think you can come by the house? I'll make dinner for us. You'll be astonished at what I have to show you. It's actually quite amazing, but disturbing as well."

"Sure. Dennis won't mind. It's Tuesday night. He doesn't teach class again until Wednesday afternoon, so predictably, he'll end up staying at the other house. If he doesn't have to teach, he just stays at the other house after working late in his woodshop," Jen chided.

Picking up on Jen's sarcastic tone, Marriette questioned, "And, you don't seem too happy with that?"

"Well, he does spend a good deal of time there."

"Perhaps, we should talk about this sometime?"

"Mmm, maybe. So, yes, why don't we leave from work together? Is that okay with you?"

"Yes, okay, then that's what we'll do, my dear," Marriette agreed, as the women rejoined their group.

Assured now of Jen's support, Marriette re-focused on her breathing and execution of positions. She looked out across the glistening dew-covered athletic field, concentrating on the sun rising in the morning sky. Cars began to fill the parking spaces along Atlantic Avenue as the summer activity on campus picked up.

During class, Jen shot a glance over at Marriette, signaling an understanding gaze, and blew a reassuring kiss with the tips of her fingers. After class, they walked across the street together. Marriette continued up the hill to her home. Jen ran off to the swim team's weight room before returning to her office to begin her day.

– Chapter 50 –

A Buried Treasure . . . of Sorts
Tuesday, June 28, 2016   Providence, Rhode Island

Later that afternoon, Jen knocked once on Marriette's office door before entering. Reflecting her status as a long tenured and respected faculty member, Marriette had acquired the finest office in Fulton Hall. She was recognized by her colleagues as an original thinker and major contributor to the field of cognitive behavior psychology.

Her antique desk was still in fine condition; it was one of the original desks when historic Fulton Hall was constructed in the 1880s. The funding for the building had been provided by an entrepreneur, alumnus, and former Civil War U.S. Army general officer, MacKenzie Islington. To pay tribute to this gentleman's contribution, the principals at Brown University had, at the end of the 19th century, commissioned his portrait be painted by John Singer Sargent. At one time, the original painting loomed large on the wall behind Marriette's desk, but it had long since been displayed in the University's art gallery. A quite accurate reproduction, commissioned by Marriette and executed by a former RISD student, was now hanging in its place. The terse gaze of General MacKenzie Islington appeared to focus on those who happened to have occasion to sit on the sofa across from Marriette's desk.

An abundance of light filtered in from the east, through two large paned windows. The sills had been installed six feet above the ground floor, rising a similar distance to the ceiling. Two light fixtures, with large white glass globes from the dawn of electricity, hung suspended from the tin plate ceiling. Original built-in mahogany bookcases, located behind Marriette's desk, were filled with books and other files of journals and papers that Marriette had published, edited, or contributed to during her illustrious career.

"Come in, Jenny. Get comfortable while I finish up. I'll be ready to go shortly."

Jen walked over to the little refrigerator by the window and reached in for a small bottle of water.

"Well, 'M', I'm pretty curious to find out what's going on here."

"I am, as well . . . you'll see what I mean by that soon enough. There, I'm all set. Shall we go, then?"

"Sure."

The women left Fulton Hall together. Jen followed Marriette out of the parking lot to her big yellow house on Prospect Street, a hilly, tree-lined neighborhood near Moses Brown. Turning into the driveway leading to the back of the house, Jen admired the pink and blue hydrangeas that were nearing full bloom, forming a border along the property fence line. Marriette's house felt like a second home to Jen.

The door to the workshop was open, exposing the tailgate of the red truck. Although two decades had passed, it still served as a comfortable reminder of James. On clear summer days such as this, Marriette would intentionally leave the garage door ajar, so the shiny red truck would be the first thing she noticed coming home.

Marriette prepared a light supper which was enjoyed on the porch over-looking the flower gardens in the backyard. After their meal, they returned to the kitchen where Marriette opened a chilled bottle of Sauvignon Blanc. She poured the wine into each of their glasses, then turned to face Jen. "Well, now, on to my little problem."

Picking up her glass, she gestured in the direction of the living room.

"Why don't we sit in the parlor. I have quite the presentation for you."

Jen followed behind Marriette and took a seat at one end of the large couch. Marriette placed her laptop on the coffee table, sitting down beside her.

"I've been quite troubled since receiving this email on Saturday. I'm feeling somewhat more relaxed now, having had time to think through what I'm about to show you."

"Saturday! 'M', why didn't you call?" Jen squealed in a voice an octave higher than normal.

"I felt it could wait. And, I needed time to consider my response."

Marriette opened an e-mail and clicked onto a link to a video. The source was a Paris television station. The video, taped in French, was a thirty-second news spot showing a vehicle still partially buried in gravel somewhere in Northern Ghana, with its front fender, bumper and right wheel oddly emerging from a wall of soil. Marriette began translating the commentary for Jen.

The following segment reported that the recovered vehicle was identified as a 1967 Land Rover. Unearthed, except for its flat tires, the truck looked exactly as it did the day it was buried. Jen moved closer to Marriette, leaning in, looking squarely at the screen.

"Oh, look at that!" she examined closely. "Hit pause. So, that's it!"

"Yes, indeed it is," Marriette confirmed.

For Marriette, it was a disturbing sight. Spread out on the ground, laying on a blue tarpaulin in front of the vehicle was a Kalashnikov assault rifle, a handgun, ammunition clips, an empty liquor bottle, an opened container of field rations, and an item the shape of a box, which was not identified in the reporting.

Inadvertently, the Land Rover and its contents, had been discovered during excavation on the construction site of a new hospital. The segment went on to report that the origin of the vehicle and reason for its having been buried, had not been determined.

"Holy shit, 'M'. This is really it! This is the vehicle you spoke about 20 years ago. Golly, someone found it!"

"Yes, someone found it. Wait, there's more."

Marriette read the rest of the e-mail from the French reporter, Jacques Lemieux. He stated that he had written an article, citing specific information about the vehicle, its contents, and location. The article noted that a significant amount of blood was found in the rear of the vehicle belonging to an African male. Traces of Eastern European male blood were found as well. Samples of long hair indicated the presence of a female of Western European origin.

The article went on to describe a botanical plant press, containing samples of hair from the same West European female found in between layers of newspaper from the *Montreal Gazette*, dating back to the years of 1970 and 1971. The top of the press was stamped with the inscription, McGill University, Department of Botany with the name, M. C. LaFleur.

His investigation was ongoing, as was that of the West Ghanan and French governments. Lemieux discovered the individual whose name was on the plant press had changed to Roy. The reporter said he had little difficulty using search engines to research Marriette's background and career. He went on to make it clear that the purpose of his e-mail was not to threaten her; he was concerned she might interpret his communication as threatening.

His intention, however, was to learn more about what had occurred four decades earlier. He was confident there was a great story to tell.

Jen looked over at Marriette in disbelief, "This is unbelievable, 'M'!"

"Yes, I agree. It has been a lot to digest," Marriette admitted with an audible sigh.

"You're dragging yourself back through the whole event and more, aren't you?"

"Of course ... and everything else I can conjure up as possible fallout from this recent ... unearthing!"

"Ahhh! Have you responded to the reporter?"

"No, not yet."

"Wow. Well, first of all, you've done nothing wrong except lose a plant press from McGill University."

"And I guess they can get it back," Marriette replied, wryly, attempting to interject some humor.

"I am concerned that this could become a burdensome event for me. It's possible it might even present a considerable amount of exposure that I'm not the least bit interested in. I can just see me back on *Good Morning America* and the like."

"I understand, 'M'."

"Before going any further, Jen, I want to show you some other things for the sake of completeness."

"Sure."

"It's clear that I can be linked to this vehicle. The square-shaped box next to the weapons in the video is one of my plant presses. I may have left it because it was covered with the blood of the mule. And there are plants in it. They are, indeed, wrapped in newspaper from the *Montreal Gazette* with the dates cited. I believe, I had six of those plant presses, all identical."

Marriette rose from the couch, and walked into an adjoining room, returning with an open cardboard box.

As she placed the box on the coffee table in front of them, she explained, "A treasure from the attic! I discovered it while opening a box that was placed inside a second box during one of our early moves. It has been sitting, forgotten, up in the attic, since moving into this house in 1980."

Marriette had opened only the outer box. Inside sat a second tattered cardboard box still sealed with its original yellowed, brittle cellophane tape. The top of the inside box was labeled 'Plant Press' with the repacking date, 1974, in parenthesis.

Jen looked up inquisitively at Marriette.

"Shall we open it?"

"Yes!"

Marriette carried it back to the kitchen island top. As she held onto the outer box, Jen gently pulled the older one out. Marriette slowly peeled off the worn tape, opening the disintegrating cardboard flaps.

"Look at that!" Jen exclaimed.

Marriette sat silent staring at the top of the plant press.

"There it is. Exactly like the other five, including the one left in the Land Rover."

Plainly stamped on the top of the plant press was 'Property of McGill University Dept. Botanic,' with the name, M. C. LaFleur in faded black Magic Marker. Marriette unbuckled each of the straps and removed the wooden lattice cover. She then separated the top layers of newspaper, carefully unfolding each, to examine the top of the page. There was the date of 11 August 1970. She delicately removed a folded and desiccated herbal plant, its efflorescence of white petals mostly disintegrated into ivory dust.

"Well, they were all just like this one. Look, here's one of my long brown hairs!" Marriette remarked, pulling the long singular strand from its entanglement. She compared the chestnut color to her long silver hair falling across her shoulder.

The women stood at the granite counter, gazing at the unique object from the distant past before putting the press back together and replacing it into the original boxes.

"There is one more item I want you to see, Jenny. It was too large for me to bring down from the attic. Well, not too large, but too . . . something."

Jen followed Marriette up the stairs to the second floor, through another door, and up a second flight into the attic. The space was still hot from the summer day's heat. A scratched up, olive drab steamer trunk, with stamped brass corner guards, lay on the floor near the top of the stairs.

In the dimly lit room with a single bulb hanging over the top of the stairwell, Marriette opened the trunk. After removing the blankets and tablecloths stored inside, a piece of curved wire lay on the floor of the empty trunk, untouched for decades. Marriette picked it up and used it to pry open the false bottom.

The women knelt down in front of the trunk as Marriette raised the false floor. Shifting her position to better view what was hidden beneath the trunk's floor, Jen directed the beam of light from a flashlight into the interior of the box.

"Jeez! 'M'!" she gasped. "There it is!"

There lay the other AKM, its surfaces dulled in aged cosmoline, resting ominously in its shaped nest, along with two full magazines adjacent, similarly encased.

"'M'? Was this the gun you ... ?"

"Yes my dear. It is. This is the infamous gun which saved our lives. I haven't fired it since Pete Long closed his range, well before he died, and well before we moved here.

We buried the other Kalashnikov with the Land Rover and I carried this one home with me in my brother's special trunk."

Jen reached in, cautiously touching its barrel with her fingertips, as if it were a sleeping serpent that might awaken and strike her.

She turned to capture Marriette's far away expression, probably in that moment reviewing the rather disturbing history of the weapon. After carefully replacing the stored items, Marriette closed the lid of the trunk.

The two returned back downstairs into the living room to sit again on the sofa. Intrigued by these sudden new details, Jen rattled off question after question.

"Do you think you will hear from McGill? Who else might possibly respond to this discovery? I would certainly find the unearthing of this vehicle, and all the implications of its contents, fascinating. I can understand why the reporter is so interested. He must be dying to get at the story. If only he knew!"

Marriette now responded with reservation, "Jenny. I feel I'm getting too old for this kind of attention. I'm not sure how I want to handle it."

"I completely understand, 'M'. Maybe you should alert our attorney tomorrow. She might help to contain a lot of this."

"I agree dear. I'll call Francine tomorrow. I don't want to get too far ahead of myself, but over the weekend I began to consider the idea of taking a leave of absence."

"Well, if necessary, 'M'. If that makes sense."

"It's getting late, Jenny. Would you like to stay over tonight? We can put a hold on this and sit out on the back porch to enjoy the rest of our evening."

"That would be nice. A little quiet time. Yes. Let's just put this on the shelf for now. I'll give Dennis a call."

– Chapter 51 –

Something's Happening Here

Wednesday, June 29, 2016
Prospect Street, Providence, Rhode Island

Jen's phone alarm woke her up at 6 a.m. For a moment, she forgot she had stayed the night at Marriette's. The sun was just beginning to rise above the rooftop next door, streaming bright sunlight into the bedroom. Sitting up on the edge of the bed, she placed a good morning call to Dennis. Without going into too much detail, Jen explained that she and Marriette had been up conversing until 1 a.m. She would soon leave for her office, before heading over to the VA clinic for the morning.

Marriette was already in the kitchen making breakfast, when Jen arrived downstairs.

"Good morning 'M'!" Jen greeted Marriette cheerfully.

"Good morning, my dear. I hope you slept well. I kept you up very late."

"I fell asleep right away. I might still be sleeping if it wasn't for my alarm. I'm going to run off to school. Going to the weight room first."

"Would you like something to eat? Maybe some tea?"

"Yes, tea please."

"How about an English muffin? I'm having one."

"Ok, thanks. A couple, if you don't mind. And some peanut butter, please? I have other things for later."

"Sure. And bananas for the road?" Marriette quipped, knowing Jen's routine.

"Yes, of course, thank you!"

They sat together at the counter, enjoying breakfast, with the box containing the plant press still occupying a corner.

Holding her mug of coffee to her lips with both hands, Marriette looked over at Jen.

"Jen, I guess I can't consider this as unexpected, but I had a nightmare last night, a flashback. Certainly not the vivid dreams I experienced twenty years ago, but interesting," she reflected.

Pointing to the cardboard box sitting on the counter, Jen responded thoughtfully, "'M,' try not to revisit any of this today. Put the plant press away. And, you don't need to watch the video, either. But let me know if you receive any other communication. Don't wait this time; tell me right away. Will you agree?"

Smiling, Marriette answered affectionately, "I know what you're doing, Jenny. You're right. I will be disciplined, I promise."

"Why don't you come over to my place on Friday evening," Jen suggested, "so we can really focus on what should be done? Maybe you'll have more information by then."

"Let's talk about Friday night later today," Marriette replied. "Thank you, dear."

"Had you thought of responding to the reporter today?" Jen inquired.

"I was considering sending a short reply. Something to the effect, 'Thank you for your inquiry. A response will be forthcoming shortly.' How does that sound? As we discussed, I will speak with our attorney first."

"All right. I like that," Jen answered. "Should hold him over for a while, I hope, but run it by Fran first. Oh my, look at the time, I'd better scoot. See you later?"

"Yes, I'll call Fran this morning, dear. See you later on." She left by way of the back porch, and out to her Jeep. As Jen covered the short distance to the University, she wondered what might happen next.

– Chapter 52 –

Do You Want to Know a Secret?

Friday, July 1, 2016
Rocky Points Rd., Denessen, Rhode Island

Friday evening, Marriette drove along the coast to Jen's place. Denny made a brief appearance long enough to say hello to Marriette, before heading off to his workshop. The women moved onto the back deck to settle in as the sun set on the estuarine landscape. Jen slid one of the cushioned Adirondack chairs closer to Marriette.

"So, where are things at this point, 'M'?" Jen inquired.

"I had a lengthy conversation with Fran today," Marriette answered. "The plan now is to filter everything through her. Even though I gave her the short version of the story, it still took an hour. She was astounded. Then, of course, she remarked that this could be material for another book."

"Of course. Why am I not surprised?" Jen chuckled with measured sarcasm at their publishing attorney's assumption. "I can see those blue eyes popping right out of her head."

Francine Burnette's eagerness for another book perked Jen's interest as well. However, considering Marriette's present predicament, she curbed her enthusiasm.

"I also heard from the reporter today," Marriette continued. "He thanked me for my response and requested an interview. I quickly returned an email informing Mssr. Lemieux that our attorney, Francine, would be in contact by Monday."

"Okay, so, it seems like things are organizing fairly well. Are you more comfortable now, 'M'?"

"Yes, I am. We'll wait to see what happens next."

Marriette stood up from her chair and paced around the deck, stopping to lean against the railing. Pausing, she removed the clip from her long hair, letting it fall free, before reworking the French twist on top of her head.

"Something else has been on my mind, Jen. It's almost as though I need to hear myself say the words."

"What's that, 'M'?"

Raising a palm to her forehead, Marriette audibly sighed, "Oh, Jenny, why did I ever keep this a secret for so long?"

"Buried secrets," Jen mused.

"Mmm . . . Buried secrets!" Marriette repeated. "I can't help but find that notion somewhat humorous. I'm now realizing that so much more of the intangible was buried - more than what was arrayed in front of the truck in that video."

Jen, sensing where Marriette was heading in their conversation, nodded in agreement.

"Maybe," Marriette quipped, 'this is all just a really good story about a 75-year-old professor, now quite easily distinguished from the partially naked, assault-weapon-brandishing 29-year-old girl."

Laughing out loud, Jen commented, "That creates quite an image, 'M', like a Mort Kunstler cover on some paperback novel from the 50s."

Getting up from her chair, Jen walked over to where Marriette was leaning against the railing. Although Marriette's intention was to add humor, Jen recognized that the thoughts running through her mind were not. Placing a hand on Marriette's shoulder, she offered an apology for laughing.

"I get it," Marriette smiled. "My goodness. It does."

"So, since learning of the unearthing of the Land Rover, I've had a plethora of forgotten feelings and memories swirling around in my head – many of them negative, unfortunately. Most likely, I probably would not have revisited them but for this revelation."

"Well, of course, but here you are, 'M'," Jen stated.

"Do you mind hearing me out for a bit, Jenny?"

"Please, go ahead."

Returning to their chairs, Marriette settled in and closed her eyes, allowing for the story and feelings to surface once again.

"Although my last three months with Havra and the tribe were beautiful in so many ways, I felt fearful every day, – especially at night, believing someone would be coming for us. I felt somewhat safer the day my return was under-way, and then safer still when I arrived at the airport at Gibraltar. I was quite relieved when I finally landed in Montreal, but then my father gave me the bad news about my brother, and I did not sleep soundly again for many weeks."

Leaning forward on the large arm of the Adirondack chair, Jen pointed out, "The discovery of the Land Rover was bound to open up many of those old wounds, thoughts, feelings."

"Yes, it has, Jen. At least now I understand how to manage them. I suspect I'll find myself talking about this in the months ahead. I know I can deal with the old images, but what I don't want is the notoriety which is bound to emerge from the news story. I have long since redefined the meaning of those images, though."

"What specific images are you referring to, 'M'?" Jen questioned.

Marriette calmly described the troubling images held deeply within her, "Over these many years, I occasionally experienced nightmares re-envisioning the Russian's face looming over me, wondering if I was going to die when he was through with me . . . or . . . seeing the chest of the other mercenary exploding, and minutes later picking up bits of his body to hide from anyone who might come looking for him . . . or . . . the image of my executing the other bastard as he lay wounded at my feet . . . and then . . . of course, I can still see the fatal head wound inflicted on Havra's young son."

"That seems like a lot to carry, 'M'."

"Yes," Marriette explained, "it's all still there, but I have since learned to redefine those images as harmless, habituated, and modified, to the point where they have become surreal. It's been so long now, it's as though they're from someone else's life."

"What was going through your mind as you resettled back into Canada that summer?"

"Back then, I was afraid about what might happen if McGill learned of my involvement in the killing of those two mercenaries, and of the death of the young boy, Tave, a member of the tribe my school had been studying for decades. I was concerned there would be legal consequences, or at the very least, my career would be affected for the long term, in very negative ways."

Quietly considering a past rarely visited, Marriette hesitated, rubbing her face in her hands.

She then looked out onto the marsh, taking in a deep breath. "I never spoke about it after returning to McGill, but I always had the feeling of waiting for the other shoe to drop . . . I imagined being handed a note to report to the department chairman.

"I was 29 years old then and wasn't sure how to handle it ... or maybe I did and didn't feel I could trust anyone. I wanted to talk to my brother - only to my brother. With his death, I felt completely alone in my predicament."

"The discovery of the Land Rover is a powerful trigger for those memories to resurface," Jen reminded her. "You certainly had a lot on your mind when you met James."

"Yes, I did," Marriette agreed. "You can see how important my relationship to James was, right from the beginning. Eventually, I became a Clinical Psychologist. Self-treatment only – until you and I began working together."

"Pretty damn good original self-treatment, by the way!" Jen interjected. Can you believe it? It's been 20 years since you first shared this story with me!"

"Yes," Marriette recalled. "You walked over to my house during that winter snowstorm."

"I remember the day well, 'M'."

"The first person I confided my story to was James. We concluded it was best not to tell anyone about my experience in Africa. So, I made the decision to store it away and go on with my life. What I regret now is that I didn't entrust the story to Harris and Jake as they became young men. If this news should become public, it is imperative that I tell them first, which I plan to do very soon."

"Yes, it seems to be the most important thing to do right now," Jen agreed.

"I also wonder about how Brown University may react, discovering their well-known faculty member's implication in a very strange incident, even though it happened 40 or so years ago. Wouldn't that precipitate bad press?"

"'M', please, don't get too far ahead of yourself. If Chancellor Graham ever gets wind of this, and he probably will, I suspect you'll receive a friendly and respectful call from him. And, don't forget, Françine is your gatekeeper. She will buffer everything."

"We shall see ... We shall see ... Damn it, Jenny. How I wish it had all just remained buried!"

Feeling the exhaustion of it all, Marriette moved back to a chaise. Suddenly, Jen lit up with a spontaneous and curious notion. She jumped up and plunked herself down next to Marriette.

"'M'. Here's a thought, Jen blurt out. Geez! Wouldn't this be wild! . . . What if Havra is still alive, and he's in a position to also learn of this new information? Might be a possibility! Don't rule that out."

Still feeling gloomy, Marriette responded, "I suppose, but hard to imagine ..."

Pulling her sweater across her shoulders, she stared out onto the marsh.

Sighing deeply, she repeated, "I'm really not up for this, Jen. I feel as though I'm at a stage in life where I don't want to deal with the public."

Trying to pull her thoughts together, Marriette began to ponder the upcoming weeks. She would need to start putting together a plan.

"I think I will make a trip to see Harris," Marriette thought aloud. "Maybe we can meet at Rutgers. I don't want to involve the rest of the family just yet, not before first informing him."

"And perhaps I should take a leave of absence beginning in September. Maybe think about retiring?"

Jen looked over at Marriette with loving concern, recognizing her vulnerability, and how the accumulating stress was weighing so heavily on her.

"Easy now, 'M'. Let's just see what next week brings. It's getting chilly. Come on, let's go back inside."

Back in the kitchen, Jen left to grab a sweatshirt from her bedroom. Marriette got up to check her email as she had not done so since lunchtime.

An earlier entry at 2 p.m. immediately caught her attention. She re-read it a second time before shouting to Jen.

"Je ne peux pas le croire! Jenny! Viens ici. Il m'a trouvé! Il m'a trouvé!" (I cannot believe it! Jenny! Come here. He found me! He found me!)

Jen came running in from the bedroom. "'M'? What is it?"

"Havra! il m'a trouvé!"

"What?"

"Goodness! Jenny! This is unbelievable! You were right! You were right! Look at this!"

Astounded, Marriette flopped down onto one of the barstools. Jen took the phone from her hand and read the email.

"Jenny. Please. Read it aloud, would you? I can hardly believe what I've just read!"

Jen began:

1 July 2016

Dear Prof. Roy,

For the sake of introduction, my name is Neville Peters. I am a professor of molecular genetics at the University of Nottingham. However, my reason for contacting you is not one of a professional nature.

You may or may not be aware that a 50-year-old Land Rover was recently unearthed in Northern Ghana. I would venture to say, exactly where you left it in 1972. I am including a video link and a link to an article in Le Monde, *in case you aren't already aware of this.*

I am writing on behalf of my good friend, Havra Emerson, who felt that taking this introductory approach, after all of these years, would be the most appropriate.

Havra is alive and well, living north of Paris. He has quite a story to tell, I assure you. I have known him since 1985 when he converted his big game hunting business into an ecologically sane, wildlife conserving one. He helped put Eco-tours on the map in Africa. He is an attorney and has recently retired from his position as Director of the International Wildlife Fund of France.

Havra has become a close friend and is a most remarkable man.

Over the past few weeks, we have learned much about your accomplished career, all of which, of course, is public.

Havra was hoping you might want to re-acquaint.

If, however, you find this communication intrusive, he then wishes to offer his sincere apology.

> *Sincerely,*
> *Neville Peters*

Addendum: Attached are a few recent photos of us outside his home in Normandy.

Marriette and Jen stared at each other in matched expressions of astonishment.

"Oh, 'M'!" Jen cried out, "This is incredible!"

"There he is," Marriette gasped studying the photo. "That's Havra. There's the eagle tattoo on his neck. See it? Oh, my, Jen. I'm at a complete loss. Really, I am!"

Jen slid her barstool closer, as Marriette firmly held Jen's arm, their heads together, peering at the images on her phone.

"It's really him!" Marriette repeated. "It's really Havra!"

Jen looked at Marriette, sporting a wide smile.

"Seems Havra is not only accomplished, but very handsome, 'M'. Wow! He's been out there in the world, all this time! Oh, and his friend, Neville, is adorable."

"How ironic, Jen, that he finds me!" Marriette uttered in disbelief.

Jen continued to examine the details in the photos.

"Oh, 'M'! Look at them with their Martins – and the beautiful French country-side in the background. Their Martins! Musicians! And the ocean! Looks like Havra did all right for himself," Jen observed.

Marriette's mind raced to fully grasp the magnitude of the moment.

"Jenny, this is Harris's father! Harris will be able to meet his biological father . . . and Havra is going to learn he has another son!"

Marriette stood up from the counter, her eyes filled with tears of joy and disbelief, as she embraced Jen.

"Oh, Jenny, I really need to collect myself. Please, help me draft a thoughtful response right now, will you?"

Trying to calm herself, Marriette sat back down at the counter.

"'M', wait. I'm going to open a great bottle of Cabernet," Jen proposed, as she disappeared into her pantry. The women took the wine with them into the living room, while exchanging a few ideas before drafting the response.

1 July 2016

Dear Neville,

I opened your e-mail only moments ago and am thrilled beyond measure with the wonderful news you bring to me.

Yes, I have been aware of the discovery of the Land Rover for about a week. I am somewhat concerned that it might provide me with publicity that I don't desire at this point in my life.

However, the greater point is that the discovery brings a most important person back into my life.

Neville, would it be possible to arrange a phone call between Havra and me? I would love to speak with him. Perhaps this weekend?

This evening, I'm at the home of a dear friend, Jen Walker. I will forward a photo of us taken tonight.

Thank you so much.

Sincerely,
Marriette

As Marriette hit *send* on the e-mail, the women clinked their glasses of wine together in celebration.

"My dear. This has been quite the evening. I think I'd better head home."

"Should you spend the night?" Jen offered.

"Thank you, but I'd best be home just in case."

"Yes, of course."

Jen walked Marriette down the spiral stairwell and out to her car. The sky was bright with stars. There was little wind, and the insects could be heard calling loudly from the surrounding vegetation.

"Pay attention on the way home, 'M', and please let me know if you hear anything. I'm so excited for you!"

"Yes, dear. I will. I'll let you know right away, as soon as I get a response. I love you, Jenny, my dear."

"I love you, too, 'M'. Be safe. Let me know when you're arrived home, okay?"

As the taillights of Marriette's vehicle disappeared around the curve in the driveway, her tires could be heard crunching along to the main road. Jen viewed glimpses of the headlights shine through breaks in the woods, as Marriette's Volvo accelerated into the distance.

Inspired by the beautiful summer evening, Jen decided to run upstairs, grab her keys, and drive down to Dennis's workshop to share the exciting news.

After arriving in the driveway of the other house, Jen walked into the backyard toward the barn. The sliding door to the barn was open with the lights on, but Dennis wasn't there. She returned to the house and peered through the windows into the living room, pressing her nose against the pane. The television was on, tuned to the Red Sox game. Dennis was asleep on the couch, his back toward her. An empty bag of Fritos and a pint of Häagen-Daz Cherry Garcia ice cream, with a spoon still in the container, rested on the coffee table beside him. Jen chose not to bother him. She got back into her Jeep and drove home.

As Marriette passed through Providence on NB I-95, she rounded the curve before the exit that would take her home. For years, she had avoided driving this patch of Rt. 95, following Route 1-A through Cranston, instead. Hundreds of excursions later, she again, automatically shifted into the passing lane to avoid the location where James's red truck was crushed 20 years earlier.

– Chapter 53 –

Havra Meets Neville

1985   Somewhere in North Benin

Originally from England, Neville Peters never intended to leave his native homeland to attend college, but after a casual conversation in a local restaurant, he was left with a very positive impression of Emory University in Atlanta. Ultimately, it became the only foreign school he applied to. He was accepted and offered a scholarship that he couldn't pass up, so, in the fall of 1979, Neville set off to the States.

Being the odd man out in his family, Neville scored exceptionally well in his AS Levels. Throughout his secondary education, he had developed a love of nature and biochemistry. Both parents were musicians, as were several cousins – one with an iconic reputation. He himself was accomplished in that respect, but came to the conclusion early on that he wasn't cut out to make music his career. He was tempted once to change his mind – during his freshman year at Emory. But he didn't go through with it. However, he made some interesting connections.

As Neville was settling into the freshman double assigned to him, his room-mate, Rick, arrived dragging a large trunk in one hand, while grasping a guitar case in the other. As they introduced themselves, Rick noticed Neville's guitar case propped up against a wall. The two quickly became good friends.

The roommates enjoyed playing guitar together so much that they soon began jamming with friends on campus and playing in nearby University of Georgia and Atlanta clubs. Freshman year proved to be an academic struggle for both of them. The extracurricular activities drained time from what they should have attended to. Neville's grades were not what his parents had expected. However, somehow he survived his first year. Fortunately, for Neville's biochemistry career, Rick transferred from Emory, moving to nearby Athens. Separated from his musician friend, Neville refocused on his science curriculum.

Meanwhile, Rick made new friends in Athens and formed a new band. Occasionally, Neville traveled to Athens to sit in on their sessions. All friends grew close, with Neville familiarizing himself with their material. When one of the band members broke his arm, Neville sat in for him, leaving school for the fall semester to tour with the group. It was the second time that he had to make a choice between science and music. Rick and his band were clearly going somewhere, but the brief detour into the music scene confirmed to Neville that he did not have the passion or commitment for the rock 'n' roll lifestyle. He returned to refocus seriously on his studies as the winter semester began.

As a senior studying population genetics at Emory, Neville began investigating genetic shifts in allele frequency, working with a professor at the medical school. He then chose to pursue similar work at Cornell University. In 1985, as a new graduate student in the Department of Ornithology, he accepted the invitation to pursue his interest in population genetics, using the tools of molecular biology to drive his research.

Neville learned of a species of colonial sparrows exhibiting social behavior that fit the needs of his thesis. It was an ideal species in which to investigate evolution within its colony and adjacent colonies. The species was endemic to Benin and adjacent countries. Neville investigated a guide business in that region owned by a man named Havra Emerson and inquired if he might consider hosting graduate students. Havra responded favorably to his letter.

In their first communication, Havra confirmed that he was able to provide the necessary services, however, he also requested more specific information on the sparrows. He was familiar with the bird Neville referenced and wanted to familiarize himself with the locations of the colonies, plus the behavioral characteristics of the species. Havra thanked Neville for his interest and emphasized that he was currently directing his business away from hunting and was, instead, seeking clients who were more interested in observation only.

Within three months, Neville arrived in West Africa with an array of equipment designed to catch, band, and release individual birds, along with the tools for drawing blood samples that would be sent back to Ithaca. Havra made certain to make time available to guide Neville, whenever his schedule allowed him to be on site. Neville was amazed to discover that Havra had researched additional information and had devoted time to observing the local colonies prior to his arrival.

Spending their first day together, Havra drove Neville out to a colony location, showing him favorite feeding grounds and likely places to establish mist nets for capture and banding. On subsequent days, he pointed out stray individuals flying between colonies, outside of their predicted breeding pool. Havra's knowledge surprised Neville, and he began to appreciate this man's intimate connection to his surroundings.

One afternoon, during Neville's first week, while out on an excursion, he and Havra were standing in deep brush under a tree not far from a mist net they had erected. They were waiting patiently to capture sparrows that were leaving a favorite feeding site to fly back to their colony. Holding binoculars up to his eyes, Neville watched for birds in transit.

Suddenly, Havra spoke in a calm, hushed, but directed voice, "Do not move, Neville. This is very important. Do not move. Do not speak. Keep the binoculars to your eyes."

A long chestnut colored snake with a creamy belly had maneuvered down from an overhead tree branch. The snake coursed along the top of Neville's backpack and up across the nape of his neck.

"Yes, that is a snake you feel moving across your back. She's going to realize there's no place to go, nothing to eat, and return to the branch above you. As she extends her neck further, she will probably look around near your face. You may feel her tongue flick against the side of your hand. Do not move. She is just exploring. There is nothing she wants here. She will leave."

The snake's shiny brown head was now visible in shadow, as Neville's eyes stayed pressed into the ocular cups. He continued to breathe gently, and evenly.

"Remain motionless, Neville. She's retreating."

The snake arched in reverse, looking at Havra as she turned, before stretching back up toward the next branch. Neville began to feel her weight lift from his backpack.

"Don't move yet, Neville. I'll tell you when it's safe to move."

The brown snake moved gracefully back onto the branch in the direction of the upper trunk of the tree.

"Step casually to your left, Neville, away from the tree trunk."

Neville did so, while slowly lowering the binoculars from his eyes. At the same time Havra also slowly stepped back from the trunk.

"My young friend ... you handled that well!"

Neville turned to face his guide, who was grinning at him. Neville smiled, shaking his head in amazement.

"Thanks, Havra," Neville answered, as he searched the upper branches of the tree where he had been standing.

"What was she?"

"We may never see another, Neville, but we still need to be mindful. This may be her tree. I would have anticipated her appearance, if we were near the actual colony location, which happens to be a good hunting ground for her and her family. Extremely poisonous. Hemolytic. We will have to be very careful there. I carry anti-venom in the truck, in the cooler, but, have never had to use it. If you had flinched, we may have had to test the serum for the first time."

Neville recognized how calm he felt throughout the long minute or so the snake was within fatal striking distance. Havra's manner and tone had provided Neville with a confidence he hadn't had to think twice about.

"This was quite an interesting introduction to sharing the same shady spot with another creature," Neville commented. "A female? Big girl . . . heavy on my neck."

"Almost two meters," Havra remarked. "The male is smaller."

Neville continued looking up into the branches. She was no longer visible.

****

At the end of the day, Havra prepared a hearty supper of antelope, faro, and spiced steamed greens. The complex was quiet as no other clients were present. With dinner concluded, Havra mentioned, "Neville, I noticed you brought a guitar with you."

"Always bring my traveler with me. It's a little 0018 NY . . . you play?"

"I do. I began to study about five years ago. One of my longtime clients and mentor, Oskar, is a jazz guitarist, and frequent guest. He makes regular visits to experience solitude – and write his music. He was born in Benin, but now lives in South Africa. When I travel back to Paris, I take lessons there as well. Most evenings, when Oskar is here, we usually go out into the field behind the house to play our music and enjoy the sunset on the grasslands. Would you be interested in doing that?"

"Yes, of course. I'll go get my Martin."

Ten minutes later, the men walked together along the well-worn path, through dense foliage, then out onto the open grassland, with their guitars and cans of beer in hand. They sat comfortably on a large fallen tree trunk; the view looked eastward, with the sun setting behind them.

"After I purchased this property," Havra explained, "I would often come here to find solitude, when my workday was done. At first, it was a struggle to find refuge from my day to day dealings with civilization. Don't misunderstand me ... I was happy and grateful for my new life, but it was a grand departure from the life I led prior to 1973. I missed home.

"So, I would sit here," Havra gestured toward the tree trunk, "sorting through my thoughts, reflecting on my origins. After guiding a hunt for the simple amusement of our customers, my meditation at dusk fulfilled a way of working through the guilt that accompanied the hunting activities. Twelve years after I began operating this business, it's finally on the right track."

"And, what is the right track, Havra?" the young Neville inquired.

"Right from the beginning, I began to accumulate clients who only wanted to observe and photograph the animals. These were exactly the clients I wanted.

"Others returned as well, who had hunted before, but now chose only to photograph. Instead of arriving with their expensive rifles, they carried expensive still and movie cameras. The information was passed along to like-minded friends who also became clients. This new group of clients had different requirements. They wanted more comfort, convenient living conditions at the home base, along with better food. Our trucks needed to be refitted for photography, both film, and now video. We directed our profits toward making these improvements."

"I'd say your accommodations are pretty nice right now. I had wondered if I might be staying in a tent for six months."

Chuckling, Havra continued with his story, "A few months ago, a certain incident brought an end to the hunting for good. I'll fill you in about it sometime. Right now, we still have a few remaining clients with previous hunting agreements. Although we're honoring those contracts, when they're up, there will be no more.

I've been fortunate ... extremely fortunate. Thirteen years ago, I was wearing goatskin. Today, I have a thriving, and successful business. My employees are diligent, conscientious, and dependable. JP is my right-hand man, and on site full-time. I'm able to schedule my embassy duties so I can be here for one or two long weekends a month."

"Fortunate for me, I'd say," Neville added.

Looking over at Havra's guitar, Neville remarked, "Beautiful D-35. Do you play every day?"

"I try to. This particular guitar was a gift from Oskar. I'll play one of his instrumentals for you ... if you'd like."

"Sure, I'd like that."

The full sound of Havra's big Martin faded off into the savannah, echoing back from the dense foliage behind them. After Havra finished his song, Neville noted, "Havra, I haven't known you very long, but I appreciate the intimate relationship you share with your surroundings. In fact, I envy it, actually. I might've panicked with that poisonous beauty crawling across the back of my neck this afternoon, but I didn't. Your instructions were precise, and calming. It's become clear to me that you share a mutual respect with the snake and other beings inhabiting the land. I admire that."

"Thank you, Neville."

"With regard to my relationship with living things," Neville went on to explain, "I understand my place and value theirs as well. You and I appear to arrive at the same position. We come from different directions, but the essential respect is there."

"Yes," Havra agreed. "You are correct about my position, but tell me more concerning yourself? I'm curious."

"I'd guess we have another thing in common, which is, curiosity. Understanding how life evolved on this planet reveals so much about ourselves and how we arrived here. To be succinct, but not to diminish the grandeur, we and all living organisms are merely complicated chemistry. It can be mysterious at times, but it's all there to figure out. There is beauty in that. Do you have a general idea of how organisms evolve at that level of complexity?"

"I do, Neville. During my last year in college, having fulfilled my law degree requirements, I took an introductory inorganic and physics course. Perhaps, I'll pick up a biochemistry text when I'm back in Paris."

"Great ... and pick up a good primer on evolution. Let me share with you my simple summation. Given a whole lot of time, life begins with simple molecules in a process of differential successes in the environment at hand. Life builds itself uniquely, generation by generation, niche by niche, job by job ... becoming more complicated as time goes on. One life form is, in a way, a subset of the next. The way a bacterial cell functions is not unlike how any cell in our body functions. The cell chemistry is conserved throughout life. Complicated things come from a relatively simpler history. The next level of complexity is built with adaptive modification of the structure and function of the previous. You can count on it. Molecular problem solving. Modifying what is already in the toolbox."

"Elegant, isn't it?" Havra reflected, stretching his long legs out in front of him.

"Yeah. Beautiful . . . gives me goosebumps," Neville agreed, shuddering his shoulders. "Because most people haven't been educated well enough in the sciences, they believe humans are set apart from other living things . . . as somehow different and special. They say, 'We're not animals, for heaven's sake!' Well, that is a dangerous way to comprehend life."

"Neville, I find your observation about how people separate themselves from other life forms is correct, and yet troubling. During my rapid transition from living in Africa to attending school in Paris, I was shocked to learn how modern Civilization completely separates itself from the rest of the living planet. It functions as if natural resources are infinite and can never be harmed. Even though I'm of the belief that most people are spiritual in nature, possessing a natural sense of wonder and awe, it becomes a danger when spirituality is captured by false ideology and dogmatic traps."

"I agree with your assessment, Havra. We could talk about that one all night."

Neville straddled his leg over the log to face Havra.

"This is what draws me to science, Havra. Good ideas emanate from rational thought and honest discourse. Gathering knowledge requires a process that arrives at conclusions we can count on. It comes from the common consensus of objective, independent thinkers. This is belief with evidence. No faith is involved. There is no pretending to know things you don't know about the world. We would not have evolved to this present moment without truth seeking behaviors. It's the only way things get better in our world."

"Well stated and so true," Havra acknowledged.

"The more I learn about the intricacies of how living things function," Neville added, "the more in awe I am of all life forms and, subsequently, the more I respect what all life forms have in common. It is imperative to understand that we are intimately a part of the whole process, not separate from it."

"Yes. Neville," Havra agreed, "if everyone understood this, the world would be a better place. You know, I think we have the start of a beautiful friendship."

The sun was just beginning to disappear behind the hills. The sky to the west was still light with the moon rising in front of them.

"My turn for a song," Neville offered.

Havra and Neville were now facing each other, leaning on their guitars.

"This is a song written by James Taylor. It's about heading out onto the road of life, looking for direction and meaning. We all do it, don't we? Make transitions. It's about taking chances and hoping to get it right. Here's 'Sweet Baby James's."

"There is a young cowboy," Neville began, "he lives on the range . . . His horse and his cattle are his only companions . . .'"

When he had finished, Havra remarked, "Beautiful song. It speaks to me of days gone by, for sure."

As the last rays of sun fell below the treetops behind them, long shadows stretched far out onto the grass land, fading into the darkness. Havra played a quieting instrumental as the first stars appeared, before the men got up and headed back to the compound.

– Chapter 54 –

You Stepped Out of a Dream
Saturday, July 2, 2016
Prospect Street, Providence, Rhode Island

Waking up early on Saturday morning, Marriette rushed down the stairs, feeling like a child on Christmas morning. She went directly into the kitchen and opened the anticipated e-mail from Neville.

'Dear Marriette,

Thank you for your rapid reply. Would you consider receiving a phone call from Havra this afternoon? That would be 11 a.m. your time. He is looking forward to it. This must feel like a momentous occasion for both of you. I've known Havra for a long time. He is an extraordinary person. You are, too.

Let me know if 11:00 works for you.

By the way, Marriette, I'm extremely curious about the red, white, and blue telecaster hanging on the wall in the photo you sent. I'm guessing Jen is a musician? Would she consider making contact with me?

Neville

Marriette immediately responded that she would be waiting for the much-anticipated call from Havra. She messaged Jen about the plan, along with Neville's request, then decided to take a long walk around campus to exhaust some time and nervous energy.

✳✳✳✳✳✳

As Marriette returned up the hill, turning the corner onto Prospect Street, she glanced down at her phone. It was only 10:45. Lingering near the driveway of her big yellow house, she attempted to leisurely examine the new blooms on the hydrangeas. By the time she entered the kitchen, it was still only 10:50. She picked up a professional journal resting next to her phone on the countertop and began to flip through its pages. Unable to concentrate on the abstracts, she closed the magazine and slid it away from her.

Marriette looked up at the old-fashioned black-and-white cat clock ticking loudly on the wall over the sink. 10:57. Picking up her phone, she immediately put it back down, amused at her seemingly out of character lack of patience. Standing up, she stretched her arms over her head and began to pace the kitchen floor. All the while, she continued to stare at the phone's illuminated face, as the last few minutes crept by. At exactly 11:00, the phone rang. Breaking into a smile, she took a deep breath and answered, speaking in French.

"Havra?"

"Marriette. Good morning."

"Oh my, Havra. Somehow it sounds like you. This is so hard to believe," Marriette responded nervously, as she wandered out onto the porch.

Finding it difficult to still herself, she brushed her fingers through her long gray hair, inadvertently jostling open the clasp securing her hair at the back of her neck. Bouncing off the tabletop, the barrette landed on the floor, rolling under the table. In pursuit of the clasp, but finding it out of reach, she elected to just sit down on the floor of the porch. Resting her back against the wall under the jalousie windows, she found herself mesmerized by Havra's voice.

"Yes. It is really me. It's not so often a 76-year-old can feel this excited."

"I am as well. My heart is racing."

"I can hear it from here, or is that mine?" Havra quipped.

"Havra!

"By the way, Neville gave you quite the introduction, and we certainly do have stories to tell one other, don't you agree?"

"Yes, we do, Marriette. There is much to tell."

Struggling to calm herself, Marriette laughed gently, "Where do we even begin, Havra? I must admit, that just prior to receiving Neville's email, I was conveying to a dear friend, my displeasure of the discovery of something I very much would rather have remained buried. My goodness, Havra, how instantly I experienced a 180° shift in my emotions."

"I felt a similar reaction, Marriette. I already love saying your name. When I first informed Neville of the discovery of the Land Rover, only minutes into our call, he cut me off mid-sentence! 'I found her! Marriette LaFleur is Marriette Roy!' The sleuth, that he is, was already busy searching the Internet.

"He then spent the next several minutes relating what he had discovered about you. After a while, I realized I wasn't comprehending a word he had spoken. I was still processing his words, 'I found her. I found Marriette.'"

"Havra. It seems like you stepped out of a dream. It's really you."

"It is!"

"My dear Havra, let me share a little bit of what you don't know. I was married to a wonderful man and father of two boys. James was killed in an automobile accident nearly 20 years ago."

"Oh, Marriette."

"The older son, Harris, now 43, is a neurosurgeon in Maryland with two boys of his own. My younger son, Jacque, is 42 and a CPA, north of Boston. He has a son and daughter. As for me, I have never remarried."

"Marriette, first let me say, I am so sorry for your unimaginable loss. I have had a different kind of life over the past 40 years, with several short-term relationships, but nothing enduring. I've been comfortable being on my own, having a few good friends. My work involved considerable travel to and from West Africa, France, and throughout Europe; thus, not exactly a life conducive for settling down, but I've had a good life and love where I live now."

"Where is that, Havra?"

"My home is in northern France, near the channel, about an hour and a half train ride from Paris."

"Lovely. Perhaps, someday I might see it."

"I'm hoping so, Marriette."

Changing her tone to one slightly more urgent, Marriette suggested, "Havra. There is so much for us to share. I would prefer to have the opportunity to do so in person. Do you agree?"

"By all means, Marriette, I agree."

"I'm able to fly to Paris anytime. Havra, would it possible to meet next Tuesday for lunch at Hotel Pont Royal in Ste. Germaine? I can make reservations this afternoon."

"Why, yes, Marriette. Pont Royal. I know it well. That would be wonderful! Let's plan to meet there on Tuesday at noon. This gets more intriguing all the time, doesn't it? Then, until Tuesday, my Marriette?"

"Until Tuesday, dear Havra."

Marriette returned to the kitchen placing her phone on the counter as she continued to stare at it, basking in the beauty of the moment. Pouring herself a glass of iced tea, Marriette returned to the porch to sit in the big wicker armchair, still hearing Havra's gentle voice echo in her ears. Closing her eyes, she sat in silence, savoring each word of their conversation.

A few blocks away, the bells in the old Union Church tolled noon, bringing Marriette's thoughts back to the present moment. Realizing she had yet to call Jen, she went back into the kitchen and picked up her phone. "Jenny, darling."

"Hi, 'M'. Yes?"

"Havra sounds wonderful," Marriette reported, her voice dreamy.

"And ...?" Jen pressed.

Suddenly a dose of reality set in, and Marriette hastily answered, "I feel I should leave for Paris 'tout de suite'. We agreed on Tuesday!

"Wow!"

"I must talk to Havra in person."

"Yes, of course! He sounded excited?"

"Oh, yes! I mean we had a great conversation to start, but the rest is too important."

"Yes, 'M'. You should leave tomorrow night. Get there a day early. Better to deal with some of the jet lag up front."

"Good point. Will you come over? Help me get things together?"

"Of course. I'll be over in an hour."

"Thank you, dear. Have you had lunch yet?"

"No. I just finished my swim, but I'm starving."

"Tide yourself over and then we'll go out to lunch."

"Yes, 'M'. See you soon. Love."

"Love."

– Chapter 55 –

A Shared Curiosity
Sunday, July 3, 2016
Route 95 SB, Foxboro, Massachusetts

With the railroad station visible in the distance, Jen exited Route 128, traveling the sweeping curve to the right, heading south on Route 95 to Providence. Prior to leaving the parking area at Logan Airport, she had sent off an email to Neville, remembering she hadn't yet returned his request.

> *'Hi, Neville. I just dropped Marriette off at the airport. She is on her way to Paris and is very excited! All of this continues to amaze me! Please, feel free to call me anytime.*
>
> *Yes, that is my Telecaster on the wall, and, I certainly noticed your D-35.*
>
> *Jen'.*

Within minutes, as Jen passed near the stadium in Foxboro, Neville's number flashed up on the screen in front of her.

"Hello, Neville?"

"Jen?"

"Yes. How nice to hear from you. Wow! That was fast!"

"Well, you did say anytime. Is this a good anytime?"

"Yes, actually it is. I'm just driving home from the airport."

"Do you have plans for the big holiday tomorrow?" Neville inquired.

"Not really. Pretty quiet here. I do have to swing by my office at the University when I get back to Providence, but other than that, the plan is to stick around the house. Back to work on Tuesday. How about you?"

"Similar schedule actually, but without the holiday. I just came back from the University lab a short while ago. Checking on the graduate students."

"What type of work do you do there, Neville?"

"Molecular genetics," Neville answered. "Simply put, we are investigating gene sequences associated with simple behaviors in a very small marine worm.

"These are such exciting times in your field, Neville. It seems as though the future of the past is upon us. So much promise."

"Yes, absolutely."

"Well, what an amazing moment is coming up for Marriette and Havra!" Jen remarked. "Havra will have quite the story to tell you later this week."

"I'm sure he will. I've never seen him so enchanted, Jen."

"I'm still trying to get over the fact that Havra was once this primitive tribesman," Jen remarked. "I should mention, that Marriette has shared in quite some detail, the events which took place during her time in Africa."

"Havra has shared those stories with me, as well. Yes, the tragedy. The loss of his only child can still haunt him," Neville added. "You know, Jen, it is so long ago now, that Havra's early years have rather become a footnote. In fact, he never really was a primitive. Just looked like one."

"So, Neville, how did you meet Havra?"

"Well, in the mid '80s, I was at Cornell, interested in studying an avian population genetics problem. I knew there was a colonial species of sparrows in West Africa and wanted to identify their mating habits, to learn how it affected their gene pools.

"I ran across an acquaintance who mentioned that a man, by the name of Havra Emerson, operated a guide business for hunters in that region. He went on to disclose that Havra was redesigning it to a wildlife eco tour business."

"Emerson? That doesn't strike me as the last name of someone born in Ghana."

"Yes, it sounded a bit curious to me too. Apparently, it was required that he have a last name for his first job as a protocol assistant at the French embassy in Benin . . . so with some expedience, Havra adopted the surname of the philosopher he so admired from Concord."

"Really!"

"By the time I met him, he and a business partner had developed a rather lucrative hunting guide business. Sensing the growing interest in conservation, and in keeping with his values, he built a posh guest lodge for the first wave of tourists, solely interested in the observation of wildlife – along with photographers, artists, writers, scientists, and the like."

"How different, Neville."

"Absolutely unique at the time. Here is another Havra surprise. He is an excellent guitarist with a great voice … loves jazz, but also classic American country and western."

"No kidding!" Jen replied, feeling an immediate connection.

"A few years after retiring, he began to show up at a bar in Cherbourg featuring acoustic musicians. He has a pretty good catalog of country and western songs. I'm always awestruck at how this Frenchman can handle the C & W twang."

"Geez, Neville, you have no idea how interesting this is getting."

"So, I began to join him at these gigs," Neville continued. "Havra was aware that I played in clubs around campus here in Nottingham."

"You do?"

"Yes, every so often, I play with bands who are looking for someone to sit in. I love doing it."

"What fun that must be!" Jen exclaimed.

"I guess Havra thought, 'well, if Neville can do it', he could, too," Neville added.

"Really!"

"Sounds as though you and Havra are very close."

"We are, indeed."

As the two continued to converse, Jen passed through Attleboro and was well into Rhode Island.

"My goodness, Neville, it just goes on and on and on! Oh, I just pulled into the parking lot outside my office. I need to go in. Meeting up with another faculty member in a few minutes. Sorry I have to cut this short, but maybe we can continue our conversation another time."

"Sure, but before you go," Neville replied, "I'd really like to know about the unique red, white and blue Telecaster hanging on the wall behind your piano. Must be a story there."

"There is. I grew up immersed in the music scene, country and western, playing in Nashville clubs with my parents. The Tele' was a Christmas gift when I was around nine."

"Wow, really! The red, white, and blue pattern strikes me as oddly familiar … just can't place it right at the moment."

"Yes, Neville. Red, white, and blue. That's a big hint! It was a present from Buck Owens."

"Oh, you really must tell me about that!"

"Yes, sometime."

"Looking forward to it, Jen."

"Nice talking to you, Neville."

"Enjoyed talking with you, as well, Jen. Bye."

"Bye for now, Neville."

– Chapter 56 –

And Safe in My Heart
Tuesday, July 5, 2016   Ste. Germaine, Paris

Arriving in Paris on Monday morning, Marriette leisurely strolled along the Seine, through the Ste. Germaine neighborhoods. In the afternoon she spent a few hours at the Louvre. Anxiously awaiting the moment of her reunion with Havra, Marriette found distraction to be difficult, despite numerous attempts. She quickly fell asleep on Monday night, only to awaken several hours later, finding sleep elusive, as she lay in bed imagining what their first encounter after decades would be like.

At the stroke of noon on Tuesday, Marriette walked down from her room in the hotel, wearing a smart sleeveless summer dress, purchased the previous afternoon at a local boutique. As she entered the small, dimly lit bar room, she spotted Havra sitting alone at a table, his back toward her. Pausing briefly to study him, she noted his broad shoulders filled the back of the dark cherry leather chair.

"Havra?"

"Oui, Mademoiselle."

Havra rose and turned to face Marriette. He was a handsome man, tall and straight, wearing a peach-colored golf shirt, revealing an athletic physique still present in his eighth decade. Both stood motionless, looking at each other, as if waiting for 44 years of absence to catch up to them.

Smiling gently, Havra stepped closer to Marriette and put his arms around her. They lingered momentarily in an embrace, without spoken word, her head resting against his shoulder.

"This is a day I never thought possible, Havra," Marriette murmured softly, breaking the silence.

"Yes, Marriette, this is a gift folks our age don't often receive."

Stepping back, they faced each other at arm's length, holding hands, savoring the moment.

Havra then motioned toward a smaller table in the corner, where the couple sat across from one another at intimate speaking distance. Marriette removed an iPad from her bag, placing it on the table as she sat down. Her nervousness swiftly began to fade as his quiet voice and gentle demeanor calmed her.

"I found you, didn't I?" he interjected softly.

"Yes! It is you who found me. I imagined you had disappeared forever. Oh, it is so strange a feeling to be here with you now, only minutes removed from my memory of leaving you, so many years ago."

"Yes, Marriette. We are older, but you are still a very beautiful woman. Look at your lovely long silver hair."

Reaching up, Havra gently touched her temple with his fingertips.

"Thank you, Havra. You are a handsome man. Dressed somewhat differently than I remember."

"Yes. Things do change, do they not, Marriette? Let me tell you how I first learned of the Land Rover discovery. Near the end of May, a friend and former colleague, e-mailed me from Benin, to inform me of a fantastic story, which included a link to a video."

"Yes," she confirmed with a nod. "I have seen it, as well as an earlier June article in *Le Monde*. It was sent to me from a French journalist just last week, prior to Neville's email arriving. I directed the journalist to contact my publishing attorney."

"Yes. That journalist is Jacques Lemieux. I met with him only yesterday."

"You did? How would he . . ."

"He didn't know of me, of course, but I made some assumptions and was correct. Neville mentioned your comment about potential unwanted publicity, so I made the decision to intervene.

"Lemieux is a professional," Havra continued, "and I didn't want him harassing you. Not that he is mean-spirited; he is not. I told him I was meeting you this week, and that we might give him exclusive rights to the story, depending upon your approval."

"Oh, thank you, Havra. You are steps ahead of me."

"Marriette, it will all work out. It is business we shall attend to later. Are you worried?"

"I think not. Not now. Besides, there are much more important things to talk about."

Reaching across the table, Marriette took Havra's hands into hers, as they searched each other's eyes, seeking to absorb this new reality.

"Marriette, let me share what has been running through my mind these past few days. Over and over, I have envisioned our last few moments together; you leaning out of the truck window looking back at me, as I watched the vehicle disappear into the dust. When the dust settled, you were gone. I knew it was going to happen; yet it was another loss."

"That is exactly how I have remembered it," Marriette acknowledged. "I've imagined our final kiss, holding onto your hand for as long as possible, before the truck pulled away."

"My dear Havra, there is something important I need to tell you," Marriette paused, looking anxiously up at him.

Sensing her hesitation, Havra squeezed her hand in support.

"Perhaps you can show me, my Marriette?" he offered, pointing to the unopened iPad.

Marriette took in a deep breath and opened the case, tapping onto a recent photo of Harris, while still grasping Havra's hand.

"Havra, this is our son, Harris Tave Roy, our child," she said, looking directly into his eyes, as a tear splashed onto the screen. Havra silently moved from his chair to sit beside her, staring at his son's image.

"This . . . this is our son? Our . . . son?" he repeated, "Harris Tave."

"Yes, Havra. Harris is our son. Doesn't he look so much like you?"

Moving his eyes slowly back to Marriette, he asked, "Marriette. Does he know I am his father? I mean, his African father?"

"Yes, Havra, he does. It has never been a mystery. The mystery was only in your whereabouts."

"Our son, Marriette. Harris is our son. I have another son."

Picking up Marriette's hand, he kissed it gently.

A waiter came by to check on them. "Monsieur, Madame. Is there anything I can serve you, please?"

"Yes, sir. Thank you. Would you please bring a very nice bottle of Burgundy . . . and perhaps a cheese plate . . .and baguette?"

"Yes, of course, right away, Monsieur Emerson."

"Merci."

"Come, Marriette. Why don't we take everything upstairs to your or my room where we can talk in a more private fashion?"

"Yes, let's."

They entered Havra's suite and sat at a small table in front of a window looking down onto the street towards the Seine.

"Marriette, I need time to absorb these images thoughtfully. There is no hurry, yes?"

"There is no hurry, Havra," Marriette answered, her heart filling with a desire for reconnection.

Returning to the open album, Marriette pointed to a photo James had taken of her while pregnant with Harris, a month before he was born.

Adjacent was one of Marriette, in jeans and a striped T-shirt, sitting with James on the open tailgate of his yellow pickup, taken a few months after returning from Africa. Her long brown hair was braided and draped across a shoulder, as he kissed her on the cheek.

"Havra. This is James. He came into my life when I needed him most.

"I suspected my pregnancy in early August of '72. It was a tumultuous time for me.

I had just returned home from Africa after two years, having had limited contact with my family. Three months prior to my return, my brother, Pierre, was killed in the Vietnam War, and already buried before I arrived."

"I'm so sorry, Marriette," Havra offered tenderly.

"I was still coming to terms with the recent trauma of that horrific day in Africa and confused about my direction in school which was scheduled to begin that fall . . . and then there was the pregnancy.

"It was challenging at first for my parents to accept the fact that I was carrying a child of mixed race. Our culture, at that time was not so understanding. However, as expected, they proved to be devoted grandparents, as were James's parents, and adored their grandsons, thrilled to have their new family.

"Before James and I became intimate, I informed him about you and the significance of our relationship – and that I might be pregnant. After deep reflection, he said he loved and supported me. James was an incredible father and, in many ways, Harris's best friend.

As I mentioned before, Harris has always known that James was not his biological father, and believed, as I, that your whereabouts would never be known."

Havra carefully studied each photo, posing questions, as he slowly moved through the succession of his son's photos, from infancy to young man.

One photo of Harris at age 16, taken on the beach with his brother in 1989 near Point Judith, was of particular interest to Havra. The two brothers, with contrasting skin tones, stood side by side in the bright sunlight. Each held a kayak paddle vertically in hand, much as a spear, or tall walking stick. Havra concentrated for a long moment on the image, as it suggested a strong likeness to his deceased son, Tave, at a similar age.

Recognizing his lengthy silence, Marriette gently inquired, "Havra, do you see Tave? Yourself, perhaps?"

"Indeed, I do, Marriette, indeed I do. It is especially easy to see the similarities through my traditional lens. I will afford myself that luxury."

"Yes, dear Havra. I do believe Harris received the lion's share of your alleles."

"Marriette, I'm feeling a great sadness at having missed all of this."

"How could things have been any different, Havra?"

"Yes, of course," Havra answered. "It's just a thought pressing upon me at this moment. Despite being the consummate rational, I can also find comfort in the Ancestral spirits giving Tave his next chance so rapidly."

"What a lovely way to express it," Marriette acknowledged.

"I can't tell you how many times I, too, have imagined the same. There is an ancient beauty to it."

"And his brother, Jacques . . ."

"In the states, he is referred to as Jack or Jake, however, we have always called him Jake . . ."

"Jake. How did the boys get along growing up together?"

"I would say, as lovingly competitive brothers. Jake always wanted to keep up with his older brother. They often found themselves playing on the same sports teams. Both played soccer in the fall, hockey in the winter, and baseball in the spring throughout high school. Are you familiar with baseball and hockey?"

"Yes. Neville introduced me to baseball . . . Atlanta Braves fan."

"Certainly, apart from sports, the brothers were teammates 24 hours a day. They're still the best of friends. Jake was also very protective of Harris's uniqueness. Anyone who looked at Harris in the wrong way had to deal with Jake. Not that Harris needed any help."

Sometime mid-afternoon, Marriette and Havra left the hotel, and strolled casually around the neighborhood of Ste. Germaine. If a certain café appealed to them, they would stop and sip a glass of wine. Marriette continued to share family stories, some of them serving to explain her long and interesting history. At one point, while lingering in one of the cafes, they came upon two successive images of Pete Long.

"And who is this?" Havra inquired. "Grandfather?"

The photos reflected a striking contrast. The first image, taken of Pete and Marriette together at his shooting range in the fall of 1972, showed Pete sporting his earlier scruffy appearance. The next, a photo taken a few years later at the VA hospital in Vermont, presented Pete as a much healthier, professionally dressed man, holding 3-year-old Harris in his arms.

"Pete Long, a World War II combat veteran, and dear friend of my brother Pierre's," Marriette explained, "worked with me at the Veterans Administration Hospital. His experiences during the war, as with most combat veterans, left him traumatized, to the extent that his life was ruinous for more than 25 years after the war ended. You can imagine . . . failed relationships, alcoholism and nicotine addiction, etcetera." He ultimately joined our clinical research program at the VA as a counselor and worked with veterans for 20 years before passing away. Pete's commitment and dedication to helping other veterans avoid a lifetime of misery, was his salvation.

"The consequences of my traumatic experience in Africa, also guided me into the direction of my career, Havra. I was convinced that people who experienced this type of stress needed treatment which was, in my opinion, not available at the time. I combined my own observations, along with my intuitive sense, to test this theory in fulfillment of my PhD in clinical psychology. That was only the beginning.

"My endeavor was to research and understand the psychological effects of trauma on an individual. Teaming up with notable others in the field, we developed efficacious treatment programs. It has been my life's work for the last 44 years."

By nine p.m., the couple had returned to the hotel. Before retiring to their rooms, Havra took Marriette's hands into his.

"Marriette. I have a request. Would you consider traveling with me to my home in Normandy? We could take the train in the morning. I have a country home there, with plenty of room. We still have much to talk about, and I have much to show you. Would you feel comfortable in doing this?"

"There is nothing I would rather do, Havra."

"Wonderful. I will arrange for the tickets tonight. There is a 10 o'clock train in the morning, Mademoiselle."

"Yes, dear Havra. Shall I reschedule my flight to Saturday morning? Is that too long?"

"Yes, and no, I'm in no hurry for you to leave . . . and there is a surprise, something I have yet to tell you."

"Oh?"

"I am scheduled to deliver a TED Talk here at the Sorbonne on Friday evening. I would love for you to accompany me."

"My goodness, Havra. That sounds marvelous! Of course I would love to go with you."

"I realize I should have mentioned it earlier," he added, "but there was so much of importance to cover first. Your presence could not be more timely and significant, considering the subject I will be addressing."

"Really? What is your topic, Havra?"

"As you may well appreciate, Marriette, this journey of mine into the culture of civilization, along with my efforts in conservation, are of great interest and importance to many in the public. My presentation provides an international opportunity to address global existential concerns. Possibly, it may also reach to others less informed . . . I would only hope."

"A wonderful reward that speaks to all of your accomplishments, dear Havra."

"Thank you, Marriette. Actually, your rediscovery is my precious reward."

"My goodness, Havra . . . at this moment . . . it all seems like a lovely dream."

"We could conclude our evening back here on Friday, and I'll drive you to the airport on Saturday morning."

"It sounds like a wonderful plan, Havra. I'll contact Jen in the morning, to let her know about our change in plans."

Arm-in-arm, Marriette and Havra walked together through the lobby. Sharing a kiss goodnight, they agreed to meet at eight the following morning.

– Chapter 57 –

Early Days in Civilization
Wednesday, July 6, 2016   SNCF Train North from Paris

Havra escorted Marriette to the First Class section of the railroad car, and they settled into comfortable reclining seats across from one another. Watching the French countryside rush by at 200 miles an hour, Marriette looked over at Havra.

"Please tell me more about the days leading up to your departure from your tribal community."

Stretching out his long legs diagonally, Havra leaned back and closed his eyes.

"For decades, I heard the McGill graduate students speak of their lives growing up and their plans for their future. It appeared, for the most part, that the students enjoyed their experience with us, but when their time was up, they were ready to leave. Africa was not home to them. The novelty of their African adventure was well diminished by the end of their schedule. Now, they looked forward to their future assignment, new job, or simply knowing they would be returning home."

As Havra spoke, Marriette studied the handsome well-dressed gentleman sitting across from her, and subtly adjusted her legs, so they rested against his. Havra took note and, with a twinkle in his eye, flashed her a smile.

"Some found the natural surroundings afforded them in Africa appealing and knew where to find analogous environments in Canada. Others had no affinity to it. A few spoke of the Native North Americans' clash with those of European civilization who openly disregarded the Native culture's sacred feelings for the earth. It was with this primary sanctity to which I identified. In fact, I recall one particular native Canadian student who had joined us for a year. I may have been around the age of 12 at the time. I immediately felt an affinity toward him."

"Do you remember his name?"

"Yes. Still remember. Jesse Crowwing. He seemed to feel at home in our culture. I often wondered if, in my own departure, I would begin to feel a loss with my connection, and find it so disconcerting, that I would abandon my own journey. As things turned out, my contract to work with the French government in West Africa, allowed me to maintain my connection to my roots, which I valued."

"When did you finally leave?" Marriette questioned.

"Sometime in the fall of 1972," Havra answered.

"For the first few days, Seeba and I walked from one tribal community to another. Initially, I was familiar with the people along the trail, but as we traveled further south, I became a stranger. On the third day, Seeba chose to remain behind with a tribal family with whom she had close relatives."

"What happened to Seeba?"

"I never saw her again. I returned to the area in the mid '80s. Much had changed, as I had expected in that part of Africa, however, I encountered no one who knew of her. The time was during the AIDS epidemic. It was a common observation that when people were taken to hospitals, they were often never seen again.

"When I departed the original territory, I carried my few belongings from civilization in a backpack a student had left behind. I remained in traditional dress until I was far beyond the indigenous regions. Because of the distance I was traveling, I wore the hiking boots a student had given me a few years earlier. I also wore an Expos hat."

"A Montreal Expos baseball hat?" Marriette laughed.

"Yes, of all things! I had sunglasses, two khaki shirts, cargo shorts, and an algebra II book which kept me busy when I wasn't on the move. I also took my Emerson book, 'On Nature'. I still have it. I carried a knife, that Soviet revolver with an extra magazine, and a small bow with a few arrows to hunt for meals.

"It wasn't until my second week of walking that I encountered my first vehicle. I had been traveling along a pathway displaying tire marks. As the vehicle passed, I hid well off the path."

"That must've made your heart beat quickly," Marriette interjected.

"Yes, actually, it did. I reached into my backpack and placed my hand on the revolver, but there proved to be no threat. It turned out to be two African men occupying a vehicle loaded with boxes. Later, in the afternoon, I heard another vehicle approach. This time, I chose to remain closer to the side of the road. The vehicle was driven by a native man, with two Caucasian men sitting in the back. The driver stopped and addressed me in native dialect. He said he was leading the two men on a hunting expedition. One of them had targeted a buffalo, but the animal ran off wounded. The driver inquired if I had seen the beast. I answered that I had not. As we conversed, one of the men in the back-seat, speaking in English, complained to his companion that the guide appeared to be incompetent, and that he was disappointed that he might lose his trophy.

"When I turned to address the man in English, he was taken by surprise that I understood his comment. The driver then quickly confided to me, that he was experiencing difficulty communicating with the tourists, as well as tracking down the wounded animal. He asked if I might be able to join them to help translate, as he understood very little French, and was afraid he might lose his job. The driver, Jean-Paul, offered to compensate me for my assistance. I glad-ly agreed and climbed into the vehicle beside him, thus beginning a lifelong friendship. Jean-Paul managed our business until retiring just a few years ago."

"Very interesting," Marriette remarked, fascinated at hearing these details for the first time.

"So, as I continued to converse with the two men in the backseat, I learned that the Frenchman worked for the French government and was assigned to the embassy compound in the capital. The other, an Englishman, was a guest of the French Embassy. Both were astonished to find that I was also able to communicate fluently in French.

"J-P drove back to the location where the buffalo had been wounded. We tracked the animal on foot through the brush and trees to where it had died. Not really a full-time guide, J-P had exaggerated his capabilities; how-ever, the Englishman received his trophy after all, and we harvested the meat before hauling it back to town.

"Later that evening, after returning to the embassy compound, the Frenchman, Claude Mongeau, asked if I might join him for dinner. We dined at a nearby café... an interesting first restaurant experience."

"He wanted to know more about me and was curious why I was in the middle of nowhere, fluently speaking two European languages. So, I shared my story with him."

"It sounds as though it was a lucky day for you, Havra," Marriette noted.

"Yes, it was, Marriette. He asked if I was looking for work. Did I have a place to stay? For the next several nights, I stayed in a plush, by anyone's standards, embassy guest quarters. I can recall that first night, laying in a soft bed, tired, yet too excited to easily fall asleep. I was surprised at my immediate good fortune. Somehow, I must have impressed Claude because he took me under his wing.

"He instructed me on the basics of life in a small city. He introduced me to clothing stores, customary grooming habits, and the everyday paraphernalia of civilization. It felt like an expedient finishing school," Havra laughed.

"Claude explained his position at the embassy, initially assigning me to work with Jean-Paul. I was soon entrusted with other jobs around the embassy. Management was pleased with my abilities, and, within weeks, I was dressed in a suit and tie like all the other embassy personal, primarily employed as a protocol assistant and translator. Speaking three languages fluently proved to be a huge point of difference – my ticket to success."

"Oh, my goodness, Havra. Imagine that!"

"I received a salary every two weeks," Havra continued, "putting most of it into the bank . . . that is, after Claude explained the banking process. He left few stones unturned. He also warned me to be cautious with women . . . introduced me to condoms and gave me a few. He said . . . I still remember, 'Just open one, you'll figure it out . . . but if the occasion arises, don't fail to use it'.

"Claude and I soon became good friends. One day, many months later, he excitedly shared a notification he had received from the education branch of the embassy system. The correspondence described a newly created program, offering a four-year college education with room and board to residents of Benin who qualified. Claude encouraged me to apply. He didn't need to ask twice. I had already established residency in Benin . . . which was quite simple in those days. When I learned that I needed a surname, I immediately thought of Ralph Waldo Emerson and adopted his. Claude helped to prepare me for the French Baccaulauréat examination, similar to your SATs. I did extremely well. By September of 1974, I was on my way to Paris and entered the Paris-Sorbonne."

"One day you're in West Africa and the next in one of the world's greatest cities!" Marriette exclaimed.

"I was surprised at how much I had absorbed of the academic environment, growing up for so many years around graduate students. I realized I had been given a very unusual private education. Although it would take an extra decade of experience and learning, I ended up being well prepared. How I had acquired the knowledge, however, was highly unusual."

While Marriette listened quietly to Havra's recapitulation of his earlier history, she made a study of this mild-mannered man and father of their son. Images of moments together, now so many years ago, flashed through her mind.

"How did you accomplish the adjustment to university life, Havra?"

"I was fortunate to have several people looking out for me. I became the pet project of the French Embassy system. Although I experienced a few struggles my freshman year, every year thereafter my QPR improved. After I graduated in 1977, I remained on campus and attended law school for an additional three years. I graduated third in my law school class. Having a much different perspective now, I can still remember being disappointed that I hadn't graduated first."

Marriette leaned forward, tapping Havra on his knee in admiration, "Havra, I believe that all people need is the right opportunity. You took advantage of your opportunity, as I did of mine."

"Marriette, I never forget how fortunate I have been. Although I owed the French government ten years of service to pay off my education, I worked in the embassies of the former French colonial countries for 28 years before taking a position with the International Wildlife Federation in Paris. After I achieved the 20-year mark of government service, I took a sabbatical for two years and pursued a legal fellowship in environmental law. That led me to my job with the IWF. I was COO of that organization for three years prior to retiring."

"So, what actually led to your starting the ecotourism business?" Marriette asked curiously.

"Throughout my governmental career, I was able to spend sufficient time in Benin, actively participating in co-management of the guide business with JP. I'm not sure I would have been content living solely in Europe. Traveling to and from West Africa allowed me to keep in touch with my roots. Civilization is the antithesis of its absence.

"Running the guide business was a bit of a compromise. I was disgusted with the wasteful slaughter of animals for the amoral and careless pleasure of rich white men. However, it became a path to something significantly better. It kept me in touch with my natural environment which I hold sacred. Eventually, I converted the guide business to an ecotourism one. That's an accomplishment I'm proud of."

"Yes, indeed you should be.

"Have you ever traveled to the United States, Havra?"

"I've been to Washington, D.C. on several occasions for business. And in 2014, I spoke at the United Nations, representing the IWF."

"Why, here we were so close!" Marriette declared.

"Yes, we were! Here's a special memory, Marriette. Do you remember our conversation that night, so long ago, when you pointed to a passing satellite overhead in the starry African sky? You informed me of the missions to the moon, scheduled that year, Apollo 16 and 17."

"Of course I do, Havra. I remember the night well. We were lying together on a blanket, studying the sky, watching for satellites."

"Yes, well, in 1998 I flew to Miami and drove up to Cape Canaveral, staying a couple of days to experience the space shuttle STS-88 launch. I thought of you that night."

"You did? I saw that launch, as well, Havra. It was in December. Jen's husband had invited us to the school observatory. We viewed, quite clearly, the fire coming off the Shuttle's booster rockets, just seconds after its launch, as it made its way up the Atlantic coast. Oh, Havra, who would have thought?"

"Marriette, I have tried to make a practice of experiencing as much as possible of the opportunities afforded me. Back in earlier days in Africa, whenever a graduate student discussed an exciting idea or related an interesting story, I made a mental note to explore those things I felt were worthwhile. A good example was playing the guitar well. After my friend Oskar introduced me to the guitar and jazz, I made a point of taking lessons and practicing regularly. It's been 35 years since I began that project, and I'm still working at it. It's also been an integral part of my relationship with Neville . . . and, speaking of him, it was Neville who suggested I study the life sciences, which significantly influenced my comprehensive worldview."

"I'm guessing this will be addressed in your TED presentation on Friday evening?" Marriette speculated.

"Yes, it will, indeed . . . but for now, suffice it to say, I believe it involves internalizing the sanctity of all life on our planet. It is what I intuitively understood during my primitive days, as have all primitive peoples, yet has come to mirror what I understand now, from the study of life sciences. All life is intimately interconnected and ultimately fragile. We are the species that dominates this planet, and the ecosystem demands our supreme respect and stewardship. In my view, there is no other concept as important as this."

"Well stated, Havra. We should be doing a much better job. The world has become a better place since the beginning of scientific enlightenment. However, there is much resistance from those who do not comprehend this, those who are not committed to a rational thought process."

"It's so ironic, isn't it, Marriette? Sadly, these days, we are living in a strangely anti-science culture. People place so much dependency on science to provide them with those things that make their lives better, yet when it doesn't suit their immediate needs, there is a disconnect."

"Because of that," Marriette quickly added, "the three great existential threats to our planet are not being addressed. They're not even near the top of anyone's list."

"No, not close!"

"For example," Marriette explained, "in the upcoming American presidential election, no candidate of either party has addressed, or expressed, a defined policy on global warming ... or on the presence of nuclear arsenals ... or the impact of automation and artificial intelligence. Apparently, the absence of these considerations appear to be, in their view, inconsequential ... unimportant. Troubling! These threats to our civilization, to our planet, need to be and can only be addressed with global cooperation. This stewardship is critical for our very survival!"

Leaning closer to Havra, Marriette gestured with her hands, "Will it take a disaster, or near disaster, to reach a tipping point when humanity begins to feel a nationalism toward the planet, rather than to the country they pay taxes in?"

"Unfortunately, Marriette, I believe we're not that far away from such a tipping point," Havra contended. As he sat back, folding his arms across his chest, he was struck by a strong sensation of re-connection emerging.

Travelling in the opposite direction, a train passed as a sudden rumble of silver blur, startling Marriette. "My goodness, Havra. I assume that is the train going to Paris?"

"Yes,' he answered, "disconcerting, unless one is accustomed to it."

Moving on to another topic, Marriette posed a question of a more personal nature, "Havra, you mentioned you never married again after leaving Africa. Were there any relationships of significance?"

"Well, yes, I did have a 10-year relationship with a woman from Paris. Julia was her name. She also worked in the embassy system. We both traveled extensively and were never able, however, to fully develop a committed relationship; no promises made. We were more romantic roommates, so to speak. A few years after we parted, I learned she had married. I believe yours was a different situation, Marriette?"

"Yes, I was 53 when James died," Marriette answered. "About the time of my

60th birthday, one of my sons inquired if I might ever consider dating again. I believe it was Jake. He wanted to make sure I understood that he and Harris supported me, should I decide to pursue that path. It wasn't the case. I just had no interest. I dated occasionally throughout my sixties, afraid I might feel regret if I denied myself those opportunities ... you know, before getting too old. Silly, I guess. Frankly, I found it extremely difficult to separate my intimacy with James, from other men with whom I just didn't feel a connection."

Looking out the window, Marriette returned their conversation back to the present, "Are we getting close to Cherbourg?"

Orienting himself, Havra answered, "Yes, I'd say we're about 20 minutes out."

After several moments, Marriette brought up the topic of the news story, "Havra, may we talk about the French reporter?"

"Yes, of course."

"I have some lingering concerns. Considering the subject matter, I think it may create a bit of curiosity in France and the United States. At this point in my life, I'm not particularly interested in that kind of circus. I realize it's a novel story that people might want to hear ... with a happy ending ... I might add, but I'd like to know what the reporter has in mind. Perhaps you can make contact with my publishing attorney? Would you mind handling this, Havra?"

"Yes, I'll be happy to. We'll get the two attorneys talking. That is, your attorney and me. Well, both of your attorneys," Havra laughed. "Maybe, we'll give him permission to write the story within certain parameters, as long as we have final say of the content. Apart from that, wouldn't you say it might make a pretty good movie?"

"And the theme of the story is a most unusual reunion," Marriette added, with a wink.

"Indeed. Maybe we can play ourselves!" quipped Havra.

"Oh, goodness!" Marriette laughed, as she looked back out the window. "The train seems to be slowing down."

"Yes, we're coming into the city. Just a few more minutes."

Within the half hour, they were settled in a taxi for the 20-minute ride to Havra's home east of Cherbourg. The vehicle quickly entered into farm country on D-116 heading toward Fort Joret.

As they passed along a tree-lined stretch of road, Havra leaned forward from the backseat and spoke to the driver.

"It's up there on the left, next to the column on the road."

The driver nodded, as he turned into the driveway and stopped in front of the garage.

As Havra settled up with the driver, Marriette remarked, "Havra, my dear, what a beautiful home! I love it right away!

She then turned full circle to examine the rest of the grounds from the gravel driveway.

"It's so lovely. How long have you lived here?"

"About 10 years," Havra answered. "It was a typical old French country home that needed lots of work. I had it completely renovated, keeping the authentically old facade on the outside, but everything else new ... and wait until you see the back yard!"

Walking in through the front door, Marriette instantly felt at home.

"I love it!

"Please, come into the kitchen, Marriette."

The open kitchen, with high ceilings was incorporated into the long sloping roof on the back end of the house. The outer wall, comprised of a series of paneled doors, offered a full view of the landscape behind the house. The couple walked out onto the patio and along the rear of the building. A vast grassy meadow sloped down to a lesser traveled local road further down the hill. A distant view of the Atlantic Ocean filled the horizon, appearing softened by the coastal mist.

"My property extends just about halfway down the hill, toward the road," Havra explained. "Most of the land is set to grow hay. I keep the grass long for a hundred meters or so, the rest is cut twice a year, contiguous with the land around mine."

Marriette moved up to Havra, putting her arms around him in a hug. "This is so beautiful, Havra. I had no idea what to expect," she marveled, gazing out toward the horizon.

"I hope you will enjoy your stay here, Marriette – and want to come back. I love your being here."

As she turned to look up at him, Havra moved closer. They shared a kiss, filled with promise.

"This still feels like a dream, Havra."

"Yes, Marriette, it does, doesn't it?"

– Chapter 58 –

On The Beaches of Normandy
Thursday, July 7, 2016   The American Cemetery

"Are you ready to go, Madame?" Havra beckoned, standing in the doorway leading into the garage.

"Here I come," Marriette answered as she attended to the braid woven into her long silver hair, in anticipation of a windy ride in the convertible. As she stepped into the garage, she looked around at its contents. Havra was busy lowering the convertible top on the BMW.

"What's under the car cover, Havra? Is that a 911?" Marriette inquired, observing the shape of the vehicle beside her.

"No, a 993. I took the train to Stuttgart and drove it back from the factory in '95. It's become the classic 911 Porsche. We can take it out tomorrow, if you wish. You'll have fun driving it along these country roads."

"Goodness! A Porsche 993. The Holy Grail of Porsches!" she laughed.

"How did you happen to know that?" Havra asked, grinning.

"Your son has been talking about wanting one since college," Marriette answered.

"Really! Well, if Harris can be patient, he will have this one."

"No hurry on that, please," Marriette quipped.

"Interesting how that last statement seemed to roll off my tongue so easily, Marriette. I am really excited to meet Harris."

Havra stopped for a moment, looking directly at her, "I will come to the States soon."

"And I'll arrange it with Harris, just as soon as I let him know you actually exist. I'm just as excited," Marriette sighed, holding her hands to her heart.

Spotting several sets of skis and poles hanging neatly along the garage wall, Marriette reached toward them.

"Havra, do you ski? Still?"

"Don't you?"

"Ah, I haven't since James died. Of course, we all skied at one time, more often when we lived in Vermont. After we sold my parents' bakery, we purchased a house not far from Okemo Mountain in Ludlow. Harris and Jake own the property now. The boys still ski with their families."

"Well, I haven't skied in over 10 years," Havra admitted. During the late '80s and '90s, I visited many of the ski areas in Germany, Switzerland, and France. Spectacular!

In '06, I dislocated my right shoulder and needed a repair. At 76, I hadn't planned to start up again."

"But, reconsidering," Havra paused, "perhaps next winter we might try the beginner's slope at Saint Moritz."

"Can we? I do think we should give it a try," Marriette agreed. As they left the driveway, Marriette caught a glimpse of the Atlantic off in the distance.

Soon they were comfortably cruising along a beautiful a country road, moving in and out of the shade of deciduous trees that hugged the roadside. Along the route were views of picturesque farmland, and intermittently, peeks of the Atlantic coastline to the east and north. After a short time, they neared Utah Beach.

Marriette kept her eyes focused on Havra, noting how handsome he still was. She was amazed at how much he had accomplished since she last saw him – decades ago.

Quite spontaneously, she posed a question, "Havra, do you think we're still married?"

Taken by surprise, he glanced over at her laughing, "I believe so, Marriette. Do you still have your tattoo?"

"Of course I do!" Marriette giggled, shaking her head at the personal nature of the question, and the unique situation they now found themselves in.

"Yes, the tattoo. It has been the source of many inquisitive looks from gynecologists over the years. I made up a different story each time."

Havra smiled, keeping his eyes straight ahead on the road. The evening before, Marriette asked if they could visit the beaches where the American forces had come ashore, as the Northlanders had many centuries prior.

They neared the town of Formigny. Before arriving, they stopped at a café with a view of the rural landscape, a view that stretched several miles out to the ocean.

Sitting at a cozy table on the patio at the back of the restaurant, they enjoyed their coffee - and conversation.

"Havra, I'd like to tell you more about Pete Long, the World War II vet I spoke of yesterday. I showed you a couple of photos of him."

"Yes," Havra recalled, "the gentleman I mistook for Harris's grandfather."

"Yes," Marriette explained, and gestured in the direction of the ocean. "Quite soon, we will pass through the town Pete parachuted into early on the morning of 6 June 1944.

"The C-47, carrying him was hit by ant-aircraft fire well before the drop zone as the plane passed over the cliffs at Utah Beach. Only a few on that plane survived. Pete's mission had been to set up radar equipment, but it was destroyed in the crash. He and another soldier, Tech Sgt. Kevin Youngs, sheltered in the cellar of a building, waiting for dawn. They shared personal stories and manage some sleep.

"At first light, they emerged from the cellar. They soon discovered other members of their group in the middle of a town, rather than at the planned drop zone. The soldiers then moved door-to-door, advancing with caution through the town.

"While Pete scanned the narrow street ahead, Sgt. Youngs moved into a doorway for shelter and lit a cigarette. As Youngs did so, he was instantly killed by a sniper's shot. Pete quickly located the sniper and killed him. Later, as Pete examined the enemy soldier's identification, he discovered they were only months apart in age and had remarkably similar facial features. This was the first combatant Pete would kill.

"Pete's parents had immigrated to the United States in the 1890s. In the process, their last name had been changed from the German, Langer, to Long. The two deaths, especially Pete's encounter with the young German sniper, as he lay dying, haunted him forever.

"Later on, when the area had been cleared of enemy soldiers, Pete returned to find Youngs' body before it was loaded onto a truck with others killed in action. He removed a letter from Youngs' uniform shirt pocket, written only hours before. Pete later forwarded that letter to the soldier's young wife. At the same time, Pete removed one of Youngs' dog tags, which he always kept in his possession, without really understanding why.

"However," Marriette concluded, "there was a happy ending, a salvation of sorts for Pete. When I began my graduate program at the University of Vermont, I designed research studies for veterans returning to the VA hospital who were diagnosed with combat stress induced trauma. Pete was involved in the program from its inception, helping in the development of the interview process and treatment protocol. He filled the role as the initial contact with Vietnam vets, and, to a lesser extent, Korean War veterans. The men were much more willing to confide in Pete once they became aware of his combat experience and the life changing results Pete realized through his own participation in the program. For the first time in decades, Pete found he really wanted to live. Eventually, he went back to school and earned a graduate degree in clinical psychology.

"How fortunate for Pete that you came into his life," Havra commented.

"Yes, then something else happened, Havra, something that further enhanced Pete's new outlook on life," Marriette went on. "Early on in the spring of '73, Pete had a chance encounter with a troubled young soldier returning from duty in Vietnam. Incorporating the methods I was still developing, along with Pete's intuitive sense of what the young man needed, Pete helped to change the boy's life. Will Mueller, then 20 years of age, is now a clinical psychologist at UNC Chapel Hill. Pete became the father Will never had – and eventually married Will's mother."

"What an amazing recovery story, Marriette."

"Yes, Havra, it was. Sneaky Pete, as my brother had affectionately referred to him, passed away in 2006 from lung cancer."

Before Pete died, he made a request that if I ever visited Normandy, I would place Youngs' dog tag, along with his, and the lower half of the German sniper's I.D. tag all together on Kevin Youngs' cross at the American cemetery."

A teary Marriette removed the chain from her pocketbook and held it at length in front of Havra before handing it to him. On the chain there were four I.D. tags.

Examining them, and noting a fourth tag, Havra looked up at Marriette, "One of these is Pierre's."

"Yes," Marriette acknowledged. "Pierre was born on 6 June 1944 . . . for what it's worth. The fact that he was born on this day was always of great importance to my brother. In his will, Pierre specifically asked that the phrase 'Born on D Day' be engraved on his headstone. And it was."

Listening intently while, at the same time, still enamored with Marriette's presence, Havra let out a deep sigh, "We both have some amazing stories, don't we?"

Gathering up her hand from the tabletop, Havra placed a kiss on her fingertips. Without taking her eyes from his, Marriette released the chain with the attached tags and placed her other hand over his.

A short time later, they were back on the road, stopping at Omaha Beach. The couple spent the next few hours walking the infamous stretch of shoreline in bare feet, taking moments to linger and reflect.

They lunched on a simple fare of wine, cheese, bread, and fresh raspberries picked from Havra's garden earlier that morning. Facing the cliffs, as they looked up toward Point Le Hoc, Marriette imagined Pete's wounded plane passing overhead with its starboard engine and wing on fire, losing precious altitude. She could feel the young soldiers' confusion and horror - and their blind jump into a burning village.

Hand-in-hand, Marriette and Havra followed the path up to the top of the cliffs. Passing through the gates of the American Cemetery in late afternoon, they surveyed the 172 acres and nearly 10,000 alabaster crosses, representing the physical deaths of the men and three women who saw action in the invasion and the ensuing combat operations of World War II.

After a long walk through the sea of alabaster crosses, they came upon the grave site of 21-year-old Kevin Youngs. In its stark simplicity, the presence of the lichen encrusted alabaster marker proved powerful and chilling. Marriette draped the ball-link chain over the top of the cross and arranged the dog tags of Kevin Youngs, Pierre LaFleur, Peter Langer, and the young German sniper, Wilhelm Millar, whose indelible reflection looked so much like that of the young soldier who took his life. Three of the men had died in wars in which they were engaged. The fourth returned home alive physically, but dying a little at a time, day by day, in a peace time that took him so long to find.

– Chapter 59 –

The Recovery of Connection
Thursday, July 7, 2016   The Normandy Coast

A faint saltiness suffused the evening air, joined by an uninterrupted chorus of cicadas calling from the trees, as Havra and Marriette traveled the road back home. Havra stretched out in the backseat with his guitar, playing songs for Marriette as she drove. Providing directions, while monitoring their route, Havra found watching Marriette captivating. At 76, he was in love with her again.

Arriving home, they spent a few moments in the house before moving outside to the back courtyard. The summer evening was warm and still, without a hint of breeze from the nearby Atlantic. The couple sauntered down the gentle slope along a path of freshly mown grass, through the hayfield, and onto a leveled stone patio.

On so many summer evenings, the patio had been a private place where Havra could go to be alone, to think, to play guitar. It was, in a manner of speaking, the comfortable substitute for the fallen tree on his African property. It even had a view to the east at sunset.

Havra had brought his guitar and bottle of wine with them. Marriette, now wearing a long flowing summer dress, carried their glasses and a ceramic bowl filled with ripe mission figs. The sun was just beginning to set behind them. A golden glow was cast down the slope of timothy grass, not yet in shadow.

"Well, look at that, Havra. You have barn swallows here!"

"Yes. Same species as in North America. Aren't they handsome? I would like to think they are enjoying the evening as much as we," Havra remarked, winking at Marriette.

Dozens of fork tailed swallows, feeding on insects, swooped down over the great expanse of grass, darting closely at times, seemingly oblivious to their presence. Distant waves were clearly visible as tiny spots of white, only to disappear in the coastal mist.

Havra sang a traditional folk song for Marriette, as she gazed out over the Atlantic, her thoughts wandering back to their afternoon visit to the cemetery, trying to imagine the pastoral landscape before her, during much different and dangerous times.

Leaning back in his chair, Havra placed his legs up on the coffee table, still holding his guitar in his lap.

"Marriette, you have yet to tell me the story of Harris's birth. You mentioned he was born in Canada, although I thought you and James had moved to Vermont?"

"Yes, that's right, but Harris arrived two weeks earlier than expected. We had traveled to Montreal to visit friends and were staying at the Mount Royale Hotel. Upon returning to our room after dinner, I began to experience contractions. By three that morning, it was clear Harris was on his way. We drove to the Hospital Royal Victoria where Harris was born at 9 a.m. the following morning on 23 March. We stayed for a few days before returning to Burlington, so Harris could be a dual citizen."

"It must have been a difficult time for you, my Marriette," Havra speculated.

"Well, actually, it didn't seem that way. James and I were doing well. It would have been extremely difficult without James. He was fully invested in our future together."

"When did you move to Vermont?" Havra inquired, laying the Martin down across the coffee table. Plucking a few figs from the bowl, he handed one to Marriette.

"It was during the Christmas holidays of '72. By that time, James had a teaching position at a Burlington area high school. We were able to purchase a house near the university. The subject of marriage became a serious consideration in late November, once my pregnancy began to show. However, it was Harris's eminent birth that pushed an issue we otherwise would have taken longer to consider.

"James and I married in a civil ceremony the day after Christmas with our parents and James's two brothers present. Brother Jacques came along when Harris was just sixteen months old."

"Were either of the parents disappointed with Catholic rituals being absent when having a child?" Havra wondered.

"It really wasn't a problem. I happened to be raised in a secular environment, so our relationship with the Catholic church was essentially ceremonial."

"Religion was viewed much the same way with James's family. James's mother was a math and science teacher at Seminaire De Sherbrooke, where he attended school. His father worked for the local hockey equipment manufacturer, Sher-Wood, for 30 years and was an assistant hockey coach at the school. Canadien Hockey was his religion and the Montreal Forum his cathedral."

"So, it sounds as though you and James were noncommittal about organized religion." Havra suggested.

"Yes. Growing up, I never really thought much about our religious heritage. It wasn't until I spent the two years in Africa that I began to question my own source of spirituality. I carefully observed your seamless connection to your natural surroundings. It was something I watched very closely and began to recognize and nurture within myself. I never again felt separate from other living things . . . and my knowledge of science only served to reinforce that understanding.

"Havra, I thought of you often when Harris was a young child. He consistently served as a reminder of our relationship. Although that connection slipped into the background as we carried on with our lives, it never completely disappeared. Did you ever think about me?"

"Yes . . . considerably at first. I felt alone in so many ways and I missed you. There was a certain ease about being in your presence – one I had never experienced since. You also personified a template of where I wanted my life to go. I had become much more a part of your culture than of mine. Marriette, you were the right woman at the wrong time. Then you were gone. Tave was gone. It was a very lonely time."

Marriette reached over and affectionately took his hand, her eyes misting, as he confessed his long-held sentiment.

"Why I never tried to find you, especially as technology made it more a possibility, I don't really know," Havra went on.

"I assumed it would be intrusive. You had your own life, and I believed my sudden appearance might be disruptive. The reappearance of the Land Rover certainly altered that. Even then, I was careful to have Neville make the initial contact. I believed speaking directly to you might be too much of a shock . . . perhaps for both of us. I'm pleased with the way our reunion is unfolding. I realize now that I've always carried a part of you. It never went away."

"Yes, dear Havra, it never did go away, did it?"

Before the last color in the western sky faded to navy and starlight, they strolled back up the hill and into the house. The last three days had brought them close again. After Havra ignited the gas log in the fireplace, they curled up together on the couch facing the hearth. Comfortable and quiet, they held each other and kissed.

"Our time together has passed so quickly, my dear Havra. What a lovely thing is happening between us."

"Yes, my Marriette, and how easy it has been. I love saying your name, again. I love being with you . . . it feels like a new beginning."

"Yes, it is. Havra."

Marriette paused momentarily, assuring eye contact. "I'm hoping we might be together tonight . . . if you are comfortable."

"Yes, I am."

"It's been a while for me."

"For me, as well, my Marriette."

– Chapter 60 –

Havra at TED
Friday, July 8, 2016   Paris-Sorbonne University

"Good evening, ladies and gentlemen, and welcome to this TED presentation. Our guest is here tonight to share his philosophical perspective developed along an extraordinary life journey. He recently retired as executive officer of the International Wildlife Federation of France. I give you, Havra Emerson."

With grace and confidence, Havra acknowledged the applause from the capacity audience.

"Thank you, and good evening. I would like to share the experience of a somewhat unusual journey over 76 years of living on this extraordinary planet. I was born into a semi-nomadic tribe, living a modified hunting and gathering existence in West Ghana. The tribe's original culture had been chosen as the subject of observation and study by the anthropology department at McGill University, beginning with my birth through my 30th year. Growing up under these circumstances, this study, made this journey possible for me. Here I am in Paris, offering 'an idea worth spreading'.

"Yes, my name is Havra Emerson. An apt surname for an environmental attorney, don't you think? In my Original culture, a last name, as such, was not required. After I arrived in the culture of Civilization, I soon learned I would need a surname. A McGill University student had gifted me with a copy of Emerson's, 'Nature'. I was so impressed with the perspective of the gentleman from Concord, Massachusetts, that I adopted his last name. I had hoped there were others who felt the way Emerson did, and have encountered many. However, I wish there were more.

"In my Original culture, Nature did not exist as something separate from our lives. We were Nature. This was true for all of my ancestors, and is, of course, true for all of yours. Original culture shared an interdependency with all living things inhabiting the Biosphere. We had no philosophy or dogma that separated us as humans from Nature. A cultural respect was shared for the resources necessary to be alive and well. All of Nature was perceived as sacred, providing us with a universal sense of awe and sanctity. Yes, there were traditional deities recognized in our customs and celebrations. However, those deities had their origin in, and not separate from, Nature."

A slide is projected onto an overhead screen showing Havra as a young man, tall and sinuous, shirtless, wearing a goatskin wrap, resting on a walking stick.

"This photograph was taken in 1969 or thereabouts, of me as a young man. I most likely wasn't considering giving a TED talk at that point, but I was aware that two men from the United States had walked on the moon."

Laughter arises from the audience as the next image appears on the screen.

"Here I am with two of the McGill University graduate students in 1971. The lovely French Canadian girl on my right is here with me tonight. We were recently reunited after a 45-year separation."

The crowd bursts into applause as Havra gestures towards Marriette. "Dr. Marriette Roy."

Marriette stands briefly as the applause swelled.

"It was only a year later that I became convinced that my Original culture was under such great threat, that it was time to leave it and confront Civilization on my own. I was determined to catch up to my modern con- temporaries and succeed. I was then, as I am now, hungry for knowledge. I was fortunate to have exposure to abundant samples of Civilization from 61 different graduate students who lived among us, rotating every year or so until 1972. My experience with these scholars gave me glimpses of a world beyond mine – as well as the ability to learn to speak both French and English fluently.

"I grew up in a remote area. It took 12 days to walk from my wilderness community to the outskirts of civilization. Then on a very lucky day in my life, because of my language skills, I was given an opportunity to become a translator at the French Embassy in Benin. Later, another remarkable door opened. I qualified for an excellent French government program designed to educate young people of the former French colonies. This led me to Paris-Sorbonne to attend college, and then on to law school. To fulfill my obligation to the French government, I worked as an attorney in the embassy system of the former French colonies for 24 years before retiring. During that time period, along with a colleague and supportive investors, I developed one of the original ecologically friendly wildlife tour businesses in Africa, which now, as an industry, has nearly eliminated the thoughtless slaughter of our native wild animals."

Spontaneous applause erupts as the audience stands in appreciation.

"Thank you ... but let me now share a much more important consideration. During my time in civilization, I discovered that, as a species, most humans do not regard all life as sacred. Over the last 10,000 years, the human population has become increasingly separated from its natural environment of origin. A universal cultural disconnect has developed which is destroying our planet.

"Despite our having innate tendencies to feel awestruck, reverent, and sanctimonious, we have tragically directed away from these values which are essential to our survival. Instead, our modern culture has committed to irrational and reckless ideas; fictitious entities. The result of this way of thinking has, apparently, given permission to humanity to do whatever it wants with the Biosphere, thus giving rise to a human culture that ignores responsibility to care for the fragile and finite place we would call home."

Another slide appears on the overhead of an image of the Apollo 8 Earthrise. The photograph is folded and worn, but nicely framed on a wall.

"You see here Major Bill Anders' famous color photo, which is in my estimation, the most important iconic image ever recorded. This particular copy, now gracing a wall in my home, has been well-traveled. I kept it folded in an Algebra II book for years until finally finding a permanent location for it. This image caught my imagination the moment I saw it, and it took several years of educating myself before I fully understood the depth of its importance. It has been said before, but is forever worth repeating . . . here is our planet . . . blue and alive . . . our only home, surrounded by a deep and infinite blackness. The thin membrane of life, spread over our Earth's surface, is measured in only a few miles of thickness. That's all.

"There are those of us who do understand what stewardship of our planet should be, yet too many who hold control absolutely ignore our responsibilities. Scientists, along with other rational thinkers, know exactly what to do to right this foundering ship. However, they do not have the political power to do so. Few in power are capable of seeing beyond the next quarter. Because of this, their leadership is appalling. Their attitudes amount to chronic intractable ignorance founded in their maladaptive decision-making. Even with the dangers of a warming planet well upon us, these scientific facts remain unfathomable to them. This is the tragedy of the current human condition."

Pausing, with a finger placed to his chin, Havra sauntered to the opposite side of the stage.

"Belief without evidence is enormously dangerous. Civilization must abandon irrational and delusional approaches to gathering knowledge. When such epistemological nightmares are introduced to a young mind, it can taint decision-making for a lifetime.

"Our species has an innate tendency to rely on our gut feelings, otherwise known as intuition. This was once a valuable behavioral tool when, in our environment of origin, rapid decision-making was frequently crucial. Civilization, however, requires a more thoughtful approach. The need for critical thinking is essential for our survival. This method of processing information, however, needs to be learned. Parsing out fact from fiction is a deliberate process. I suggest to those of you who have never taken a course in critical thinking, to do so. The more factual information one seeks out and incorporates into one's decision-making, as individuals or groups, the safer and healthier our planet will be. Then, given this approach to learning, one can become more familiar with the basics of the physical and life sciences. With this foundation of the intricacies and interconnect-edness of life . . . all life becomes sacred . . . and . . . the more connected we are to our planet.

"Like everything else that is living, we humans occupy a unique niche built upon the structure and function of life that preceded us. We share so much with every life form, from microbes outward, along every branch of the tree of life. Life's complex biochemistry is a continuum, and it is real. There is great reverence and beauty in that. We, as humans, are not separate from, nor can we exist without, a healthy Biosphere. Discern from life what you are able, as thoughtfully as possible. Take the time to do this. It is a beginning.

"We are ordained by no one to be the gods we may think we are.

"We are special only in that we are the first species on this planet with the potential to control our existence and well-being. The question is: are we indeed capable? We are, and always have been, interconnected with all living things. My great hope is that one day humanity will achieve a universal spiritual foundation, springing forth from Nature . . . from life itself. What could be more natural, indeed? We exist in no one's image. Life . . . itself . . . is the greatest story ever told."

– Chapter 61 –

Future Plans
Saturday, July 9, 2016
Logan International Airport Boston, Massachusetts

Jen arrived at Boston's Logan Airport just as Marriette's flight from CDG was scheduled to arrive. Driving into the Terminal E parking lot, she was happy to find a shady spot on this hot July afternoon. She trotted across the access road into the International Terminal and proceeded to the baggage carousel.

Waiting patiently, keeping her eye on the schedule board, Jen reviewed the daily texts Marriette had sent throughout her stay in France. She hadn't written much, but forwarded photos taken of all the places visited, mostly as selfies with Havra. Jen was looking forward to hearing Marriette's stories on their ride back to Rhode Island.

Another 45 minutes passed before Marriette walked through the doors at U.S. Customs. Jen ran up and gave her a welcoming embrace, as the crowd continued moving around them toward the baggage area.

Taking a step back, Jen held onto her ponytail with both hands, in anticipation of Marriette's first comment.

"He's wonderful, Jenny! Havra is wonderful!"

They hugged again, both squealing at Marriette's revelation.

"Jenny! I think I'm in love. I know I must move forward carefully . . . but it feels very good right now."

"Wow! Really?" Jen giggled, her body animated in excitement.

Attempting to assume a more rational composure, Marriette asked, "Do you think I'm too old to be in love?"

"No 'M', not at all! It's thrilling to see you so happy! Well, you know . . . I suppose you should take it one day at a time."

"Yes, of course, my dear."

After collecting Marriette's luggage, they exited the building, crossed the road to the parking lot, and loaded the bags into Jen's car. Within minutes, they were through the Ted Williams Tunnel and onto Expressway 93 South, heading toward Providence.

"'M'," Jen began, "not that I don't want to hear everything, mind you . . . but, can you give me your thumbnail impression of Havra?"

"Well . . . he's gentle . . . very wise . . . well-educated, as determined as ever, and incredibly energetic. How's that?"

"Sounds like you hit the jackpot!"

"Not that I was looking to, but it certainly does seem that way."

"Anything else?"

As Jen drove past Sister Corita's gas tank, she glanced over at Marriette catching her grinning from ear to ear.

"Yeeesssss?" Jen pressed.

"He's handsome and fit too. I know that for a fact," Marriette winked, looking back over at Jen.

"Oh, 'M', you're blushing?"

"My goodness, Jenny. We made love. Twice!"

"What?"

"Yes! I never thought I'd experience that again! It was wonderful."

"Wow, how beautiful, 'M'. Isn't this all so amazing?"

"It is amazing and, you know, I don't have to concern myself with the Land Rover fallout any longer. Havra is going to take care of everything. He's been in touch with the reporter. He and Francine plan to negotiate an agreement, so I'm not going to give it a second thought. I've decided to just enjoy what is ahead of me . . . and, my darling, I've made another decision."

"What's that, 'M'?"

"I plan to finish teaching my two courses this fall, and then that will be it. On to the land of 'emeritus'."

"Oh my! It really is a new day, isn't it?"

"Among the things on my list to do this week, is to give my notice of retirement to the University, which reminds me, I believe you're next in line for my office, Jenny."

"Just what I've been waiting for," Jen chuckled. "When do I get to meet Havra?"

"Soon, I hope. I've made arrangements to see Harris next weekend. I plan to meet him in New Brunswick, which isn't a bad drive for him. I'll fly to

New Jersey on Friday and stay in one of their cozy guest bungalows. Havra wants to travel to the States as soon as possible to meet his son. We haven't talked specifics, yet. I'm waiting to see what Harris comes up with. As I keep reminding Havra, I have to first let Harris know that his father actually exists!"

"I love all the photos you sent, 'M'. What a beautiful home Havra has. I wouldn't mind a house like that!"

"Yes. I immediately felt comfortable Jenny . . . and the view from the back-yard . . . glorious!"

"I also loved the short video of Havra playing his guitar. What a great voice! Is he from Tennessee, too?" Jen teased. "Gee! My father would love him."

"I know," Marriette laughed. "Neville calls him 'Ray Price II'.

"By the way, were you able to get in touch with Neville?"

"Yes, I was . . . We had a nice conversation, and I liked him right away. Very easy to talk to. I suspect he's a really good musician too . . . which is quite interesting. He and Havra seem very close. Maybe as you and I are."

"Yes, they are. Havra expressed that Neville is an accomplished musician and vocalist – and would just as soon focus on his music more than anything else right now. Maybe you've already picked up on that . . . I see a twinkle in your eye, my dear."

"You do, 'M'?" Jen smiled.

– Chapter 62 –

The Word is Out
Monday, July 11, 2016
Fulton Hall, Brown University, Providence, Rhode Island

Marriette's phone rang as she walked into her office. Placing her briefcase on the couch, she reached across her desktop to pick it up.

"Marriette Roy. Bonjour."

"Good morning, Professor Roy. Jim Graham calling. Chancellor Graham."

"Oh, my goodness! Am I being called into the principal's office now?"

"No, Ma'am," he laughed good-naturedly, addressing her with his southern politeness. Hailed from Birmingham, Graham had recently been appointed Chancellor.

"Actually, Professor Roy, I was hoping I might walk over to Fulton Hall to pay you a visit. Would that be possible, Ma'am?"

"Why, by all means, Dr. Graham. Since we haven't met yet, I believe this would be a good opportunity. Frankly, I have an inkling of what may be on your mind. We shall see. I'm free for the next two hours. Would that work for you?"

"Why, yes, Professor, thank you. Please call me Jim."

"If you please, Marriette is fine. Can you come by in 30 minutes then?"

"I'll be there in 30 minutes. Thank you. Your office is ...?"

"First one down the stairs on the left, coming in from the parking lot. See you shortly, Jim."

"Yes, see you soon, Marriette."

Hanging up, Marriette immediately sent a text to Jen.

Still in a meeting with her research group at the VA, Jen noticed the light flash on her phone which had been discreetly positioned in the open drawer of her desk, and quickly read the message, *"Call me as soon as you can. Love"*.

After the meeting ended, she phoned Marriette.

"'M'? I called as soon as I could."

"Yes, dear, thank you. I just received a call from our Chancellor Graham. I assume he has information, or rather . . . questions for me. He's walking over to my office in a few minutes."

"What did Francine advise?"

"Fran said she would prefer to be in attendance for any interviews. Of course, that's what they always say. Anyway, she suggested I politely listen, and provide more information to her later. Havra will arrive next week, and I'm hoping we can all get together then with Fran. I've decided to take her advice and listen to what Jim Graham has to say. Would you be able to come by later? I'll let you know when he leaves."

"OK, sounds good. I have a client interview in a few minutes. Probably waiting outside now. I'll be through in about an hour or so. I'll wait for your text. Bye. Careful."

"Bye for now."

In a matter of minutes, a gentle knock on the antique door gave rise to its typical rattle produced by the large pane of opaque glass. Marriette opened the door and welcomed the University chancellor into her office. They shook hands; she offered him a seat on the couch, then settled into the armchair across from him.

The large portrait of the steely looking bearded man hanging behind Marriette's desk caught the Chancellor's eye. Marriette's facial expression gave way to a faint grin as he refocused his attention toward her.

"Professor Roy, it appears you have a John Singer Sargent portrait in your office."

"If someone happens to notice," Marriette answered, now full smile, "I always enjoy their initial reaction.

"To make a rather long story short . . . about 10 years ago I commissioned a local portrait painter, a graduate of RISD, to paint this reproduction for my office. The original, painted in 1894, had previously occupied that same spot," Marriette explained. "The authentic one is now secure in our Daniel Winton Bell Museum, these days."

"Interesting. Could have fooled me. I'll have to make a point of visiting the original," Jim Graham remarked, smiling back.

"Well, Jim, I don't ever recall a university Chancellor honoring me with a visit to my office. Welcome. This should be interesting – for both of us."

"I would say, Marriette, this may be one of the more enigmatic issues I have yet had to address," Graham began.

Cocking her head, Marriette nodded, repositioning her long silver braid over her shoulder.

"This morning, I received a call from my counterpart at McGill informing me that he was sent an e-mail from a French journalist, Jacques Lemieux, followed up by a phone call. Lemieux had been in touch with the McGill anthropology department concerning a recent most unusual discovery in West Ghana."

"And what was the nature of this said discovery, Jim?" Marriette inquired, absent any change in her demeanor.

"It was reported that, while excavating for a foundation, construction workers at the site uncovered a buried Jeep ... actually, an old Land Rover to be exact, built in England. In this military vehicle were found ..."

Graham began to read an inventory originating from a document held in his hand. "... one AK-47 assault rifle of Eastern European origin with serial numbers traced to Belarus in 1964 along with 200 rounds of ammunition, an early Soviet sidearm with 50 rounds, traces of Eastern European origin blood, male ... a copious amount of African origin blood, male, and a botanical plant press with various species of intact preserved herbaceous plants, spattered with non-human, equine mammal blood ... Montreal newspapers dated in 1970 and a considerable amount of long, brown Western European hair, female, present among the plant specimens."

Maintaining her neutral composure, Marriette listened silently.

"McGill records locate you in that area from 1970 through 1972. And there is a record of a master's thesis researching sources of primitive native pharmaceuticals authored by one Marriette C. LaFleur. Same last name as on the plant press."

With a slight tilt of his head, Graham looked up at Marriette, raising an eyebrow.

"How interesting," Marriette noted. "Let me be as direct as I can for now, Jim. Yes, I was there during those dates. Approximately four weeks ago, I received an email from the same journalist, Mr. Lemieux. He was associated with the news story in LeMonde, and planned to continue to investigate this, to use Lemieux's words, 'compelling' story.

"I can tell you this much. I was not involved in any nefarious behavior. There is, however, an interesting story that will indeed unfold. As soon as I have further consulted with my attorney, I will provide you with more details. There is no reason to do otherwise. My sense is the report will not affect Brown University in any negative way. But Administration may have to deal with the media for whatever lifetime this story will support. My involvement with this issue, and the attention it might generate, may necessitate my taking a leave of absence, or perhaps pursuing retirement, which, Jim, I was considering anyway. I have no definitive plans thus far. However, once I have made a decision, I will work through the chain of command. I fully understand my obligations to Brown and am quite confident the outcome will be seen in a positive light."

Satisfied with her response, Graham assured Marriette, "As far as I know, you and I are the only ones at Brown who are aware of this matter. You have a stellar reputation here. I have a strong sense that when the facts are unveiled, it will only be enhanced."

"I believe your assessment will prove correct, Jim."

With that, Graham stood up from the couch, offering his hand to Marriette.

"It's been a great honor to finally meet you, Professor Roy."

"Thank you. One for me, as well," Marriette reciprocated. "I will be in touch soon, Jim."

"Thank you, Marriette."

Opening the door, the Chancellor let himself out, closing the door behind him. As the glass pane rattled, Marriette took in a slow deep breath, exhaling a long sigh.

– Chapter 63 –

Marriette's Revelation to Harris
Saturday, July 16, 2016
Rutgers University, New Brunswick, New Jersey

Marriette peered out between the living room window curtains of the guest house, anticipating Harris's arrival. This visit would be different from all others as it would announce the revelation of Harris's biological father. Saying 'our son' now engendered a new depth of feeling.

As Harris pulled up in front of the house, Marriette walked out into the hot and humid early summer afternoon to greet him. Emerging from his vehicle, he opened the back door of the car to remove his suitcase. A handsome man in his early forties, Harris had inherited his mother's smoky blue eyes and a lighter version of his father's dark skin. Looking up and seeing his mother, he greeted her in his typical calm manner, "Hi, Mom. It's a beautiful day at RU."

Throwing his travel bag over his shoulder, Harris turned his large frame full circle, surveying the campus he was once so familiar with. He then smiled at his mother with the same gentle smile that Marriette had witnessed only days earlier on his father's face.

Walking around the car and up the walkway to where she stood waiting, Harris embraced Marriette a little longer than usual. Not only because they hadn't seen each other in several months, but because he sensed a stress in her. He wasn't privy to its origin but felt the need to comfort her from the moment he arrived.

Harris had grown closer to his mother since James's death, offering increased attentiveness, trying to compensate for his father's absence.

"Thank you for responding so quickly, my dear," Marriette said, still processing the new revised sense of family.

"Of course, Mom. But I will tell you, this is a mystery. You are all right, aren't you?"

"Yes, my dear boy, I am very well. I was hoping to walk around campus and talk, but it's too hot. Why don't we go inside for now? I have a lot to tell you."

Built in the 1920s, the neatly kept bungalow was one of several guest houses available to visiting faculty and other guests. The front entrance looked out onto a heavily treed quadrangle, located on the south end of campus. A porch, supported by thick cylindrical columns, provided welcome shade from the hot afternoon sun. Marriette felt at home as she had occupied the facilities on many occasions in the past. She escorted her son upstairs to one of the bedrooms to settle in. When Harris returned and walked into the parlor, Marriette was already sitting in one of the armchairs waiting for him. Both felt a slight twinge of anxiety arising, originating from different sources of anticipation.

Harris sat down on the couch and put his socked feet up on the coffee table. Without further hesitation he came straight to the point, "Mom, you've reassured me you're all right. I'm interpreting that to mean you are fine medically, apart of course, from experiencing stress about something. Whatever's going on, I'm here to listen and help you in any way I can. Everything is fine at home, so there's no rush for me to get back. I don't have patients scheduled until Monday afternoon, and, if necessary, one of the PAs will cover for me, so please, tell me what's on your mind."

"Thank you, darling. I love you, Harris."

"I love you, too, Mom."

"Yes, dear. I'm medically fine, but there are a few unanticipated issues that have arisen in the past few weeks."

"That's a great start, Mom."

"Harris, you've always known that when I was young," Marriette slowly began, "I had an intimate relationship with your biological father when I was a graduate student living in West Africa. From time to time, you've asked me for more details about him. Until very recently, it was my understanding that his whereabouts would likely remain unknown."

Harris's eyes widened at the potential implication of his mother's last remark. Marriette took in a slow deep breath as she reached into her briefcase to remove her iPad.

"Darling, your father James was my loving and dedicated partner for 22 years. Who he was, what he did, and what he meant to all of us will never be replaceable. Never. I continue to miss him every day."

"I'm listening, Mom."

Pausing a moment to deliberate, Marriette opened her iPad and tapped onto a photo taken only days before in Normandy. She handed the screen to Harris.

"This, my son, is a recent photo of your biological father, Havra Emerson."

"Really!" Harris reacted, drawing in a deep breath. "Really!" he repeated, holding the iPad out at arm's length.

"Amazingly, it was your father who recently found me!" Marriette added. "He is alive, well, and living in northern France."

Stunned, Harris continued to stare at the photo.

"Two weeks ago, I was contacted by a long-time friend of his, Neville Peters. Last Sunday, I flew to Paris and spent four days with your . . . your other father," Marriette explained, with tears now flowing down her cheeks.

Harris stood up and knelt beside his mother, gently pressing his head against hers as he set the photo down in front of them.

"Mom, Mom. It's okay. I'm with you," he whispered into her ear. Lightly grasping her arm, he silently studied the image of his father.

"Harris, so much has come about in the past three weeks. I'm feeling overwhelmed. I always assumed it would be next to impossible to find Havra . . . your father . . . and now . . . he found me. During my time living in Africa, Havra was a tribal leader. I never fathomed the incredible things this man would accomplish since last seeing him over 40 years ago.

"Havra has been told that he has a son . . . a happy and successful son in the United States. To be brief for the moment, his only other son, Tave, was murdered three months before I left Africa. I was witness to that tragic day. Havra was not. Through quick action and good fortune, my life was saved along with several others. We had to deliver Tave's lifeless body back to the tribal village."

"Oh, Mom! What happened? Tave . . . that's my African middle name."

"Yes, it is, darling," Marriette quietly acknowledged, "Yes, it is. I will explain everything about that horrific event in detail later to you."

Harris moved to sit on the edge of the coffee table, across from his mother. Taking her hand into his, he gently said, "Mom, tell me everything when you're ready. There's no hurry."

"Thank you, Harris. I would like to begin by telling you about your biological father. Shortly after he was born, students from McGill University anthropology department began arriving to study Havra's tribal community, usually one or two students at a time. The objective was to study what was then a relatively untainted primitive culture in West Africa. The program began in 1938 and ended in 1972. I was the final student to participate. The students' academic presence created an environment that exposed your father little by little to modern civilization. During the years that the McGill program was active, Havra was mentored in varied and unique ways by no less than 60 students.

"From infancy on, Havra was exposed to the spoken languages of English and French. More fascinated than most other members of his tribe, Havra regularly sought out the graduate students, absorbing everything he could about their culture. By the time I met your father, he spoke French and English fluently, and had learned to read and write to at least the level of a high school senior. In his early twenties, he was tempted to leave Africa with one of the returning students, but at the time, despite an insatiable curiosity and desire to experience a different life, he elected not leave his people.

"Eventually, though, he did make that journey into Civilization. It was astonishing to learn that, less than two years after my return home, Havra was already living in Paris and beginning an undergraduate degree in economics. He then attended and graduated from law school. He has recently retired after three decades of serving as a government attorney, addressing legal matters involving the former French African colonies.

"Your father now lives on the northern coast of France. He is a wonderful man, Harris. It's a relationship I wish to re-establish. I know that already."

Harris stood up and began to pace the living room as he tried to comprehend this stunning information. After a short while, he settled back down onto the couch.

"There certainly is a lot going on here," he acknowledged, shaking his head. "Apparently, Mom, I seem to have had two incredible dads. When do I get to meet him?"

"Hopefully sooner, rather than later," Marriette answered. "It's up to you, darling."

That afternoon, with the sun's angle not so severe, mother and son left the bungalow to wander throughout the relatively quiet summertime campus as Marriette revealed the depths of her African story to Harris. They would saunter a while, then rest on a park bench or granite wall until moving on to another location. As evening approached, they patronized a local restaurant they had enjoyed in past years and settled into a cozy booth for dinner.

Marriette explained that she planned to take a leave of absence for at least the fall semester and was likely to retire. Circumstances of the last three weeks had greatly influenced her decision. She didn't offer details, but said, "I'm exhausted, Harris. I prefer to finish telling you about those last months in Africa tomorrow. I think we have both had enough for tonight."

Trying to comfort his mother, Harris remarked, "Listening to this incredible story, Mom, I don't know where to begin with questions. I didn't know, or don't remember, that you've had issues with traumatic stress. I can fully appreciate why you wouldn't want to speak of the death of Havra's son . . . my brother . . . or complicate Jake's and my relationship with you by disclosing your experiences. I know you love me, and that the decisions you and dad made were in my and Jake's best interest."

"Thank you, dear."

"It's interesting how things happen in life. What I'm feeling right now, Mom, is pride. Wow! What a remarkable job you did in handling an impossible situation. How terrifying . . . and, as I speak these words, I can easily understand why you needed to bury it all . . . along with the Land Rover."

Moving his dinner plate off to the side as he leaned closer to his mother, Harris emphasized his next words. "It makes a huge difference knowing this about you – and hearing how I arrived here. It's also a beautiful gift to learn I have an incredible new dad. Occasionally, as a youngster, I would imagine a man suddenly appearing, claiming to be my father and fearful that it would interfere with my relationship with Dad . . . that it might ruin our family. I wouldn't say it was a constant worry, but it did frequently cross my mind, especially later in grade school. But . . . all that is in our distant past. I'm looking forward to meeting my father."

"It will be quite the day, will it not, Harris?"

"Yes, Mom. Indeed, it will be. My concern now is for you."

"Thank you, my darling. I am so relieved to finally get this off my chest. My next job is to inform your brother."

"Mom, let me do that," Harris quickly proposed. "Let me get the initial word to Jake. I'll fly up to see him next weekend. You and I can talk later to coordinate our efforts. I'll make it clear to Jake that it was I who chose to do this rather than you. He'll understand how uniquely personal this is to me. On another day, you can tell Jake the story yourself."

"Thank you, dear Harris. Havra wants to fly to the States soon. He is very excited and anxious to meet his son. We'll see what works with everyone's schedule."

Sensing Marriette's fatigue, Harris made a suggestion, "Mom, let's put this aside for now and sit out on the porch when we get back. Let me do some talking. I'll get you caught up on your grandsons."

"That sounds like a perfect idea, Harris, my darling."

– Chapter 64 –

A Defining Moment
Sunday, July 17, 2016
Rutgers University, New Brunswick, New Jersey

When Harris went to bed that night, he was not of the mind to sleep. His thoughts meandered back through the day's conversations with his mother. He imagined meeting his newly discovered father for the first time. What would it be like? What would he say? Harris's thoughts then drifted to James, the father who raised him – and to memories of childhood experiences that he encountered as a result of looking different than his parents or brother.

Harris recalled being asked questions from elementary school classmates or, on occasion, from an inappropriate adult. His parents had prepared him well with answers that he could deliver confidently during those awkward moments. He also became skilled at anticipating questions before they arose from someone's stray glance.

Being raised in a university environment afforded Harris and his younger brother exposure to an enlightened population of adults and their families. Individuals came to the Brown community from all parts of the globe, providing the brothers with an opportunity to experience ideas and cultural expression not always the same as their parents' perspective. There were other children of mixed races and what seemed to be an acceptance of all in the relatively progressive campus atmosphere of the seventies and eighties. If ever an issue arose for Harris, it usually happened outside this cocoon of acceptance.

Both he and Jake played on youth hockey teams in the greater Providence area. Harris grew in size rapidly and was uncommonly coordinated, making sports, or anything requiring an athletically wired nervous system, come easily to him. One year for Christmas, possibly his eighth, an uncle sent him a set of juggling balls. When Harris asked his father for instructions, James admitted right off that he could not juggle, and suggested waiting until his uncle next came to visit and he could certainly teach him. Not willing to wait, Harris quietly disappeared into another room, returning only minutes later, walking and juggling the three balls with ease.

The home youth hockey rink, located on the western outskirts of the city, was a dark and damp old place run on a shoestring budget. A bent and rusted chain-link fence provided protection from stray pucks sailing over the splintery, delaminating plywood boards. One Saturday in January, when the locker room bathrooms were no longer being heated, players found the toilet bowls covered in a solid layer of discolored ice, filled with incarcerated cigarette butts.

As Harris lay in bed with sleep still evading him, he remembered a defining moment during a late October hockey practice at the dilapidated hockey rink. Harris was 11. He, along with some of his teammates, stood in the bench area along the dasher, awaiting instructions from the coaches who were nearby, but still on the ice.

One of Harris's squirt level teammates standing beside him, turned and sarcastically commented that he "didn't think niggers played hockey." Without a moment's hesitation, Harris removed a glove and punched the helmetless adversary squarely in the nose, spilling blood. The boy began to cry, screaming between syncopated breaths, "You nigger! Nigger! I hate you."

The coaches quickly gathered around them, as the parents of the two boys rushed toward the bench area. There were no immediate questions posed, as the kid with the bloody nose had emphatically incriminated himself by making his offense public with his statement.

James swiftly arrived at his son's side. Harris recalled looking up at the other boy's parents, as the mother flashed a fiery glance at him, attending to her son's bloody nose which was dripping profusely onto his white uniform sweater. The assistant coach strongly suggested that Harris apologize to his teammate. Harris always remembered his response because James had reminded him of the comment later.

"I'm sorry this happened, Coach, but ... I ... don't have anything to apologize for."

James quietly advised Harris to be cool over the confrontation, but his directive proved unnecessary. Harris calmly informed both coaches that he had done nothing wrong and was ready to get back on the ice. Taking control of the interchange, the head coach cut in, saying, "Absolutely!"

Harris nodded the affirmative, as the coach gave him an encouraging tap on the back, instructing, "Let's move on from this. We have a practice now. We'll all talk about it later. Get out there and skate hard, Harris!"

Harris put his helmet back on and fastened the chin strap, mumbling with his mouth guard in place, "Okay, Coach. See'ya, Dad."

Harris gave a thumbs up with his glove as he jumped over the dasher with coach right behind him. As his son hit the ice, James yelled out in their native tongue, "Soyez votre meilleur! Intensité, Quatre." (Be your best. Skate hard, number 4.) And he did.

After practice, while driving home from the rink, father and son discussed the regrettable incident and the lessons that might be learned.

And now, years later, Harris revisited the conversation as clearly as if it were yesterday:

"So, Harris. How did all that start?" James inquired, having already heard the other boy's subsequent remarks.

Harris answered his father by repeating his teammate's initial comment.

'Did I do the right thing, Dad?"

"To begin with, Harris, I'm sorry this happened. Those were very hurtful words," James answered glancing over at his young son, buckled into the front seat of the Blazer.

Possessing a lifetime of familiarity with the hockey environment, James lightly jested, "If you had been at a tennis match, maybe you might have given him an opportunity to correct his statement . . . but this is hockey practice. There is a hockey honor culture among teammate, which he violated. I guess I can't disagree with how you reacted. It sends a message . . . to Brian and everyone in the building."

James then paused momentarily, emphasizing his next words, "And how you handle this matter going forward will send an even stronger message about who . . . you are . . . remember that, Harris, my boy. Let me tell you what I mean by that."

"OK, Dad," young Harris listened, as he turned in his seat, leaning up against the truck door to face his dad.

"What is important now is that everyone learn something from this incident. And it begins with you, Harris. You lead the way. That's how life is. Sometimes one person needs to lead the way, and I know you can handle it."

"I think I can, too, Dad."

"It's also important to remember how those words made you feel. You should always keep it in mind if you ever have an inkling to say something of that kind to someone else . . . not that you ever would."

"Yeah, I didn't really think about it during practice, but afterward, when I was getting dressed, it made me feel sad. It shouldn't have happened."

Removing his new Pawtucket Red Sox cap from his head, Harris examined it as he continued to speak to his father.

"One of my teammates came up to me as we were leaving the locker room and told me how cool it was that I made Brian's nose bleed and everything. I know he doesn't like him. Brian is hard to like. I told him I didn't think it was that cool but thanked him anyway."

"Good ... good on both points ... and Harris ... also consider that Brian's comments were not well thought out. Not a hint of forethought. Those words probably, and unfortunately, originated with his parents or someone close to him. He had to learn them somewhere."

"Yeah, I suppose."

"I wonder how Brian's parents will handle this," James proceeded, "I saw Coach Barry go back and talk to them before they left the rink."

"Do you think the coaches will kick Brian off the team?" Harris wondered.

"Think they should?"

"I don't know, Dad."

"What if Brian thought about what he said, understood he had made a mistake, and was truly sorry? Would he deserve a second chance, Harris?"

"Yeah, but how can I tell if he really believes he made a mistake, Dad?"

"Maybe you can and maybe you can't ... but I think he deserves a chance to prove it. This is important, Harris, he needs to make his own statement. His not having the opportunity to reconcile his mistake might become the worst part of this whole mess. Who will this young guy be going forward? This is how we all grow up ... choice by choice."

"It's not so simple, is it, Dad?"

"No, it isn't, Harris. This predicament is not simple. An adult will probably suggest, or rather insist, that he apologize, especially if he is going to stay on the team. Brian will have a choice to make. Hopefully, he can figure it out and separate himself from the source of his racist remark. Either he will become more thoughtful about what he says or he will continue on the path of being a jerk for the rest of his life. This can be a big fork in the road for Brian."

"Yeah, Dad, which direction do you think he will choose?"

"Harris, you can help him go in the right direction. Remember, his words reflect his own problems. I know ... it's difficult not to take personally, but his problems don't originate with you. His comments are about his life, not yours. This is your chance to show some leadership. It's a really valuable opportunity for you. Don't underestimate it, Harris. You too have a choice.

You can remember this day as a bad one in your life . . . or one that is meaningful for you and maybe for someone else, as well."

"Do you think he'll apologize at the next practice, Dad?"

"Well, I think he'll be given the opportunity to apologize. I'm hoping Coach will take the time to counsel Brian privately. That might help . . . I imagine before the next practice, Coach Barry, Brian, and his parents will probably gather together with us, away from the rest of the team. I've seen this play out before, as both a player and a coach. It will be embarrassing for Brian. Imagine how you might feel. I suggest at that point, you pull Brian aside, away from everyone else, and give him a chance to say his thing – with as much privacy as possible. As long as he attempts to apologize, offer to shake his hand. Ask him if 'we can be better teammates now'? That might really surprise him. Perhaps, given a chance at redemption, he will want to be your friend forever. As much as you might like to have an apology, he may want your forgiveness even more. What do you think about that?"

"Thanks, Dad. I get it."

"I love you, my boy."

"Love you, Dad."

Harris was quiet for the rest of the ride home, as he stared out at the road ahead. By the time James pulled into their driveway that evening, the October sun had set, and young Harris was sound asleep.

Now, some 35 years later, Harris lay awake in the little bungalow, alone with his thoughts. He got up from the bed and walked over to sit near the window and look out onto the familiar campus. He thought more about his mother's story. He thought more about his father, James, and his influence on the man he had become.

A thunderclap rumbled in the distance. It was gently raining now. Harris pushed the window wide open. Sheet lightning illuminated a cloud bank to the north. Resting his forehead on the window sash, he sat quietly, transfixed on the scattered light of the streetlamps through the wet screen.

He finally crawled back into bed, slipping into the unconsciousness of sleep, until hearing his mother's call at 9 a.m. the following morning.

– Chapter 65 –

Harris and Laine
Sunday, July 17, 2016   Towson, Maryland

Harris acknowledged his mother's call from downstairs to awaken him with a polite shout from his bedroom, "I'll be down in a couple minutes, Mom." Hearing her voice was reminiscent of her calling him from the base of their stairwell when he was a child.

As he lay in bed considering how to tell his wife about these extraordinary new circumstances, Harris heard his mother coming up the stairs. Harris glanced over at the clock as Marriette poked her head in the door, finding him propped up on a pillow with both arms behind his head.

"Good morning, darling. It's 9 a.m. Sleeping in?"

"Good morning, Mom. I can't remember the last time I slept this late. I was awake for quite some time before falling asleep last night."

"There's a lot on your mind, my darling."

Marriette sat down on the edge of the bed and looked into her son's eyes, "How are you doing with all of this?" she gently inquired, feeling the relief of the evening before now somewhat uncertain. Harris read her expression and reached out placing his hand over hers, intent on resolving any concerns.

"Really, Mom," he answered with a smile. "I'm good with all of this. There is a lot to process, but I dare say, I feel it's a surprise gift for both of us, with much more to look forward to. Right? That's the way I see this."

Marriette continued to gaze at her son with only the love a mother can have for her child.

"Mom, please, ease your mind. We have this entire day to spend together, so let's just wander around campus and talk about what comes to mind. I want to hear the rest of your story. We rarely have an opportunity such as this to spend time alone together. Let's take advantage of it – and the beautiful day."

"Yes, you're right, dear."

"And Mom, I want to know everything you can tell me about my new father. It's apparent that you are very happy with the time you've spent together.

I can tell that he is someone very special. I already feel a closeness through you."

Recovering her sense that Harris was comfortable, she leaned over and placed a kiss on his cheek. He wrapped his arms around her.

"Yes, Harris, darling. While you get ready, I'll go out for a walk to stretch my legs. I'll be back in half an hour or so. I'll have my phone with me."

"That sounds perfect, Mom. Enjoy your walk. I love you so much!"

"I love you, too, darling."

As Marriette left to go downstairs, she leaned back over her shoulder and blew Harris a kiss.

After showering, Harris went down to the kitchen and poured himself a cup of coffee.

Settling into a comfy chair on the front porch, he opened his tablet with the intention of checking his email. Suddenly, he realized he hadn't yet called his wife. She was waiting for an explanation of Harris's rush trip to Rutgers. It was a little after 10 a.m. when he reached her. Laine had taken their two boys to an instructional summer baseball clinic and was positioned at one of the fields watching the older of the two, 11-year-old Brooks, playing in a game. Like his father, Brooks was big for his age, possessing the grace and body type of a younger adult, rather than that of a boy. Laine's phone rang several times before she picked up.

"Hi, Doc!" she answered, playfully. "Is everything all right? I've been wondering when you were going to call. The boys have been asking about you non-stop since they woke this morning."

"Sorry, Baby. Everything, everyone is fine. Please let the guys know that as soon as possible, all right? I was up quite late last night mulling things over. I surprised even myself; I didn't get up until Mom woke me just a few minutes ago."

"Okay. So, can you tell me what's going on, Harris?"

"It's all good news, Laine. There is a big surprise, however."

"Jeez, Harris did your mother hit the lottery?" Laine teased, not taking her eyes off the game.

"No, no, no ... well, a different kind of lottery. I have..."

Suddenly, Harris was interrupted by a loud squeal from his wife.

"Oh, wow! Jeezuzz! Whatta catch!" she yelled out at Brooks, followed by more screeching and screaming, now no longer directed into the phone, but still audible. "Brook-zee! Amazing! Wow! Great throw! You got 'em. Shit. Ah, he got back. Great stuff, Brook-zee!"

Laine was excitable, especially when it came to sports. A New Jersey city girl, Laine was an athlete, blue-eyed, with auburn hair and freckles. Before med school, she had played soccer at Duke, and still played on a women's team every fall. The couple met at Rutgers during their second year in medical school. Laine had become a pediatrician and molecular geneticist at Johns Hopkins.

Still quite charged, Laine got back on the phone and blurted out the replay so quickly in her heavy Jersey accent, it sounded like a run-on sentence.

"Harr…ris! Brooks just made this freakin' amazing catch…right in front of me …living up to his name, yeah? Frozen rope down the third baseline four or five feet in the air…His whole body stretched out parallel to the infield… caught it back hand! The instructors are freaking out! Saved two runs…as soon as he landed, he had the mind to set himself and throw back to second …almost got the kid. Unreal, Harris!"

Pausing, she took in a deep breath to settle herself down, "Sorry, Harr. What were you saying?"

Still amused with her staccato replay, Harris remarked, "Sorry I missed that, Laine. Can't wait to hear what Brooks has to say. Probably not much. Hey, darling, I can tell you all of this later if you want?"

"No, honey. Please. Tell me now."

"Well, get yourself ready for more excitement."

"More excitement?"

"Yes! My mother was recently reunited with my biological father, Lainey. He's currently living in northern France, and the back story is quite amazing."

"Oh, my God! What? Really? After all this time? How? You're kidding me! Why now? Jeez, Harris! Your father! That's unbelievable!"

"Oh, Harris…wait…that was the third out. Brooks is running over. He's giving me the hurry up sign. He must know it's you. Wow, Harr! Here's Brooksie."

A handsome young man, olive skinned and blue eyed like his dad, Brooks took the phone from his mother and calmly greeted his father, the front of his uniform covered in red clay dust.

"Hi, Dad. Are you still visiting with Grand-Mére at Rutgers? Everything okay with Grand-Mére, Dad? Are you coming home soon?"

"Hi, Fella. Yes, I'm still here. La Grand-Mére est très heureuse. (Grandma is just fine.) Everything is very good. I have a big story to tell you and Case when I get home. I plan to be back around noon tomorrow. What about this catch Mom is screaming about?"

In his matter-of-fact manner, Brooks described the play to his father, "I caught a rope over the third base line ... just missed getting the double play at second. Took me too long to get set after I crashed. Threw it from my knees though ... really close. Dad, the coaches are waving at me. Talk to you later. I'll give you a call. I love you, Dad. Wish you were here, Dad."

Before Harris could get in another word, Laine was back on the phone. Sitting down on the grass along the outfield third baseline, she finally directed her full attention toward her husband.

"This is quite the revelation, Harris. I imagine there's an interesting story that goes along with this. Am I right?"

Definitely, definitely, Lainey. It's one of the most amazing stories we will ever hear... and Brooks and Casey now have a grandfather living in France."

"Tell me, Harr."

"What I've learned so far, is that my biological father, Havra Emerson, was an attorney for the French government for 25 years, speaks several languages, owned a successful ecotourism business, plays country and western music in cafés, and lives in a country home in Normandy. I can imagine how surprised he must have been to learn about me ... and Lainey, I look just like him!"

"What? For once, Harris, I'm speechless."

"Mom just returned from France after spending several days with him. My father will be flying to the States in a few weeks. I'm just beginning to contemplate what I want to say to him when we first meet. Anything going on tomorrow we can't rearrange? My plan is to arrive home around noon."

"This is incredible, Harris! I'll clear out the schedule ... kind of prep the boys. Call me later, Harr? I need to check on Casey. He's at the other field. OK?"

"Sure, Doc," Harris laughed.

"Talk soon? I love you, Harris. Love to Marriette."

"Yes ... and I'll call Casey ... first thing on the drive home. I love you, Lainey."

– Chapter 66 –

Harris, Emerson, & Lincoln
Sunday, July 17, 2016   Trenton, New Jersey

Later that afternoon, Harris drove his mother to Mercer Airport in Trenton for her return trip home. He brought up the topic of his future meeting with Havra.

"Mom, I've been carefully considering how my father and I should meet for the first time," he began. "In every way possible, I want this to be a very special and memorable moment."

"Yes, of course, my dear."

"I'd rather not communicate directly with Havra yet … or should I call him dad? Probably not. I'm not sure about that either."

Harris briefly glanced over at his mother, "Would you help arrange a date and time when Havra can fly over? I want to meet at a place worthy of the occasion. You mentioned he has been to Washington a few times."

"Yes, he has. I believe I have an idea of what you're thinking."

"It isn't that I don't want to communicate. What I think I'd prefer is that the first time we meet is the first time we speak. An email or phone conversation ahead of time just isn't personal enough."

"I know exactly what you mean, Harris. I felt the same way."

"I've been thinking I'd like to meet him at the Lincoln Memorial. Is that too much of a stretch?"

"Not at all, Harris. I like the idea."

"Good, Mom. I envision us sitting together on the steps of the Memorial at Lincoln's feet. I find that appealing. We can sit right there and get to know each other – or wander off to another interesting location. Havra can take a cab directly there from the airport and store his bags until we pick them up later. Don't most of the planes from Europe arrive later in the morning?"

Marriette listened intently, watching her son think aloud. "Yes, they do."

"Of course, I want you to come to Washington, too, Mom, but give us an hour or so alone together. Maybe we can then meet you at the National

Gallery? How's that? Why don't you explain the plan to him that way? Later, the three of us can drive back to Towson to meet Lainey and the boys. Do you think he might go for that?"

"Yes, I do. I believe Havra will appreciate your thoughtful approach. I love your plan, my darling."

******

Saturday, July 23, 2016   Lincoln Memorial, Washington, D.C.

Marriette's flight from Providence to Washington D.C. arrived with enough time for her to make her way to Customs to meet Havra. They had communicated several times during the previous week. Excitedly, she watched as Havra emerged from U. S. Customs. Running toward him, they caught each other in a long embrace.

"My goodness, I missed you," Marriette sighed, kissing him as if they were young lovers.

"I'm thrilled to finally be here with you," Havra whispered lovingly into her ear.

Following the signs for ground transportation out to where the taxis gathered, Havra watched Marriette as she walked in front of him pulling her luggage, weaving their way through narrow openings in the crowded corridor. She was tall and elegant in her cerulean and white striped summer dress. Her long silver hair, secured in an ornate clasp at her neck, reached to the middle of her back.

Havra moved up beside her as the crowd thinned, complimenting, "How lovely you are, my dear."

"Thank you, Havra. Today, I feel as though I'm in my thirties!"

She slowed her pace, reaching up to kiss him again. The couple stored their bags and boarded a taxi directing it to the Washington Mall.

"How are you feeling right now, Havra?"

"I've been pondering this day all week, my Marriette. I'm not sure I can put words to it. I can't help but see the striking similarities to Tave in the photos of Harris you've sent me. It tugs at my ancestral past, tempting me to think of them as one and the same. When I meet Harris, what I hope for, is to let all those impressions seep in as they will."

As Havra angled himself in the backseat of the cab, trying to comfortably place his long legs, he continued his thought, "Harris was raised by a wonderful man who helped him become the person he is today. I missed that opportunity. It's a loss I must accept and put into its proper perspective. I can only move forward now – and get to know my son to the fullest extent possible."

"Yes, dear Havra … and might I remind you, we also have the grandchildren. Brooks and Casey suddenly have another grandfather. This is our time to experience as much of them as we can, and I'm hoping we will want to do it together."

"I certainly do, Marriette," Havra replied, as the cab pulled up to the curb in front of the National Gallery.

"Text me when you and our son are on the way. I'll meet you at 'Lavender Mist'," Marriette instructed, as she kissed him and got out of the cab.

"Lavender Mist?"

"Yes, Havra, Lavender Mist."

Havra watched Marriette walk towards the granite staircase of the Gallery as the cab pulled away on route to the Lincoln Memorial. Quickly googling the meeting location, he chuckled to himself as he discovered the image of Pollock's 1950 work. "Fractals! 'I am Nature'," Havra murmured, studying the painting's image and recalling Jackson Pollock's description of himself.

"Yes, I am Nature," he quietly repeated.

****

Harris had arrived early at the Lincoln Memorial on purpose. After pacing the stone floor of its vast interior, he sat on the granite stairs at the base of Lincoln's feet. Few people coursed through the Memorial this hazy summer noon. More than once Harris walked out to gaze upon the reflecting pool, standing on the very spot where Martin Luther King, Jr. once stood. He returned and centered himself on the stairs between Lincoln's boots, resting his forearms on his knees, staring at the granite surface in front of him.

When next he looked up, a tall man stood facing him at the edge of sunshine and shadow some 20 paces away. The clarity of his image was obscured by the glare of the hazy summer sun behind him. Raising a hand to his brow to shield the bright light, Harris rose from where he was sitting and began walking toward the image. As the men approached each other, the older of them smiled, calling out in French, "Dr. Roy?"

Only moments earlier, Harris had been mildly anxious, uncertain of the reaction he would feel. Now he smiled broadly in response, "Attorney Emerson, my father."

With each step moving closer toward one other, they recognized their uncanny similarity in appearance and manner.

"My son."

The extended handshake soon moved into an embrace. Their similar height positioned them eye-to-eye, so as to smile upon each other without words. Havra was first to speak, his large hands clasping his son's shoulders.

"Where did you get those smoky blue eyes, handsome?" he inquired, his eyes twinkling.

In the days leading up to this, their first encounter, Marriette had provided both father and son with much history. Now, as the two conversed, being in each other's physical presence transported their experience to a new level. In an inexplicable and beautiful way, a deep thread of connection was suddenly experienced among father, son, and the ancestral presence of Tave.

Speaking with ease, they sauntered along the edge of the Reflecting Pool, moving from the Memorial and in the direction of the National Gallery. As they approached the Gallery, Havra directed, "We're going to the East building upper level. It says here, gallery 407B."

"What is Mom having us do?" Harris quipped.

"We are going to meet your mother in the presence of Jackson Pollock."

"Interesting," Harris remarked.

Turning from the hallway, the men entered into the gallery. There, Marriette stood in front of the large textured image, 'Lavender Mist', its sharpened lines forever branching to infinity, bathed in a subtle reflective mauve.

Father, mother, and son entered into a silent embrace, their heads together. The power of the moment brought tears of joy and a profound sense of thankfulness. On this momentous day, that which was lost was now recovered.

– Chapter 67 –

What Once Was Then, There Is Again
Thursday, September 27, 2018   Normandy Coast, France

The September sun was beginning to set over the slate roof of the French country home. Havra moved quietly in the shadowed backyard, sweeping up grape leaves, which had begun to fall from the arbor covering the bluestone patio.

Earlier that day, he had returned a signed contract to his attorney in Paris. His remaining shares of the ecotourism business in Benin were now sold. He held no regrets. The business was in capable hands. Havra doubted he would ever return to Benin and felt no desire to do so. The last page of that chapter had been turned.

Throughout the day, however, the sale, brought to mind old memories of his life in Africa.

Havra stopped sweeping to sit on the short stone wall enclosing the edge of the patio. Leaning his chin on the top of the broom handle, he gazed beyond the grassy slope below and out to the English Channel. At the eastern horizon, the first stars were beginning to appear in a clear navy sky.

Havra recalled one sunset long, long ago, as he began the journey from his native homeland to this very different world. He remembered the loneliness he felt on that particular evening, coupled with the uncertainty of the future he faced.

Although he fared well in his new civilization, a loneliness had continued to occupy a depth in his soul. Decades had now passed since he witnessed that last African sunset at elevation, seated on a dusty red rock, leaning on his walking stick. Havra recalled imagining the image of the young woman from Canada climbing up the embankment to join him as the sun fell on the African savanna – but believing in his heart she was gone forever.

His gaze now turned from the Normandy horizon to the grassy path below, in shadow, as Marriette appeared carrying glasses up the hill from where they had left them on the little patio below. She was with him once again. No longer was there that feeling of loneliness, but a treasure recovered.

Walking up to Havra, Marriette put the glasses down. She gently took away the broom, moved onto his lap and into his arms. They looked up at the sky as a shooting star passed overhead, far out over the channel. A tender kiss was shared before retiring together to the cottage for the night.

– Epilogue: The Circles Are Closed –

The End . . . The Beginning
Tuesday, November 10, 2020
Somewhere in West Ghana, Africa

It is after 6 p.m. and Harris Roy, M.D. has finished his last case of the day. Removing his gown and gloves, he leaves the operating room, passing through the center core, and dons a long white lab coat with the emblem 'Doctors without Borders' imprinted on the left chest pocket. Removing a bottle of water from the small fridge in the lounge, he proceeds out of the surgical suite into the main corridor. The late afternoon sun streams in through the windows. At the end of the hall, Harris opens a door to an outside concrete stairwell and climbs the three flights up to the entrance of the rooftop.

The surface of the building top is still hot from the heat of the sun. It offers an unobstructed view toward the west over nearby treetops. It was here, four years ago, that the nefarious Land Rover was unearthed – during the excavation of the foundation for this very hospital. Dr. Roy looks out over the breathtaking West African savanna where his father once roamed as a young man – where he himself had been conceived 48 years before.

Resting his hands on the top of the short concrete wall, Harris gazes out onto a vast grassy plain glowing orange in the setting sun, a long view stretching to the horizon.

Rob Ritchey is a portrait painter, a writer, and a surgical podiatrist. He graduated from the California College of Podiatric Medicine in San Francisco. He went on to postgraduate training in foot and ankle surgery in the United States Army, where he served on active duty for eight years.

Rob and his wife, Maricris, live on Cape Cod where he continues his medical practice. After 45 years, he is painting again. And he has started writing. This is his first novel. A second is in process.

This book was designed and typeset by Nancy Viall Shoemaker of West Barnstable Press using ITC Caslon No. 224 inspired by the serif typeface Caslon by William Caslon of London in the 18th century. Ed Benguiat created Caslon 224 in 1982. Although very different from William Caslon's design, it shares the readability of its predecessor.

Benguiat was born in Brooklyn, New York in 1927 and started his working career as a jazz percussionist. He served with the Air Corps and used the GI bill to attend the Workshop School of Advertising Art. Ed went on to teach at the School of Visual Arts in New York and has designed over 600 typefaces, as well as logotypes for *New York Times, Esquire, Sports Illustrated*, and *Playboy*. He continues to enjoy flying.

www.westbarnstablepress.com